STIRCHLEY LIBRARY
Bournville Lane B30 2JT
TEL: 0121-464 1534

Loans are up to 28 days. Fines are charged if items are
not returned by the due date. Items can be renewed
at the Library, via the internet or by telephone up to
3 times. Items in demand will not be renewed.
Please use a bookmark

Date for return		
2 5 NOV 2006		
0 8 JAN 2007		
Renew 6|2|07	1 0 FEB 2011	
2 8 JUL 2007		
2 3 APR 2010	2 1 OCT 2011	
	2 4 MAY 2012	
	0 5 FEB 2015	

Check out our online catalogue to see what's in stock,
or to renew or reserve books.

www.birmingham.gov.uk/libcat

www.birmingham.gov.uk/libraries

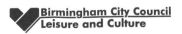
Birmingham City Council
Leisure and Culture

Birmingham
Libraries

Gigi Levangie lives with her film producer husband and four children in Los Angeles, California.

Visit the author's website at
www.gigigrazer.com

THE STARTER WIFE

When her husband dumps her (by cell phone) just before their tenth wedding anniversary, Gracie Pollock is left reeling. Though her role as the wife of a semi-famous studio executive often left her cold, she had become accustomed to the unique privileges extended to Tinseltown's elite. Gracie really believed that she and Kenny were different from other Hollywood couples. She never thought she'd be a *Starter Wife*. But now that her marriage is over, she's a social pariah and things go from bad to worse when she learns (via her florist) that her husband has upgraded: Kenny is dating a famous blonde pop starlet. What will Gracie do next?

GIGI LEVANGIE

THE
STARTER
WIFE

Complete and Unabridged

CHARNWOOD
Leicester

First published in Great Britain in 2006 by
Bantam Press
London

First Charnwood Edition
published 2006
by arrangement with
Bantam Press, a division of
Transworld Publishers
London

The moral right of the author has been asserted

British Library CIP Data

Grazer, Gigi Levangie
   The starter wife.—Large print ed.—
Charnwood library series
   1. Divorce—California—Los Angeles—Fiction
   2. Hollywood (Los Angeles, Calif.)—Fiction
   3. Large type books
   I. Title
813.6 [F]

ISBN 1–84617–465–1

Published by
F. A. Thorpe (Publishing)
Anstey, Leicestershire

Set by Words & Graphics Ltd.
Anstey, Leicestershire
Printed and bound in Great Britain by
T. J. International Ltd., Padstow, Cornwall

This book is printed on acid-free paper

To Brian

Author's Note

This book is a work of satirical fiction. The characters, conversations, and events in the novel are the product of my imagination, and no resemblance to any actual conduct of real-life persons, or to actual events, is intended. For the sake of verisimilitude, certain public figures are briefly referred to or make appearances in the novel, but their descriptions, actions, and words are wholly fictitious and are not to be intended to be understood as descriptions of real or actual events, or to reflect in any way upon the actual conduct or character of these public figures.

Acknowledgments

Thank you to the team: David Rosenthal, Marysue Rucci, Jennifer Rudolph-Walsh, Sylvie Rabineau, Stephanie Davis, Tara Parsons, Kerri Kolen, Victoria Meyer, Michael Selleck, Aileen Boyle, Louis Burke, Katie Finch, Lynn Goldberg, and Megan Underwood. I'd also like to thank that very nice man at FedEx. Thanks for all the support from my friends, Julie Jaffe, Leslee Newman, and Julia Sorkin. Now you can read the rest of the book. Thanks to Michael Smith for obvious reasons (you'd have to know him). Thank you to my family, my three sisters, Julie Levangie Purcell, Mimi Levangie, and Suzy Levangie Kurtz. Thank you to my mother, Phillipa Brown, who has sent me cartoons about the particular pitfalls of having raised a writer. It's a good thing she was a good mother. Thank you to my father, Frank Levangie, who looks like Paul Newman and is momentarily single. Thank you to my two step-teenagers, Riley and Sage Grazer, and my two little boys, Thomas and Patrick, for giving me so much joy and so little tsuris.

The Starter Wife

'She looks terrible. Oh my God. The girl's got skunk hair.'

Cluck, cluck.

'She's falling apart . . . hold up, is that a smile on her face? Look at those lines! Calling Doctor Botox! Calling Nurse Restylane!'

Cluck.

'She used to be a size four. Call me a liar, but you could sell that butt in Brentwood Park — that back end is lot-size — '

Cluck!

Gracie Pollock found herself standing in a half-moon contour with The Three Blondes, her Jimmy Choo stilettos sinking into damp, pricey Bermuda grass. She listened as she sucked a syrupy liquid with just enough alcohol through a straw; just enough alcohol to ward off the mental lucidity that would entice her to run for her life.

It was a fortieth birthday party for a friend. Well, not a friend, exactly, more like an acquaintance. The Wife Of . . . who was she the wife of, again? Anyway, seemed easy enough. An endless lawn filled with the ultimate in well-groomed wives. Rumors of a midday concert by Cyndi Lauper singing, what else — 'Girls Just Want to Have Fun.' Gracie thought it might even be something these gatherings rarely were: a good time. Until she pulled up in her Volvo SUV, walked along the side of the

1

Seussian Italianate mansion (cursing her choice of footwear as she slid into the muck with each step), and saw who was there.

Mean girls. The meanest of the mean in L.A. — every single woman who had nothing good to say about anybody was in attendance. There were no smiles; there were only sneers. Each one of these Evil Barbies could cut you with a look, lacerate you with one word, disembowel your confidence with a flick of their hair extensions.

And somehow, she'd found herself standing with The Three Blondes. Otherwise known as The Three Meanest Bitches in Town — Don't Even Think of Crossing Them.

They were something out of a warped fairy tale. One was short and ferocious — Gracie thought she resembled a pig with eyebrows; one was a bit taller, with an expansive bosom (they're hers; she bought them) and stick legs (ditto, above); the third loomed over the others, one feature larger than the next. Her man-hands could easily carry a sub-Saharan continent plus her ten-year collection of Birkin bags.

And they liked her. They liked Gracie, which didn't please her so much as strike terror in her soul. Where had she gone wrong? she wondered as they gathered around her like the parasitic flies that hang on cattle.

Their object of derision was the latest victim in a series of divorces that had rocked the West L.A. basin like a 6.2 earthquake.

The freshly divorced divorcée had the nerve to walk into the party without a Westside passport and, worse, without a proper escort — a current

Wife Of. She now lived in a condo on the east side of the universally recognized border of La Cienega Boulevard, and seemed to be unaware that her Westside friends had abandoned her. She had boldly, improperly, assumed that the gilded invitation sent to her before her separation still held two months later.

'The nerve,' the tall one sniffed, and sucked down her daiquiri, the straw disappearing momentarily into the recesses of her giant, giant mouth before popping out suddenly, causing Gracie to jump back. The bruises around the rim of her oversize lips stubbornly showed through the inch-thick smear of industrial-strength MAC Lipglass; she must have had her collagen shots just that morning, Gracie thought. A violation of the coda — no shots on the day of an event.

'She used to be The Wife Of,' the medium one oozed. 'Now, she's just another Starter Wife.'

Cluck. Gracie heard chickens whenever she bumped into the three. She knew it had something to do with her nerves, and would probably require a pill and an afternoon of needles punctured into her forehead at Dr. Zhu's. Luckily, she could score an emergency appointment; having sent Dr. Zhu on the requisite first-class weekend trip to Punta Mita, Gracie was at the top of the VIP list.

'Gracie.' The short one turned on her and narrowed her steel, bullet-slug orbs. 'What do you think of her?'

'Well,' said Gracie, caught between a rock and a hard-ass. She stared at the divorcée, hesitant to add to the venal brew. Time slowed. She could hear herself breathing. 'She doesn't look the same,' was what Gracie finally declared.

The three clucked with vigor and bobbed their blond heads, and Gracie asked, 'You girls want anything?' (Translation: 'Steal me away from Satan's Brides!') She scurried off not toward the bar but the freeway, serenaded by the sound of Cyndi and her band setting up. Cyndi screeched into the popping microphone, 'Forty ROCKS!' as Gracie's three-and-a-half-inch heels sank into a lawn that had obviously been watered several hours ago. For that, Gracie thought, my husband would have fired the gardener.

Gracie waited for her car in the circular driveway, watching the college-student valets run and park, run and park, and wondered about the divorcée. She *didn't* look the same, Gracie thought. She looked . . . older. She looked . . . not so blond. She looked . . . rounder, softer . . .

And something else, Gracie thought. She didn't look mean.

She looked, Gracie thought, could it be?

Normal.

'Girls just wanna have fu-un!' Cyndi sang, her signature voice and song somehow dancing around the stone, pillared behemoth, ten thousand square feet of home to two children, two parents, and nine 'staff.'

'Hi, Mrs. Pollock,' said the valet with the blue blazer and the cloying expression that tele-graphed he was looking for his Mrs. Robinson, as he jogged toward her. 'Leaving already?'

'Oh-oh, girls just wanna have fun!'

4

★ ★ ★

You can't avoid them. Don't even try. They're everywhere. Polished hair, polished nails, tucked, sucked, blown, bleached, waxed, Martin Katzed, and decked. Early morning? They're piloting their Navigators with the backseat DVDs blasting *Finding Nemo* in the car-pool lane at the Brentwood School, or crouching in a toddler circle at Mommy and Me at Bright Child comparing diamond ring settings. Ten-ish? They're IMing their Realtors searching for the illusory two-acre flat before twisting their limbs into erotic poses at Hot Tub Tony's class at Maha Yoga; after a bout of ujjayi breathing, they're hoisting soy green tea blendeds at Coffee Bean on San Vicente. At lunch, they're raking a carbless chicken-pecan salad with sterling forks at Barney Greengrass or draining Chardonnay decanters at the Ivy. Post-perc aperitif, you'll spy them trolling a Tuleh or Valentino trunk show on the second floor of Neiman's, assisted by a fluttering personal shopper. In late afternoon, the devotional worship at the Church of the Holy Mother of Upkeep: hair blown stick straight at Chris McMillan, nails French manicured at Jessica's on Sunset Plaza, Botox injected by dermos Arnie or Harold (after trying to decipher, say, Jennifer Aniston's name on the blacked-out patient sign-in board). Perhaps later they'll have their auras read by Lola the Chiropractor on West Pico, or while away the late afternoon firing a nanny because the baby called her 'Mommy' and then complaining about

5

the ensuing trauma to the tennis coach who has taught them everything but the serve. Evening? Unearth them at a Cedars-Sinai fund-raiser at the Beverly Hilton, swaying to the pop stylings of Miss Natalie Cole, or posing for a picture for *Angeleno Magazine* in the matron-chic Chanel suits their husbands loathe (they paid too much for the new breasts to keep those puppies imprisoned in tweed). Another night, they'll be attending the Holmby Hills version of the Oprah Book Club, hosted by a gaggle of blond doppelgängers eager to appear knowledgeable about something other than who the go-to girl is this week at Louis Vuitton.

And sometimes they even put their children to bed.

In the morning, the cycle begins again.

Among the numerous subcultures found in Los Angeles — the Sunset Strip Euros, the La Cañada skatepunks, the Hollywood Hills posers, the Encino Valley girls (yes, they still exist), the Echo Park graffitos, the Montebello gangsters, the Zuma surf rats, the West Hollywood buff boys, the Palisades breeders, the Santa Monica socialists, the Pasadena neocons, the Armenians, Mexicans, Vietnamese, El Salvadorans, Filipinos, Koreans, Russians, Hasids — there exists one civilization specific to its geographic origin, one which does not exist anywhere else.

The Wife Of.

The Wife Of could be married to the suit who runs the World Bank or the impotent action movie star, the elderly real estate magnate or the philandering studio chief. Powerful men may run

6

the world, but the 'Wives Of' run the powerful men.

At least, until their worst fear happens — the divorce that turns a Wife Of into a mere Starter Wife.

★   ★   ★

Enter Gracie Pollock. At every breakfast, lunch, dinner, party, school, or charity event for close to ten years, she'd been introduced as the 'wife of . . . ' In the beginning, this dubious title riled her. In one fell swoop, the wife of negated not only Gracie's existence prior to marriage, but her own contributions to the world (however feeble they may appear to, say, Doctors Without Borders). In the beginning, she would fight back by wielding her maiden name like a discus, throwing it out at whomever she met. But the hard truth was 'Gracie Peters' would draw blank stares. After a stretch, she attempted to clarify, tacking her husband's last name onto hers. Gracie became a thing unwieldy and confusing: the three-named woman.

And the blank stares persisted.

Finally, after several years of valiant resistance against the social mores, Gracie was beaten; she became so inculcated into the Wife Of culture that, like a dog who rolls onto his back at the first whiff of confrontation, she succumbed completely. The facts were cold and brutal: The Wife Of could get an eight o'clock reservation at Spago on a Friday night; The Wife Of could line jump at Disneyland; The Wife Of got 20 percent off at any of the designer boutiques on Rodeo Drive; The Wife Of got her kid into the school of her choice.

The Wife Of attained admission to The Club.

The Wife Of existed.

In the post — 'Gracie Peters' epoch, if Gracie were to have met you, at a political luncheon, a school fair, or restaurant opening, she would have automatically, graciously, casually, introduced herself as the 'Wife of . . . '

But there was nothing casual about her decision.

WIFE NUMBER ONE

The former soap star married to an Oscar-winning producer was looking forward to an annual Oscar party. There was only one glitch: She had gained fifteen pounds in the last year. 'Baby weight,' she sighed to her stylist as she struggled into a Narciso Rodriguez floor-length gown. 'You have no idea how hard it is to lose.'

Her bouncing baby girl was almost nine months old.

She had been born to a surrogate.

1

Married, With Onion Rings

Cellulite massage is not for the faint of heart. Which is what Gracie Pollock was thinking as her thighs were pounded by the grunting Russian woman who left her bruised, swollen, and otherwise disfigured every other Monday at three o'clock for the last five years. Gracie's calendar was filled with benign-sounding yet brutal 'treatments': Tuesdays were hair (blow-dry, cut, and highlights, if needed), Wednesdays were waxing or plucking, Thursdays belonged to dermabrasion or acid peels or any variety of activities involving needles and the hope of Insta-Youth, Fridays were off days, save for the second blow-dry of the week, when Gracie would compare her week of treatments to her friends' week of treatments over lunch at The Ivy.

You want irony? For the privilege of emerging from a session with Svetlana looking like she'd been locked in a freak dance with Mike Tyson, Gracie would write a check out to 'Cash' for $250 and hand it over with shaking hands.

Svetlana left the room, leaving behind an imprint of garlic cloves and generations of suffering on the air. There were countless other Wives Of to punish, those who bought into the myth of defeating the onslaught of age with a pair of hardened Russian fists. Gracie groaned and leaned up from the damp, tacky massage table (a nice way of putting the modern equivalent of the rack) and onto her elbows. She willed her eyes open, her lids feeling like the only part of her body that had escaped Soviet vengeance. She slowly twisted her head to the side to assess the damage in the veined, mirrored tile lining the walls. Mirrored tile, Gracie thought, all the rage when Sylvester, the lisping Supreme Ruler of Disco, was at the top of the charts. 'For a tax-free two-fifty a pop,' Gracie muttered, 'Svetlana the Terrible could swing a subscription to *Elle Decor*.'

But the veined tile with the mirrored surface served its purpose. Here's the scoop. Gracie Pollock looked ridiculously good in that her polished exterior straddled the territories claimed by both adjectives, *ridiculous* and *good*. Each time Gracie peered at her reflection, she was startled, as though she had run into a formerly plain-wrapped high school friend who had transformed herself into a middle-aged version of Jessica Simpson. What are the odds of looking better at forty than at sixteen? Gracie thought to herself. About the same as crapping a gleaming pile of Krugerrands.

Let's start with the hair. Said hair being the color of that expensive European butter no one can pronounce. Domestic butter, according to Gracie's colorist, not being, well, buttery enough. And this hair was thick. Thick, as though somewhere in the Hamptons, Christie

Brinkley had awakened looking like Michael Chiklis with hips. Gracie's original mousy brown, tongue-in-light-socket chicken wire had been colored and wrestled and yanked and stretched and stretched again into submission by a fine-boned man of unknown sexual and other identity named Yuko, then brightened with highlights every three weeks and lengthened with extensions, rewoven every twelve weeks. Her forehead was as unlined as the hood of a new Porsche, due to the same poison found in warped green bean cans she was warned about as a child. Her lips were soft and full. Thank you, the pitiless Collagen God. The teeth? Straight and white. The teeth were hers. The teeth, she'd grown herself.

I did grow those teeth myself, right? Gracie thought.

Yes, Gracie reassured herself as she bared her teeth like a rich blond rottweiler into the veined mirror. *Those are my teeth.*

She growled at her reflection.

Let's move on. The breasts were a perfect full B cup. Gracie had given birth and breast-fed — and yet her nipples pointed due north. Nature? Or the magic hands of Dr. Barbara Hayden? You decide.

The tummy, save for the bumpy scar which Gracie had not yet 'done' above her pubic bone, was hard and as hard earned as the diamond on her left hand. The arms, brown and muscular and hairless as newborn Chihuahuas. The legs, Gracie's bête noir throughout her teenage years, were as sleek and taut as the skin on an apple.

11

Just looking at them made her weary.

Maintenance was a Mother Fucker.

Gracie stuck her tongue out at her reflection. The blond, green-eyed, perky-breasted woman rudely assessing her was not related to the soft-fleshed, brown-eyed girl she'd been more or less satisfied with for thirty years.

This Gracie, by all accounts, appeared perfect. Media friendly. Easy on the eyes and hard on the 401(k).

Then she looked down at her hands. *Good Lord, not the hands*, Gracie thought. The dead giveaway. The Dorian Gray painting in the attic. The skin on her hands was changing. Freckles that had once been a badge of youth and vigor were now a sign of encroaching age — the inevitable, inexorable spiraling into the Martha Raye Terra In-firma.

Gracie hadn't told anyone, not even her close friends, but in the last two years, she had failed the pinch test. Failing the pinch test is something best kept close to the bustier — if Gracie pinched the back of her hand (which she did several times an hour), the skin no longer snapped back. It slid back.

Eventually.

And those freckles. What could blast them out? Gracie hovered over her hands with a critical eye. What could possibly eliminate the speckled insurgents? Laser, acid peel, that pricey SPF 1,000 Greek sunscreen, bleaching creams, fotofacial, collagen, harvested fat cell shots. She had tried everything. And still the pinch test failed. Still the freckles persisted.

12

Gracie tucked her hands away, hiding them like a dreaded family secret. She sighed. And then she thought about her elbows. Gravity is a bitch, she thought.

'Do not' — she wagged her finger at her reflection — 'appraise the elbows!'

Gracie felt her body was a time bomb, just waiting to jump back into its normal state, should the narrowest opportunity appear. She lived in a world where people fought their natural condition on a daily basis — every day in L.A. was Halloween. Those weren't masks she'd see in the women's dressing area at Saks or in the salon chairs at Cristophe or suspended over glass noodles at Mr. Chow — those were faces. Gracie feared she'd wake up one day and the skin around her face would be pulled into a bow in the back of her head.

Gracie was on the precipice. Was she going to be the recently Asian Joan Rivers, or what once was Brigitte Bardot? She'd have to make a choice.

One pull of the pin, Gracie knew as she peered over her shoulder at her proto-human reflection, and the whole thing would blow.

★ ★ ★

The trouble started with the earring. This wasn't just any earring — like that silver Celtic cross Gracie had lost in a public toilet at Santa Monica Beach because she was so freaked out by the thought of homeless people wandering in while she peed in a doorless stall. This wasn't one of the pair of pink diamond and platinum three-carat studs Gracie and every other stuck-in-a-loveless-marriage-but-with-a-generous-allowance Wife Of had her eye on at the Loree Rodkin case at Neiman Marcus, aka Needless Markup, just waiting for her husband to slip up for an excuse to buy. No, this wasn't just any earring. This was a delicate gold-wire hoop suddenly attached to her husband's heretofore unadorned, exhibiting middle-aged tendencies (more hair, additional length) right earlobe.

File Gracie Pollock's story under 'hindsight is twenty-twenty,' with the understanding that her sight was definitely up her hind end at the time. But how was Gracie to know that the demise of her nine-year, ten-month, three-day, eighteen-hour marriage could have been foretold mere weeks ago by a tiny piece of metal in a middle-aged man's ear?

'Yo, ho, ho, a pirate's life for me,' sang Gracie, wife of Kenny Pollock, president of Durango Studios, as her ever-tardy husband loped over to their usual corner table at Ivy at the Shore, their (and every other Power Lister's) watering hole of choice. Kenny was twenty minutes late, as always. Somewhere between 'punctual' and 'rude' there was 'Kenny time': twenty minutes late. Not ten minutes, not fifteen minutes. Twenty. Sometimes Gracie wondered if he waited out in the car until half past nineteen minutes — his lateness was as precise as the creases ironed into his jeans. (How precise were those creases, you ask? So precise that Kenny measured the creases himself, with a carpenter's

14

measuring tape. If the crease was off center, bodily threats would be faxed to the dry cleaner.)

'Investors meeting at the studio,' Kenny said, kissing Gracie's upturned cheek, ignoring her rendition of the Disney classic with a shrug of his long-ago-college-football-player shoulders. Gracie noted that he did not issue an apology for his tardiness — another in a long line of power moves. She knew the drill: 'Sorry' is for people who have to care. 'Sorry' is for people who may need a job someday. 'Sorry' is for Pussies. Kenny greeted their dinner guests. 'Or were we their guests?' Gracie asked herself. 'One forgets.' The dinner had been set in November of the previous year. Most of their dinners were set months in advance — Gracie and Kenny could barely get through the first week of January without knowing exactly how their year would lay out. They knew exactly who they would have drinks at the Four Seasons bar with on March twelfth, who they'd be entertaining at home with a chef's barbecue on May seventh, whose summer vacation home in the Hamptons or Martha's Vineyard or Point Dume they'd find themselves watching fireworks from on July fourth, whose winter vacation home in Aspen, Telluride, or Sun Valley they'd find themselves skiing out of come Thanksgiving Day weekend.

The pair they were eating dinner with tonight was a married couple — the man, a slithery, amphibious, soon-to-be-unemployed network chief (everyone except for him, from the valet parkers to the Sumner Redstones, seemed to know this) and the wife, a former stripper and back-page material Playboy Bunny trying to hide her past, along with her overenthusiastic breasts, under a serious blue, aching business suit. Last Gracie checked, Jil Sander did not design in spandex. Gracie had spent the last eighteen minutes listening to the man brag about his new electric car (to augment his fleet of Escalades and his habitual use of private jets), his Tuesday-night lineup, his resting heart rate, the view from their newly remodeled Beverly Park home across from Sly, and the number of Ivy League slots taken up by his children's private school each year. His pace was breathless, skipping from self-adoring subject to self-aggrandizing subject, leaving poor Gracie to wonder what they would have left to talk about over the ubiquitous grilled vegetable salad dinner. And then Gracie remembered that Kenny was no slouch in the bragging game. Her work was done. She could retire to the master bedroom in her head.

Gracie sat back and smiled, sipping her 'rocks, salt, and quick, please' Patron Margarita. Gracie felt brave asking for salt, her guests and Gracie knowing full well that she was flirting carelessly with water retention. At her age, two weeks shy of forty-one, Gracie reckoned, retention of any kind — mental or physical — was welcome. She threw caution to the Santa Anas and indulged in her sodium-laced, liquid escape hatch, as Kenny launched into a soliloquy on the state of the three movies his studio was currently shooting. He'd just flown back from the set of the new

$150 million Civil War epic (a paean to American history filmed, ironically, in Romania). Kenny was claiming to have come up with the story for it himself one day on the stationary bike, which he rode every other morning, alternating with the dreaded treadmill, at six-fifteen for not one minute over twenty-two. He'd read in *Men's Health* (the only periodical he read religiously) that maximum aerobic benefits start to trail off after twenty-two minutes, and he was not one to waste time — his time, specifically.

Gracie wondered what the well-respected screenwriter (oxymoron?) of the epic would think of the yarn Kenny was spinning — it felt as though he was trying out an Oscar speech. But Gracie was too grateful for her husband's appearance to quibble. It saved her from probing haplessly for common ground with the ex-stripper, whose breasts were threatening a mutiny: Gracie was deathly afraid a button would pop and ruin the results of her LASIK surgery. Kenny had urged Gracie to correct her nearsightedness; the glasses he'd once loved on her made her look 'like she read too much.' As Kenny talked about the details of the Civil War that were previously unbeknownst to him and no one else on the planet ('Did you know brother fought against brother?') and the network executive chewed the ice from his gimlet (sexual frustration? Even with the boobage his prosti-wife was sporting?) and patiently waited his turn to talk about last week's rare-as-a-spotted-owl ratings win, Gracie slipped into a self-imposed waking coma.

Occasionally, during business dinners, cocktail parties, premieres, test screenings, and endless christenings and bar mitzvahs, Gracie would disengage herself from the physical world and picture her body floating above the shiny, glazed surface, gazing down upon her fellow inmates who looked like so many sheep in a Technicolor field. Gracie had learned years ago that all that was required of her as a Hollywood wife was to nod and smile and ask empty, flat questions and make meaningless declarations, and she had mastered those skills, which was harder than one might think.

Try it. Think of 101 Ways to Say Hello and Inquire about The Children. Or, more rash, Inquire about The Movie. To do this, you must remember who made what film. And then you must remember what movies to bring up, what movies never to mention. Otherwise, you could have a conversation that goes something like this:

Gracie, to a famous director: 'Hi, Fred. Wow, I saw your movie *The Toad in Spring* last week. It was wonderful.'

Fred, wielding a sneer, 'I fucking hated that movie.'

Becoming a Wife Of required almost as much training as first violin in the London Symphony Orchestra. Gracie often thought there should be a Juilliard for power-wives-in-training. Examples of the classes might be: 'Your Interior Decorator and You,' 'Getting to Table One,' or, a favorite elective, 'Embracing Your Inner Self, and Then Stomping It to Death.' Gracie was currently enrolled in 'Botox or Brow Lift: Stay 29 Forever or Be Replaced by Your Nanny!'

Gracie remembered that when she first started dating Kenny, it had taken months to train herself not to hurl a sarcastic comment when one of about 200 million 'Executive VPs' shook her hand while looking over her shoulder for a more important person to greet (and there was always someone more important than The Girlfriend). It had taken weeks to recover from having to reintroduce herself to a satellite player fifteen times in the same year. Finally Gracie had mastered introducing herself by name to anyone she ran into, even people who were friends. You never knew who would draw a blank at the appearance of your nonfamous face.

In the beginning, Gracie had considered herself one of the lucky ones, and not for the reasons one would think — sure, there was the money. But Hollywood was not unlike Major League Baseball: the players had a short shelf life; once a studio executive started striking out on a regular basis, they were relegated to the Minors. They elected (were fired) to move on to their own production shingles, often housed in off-the-beaten-track office buildings above Sofa-U-Love or Jacopo's pizza shop. In the milliseconds between the words 'You're' and 'out!' uttered merrily by a superior, they went from buyers to sellers, and for the most part never made another movie in their lives. The local college extension courses were full of former executives teaching 'Screenwriting 101' and 'An Insider's Guide to Hollywood II' (with prerequisite).

But even if one were a success in Hollywood, try keeping up with the Joneses (there are no Joneses in Hollywood) when the Joneses are chauffeured in their Maybachs to the Polo Lounge for breakfast. Try keeping up with the Joneses when a beach house in the Malibu Colony costs $80,000 to rent in July (which is when everyone who is anyone is there). Try keeping up with the Joneses when the Joneses haven't set foot in LAX in a decade, because they've got their G-5 gassed up and awaiting flight plans at the Avjet terminal in industrial Burbank.

There was not enough money in the world for people in Hollywood; someone always had more.

And they were building their mega-mansion right next door to yours.

Gracie had been able, at least for their dating years, to hang on to her own identity, separate from Kenny's. It was rare for a Hollywood girlfriend or wife to have a job — rarer still to have a career. Kenny seemed to love that she'd had both. For a time, he'd brag to his coworkers, stating that he was planning on retiring on Gracie's income — that maybe she'd be the one to ask for a pre-nup. She didn't. Kenny did.

Through a lot of luck and a little hard work along with what Gracie claimed was a modicum of talent, she had become a semipopular children's book author. Right after college, she'd written and illustrated books like *Question Boy* and *Curiosity and Question Boy*, the sequel,

20

based on an autistic boy she'd befriended at a bus stop. All of six or seven, he questioned her about the nature of the 'square-not-round' buttons on her coat, why her hair was curly and his was straight, and why her left front tooth was slightly crooked and a bit yellow. His mother shushed him, but Gracie realized that here was a boy for whom every moment at a bus stop was discovery, every bus ride an adventure. She was fascinated. She'd started the book literally out of nowhere, with no background in illustration or writing, the minute she stepped into her apartment. The first words she'd written down, without taking off that square-not-round-buttoned coat, were:

Do you like buttons? I like buttons. Mommy says buttons attach our warm coats to our bodies. Do belly buttons hold our bodies together? What if we unbuttoned our belly buttons? Would we explode? What if . . . ?

Gracie created a series based on little people who were left a half-step behind on the evolutionary scale (they were light green and covered in a soft, downy fur and survived, like frogs, both in water and on land) called The Frugs. She considered herself a writer more than an artist: her drawings were simple, childlike; her colors bold and rudimentary. She drew and painted quickly before she lost interest, like the pint-size audience she was striving to reach. And then she would settle into the words.

Gracie made enough money at her career to support herself — the only goal she'd set.

She could afford a car, gas, insurance, an unfurnished one-bedroom apartment in the Fairfax district, enough dinners out at cheap, exotic, out-of-the-way places to encourage a weight issue. She made more than a school-teacher and less than an accountant; she was satisfied.

But she was also a vessel of that most common of human afflictions, loneliness. Gracie didn't work in an office where she could commiserate about the horrible boss over one-hour lunches at the Olive Garden; she didn't have a dog — wasn't allowed one in her apartment. She would write, take a walk, go get a cup of coffee, come back, write, go get some lunch . . . return. Gracie would walk into her apartment and say 'I'm home' as a joke, but also as a prayer; maybe, if she said those words often enough, someone someday would answer.

Yes, Gracie had friends, writer friends — or the occasional oddball who had a trust fund that was barely enough to pay rent on a studio apartment. But the majority of her friends worked two or three jobs, keeping themselves solvent until the big payday when their scripts would be optioned, that network pilot would be picked up, or they packed it in and went back to graduate work — or to marrying the high school sweetheart they left behind somewhere in the middle of the country.

Gracie could go days without saying more than 'I'll have the chicken soup, please,' to one of the gruff elderly waitresses at Canter's. She was an only child; her gentle, beloved father had died suddenly of a heart attack when Gracie was in her senior year at college, living off-campus. Her mother, the youngest of four girls, had never lived alone and was not prepared to do so now, in her fifties. She had moved shortly thereafter to Seattle, where her favorite older sister lived, away from the smog and the freeways and the memories and the crime. But also away from her daughter. They rarely talked. Gracie thought of herself, when dreariness and self-pity consumed her thoughts (she allowed herself this luxury about once a week), as the world's oldest living orphan.

When Kenny appeared in Gracie's life, with his grand plans, his sheer velocity, she was swept up like a tumbleweed in a desert windstorm. Gracie went quietly, as resistant as melted butter, a shining example of Stockholm syndrome. 'Tell me where to go,' her brain whispered as she looked at Kenny speaking with conviction, with energy, with life, on any given subject, any at all. 'I'll go,' her eyes revealed.

On her first date with Kenny, he'd picked her up at her apartment, knocking on her door like machine-gun fire. He was five minutes early and her dating clock was five minutes late — she'd taken a full hour to get dressed. Not counting the make-out session with the lanky college student from Germany who lived across the street, this was her first date in six months.

Gracie had quickly tugged Kenny in, away from the prying eyes of her widowed neighbor, and he'd waited in what she called her living room — a plaster square replete with a

23

two-seater couch, a small TV on a stand, and a coffee table.

She heard him poking around the kitchen as she slipped on her heels, cognizant of the scuffs that pinned her as a girl on the rise or slipping badly. She came out to find Kenny looking into her mini-refrigerator and shaking his head.

'How long has it been since you've had a good meal?' he'd asked. She looked at him, her mouth open. Gracie had almost burst into tears, for it was a question a mother would ask. A question no one had asked her in a long, long time.

Kenny had taken her to legendary Spago, where he was greeted by 'Wolfie' and where they had eaten foie gras four ways and crab cakes and some kind of architecturally challenging beet salad and drank a bottle (two bottles?) of Cabernet and platefuls of desserts, and when she spied the bill, before Kenny flipped his American Express (business) card onto it, she was shocked to see the price of the meal.

She had eaten two months' rent. And had been completely seduced. She felt like Pretty Woman; but instead of the hottest hooker on the planet, Gracie was an attractive, if a bit mousy, scribe.

Once they were married, having her own identity set her apart from her peers, her fellow wives. Sure, there were a few wives who had outside interests — baby photography, a clothes boutique — and they talked about their interests at length in various fashion magazines, where they would be photographed in the glamorous setting of the studio they rarely used, the eponymous boutique they seldom frequented. Their jobs were more like very expensive, well-publicized hobbies.

Gracie surmised that Hollywood Wives had the highest unemployment rate in the country.

Let it be said that Gracie hadn't written anything in a while. 'A while' translated into half a decade, give or take a year. She hadn't been seized with an idea that demands you run to your computer before it recedes into the fabric of what Hollywood people loved to call their 'crazy busy' lives. She hadn't met the boy at the bus stop, so to speak. Gracie had sat in front of her computer many days, jabbing at keys, willing an idea to fall out of the sky and drizzle out through her fingertips.

At first, Gracie figured it must be the demands of having a baby. She and Kenny had a baby girl almost four years ago, after years of trying. Of course a baby is a distraction. Of course a baby makes life more full, and of course a mother has less time to write than a nonparent.

But deep down, Gracie knew her dry spell, the endless desert of her unproductive days, had a different genesis. It wasn't pregnancy brain, it wasn't postpartum, and it wasn't her beautiful Jaden.

(Okay, the name. Time to come clean. Jaden was named after Jada Pinkett and Will Smith's child. Kenny, at the time, was casting a Vietnam War movie that needed a young, black, powerful lead. Will didn't wind up taking the role, of course, and Gracie in the meantime had a child whose name was looted

from movie-star offspring.)

Gracie's well of ideas had run dry. Gracie's talent, her personality, her gumption, even her anger, were fading. She felt like a pencil drawing that was being slowly, methodically erased. The demands of a life filled with petty concerns — *Why are the tennis court lights on at eight a.m.? The air-conditioning went above 72 degrees in the guesthouse sitting room! We need new flower arrangements twice a week. Why won't the remote (that cost as much as a new Toyota) turn off the Flat Screen TV in the bar? What is the proper ratio of studio to talent for a dinner party? The orchids in the foyer are dying. Should we serve lamb or salmon at our third dinner party this month? I want a phone on the left side of the master toilet. Who has (imaginary) food allergies? The pool is overflowing. Who doesn't eat meat? That painting doesn't work with the new couch. Who doesn't eat bread? I need another iPod (preprogrammed with Julia Roberts's favorites). The gardener cut the grass too low. The made-in-Tibet screening-room curtains won't open* — had devoured not only Gracie's creativity but, more important, her spirit.

Gracie's comatose state was starting to lift as she looked up at the ex-stripper, whose full figure and full attention were on Kenny as she bobbled her head like the dog figurines Gracie would see in the back of the rusty Toyotas owned by the Latina nannies in her neighborhood.

The Stepford wives had nothing on the Wives Of, Gracie thought ruefully. Amateurs.

Onion rings that everyone agreed to order but no one would eat, thanks to Zone oppression, arrived at the table. Kenny stood to greet someone famous whom Gracie didn't recognize — Gracie could tell this person was famous because Kenny had forgotten to introduce his wife. He wasn't trying to be rude. Kenny had Celebrity Alzheimer's: His brain went on the blink when approached by a celebrated face. Kenny was blinded by fame, fascinated by those on the lit side of the camera. He would often forget that his civilian wife, who would never be found in the pages of *People*'s 50 Most Beautiful! edition, was standing right next to him.

Gracie stared at this girl, a petite, anemic, pretty blonde like so many petite, anemic, pretty blondes on screen, and made a game out of trying to place her. She considered celebrity naming a sort of virtual crossword puzzle: *Is she on a sitcom? In a movie? Action movie? Romantic comedy? Is she British? One of the hundreds of Australians? (Does anyone in that country not act?) Does she sing? Under thirty? Over thirty? Dating a tennis star? Dating Ben Affleck? Just broken up with Ben Affleck? Pregnant with Ben Affleck's twins?*

After she'd turned forty, Gracie realized that she was recognizing fewer and fewer 'recognizable faces.' Gracie had no interest in a network called the WB — Gracie wasn't even sure what WB stood for — and they had no interest in her. FOX left her cold, except for that show with Keifer Sutherland, whom Gracie still expected to look like the Lost Boy she lusted after when she was young, not the grizzled Manly Man (whom she still lusted after) he'd become. NBC and ABC were passable. CBS? Gracie didn't know what that was, but apparently she would in her retirement years. And Gracie didn't understand — was it her, or were there just so many more 'famous' people than there were fifteen years ago?

And was Gracie the only one who wasn't famous?

Gracie was midway through dinner by the time she was up to her third witty remark — she had finally met her self-imposed quota. Maybe Gracie would go beyond the expected and dole out four, although she usually kept herself to three per dinner, so as to not appear as detached as she felt. During their years of courtship and marriage, Kenny and Gracie had attended hundreds of affairs and endured endless hours of small talk. So much small talk that Gracie had developed a foolproof method for dealing with it. She'd even broken down the elements of these nights into categories of engagement:

1. You Had Me at 'I Made the Cover of *Variety*': Always greet with a warm smile (bonded is good, veneers are better), a litany of your recent successes (ignore flops and wayward children), a full-body-slam hug, and finally a kiss — a double kiss if in vogue. As in dancing, let the man lead.

    They will, anyway.

2. Hair, Wardrobe, Vacation Homes: After the greet, the first ten minutes of conversation must center on these three items. As in: 'Love, love, love your new hair' (meaning, literally, 'new hair' — Japanese extensions still stubbornly all the rage), 'Where did you get that belt? (Garage sale? Your mother's closet? Prada?),' and 'Have you been to your second home in (Sun Valley, Aspen, Telluride, Park City, Martha's Vineyard, Promises rehab in Malibu) lately?'

3. Where are you going for (fill in the blank): Christmas vacation? New Year's? Spring break? Presidents' Day weekend? Where are you summering?

3a. Where are you staying? (See above.)

4. The Democrats: Politics is a fine topic to bring up in Hollywood — everyone is in agreement over who is good and who is bad. In fact, politics is considered a polite topic of conversation, and also a way to work in that one knows who the current president is.

5. The Republicans: They eat babies; they steal from grandmothers; they are awful; everyone hates them. Repeat ad infinitum. Unless, say, you are in the presence of the few Red Celebs: e.g., the still controversial Charlton Heston.

6. Where do your kids go to school? It is assumed that the child or children attends a private school, though rarely has a parent attended one. And the parents of children in one private school are suspicious of parents of children in a different private school. Why are they in that school? Why are we not in that school? Are we wait-listed for that school? Why? How many hours of home-work does your kid have? (Why doesn't our kid have that much homework?)

There are no parents more obsessed with getting their kids into Harvard than the Hollywood parent, though few had gone there themselves, and if they had, had probably been fired from their jobs by now. Here's a tip: Moving to Hollywood? Keep your Ivy League degree to yourself.

Religion? Seldom brought up unless someone was trying to get his child into a private school with a religious affiliation. For example, a person could say, 'I'm trying to get into Wilshire Boulevard, but I have to join the Temple.' Or, 'I need to be a parishioner for two years before I get into St. Stephen's.'

Kenny and Gracie had scrambled onto the guest list of every party for those between the ages of twenty-five and seventy-five. For the last few years, they had attended, without fail, four events or dinners a week.

Gracie calculated as the network executive jumped into the conversation guns blazing — four times fifty-two weeks equals two hundred and eight, multiplied by ten equals two thousand and eighty outings, not including this one.

As the network executive labored through his dubiously masculine account of a recent white-water rafting trip, Gracie experienced Past Life Regression.

Kenny wasn't always so very Kenny. Gracie was clearheaded enough to remember when Kenny would groan about having to go out all the time, even if Gracie never quite believed that he resented the demands on his time. Gracie never really bought that he hated talking marketing with David Geffen or Barry Diller. Did Gracie wonder that he was miserable being away from her on her thirtieth birthday because he had to catch a private jet with Spielberg to see a screening in San Diego? No. Did Gracie think for a moment that he hated going back to work an hour after their daughter was born because Billy Bob Thornton was fighting with the director on his Western? Not a chance.

Kenny was a low-man-on-the-totem-pole development executive when Gracie met him. He had phoned her out of the blue. 'Kenny Pollock here,' he'd said, 'Pollock like the fish.' 'Not the artist?' Gracie had asked. She'd recently been to a LACMA exhibition of the artist's most famous works. She'd stood for hours, staring at . . . what? Drops, lines, webs, colors, streams . . . And yet, she stood. Mesmerized. She'd gone back twice. The greatest emotional involvement she'd had in years — and it was with a painting.

'Artist?' Kenny had cracked. 'Don't tell anyone in Hollywood I've got an artist's name, they'll run me out of town.' He talked her up for half an hour about optioning her first children's book for no money for a never-to-be-made movie. Gracie was charmed by the way his voice cracked while toiling under the tenor of false bravado. Gracie had no idea what he looked like; she imagined he was small boned and fidgety and dark — just her type. He invited her for sushi in a place called Brentwood. Gracie had never had sushi and had rarely ventured west of La Cienega. When Gracie met him for this sushi lunch, she walked right past him toward another man sitting at the bar. Kenny tapped her on the shoulder, and Gracie turned around, stunned to see a tall galoot with football-player shoulders and a child's grin, and more stunned when he bear-hugged her and planted a big kiss on her cheek. Gracie wasn't yet accustomed to the typical Hollywood greeting; she generally consigned her kisses and hugs to family members and lovers. Gracie soon learned she was a prude, that in Hollywood a kiss carries as little weight as a blow job from a call girl. Gracie learned to hand out kisses to maître d's and studio chiefs as easily as she'd kiss her own mother. Except that she had never kissed her own mother on the lips.

Kenny wasn't her type. Period. Not least because he was the King of Exclamation. No person or activity was too prosaic to elude the Kenny Howl of Enthusiasm. Then there were his looks. Gracie didn't like handsome, didn't trust handsome, was never even a fan of handsome movie stars. Why would Gracie drool over Brad Pitt when Gracie would rather look like Brad

Pitt? Kenny was too tall, too good-looking, and, she learned as their lunch wore on, too ambitious. Gracie had heard of five-year plans, even ten-year plans — but he had twenty-, thirty-, forty-year plans. Kenny knew what studio he wanted to run, he knew the types of movies he wanted to make, he knew who he wanted his lieutenants to be. Kenny knew what he wanted in a wife and he knew how many children he wanted (two: one boy, one girl) and where he wanted them to go to school (preschool, elementary school, high school, college — graduate school!). He knew what street he wanted to live on ('Rockingham — the best views in Los Angeles'); he knew what car he'd be driving in five years (Mercedes 600SL). The man knew where he'd end up after Alzheimer's hit him in his old age (the Motion Picture Home).

Kenny, who had barely made a dent into his thirtieth year, knew he'd be cremated and where his ashes would be scattered (in the Pacific, off the Baja Peninsula).

On the surface, nothing about 'The Kenny Package' would seem to appeal to a person like Gracie. She had never shared a tuna roll with anyone who seemed untouched by the Human Condition. He had emerged from his first thirty years unscathed. Of course Kenny had been a college athlete; of course he had been treasurer of his fraternity (better access to beer funds than the president); of course he had grown up in the suburbs in a two-parent household with a younger sister and a dog named Rusty.

And of course he drove a BMW, in the

L.A.-biquitous black. He took one sidelong look at her Toyota Cressida, as though afraid of infection by the working class, and told her she'd have to sell it and buy something more hip. Gracie told him the only thing more hip she could afford would be a skateboard.

That afternoon he sent her a brand-new skateboard with hot pink wheels. She'd hugged the gift card to her chest. She could still remember the words scribbled onto the tiny card: 'To Gracie, who deserves better wheels. Love, Kenny 'The Artist' Pollock.'

Love!

Gracie had been Kenny-fected.

So despite her qualms, Gracie dated Kenny anyway and got attached to his goofy charm anyway and slept with him on the third date anyway — after all, they'd already had their first kiss at the sushi bar. Maybe she was a sellout. Maybe Gracie should have stuck out her existence on the wrong side of town, driving the wrong car and wearing the wrong clothes. ('It's a good thing you're so cute,' Kenny told her the first morning after they'd slept together as Gracie was getting dressed in her baggy corduroys and long-sleeved T-shirt, 'because your clothes suck.') But Kenny represented what Gracie felt was missing in her life — stability. He could take charge, he knew where he was going; Gracie had no idea where her life was headed. There was no five-year plan; there wasn't even a three-week plan. Gracie, who always prided herself on her independence, who had never depended on anyone, much less a man, secretly longed to be taken care of.

With Kenny, Gracie would emerge from the shell of the studious UCLA student who watched from the bus stop as sorority girls whizzed by her in their convertible Cabriolets; with Kenny, she would no longer have her nose pressed up against the plate-glass Prada window. (Except that as she got older, she no longer 'understood' Prada; what could those odd shoes and unflattering dresses mean?)

In fact, sometimes Gracie wondered if the main reason she married Kenny was to seek vengeance upon Cabriolet-driving, Master-Card-hoarding sorority girls. Not that that was a terrible reason to get married. In Los Angeles, it could be the raison d'être; anyone would understand. In India and Pakistan, they had arranged marriages; in Los Angeles, marriages were arranged by the color of your American Express card.

Back to Kenny's business dinner: Emerging from her Past Life Regression, Gracie sipped her margarita and leaned back, sucking in her lower stomach as she always did when she heard her Pilates instructor's voice egging her on in her mind — 'strengthen the core, and the rest follows.'

Thank God, Gracie thought. Thank God I'm married. I don't have to worry about a little extra tummy.

'Where are you going this Christmas?' the ex-stripper asked, jamming an ice pick through the fragile surface of Gracie's reverie.

It was March.

Gracie smiled. The margarita was working its magic.

★ ★ ★

Gracie had turned left from Sunset onto Rockingham when her cell phone rang, the recorded voice of her daughter repeating itself: *Mommy, your cell phone is ringing. Mommy, your cell phone is ringing.*

The caller ID flashed Kenny's car phone number.

'Hello?' Gracie said. 'Hello?' she repeated. She cursed; the reception in Brentwood was always bad.

'Kenny?' All Gracie heard was the maddening staccato hiccups of a broken phone connection.

'Kenny? I'm losing you,' Gracie said. She wondered why he didn't wait to talk to her until they were both home. She hung up and tossed the phone in the passenger seat. And then she worried: *What if he'd been in an accident?*

She was pulling into her driveway when the phone rang again. Three bars showed up on the cell phone. The reception would be clear.

'Kenny?' Gracie asked. 'Is everything all right?'

'I said' — Kenny's voice was finally clear — 'I want a divorce.'

The execution of their marriage was performed via Cingular Wireless.

2

The Seven Stages of a Hollywood Marriage

Kenny had proposed, as expected, on Valentine's Day. After all, they were almost three years into his five-year plan, and Gracie knew he wanted to be married before he was thirty-two. They were staying at the Auberge du Soleil in Napa. Gracie knew that something was afoot because Kenny seldom took a day off from work. Even on weekends, he would read ten scripts to be ready with notes on Monday, and watch as many demo reels and videotapes to be up on the talent pool. Kenny and Gracie were living together in his small house in the Palisades, the miniaturized ultimate in *Woman's Day* suburban living. Kenny hated the little house; Gracie thought it glorious. Kenny had his social (read: work-related social) routine: the business dinners during the week, followed by a breakfast meeting on Saturday, either at the Peninsula in Beverly Hills or Shutters in Santa Monica — there were stringent rules on where to hold breakfast or lunch meetings. Or since he'd taken up golf ('Eisner golfs!'), he'd be up and out early at the Riviera.

But Sunday morning — that was their time

alone. They would make love early in the morning, barely awake, dreamily groping for each other's body under the covers. Time would evaporate. Troubles were shunted aside. All that existed were lips and skin and Kenny's boyish scent. Gracie could have lived for days on Kenny's scent.

The sex was phenomenal. Gracie knew that she was unlike any other girl Kenny had ever dated. She saw the old pictures, the slender, dynamic blondes clutching a beer can and cigarette in one hand with troublesome ease, the tennis wrinkles already forming around their startling blue eyes. Kenny approached Gracie as though she were the northern tip of Africa, and he the Great White Hunter. She knew he'd never experienced ample thighs, her tangle of hair, her pale, giving skin. Kenny would fall asleep on top of Gracie's stomach, purring into the well of flesh around her belly button.

Gracie would run her fingers through his jock-cut hair as he slept. She would stare at the high Spanish ceiling with the watermarks and pass his locks through her fingers like a mantra. She found whole worlds in those moments.

Hours later, they would rise and jog, unsteady, giddy, down to the beach. If they were very ambitious, they could make it all the way to Venice. But Gracie was not nearly as eager to exercise as Kenny, so often they'd just stop for coffee along the bike path, taking in the sights — overly tan girls in bikinis on roller skates, chubby men in Lycra shorts on blades, babies bouncing uncomfortably in jogging strollers as their stringy, stern mothers chugged behind them. During the week, it was easy for Gracie to lose Kenny. He was at the gym on Montana by 6:00 A.M. five times a week (Jerry Bruckheimer pumps iron at five-thirty!); they would often not see each other until seven-thirty in the evening, and that was usually in conjunction with another couple — or a hundred other couples. But Gracie could fill the hours with procrastination and sometimes even the writing itself. Gracie was proud that she made her own money, though it was nothing by Hollywood standards; more than that, Gracie loved that Kenny was proud of her. She knew she was different from the other women; Gracie would never become needy, Gracie would never mold herself into the image of the proper wife.

There were a lot of things that Gracie told herself she'd never do.

And then Gracie grew up. Oh, did Gracie grow up.

Their last night at the Auberge, Kenny insisted on having dinner inside their room on the balcony. Gracie had to agree; it was a night consistent with the vestiges of winter — dark, cloudless sky, stars forming their own personal constellations. Kenny pointed his long, pitcher's arm toward the sky. 'There's the constellation Batman' or 'Do you see? There's the constellation Swollen Penis!' They laughed like five-year-olds and Gracie held on to him and had never in her life been happier.

Looking back, Gracie marveled at the fact that Kenny had picked a perfect night for a proposal.

His timing had always been faultless; he knew just when to move out of one job and into another, he knew the right moment to court press, he knew when to cut losses and people. With every major life question, he was the Titan of Timing.

They had just finished her favorite part of the meal, dessert — a molten chocolate soufflé. Gracie had eaten her half and Kenny's when he dropped down to one knee. For a second, Gracie thought he had dropped his fork, but there it was, a solitaire diamond so beautiful that Gracie had almost forgotten about the chocolate.

'Will you?' he asked.

'Will I what?' Gracie teased.

'Will you help me up?' he replied. 'I've got a bad knee, remember?'

Gracie laughed and said, 'Yes, I will help you up, and yes, I will marry you.'

He was putting the ring on her finger when Gracie asked, 'You were asking me to marry you, right? I don't want to look more foolish than I already do.'

Kenny nodded and smiled, his big, trademark grin easing across his face. He looked so happy — almost, almost carefree. Gracie kissed his mouth and they smiled, nose-to-nose, and they kissed again and then they laughed and couldn't stop laughing until Gracie cried like a baby, relieved that the world had suddenly opened its large, loving arms for her, and he begged her to stop or else he would take the ring back, and then they kissed more.

Gracie had described the scene to friends and

to acquaintances many times since, but never quite recaptured the moment. There was enough romance in that one night to last a lifetime. Whenever Gracie felt impatient with Kenny, which was often — with the demands of his job, the demands on his time, the bad romance novels Gracie read at night because there was no one to talk to — Gracie would think of that moment and hold it close. And remember why she had married him in the first place.

* * *

Puking in an enclosed garage creates a surround-sound effect that George Lucas himself would be eager to copyright. Gracie wiped damp remnants of onion ring from her mouth when she realized, through her tequila-pending-divorce stupor, that she had lived through all seven stages of The Hollywood Marriage:

STAGE ONE: Date the up-and-comer — this part can be eliminated if up-and-comer is already up and came (currently successful) or came and went (bilked studio out of hundreds of millions and living it up in Bel Air).

STAGE TWO: Marry aforementioned.

STAGE THREE: Swear you won't give up your career.

STAGE FOUR: Give up your career when the burden of being on what feels like thousands of charity boards becomes overwhelming. Children, memorize this equation before you begin Stage Four: One Charity Board = 240 uncomfortable phone calls (to ask for money), thirty lunches (to plan [some] and drink [more] Chardonnay), and one excruciatingly painful event night.

STAGE FIVE: Two kids a must. Two, not one, two! Even if the second one has to be adopted, through a surrogate, or an adopted surrogate! Two kids = triple child support = a lifetime of yoga retreats.

STAGE SIX: Begin drinking (if haven't already. But you have, haven't you. Good girl.) If possible, stick to Grandma's good-old standby, vodka. No smell, no tell!
    Or: Begin Vicodin and/or Mexican Quaaludes. Or both. Why not?

STAGE SEVEN: Decorate house(s). Hire decorator. Become decorator's new best friend that you can't live without. Pay decorator exorbitant sums to be new best friend. Fight with husband over new best friend. Husband complains to Wednesday-night poker buddies but secretly enjoys that he has money to burn on eighteenth-century Dutch étagères. Whatever that is.

ALTERNATIVE TO STAGE SEVEN: Do yoga, then do yoga instructor.
    Gracie had chosen Stage Seven (A), and had

'adopted' her decorator, Will. She steadfastly refused to have an affair with a yoga instructor until she had the self-esteem to attend a yoga class, which attracted as many nineteen-year-old actresses as an open casting call at The O.C.

STAGE EIGHT: Divorce.

★　★　★

'Over his cell phone?'

Gracie had called her closest friend, Joan, right after she'd swung open the car door, threw up inside the carpeted three-car garage, and traversed, in the dark, the maze of sharp-cornered postmodern furniture in the living room. Gracie finally curled up in the corner of the couch shaped, mercifully, like a lima bean. She didn't dare turn the light on and risk catching a glimpse of herself in the smoky mirror hanging above the granite fireplace. Gracie didn't dare acknowledge the fact that here she was, on the precipice of forty-one and a widow. Well, not really a widow Gracie thought, but one could hope. Perhaps Kenny would drive his convertible Mercedes (600 series, of course!) into an endangered California oak on the way to wherever he was going, leaving his boulder-sized head to roll down Sunset, where it would be picked up in the morning by a street sweeper.

The thought of Kenny being decapitated made Gracie feel momentarily better. Her body warmed, she felt the blood return to her fingertips.

As of fifteen minutes ago, Gracie had become a statistic. More than a statistic — Gracie was a woman who would probably never have sex again in her lifetime. Which could be some sort of statistic in itself.

Gracie thought she should move to Paris. Didn't Parisians take pity on middle-aged American women with freckles on their hands? Didn't that Olivier Martinez live in Paris? How do you say 'Take me, I'm old' in French?

'He said he didn't want to be married anymore!' Gracie screamed back.

'Over his cell phone?' Joan yelled again. 'Who breaks up with his wife over a cell phone? Who does he think he is, P. Diddy?' Gracie pictured her with her orange-red suicide bangs flipping up and down, down and up with each dramatic, exasperated breath. Joan had experienced every legal vice known to man and had stuck like glue to at least three of them, including yelling when talking would suffice.

'It was very Hip-Hop of him,' Gracie acknowledged. 'Do you realize you're screaming?'

'Calm down,' Joan yelled. 'You're hysterical!'

'Oh, God. He said . . . he actually said . . . he said we've grown apart!' Gracie was now bawling and screaming at once. 'It's like something out of a Catherine Zeta-Jones-Douglas movie! He dialogued me!' A torrent of liquid snot poured out of her nose. Lights flashed before her eyes as Gracie lost all control of her senses. The last time Gracie had felt this way, the Republicans had gained control of the House and the Senate.

44

'Bullshit!' Joan said. 'The only thing that's grown about Kenny is his head. His head is so much bigger than when I first met him. His head could eat other heads!'

Joan was a former sitcom writer on a show about two blond twins who wind up living with their therapist; it was called *Who's the Crazy One?* When the show was canceled, after the actor who played the therapist hung himself in his trailer (he was heavy into Vicodin, the Official Drug of the Millennium), Joan left the business and married a real estate magnate she'd met at a Funk Dance class at the Sports Club. An older real estate magnate. A *much* older real estate magnate. Who was bald. Not to mention older. Okay, he was freaking Methuselah. This is what happens to forty-year-old women in L.A. when they run out of dating options: they marry their grandfathers. Joan seldom wrote anymore, what with all the Georgian rooms that needed decorating and the French wine that needed drinking and the Ben Franklins that needed spending.

'I don't understand, I just don't understand — ' Now Gracie realized she sounded like she was starring in a movie. *Take My Divorce*, featuring Gracie Anne Pollock in her first ever starring role!

'Oh *God*. I'm mewling!' Gracie banged her head against the arm of the couch. 'I never mewl!'

'Is it the baby?' Joan and Gracie still called her three-and-a-half-year-old, Jaden, 'the baby.'

'He loves the baby — he says he loves the

baby.' Gracie thought about it. Did he really spend any time with our child? Any time at all? Didn't Jaden seem, well, kind of scared of her father? Maybe not scared, Gracie thought, but definitely startled when he walked into a room. Jaden, who smiled and engaged in three-minute conversations with everyone — the gardener, the poolman, the UPS guy with the granite legs.

Gracie wondered if the UPS guy was single.

'Is it the sex?' Joan inquired. Bravely, Gracie thought.

'Who? Where? What? When? How?'

Gracie had been nauseous for nine months with her pregnancy; the only time they tried having sex when Gracie was pregnant, she had had to run to the bathroom and throw up. After the baby was born, things had picked up for a while. Hadn't they picked up for a while? When was the last time they actually . . . picked up?

Ah. Oh. Hmmm.

Gracie figured Kenny was through with having sex, but maybe he was just through with having sex with *her*.

Oh, thought Gracie, here comes the headache. Just waiting patiently behind the curtain for its cue — Kenny no longer wanted to have sex with her. Yep, there it was. Hello, Headache! Come on in, join Low Self-Esteem and, next up, Diarrhea! Doesn't she look great?!

'Look, everyone knows you don't have sex after you have a kid,' Joan said. 'That's why Pappy and I are not having children.'

'Joan, no offense, but your husband is old enough to remember the Alamo, the war not the

46

movie, no one could remember the movie,' Gracie said. 'And please, for the love of God and this one conversation, don't call him Pappy.'

'But that's his name!' Joan's husband was Mike 'Pappy' McAllister of McAllister Realty, the second-largest real-estate agency in the Greater Western Los Angeles Area (according to the Paps himself, and the bus stops that bore his name and likeness from his Army photograph, circa 1944).

'Make up something else. For me.'

'Anyway, that's reason number one why I'm not having a kid. Number two being that I already own yours; I bought her off with Malibu Barbie's RV, remember?' Joan continued. Gracie had the distinct feeling she was not only talking to Joan, but to Joan plus three glasses of red. 'Number three, my eggs have dust bunnies.'

Gracie and Kenny had talked about having another baby. Kenny's plan was to have two children, one of whom was to be a male child; Kenny applying the same rules for himself as, say, a monarchy. Gracie had resisted; it had been so tough for her to get pregnant. And then her pregnancy was not a time of spiritual enlightenment, of glowing skin and glossy hair and swelling bosoms, a time of feeling connected to the world; Gracie's pregnancy was a time of elephant ankles, of hips that mushroomed into buildings overnight, of strange medical terms that required shots several times a week, of a nausea that lasted 238 days. The nausea, Gracie thought, when she envisioned another baby in her life. Imagine being seasick for thirty-four weeks, with no sign of land or medication. Now double that feeling. You're almost there.

She had brought up adoption; Kenny was adamant about passing on his genes. 'What if we got a faulty one?' he'd say. 'Didn't you see that movie?'

Gracie heard Joan's voice, through the memory muck.

'Okay, I know you're not ready to hear this,' Joan said, 'but I think you've got to ask yourself. Is it another — '

'Don't say it — '

'Eighty percent of couples deal with infidelity at one point or another in their marriage,' Joan said, 'which is why I married an older man. That and the fact that he was the first man I'd dated in five years who had his own transportation. Now, back to Kenny's insensitivity and big head and infidelity.' Joan and Gracie's friendship had no artificial flavors or colors. Sometimes this was a good thing; sometimes, Gracie could do with some fake vanilla.

'I said, *do not say it!*' Gracie wasn't ready to think about any other women just yet. Other younger women with pouty smiles and dewy skin and liquid eyes and dimples on their faces, where they should be, as opposed to where hers were starting to congregate — from the waist down, despite the hours of cellulite massage.

Gracie started to gag like a dog who's eaten too much front lawn. She decided to take solace in the fact that there was a one percent chance Kenny could be gay. Wasn't every man in L.A.?

'Can I be blamed for not having a penis?' Gracie asked.

'What? You're feeling guilty for not having a penis? I'm coming over right now,' Joan said. 'Pappy's asleep, he'll never know I'm gone.'

'No.' Although Gracie really did want someone to come over and rock her in their arms and stroke her hair and make her something sweet to eat that wouldn't make her weigh one ounce more in the morning. Kenny had bought her a Tanita fat-measuring scale for last Christmas — the romantic fool! The gift that keeps giving (her a heart attack)! Gracie knew how much each item of clothing in her closet weighed, down to the last belt buckle (four ounces), down to the last knee-high nylons (two ounces). Gracie stopped weighing herself after she noticed that she was weighing herself after every trip to the bathroom, when Gracie knew how much a typical morning bowel movement weighed (think belt buckle).

'You sure?'

'I'll be fine. I'll be fine,' Gracie said. 'I'm going to kill myself.' Gracie was joking, of course. She'd never kill herself over Kenny; she'd heard the story of The Westside Widower, the handsome, young L.A. widower (Kenny at forty-one was young; Gracie at forty-one was middle-aged — such was L.A. math). The minute his lovely wife died of cancer, leaving him with two young children to raise, he went on a dating rampage, turning up on the mattress side of Frette sheets everywhere from Silver Lake to Point Dume. He covered more area of Los

Angeles than Onstar.

The Widower's wife's death was like Viagra, without side effects. Gracie wondered if such a thing could be prescribed. 'Take one dead wife and call me in the morning. From your new girlfriend's futon.'

'I'm driving over right now — '

'What're you talking about? You're way out in Malibu. By the time you got here they'd be zipping up the body bag.'

'Where is the Kenny right now?'

'The Kenny is staying at a friend's house, some director who's going through a divorce,' Gracie said. 'Apparently it's in the water at The Ivy.'

She sat up as a realization reared its ugly head. 'He planned this out. You know Kenny. He probably knew he was going to do this years ago. He probably has another family. Maybe he's leading a double life.'

'This is crazy, it can't be over, just like that. What about counseling? Have you been to counseling?'

Gracie thought about it; they'd never been to marriage counseling. Gracie had gone to counseling in the beginning of their marriage — there were many personality issues to overcome. More or less her personality issues — the fact that Gracie had too much personality. Gracie said and did pretty much what Gracie pleased, in the beginning. Before Gracie learned The Way of the Wife.

'He just wants out,' Gracie concluded. 'He just wants out.' Without thought, her hand opened, palm up, as though she were freeing a living thing.

'You're going to need a lawyer.'

'Oh, God, I don't want lawyers. Lawyers will only make things ugly.'

'Guess what, Princess. Things are as ugly as Tony Soprano in a Wonder Bra. Tell me you don't have a pre-nup.'

Gracie paused. She and Kenny were to celebrate their tenth wedding anniversary in a month. 'Oh my — '

'God! You have a pre-nup?!'

'With a ten-year expiration date — '

The pre-nup was about to be annulled. In one month plus change, it would have been null and void.

Instead, her marriage was.

'I've been Cruised!' Gracie, slurring, meant being left by one's spouse before the ten-year anniversary mark. She'd heard that in California, if a couple has been married ten years, the wife is entitled to spousal support for the rest of her life. Allegedly, Tom Cruise had asked for divorce prior to the ten-year mark when he divorced Nicole Kidman.

Gracie burped, which she sometimes did when she was under extreme duress. How attractive. How very attractive. Men like middle-aged, freckly handed alcoholics.

'I can have him killed,' Joan offered. 'Pappy knows people. West-side real estate is a very rough business.'

'You say the sweetest things,' Gracie said.

'Seriously, Gracie,' Joan said, 'make up your

story. Make it up tonight. Before Kenny has a chance to.'

'My story?' Gracie asked.

'Not too many details, keep it on the surface. I'm a little rusty, but I can help you. Include the words: 'impotence' and 'bad investments.''

Gracie kissed Joan good-bye and hung up. When she had handed her valet ticket to the nice young Peruvian boy (single?) at the valet station, she'd still been married. Before she'd answered that call, she'd still been married. What would have happened, Gracie wondered, had she still been in a bad reception area? Or had she had the cell phone on vibrate?

She would still be married. Until the morning, maybe. But at least she would have had a good night's sleep.

Gracie looked at her ring. She forgot to ask Joan when she was supposed to slip it off her finger. Now, tonight? After the divorce was final? When?

She sat there, alone in her bad-cell-phone-call grief, wondering who else she could burden. Joan was an easy call — she had no children, and her husband, much like an infant, was asleep by eight-thirty. Most of her other friends had kids and marriages held together by duct tape. Gracie wondered at the marriage she'd thought she had. She and Kenny were supposed to be the happily married couple, they were the ones other people talked about in their thrice-weekly therapy sessions, they were the ones who were called The Power Couple in *L.A. Confidential*. How could The Power Couple break up? The Power Couple cannot break up! Gracie thought, mocking herself. We can't break the hearts of our millions of followers!

In her stupor, Gracie tried thinking back to what she could have done — did she miss a signal? Did Gracie speed through a marital stop sign? A blinking yellow light that said 'Caution! Your husband is headed-for-divorce-unhappy'? And then it came to her. The earring. Two months ago, it had appeared in Kenny's right ear like a midlife-crisis beacon. But Gracie had been distracted; she hadn't thought much of it. Why hadn't Gracie thought much of it? What would Kenny have had to do? Take out a billboard on Sunset Boulevard proclaiming himself in the throes of early-midlife-about-to-screw-someone-else crisis? Even then Gracie probably wouldn't have noticed. Gracie avoided driving down Sunset Boulevard at all costs — the Eurocafés and their midriff-baring constituents distracted and annoyed her. And when she did, she'd become so enraged at the sheer numbers of giant SUVs and Hummers choking the road that she wouldn't notice the billboard unless her car sprouted wings and flew into it.

Of course, Gracie had made fun of Kenny. Who wouldn't make fun of a forty-year-old man with an earring? Why, the great Jon Bon Jovi himself couldn't pull off the look in the early '80s. Why would her slightly paunchy, Hawaiian-shirt-wearing hubby be able to pull off the look? Gracie had thought it was a passing phase, like when an errant teenager comes home with a blue

Mohawk and a tongue ring. Gracie had viewed this new transition as an opportunity to try out her parenting skills.

First, Gracie had tried to ignore the offending item. But how does one ignore a violation of the laws of nature? Women should not have mustaches and men should not wear ear jewelry. Period.

Obviously, this step was too difficult for her. Gracie had moved on.

Next, she had tried to talk to her child, er, husband, with an emphasis on positive reinforcement. Gracie had sat Kenny down with a glass of wine and told him how attractive he was, especially his earlobes. Gracie had told him how she'd never really noticed his ears until now, and, gee, they were really nice ears. Incredibly nice ears. Ears that didn't need any help at all to look nice.

Finally, she had pleaded. 'What are you thinking?' Gracie had beseeched, spilling wine on herself as she gestured toward his stupid, insane, ridiculous ear (which really wasn't so attractive, come to think of it).

'What's the big deal?' Kenny had said, as if he were a teenager talking to his so-out-of-it-she-hums-to-Crosby-Stills-and-Nash mother. 'It's just a statement. Besides, Steve-O thought it looked rad.'

'Steve-O?' Gracie had asked, incredulous. Steve-O was a twenty-two-year-old Nike commercial director who was still living in his parents' house in Encino — and embarking on a $100-million science fiction movie starring

Bruce Willis. 'Steve-O is barely weaned! He still wears pull-ups!'

'Steve-O is a very talented director,' Kenny had said, as though she had insulted his very child.

'You look ridiculous — you're a forty-year-old man — you're successful, you're smart — ' ('ish,' she meant to add. Smart-ish.) 'Think of your dignity.'

Gracie had looked at him, in his trademark Hawaiian shirt and ironed jeans and, now, his earring. Maybe it was too late for dignity.

'My look works for me,' Kenny had said, puffing up, screaming-loud orange and green hydrangeas stretching across his chest. He looked like a proud baggage handler for Hawaiian Airlines.

'As a matter of fact,' he had told her, 'a lot of people, important people, like this look. A lot of important people.'

'Are any of them named Magnum P.I.?' Gracie had yelled as he walked away. Again.

Kenny had given up fighting with her. We used to fight, Gracie thought, we used to stake claims in battle and fight until our eyes bled. And then, oh my God, she thought, we'd make up, we'd fuck as intensely as we'd fight. Gracie thought they had grown up, that they were beyond screaming and punching at the air, that they knew that at the end of the day, at the end of the fight, they were still going to be together. Gracie hadn't known that Kenny had stopped fighting because he no longer cared.

Looking back now, Gracie could see a distinct

pattern in Kenny's repellent (to her) fashion choices, parallel to the demise of their marriage. First, there was the switch from loafers to tennis shoes, even for work. Then he traded slacks for jeans. Ironed jeans, yes, but jeans nonetheless. Gracie had even pointed out to Kenny, helpfully, that jeans are never meant to be ironed, that's the first sure sign of middle age. The second, third, and fourth being the need for reading glasses, Mylanta, and a new wife. Then there were the Hawaiian shirts. Kenny was searching for a 'look,' searching for something to make him stand out from the Armani-Prada-Hugo Boss-clad, contract-killer studio crowd. He became the Madonna of the pay-or-play populace. The fashion gambit paid off — he was soon known as the 'casual exec,' he became friends with the younger, up-and-coming crowd, the video directors who became film directors, the TV actors who were transitioning into celluloid. Why would her husband want to hang out at home with his wife and three-year-old daughter? The very people who reminded him he was getting older? Of course it made sense that he wanted out. It's a wonder, she thought, that he didn't leave earlier.

Gracie went to her daughter's room and curled up on the tiny bed next to her and played with the shiny blond tendrils of hair covering half her face, always covering half her face because Gracie couldn't bring herself to cut her daughter's crazily perfect hair, and wondered what she would say to her in the morning. 'Daddy's not coming home,' maybe. Or:

'Daddy's got an earring and he doesn't like us anymore.' Gracie would figure something out. And then, some time after that, Gracie would figure out her new life.

Tequila vapors echoed through her head, forcing her into a twitching, unsettled sleep. Too late, Gracie realized that what the female bartender at a particularly uneventful agency party (oxymoron) told her was true: Tequila is the only alcohol that is a stimulant.

The final thought that drifted into her brain haunted her sleep: Gracie had become a Starter Wife.

3

One Hundred (And Two) Clues That Your Husband is Unfaithful

Roses. The asshole sent one hundred roses to someone who wasn't his wife. Someone who wasn't his dead mother. Someone who wasn't his daughter. How did Gracie find out about the roses? Her florist.

Gracie, like all Wives Of in L.A., had a favorite florist — a messy, expensive relationship fraught with emotional potholes. The florist/ client relationship was closer in her world than the hairdresser/client relationship. The right florist could be called on night and day — and often needed to be on standby. Gracie had at least three occasions a week in which to send flowers: someone's grandmother died, someone had a baby, this person got promoted, that person got demoted, this producer has a movie opening, that producer's movie reached 100 million, this actress is having (more) (cosmetic) surgery, that actor is having a nervous breakdown, so-and-so's in rehab, it's the star's brother's wife's birthday.

The list was endless.

Gracie's florist, a human nerve ending with

concert pianist's fingers and a head as smooth as an eggshell, called the next morning asking how she liked the flowers, letting her know how to take care of them — he prided himself on the lengths he would go for that extra 'personal touch.'

'Darling, they could last over a week with distilled water, and only distilled water, and one aspirin,' he said, hyper as a whippet. 'Did you have a dinner party last week? I heard you had a dinner party last week, you know you're supposed to call me for your dinner parties, naughty girl, are you cheating on Raymondo?'

'I'm the one who needs an aspirin,' Gracie told him, unconsciously squeezing the phone like a lemon. Her forearm started throbbing. She knew it was because she wanted to wring Kenny's thick neck.

'I didn't get any flowers, Raymond.'

'What's that, Precious?' he squeaked.

Raymond was gay. Gracie wondered if he were single. Gracie wondered if gay, single men would want to go out with her.

Gracie cleared her throat of an enormous, Kenny-hating lump. 'I didn't receive any flowers.'

There was silence at the other end of the phone.

'There must be some mistake,' he finally said, with a droplet of cheer at having tripped upon an appropriate lie. 'Oh, yes.' Gracie heard the shuffling of papers.

'Oh, yes,' he repeated. Gracie had known Raymond for seven years and had never heard him, to her knowledge, lie. So Gracie waited, curious and patient. This was her new life, people stumbling on their words, and her, with the newfound ability to read their thoughts.

Gracie knew what Raymond was thinking. 'Oh, shit' was probably first in his mind, followed in close succession by 'Who the hell did Kenny send one hundred roses to?' then 'I'm going to kill my assistant,' and finally 'Wait till I tell (everyone).'

Gracie watched her girl as she stood, arms over her head, swinging her doll-sized hips, in front of the television set, watching what Gracie thought was the most famous homosexual revue in the world, The Wiggles. Gracie had tricked her daughter long ago to listen to the television with the sound turned down almost to mute. Thus, only one of her senses could be assaulted by The Wiggles at a time.

Gracie looked at the television set out of the corner of her eye; she could bear only the slimmest glimmer of Wiggle . . .

Gracie found herself wondering if any of them were single. Gracie wondered, if she married a Wiggle, about their first dance at their wedding. Would Gracie, too, be forced to wag her arms over her head, to wrestle her hips into some sort of rhythmic motion?

'Would it be all right if I called Mr. Kenny's office?' Raymond asked. The man gave suppliant ass-licker brown-nosers a bad name.

'Raymond,' Gracie said, 'we did have a dinner party last week. And the flowers were sensational.'

Gracie heard the gasp just as she hung up. She suddenly realized that if she were getting a divorce, one of the benefits was that she wouldn't have the need for a florist except for special occasions. Raymond was probably already asking Kenny's assistant how the recipient liked the roses and giving tips on distilled water and aspirin.

What does one do on the first day of separation? How should Gracie mark it on the calendar? 'Today's Wednesday, so that means Tennis, Toddler Group, and oh, yes, a Trial Separation.'

And why was she still breathing? Why hadn't Gracie died in the night? And why, why hadn't Gracie planned for this moment? Why hadn't she put away the requisite $500 cash per week into her own account, like the other Wives Of? Why hadn't she purchased more jewelry, like the wife who bought out the Cartier display at Saks two weeks before she served her husband with papers? Why didn't Gracie know she and Kenny were headed for the destination marked 'first marriage'? But Gracie couldn't even call what they had a first marriage, could she, unless she was already in her second marriage. Damn. Damn. Damn. So many new rules, so many newfangled, meaningless niceties to incorporate into her behavior. Gracie was now a Former Wife Of — a Starter Wife. Performances would have to change.

And just when she had finally grasped all the behavior patterns for a Wife Of. It was akin to telling an Olympic wrestler that he would have

61

to compete in the women's synchronized swimming event.

Another horrible feeling ran over Gracie, leaving deep tracks on what was left of her psyche. Did other people know this was going to happen? Was Gracie the only one in the dark?

Gracie grabbed at a barstool and slid her body onto it, propping herself up on her elbows on the kitchen counter. The thought of divorce had robbed her, temporarily, of any thought of eating. All Gracie desired was coffee — straight — black enough to leave her teeth looking like pieces of driftwood. And Gracie wanted it thick, thick as Anna Nicole Smith's speech pattern. Gracie wanted her nerves to have nerves. And cigarettes. Gracie would have killed for a cigarette. But no, Gracie had given up cigarettes. Kenny didn't like smoking, even socially. Even outside on a balcony at a party where smoking made a little more sense than jumping. Screw him, Gracie thought. She'd have given Kenny's left nut for a cigarette right now. In fact, she would have given both Kenny's nuts. Nutless freak. Who would want him then?

Oh, Gracie wanted to be French. The French knew how to survive Nazi occupation, McDonald's, and bad techno music and still look good.

'Honey? Do you have a cigarette?' Gracie asked her daughter, who was now Wiggled out, sitting on the floor, her legs spread out before her, her Powerpuff Girl pajamas crumpled up around her pale, bony knees. How Gracie had managed to have a tall, skinny, long-legged daughter, she did not know. Perhaps Jaden had been switched at birth, and somewhere in the city a short-legged, chubby, brown-haired daughter was being raised by Swedes.

'Bad people smoke cigarettes,' she replied. There's no one more matter-of-fact than a three-and-a-half-year-old with conviction.

'Who told you that?' Gracie asked.

'Daddy,' she said. Of course.

'Well,' Gracie said, 'Daddy knows all about bad people.'

So sue her.

'Honey,' Gracie said, 'I have something to tell you about Daddy — '

Jaden had her eyes closed, her head leaning back. 'Daddy's gone away,' she said.

Gracie looked at her. 'Who told you that?'

Jaden opened her eyes and looked straight at her mother. 'Daddy told me,' she said. 'I think on Saturday. Or Tuesday. When did I watch him get a haircut?'

Gracie started to blink uncontrollably. Her husband had told her daughter he was leaving before he'd told her — only his *wife*. 'Did Daddy tell you where he was going?'

Jaden shook her head. 'Daddy said it was our secret. And he gave me a dolly that pees and cries.'

'Kind of like Mommy, huh?' Gracie asked.

'Mommy's joking,' Jaden said.

'Of course Mommy's joking,' Gracie said.

Gracie looked around her kitchen — the Sub-Zero, stuffed with FIJI water and Plugrá butter, embodiment of the fact that they had 'made it.' Gracie, who had negative interest in decorating, had spent a ridiculous amount of time getting the exact color right for the paint — green but not too green, light but not too light. The kitchen was commercial ready; all that was needed was the Folgers lady with the disturbing accent.

Gracie steadied herself by gazing outside into her backyard, where Jaden's plethora of plastic — buckets, shovels, dolls without hair, dolls missing eyes, dolls without limbs, tiny rakes, two construction trucks for innocent, visiting boys — had gathered like multicolored congregants on the lawn. Many of these items were scattered under Kenny's favorite chaise where Gracie could almost make out his large outline in the particular indentation of the long pillow. If Gracie squinted, she could almost see him lying there, sleeping, a script open on his chest. If Gracie squinted hard, she could almost see him lying there, a kitchen knife embedded in his chest, his tongue poking at the corner of his mouth, his eyes open with the question, 'Why?'

'Why?' Gracie said out loud, 'I've got one hundred reasons why!'

'Mama, are you talking to yourself?' Jaden, her Swedish cherub, asked, looking over at her. Gracie smiled at her, which hurt about as much as a labia wax, but Gracie remembered reading something about being brave for your children in trying times.

'Of course not, sweetheart,' Gracie said. 'Mommy was talking to her coffee mug. And you know what? It answered back. Can Mommy see

64

you dance some more?'

'Mommy, I love you, but I'm not a machine,' Jaden said, her eyebrows angling down toward her nose.

'No,' Gracie said, 'you're not a machine, but Mommy's a machine. Mommy's like an old washer that you put out on the front lawn hoping someone will pick it up so you don't have to make a trip to the city dump.'

Her daughter, thankfully, had ceased to listen to her.

Gracie sighed; she felt like there should be yellow tape around her house. Our marriage, our life, the crime scene.

What were her options? Long-term: Find another man, find happiness, find herself. God, how awful, Gracie thought, I sound like a *Woman's Day* article. Worse, I sound like a letter to Dr. Phil.

Short term, however, Gracie knew what she needed to do: She needed to go to lunch, to go shopping, to show her face, to get dressed in her best 'Look at me, I'm fine, I'm more than fine, I'm *great*' outfit. To laugh in the face of divorce proceedings.

All these things she would do, right after Gracie took a nap. After all, it was now nine o'clock in the morning. Nine hours down, thousands to go. Gracie called to Ana, her housekeeper, to keep an eye on Jaden for a few minutes. She wondered who would get custody of Ana. These things, Gracie thought, are so messy for the loved ones.

Gracie realized she had officially skipped

breakfast, her first (inadvertently) skipped meal in fifteen years, and she suddenly felt better. Gracie just might come out of this divorce looking like Elle Macpherson, only shorter and without all the bothersome male attention.

And then a thought came to Gracie, floating into her head like a mantra.

Eat, the thought urged. *Eat,* it cajoled. *Enjoy yourself. Stuff your face. You've got nothing to lose.*

The thought had a voice which sounded an awful lot like Mel Brooks.

But no matter. The pin had been pulled. Gracie smiled, hopped off her stool, and headed for the forbidden room.

The pantry.

★ ★ ★

Two SESAME BAGELS (toasted, buttered, and smothered with cream cheese) later, Gracie started to drift off to sleep. And at that moment where reality encounters dream, she thought about the other ways to tell that your husband is cheating on you.

He starts shaving his balls.

And it isn't even summertime.

And he isn't even gay.

Gracie's eyes snapped open. Of course, she thought. Two weeks ago, Ana had told Gracie that Kenny's shower drain was plugged. When Gracie looked, she saw dozens of tiny pubic hairs stuck in the drain; she checked his razor — curly hairs were clinging to the blades like

66

refugees on a sinking raft.

Ana had widened her eyes and raised her eyebrows and then had left Gracie alone in Kenny's bathroom to ponder the meaning of the pube glut.

Finally, she'd called her husband at the office.

'Your drain is clogged,' she told him.

'So, call a plumber,' Kenny said. 'Are you meeting me tonight or are we driving together to that thing?'

'I called a plumber,' Gracie said. 'Can you tell me why you're shaving your pubic area so I can explain it to Joe-Earle?'

Joe-Earle was the plumber. He wore a gold socket wrench charm around his neck and talked too much about his other clients, which, while fascinating, led Gracie to believe he talked too much about them as well.

This story should be a doozy, Gracie thought.

'All the kids do it, it's a kid thing,' Kenny said, 'it's called 'mowing the lawn,' 'culling the herd.' It's, you know, cool.'

He said this with a tone which made it clear that Gracie would not know a thing about what's cool.

''A kid thing',' Gracie repeated. ''It's cool.'' The toddler volumes had taught her to repeat back certain sentences to the child, certain sentences that could be upsetting.

'Makes your dick look bigger. Did you call Rupert Murdoch's wife yet? I've got to run. Love ya.' Then he'd hung up.

He said 'ya.'

Gracie had shaken her head. Kenny was all

about staying ahead of the curve, but keeping your balls ahead of the curve could be seen as overkill. Gracie couldn't imagine that the real power players shaved their balls — Spielberg, Katzenberg, Murdoch . . .

She had wiped her mind of those images and tried to go about her day.

But now Gracie could see, this 'mowing the lawn' thing had been a sign, as clear as if Kenny had printed up bright yellow T-shirts saying I'M LEAVING YOU, SPRING 2005 in block letters.

★ ★ ★

'But you *can't* get a divorce,' Cricket sobbed when Gracie broke the news. 'What's going to happen to every third Tuesday?'

Gracie had called together two more friends, the final components of The Coven. Kenny had bestowed Gracie's circle with this nickname, which Gracie once thought was funny but now just viewed as rude.

'Why,' Gracie had asked, 'do you insist on calling my circle of friends The Coven?'

'Because they hate men,' Kenny had said. 'They remind me of the witches in that play.'

'Double, double, toil and trouble? *Macbeth*?' Gracie had asked, 'Well, at least it's Shakespeare. I guess I should take that as a compliment.'

'I love that you're so smart,' Kenny had said, genuinely admiring. 'You make me look good.'

Gracie had smiled at his remark. On a scale of one-to-ten, in a two-hundred-year-old classroom at an Ivy League college, her brains were about a seven — maybe a six and a half since her daughter was born. But at a Coffee Bean on the west side of L.A., she was pushing a nine, nine and a half, easy.

'My friends don't hate men,' Gracie had said. 'One of them is a man.'

'Yeah, right,' Kenny had said, and snickered like an underage frat boy boozing it up at a strip club. Translation of Super-Hetero remark? Will was that rarest of creatures, a gay interior decorator; therefore, Will was not entirely a man. Kenny was not waving a banner at the forefront of the P.C. Revolution.

Back to Cricket, whose remarkably large green eyes were spitting tears into her grilled chicken salad, which remained otherwise untouched.

'Apparently, I can get divorced. It's not illegal in the United States — yet,' Gracie said. 'And I've decided to title it: Operation Gracie's Divorce!'

Day 1.5, Post-Catastrophic Phone Call. Gracie, Cricket, and Will were at Barney Greengrass, the rooftop Upscale-Restaurant-Professing-to-Be-a-Deli at Barneys Beverly Hills. Gracie had wanted to go somewhere where she could see people. Well, not real people, fake people: Agent People, Writer People, Development People, Manager People, B-Level Celebrity People, Studio Executive People. A place where Gracie could put on her one Chanel suit and try out her brave face. This was a mistake. The Chanel suit had been bought a few years before her current feeding frenzy, which hadn't abated since the double-sesame-bagel blitz, and she wound up feeling like a carpeted sausage.

Cricket was sobbing about their monthly double date. 'You and Kenny are The Perfect Marriage,' she sniffed. 'Jorge and I count on you, we look up to you, you keep us in line, you're like our Elmer's glue!'

'It wasn't a perfect marriage,' Will said. 'It was a mixed marriage. He's an asshole and she's not.'

'Thank you,' Gracie said, reaching over to squeeze Will's hand.

'Now,' Will continued to Cricket, 'quiet yourself. Gracie's life is in the dumper and I want to be a supportive friend and digest every last tragic morsel.'

Why Gracie had chosen to tell her fragile friend Cricket, wife of Jorge — you know, Jorge Stewart, the whiz kid former Green Beret who became a TV producer of the raging hybrid, legal/military dramas — in a public forum, now revealed itself to be another in a long line of strategic mistakes. Cricket, mother of three children under four, was not known for her emotional or otherwise stability. Weighing in at just over 106 pounds, with not one ounce of muscle tone, she had the physical strength of a hummingbird, combined with a mental state hovering between questionable and deeply questionable. Gracie had met Cricket in a Lamaze class; she was breast-feeding her two-year-old and pregnant with twins. Their husbands, recognizing a fellow showbiz inmate, had bonded right away. Gracie had 'fallen in love' with Cricket the instant she told Gracie

70

that Lamaze was a load of 'hooey' (Cricket never swore) and that she only needed to know three words when giving birth: epidural. And: more epidural.

And here was Will, Cricket's opposite. 'Sentiment' was not a feeling found in his emotional lexicon. He claimed he'd had all sentiment beaten out of him as a child, growing up homosexual in the California Third Reich, otherwise known as South Pasadena. His father had been a football coach at USC, his mother a member of the Junior League. He had grown up attending stadium football games every week; his favorite play was the huddle. His father had disowned him after Will seduced the quarterback, who didn't need all that much encouragement. Will was an L.A.-phynate: Interior Decorator — Wife Of's Best Friend. Gracie had invited Yin and Yang for lunch and was finding neither to be gratifying, spiritually or otherwise.

'He never satisfied you,' Will said. 'Let's be frank. Speaking of which, I met a Frank the other day and I said, 'Can I be frank?' and he said, 'Will you?''

Will sighed, 'Wasn't he the clever boy?'

'Do you think we're next?' Cricket sniffed again.

'Cricket,' Gracie said, 'you can't actually 'catch' divorce.'

Cricket looked at her, pained. 'Did you hear Nick Cage got married again? To a young Asian waitress.'

'Asian is the new black,' Will said.

'Let's stick to my own car wreck of a life,' Gracie said.

People were starting to stare. A few of the overgroomed seemed to be pointing their manicured fingers in the direction of the sobbing peroxide blonde, her Chanel-clad friend with the strained seams and expression, and the boyish fellow with the careful highlights. This in a town where no one would blink an eye if a building were to blow up in front of them — a fatalistic town where disaster was waiting behind every headline in *Variety* and behind every corner, just to the right of the Polo store.

'You need to talk to my psychopharmacologist,' Cricket said, taking a business card from her Balenciaga. 'You should start off with Klonopin — it's strong, but under these circumstances, Wellbutrin is useless — '

'Wellbutrin?' Will said. 'You can't smoke with Wellbutrin!'

'Gracie's not a smoker!' Cricket yelled. 'Gracie, you haven't started smoking again? You know it's bad for babies!' Cricket was the type of mother who made hot lunches and never let another soul put her children to sleep; she was a wonderful, caring mother. Who would someday have to be institutionalized.

'Don't scream,' Will hissed at Cricket. 'You get all wrinkled when you scream.'

'Use your church voices,' Gracie said. 'I don't want to be wading in the gossip pool.' She said this even though she knew the news of her impending divorce was nearing the deep end of the rumor-ridden waters.

'No one's heard about your terrible breakup!' Cricket honked and assured her, placing her pale, younger-than-her hand on Gracie's. Gracie noted her friend's lack of freckling; Gracie noted the wedding ring. Gracie stiffened. What was Gracie supposed to do with her damned ring? She had taken off her diamond engagement ring, but she couldn't return it — wasn't there a statute of limitations on engagement ring returns?

Like the Buddhist dilettante Gracie longed to be, she tried to find the positive in the moment. So she congratulated herself on not devouring the entire passel of breadsticks that came to the table. Although Gracie had eaten nonstop in the last day and a half, the divorce diet was still working. Why, Gracie had shed 190 pounds of ugly fat in less than a day! One ninety-five, fully clothed and sopping wet, holding Ray-Ban sunglasses in one hand and a script in the other.

She grabbed the last two breadsticks and ate them.

'Gracie, maybe I shouldn't bring this up, but now's as good a time as any,' Cricket said. 'There's a whole new world out there, and I want to talk to you about labial rejuvenation.'

'CHECK!' Will screamed.

'I'm trying to save her marriage!' Cricket said. And then, in hushed tones, 'I'm thinking about doing it myself. I heard it can make your vagina look like a rosebud.'

Will put his head in his hands; Gracie was afraid he would start sobbing.

And then Cricket said quietly, 'My waxer,

Janusz, told me . . . ' She pointed to her Dolce'd crotch.

Her voice choked up. Gracie handed her a glass of water.

'Is this FIJI?' Cricket asked before she drank.

'For God's sake, what did Janusz say about your . . . ' Will said, then waved his hand down there.

'He said . . . ' Cricket hesitated. 'He said . . . ' she continued in a voice that sounded somewhere between Gorbachev (remember him?) and the guy who pumped Gracie's gas, ' 'she-a looks like-a Dumbo.' '

Will looked at her, aghast. 'The very best argument for male homosexuality,' he finally said.

'I don't care what *Redbook* says,' Cricket said. 'The vagina is never the same after having kids — '

'Mom!' Will said to Gracie, 'Cricket's reading *Redbook*!'

'Back to the topic at hand,' Gracie said, herding the strands of conversation like errant sheep. 'Cricket, it's really important to me that you keep this to yourself. No one else can know about this. It's entirely possible that Kenny and I can work this all out.' For now, Gracie thought she should stick to the abridged 'Kenny and Gracie Divorce Story' — the *Reader's Digest* version.

'Your alarm clock's ringing,' Will said helpfully. 'Wake up. Kenny and I have a better chance of exchanging vows at the Bel Air, giving birth to five biracial puppies, and working out

74

our marital issues than Kenny and you.'

Gracie snapped Will in the arm with her knuckle while Cricket zipped her collagened upper lip, the one her husband thought was hers and hers alone, though mysterious bruises appeared on them every three months. 'Your secret is safe with me,' she whispered at Broadway-stage levels. 'I won't tell a soul!'

★　★　★

'Is it true?' Sharon Adler, wife of Kenny's business attorney, Mervin, widened her already preternaturally wide eyes at Gracie — wider even in the last year because of the Brentwood-essential, thirty-eight-years-and-counting eye lift. If they were any wider, Gracie would be looking at the back of her head. Moments like these made Gracie wonder why she bothered with mascara. How could one compete by using the usual, pedestrian eye-widening tools?

Gracie was picking Jaden up from her preschool class at Tiny Miracles, the nursery school Kenny insisted Jaden attend even though the class interfered with her naptime. The place was indeed tiny, with a dirt yard spotted with tufts of dying grass that was barely big enough to accommodate five or six children, much less the fifteen connected kids in her class. Worse, it stood next to a dry cleaner that had steadfastly refused to use environmentally safe cleaning agents. Smoke billowed out from the top of the square, windowless concrete building, forming perc clouds over the preschoolers playing in dirty sand with the school mascot, the nursery founder's ancient, ornery rabbit.

So why attend? Kenny and Gracie had come to this school for a tour when Jaden was barely three months old. Kenny had immediately scoured the room for the presence of excellent trade placement; he was looking for anyone who would warrant a front-page story in the *Daily Variety* or *Hollywood Reporter*. Kenny wanted Jaden to be at a school where he could schmooze. If there was no schmooze factor at the school — for example, if the parents were mostly in finance rather than entertainment — well, then, Kenny couldn't be bothered.

Tiny Miracles' schmooze factor was off the charts. In Jaden's class alone, there was an Oscar-winning director's child, an action-producer's child, and most important, a movie star's child. Who did Jaden prefer to hang out with? The scholarship child, the daughter of a local housekeeper. Gracie called it Divine Social Justice; Kenny called it annoying and grumbled at every check they wrote out to Tiny Miracles, as though the schmooze factor should have made the tuition tax deductible.

So there Gracie was, performing her motherly duties with one other mother and thirteen nannies, even though her world was crumbling around her like an Irwin Allen movie.

And now, she had run into the rumor-mill generator, Patient Zero of The Gossip Pool.

'Is what true?' Gracie asked Sharon. 'Are you talking about global warming? Or the brave new direction of the Democratic Party?'

Sharon Adler was also known as The Local National Enquirer. Having a conversation with her was like looking at the cellulite-ridden celebrity photographs inside the *Star* — you were just happy the story wasn't about you.

But this time it was.

Sharon focused on her, and Gracie suddenly felt a familial empathy toward shark bait. 'Cricket told me,' she said. 'I can't believe it — I heard Julia Roberts left her husband for Kenny.'

'That's ridiculous. I don't know what you're talking about,' Gracie said. But Sharon the Great White smelled blood in the water, so Gracie added, 'Kenny and I are just taking a little break.'

What she really wanted to say was: 'Kenny and I are just taking a little break of his neck.'

Gracie looked at her daughter, finishing up a sand pie in the crowded sandbox. Gracie wondered what the real estate market was like in Costa Rica. She wondered what the food was like in Costa Rica. She wondered what the men were like in Costa Rica.

'Jaden doesn't know anything,' Gracie admitted, 'so I appreciate you keeping this quiet.'

'You know I'd never say anything to anyone,' Sharon replied.

'I know,' Gracie lied back.

'Someone said Kenny was gay. Is he gay?' Sharon asked.

'Sharon!' Gracie said. And then she thought for a moment.

'Actually,' Gracie said. And then she didn't say anything. But she posed a philosophical question in her mind: If a lie falls in a preschool sandbox without making a noise, is it really a lie?

★ ★ ★

'You are a bitter, hateful, pathetic — ' Kenny was calling Gracie on her cell phone. Gracie was heading back to the house from Whole Foods, an upscale, organic-enough-to-feel-good-about-yourself grocery store she was now drawn to on a daily basis.

Whole Foods had become Gracie's crack.

'And hello to you, my young friend,' Gracie said. She realized, as she swallowed the remainder of a yogurt pretzel, that she'd forgotten her thrice-weekly training session.

'Did you tell Sharon Adler that I was gay?' he said in his best demanding studio-exec tone.

'No.'

'You didn't say I was gay.'

'Absolutely not.'

'She told Ben that you said I was gay.'

'I don't know how she would have picked that up,' Gracie said, 'unless . . . '

She dipped her hand back into the yogurt pretzel bag. She reminded herself to call her trainer.

'You are a sad, sad person.'

'Actually, I'm feeling a bit better, thanks for asking.'

He hung up on her.

The truth is, Gracie was crushed. She didn't know why, but somehow, talking to Kenny was better than not talking to him. Even if they were unhappy together, even if they rarely had intimate conversations anymore, much less sex. Gracie didn't know her life without Kenny.

Gracie would have to learn.

She ate the rest of her pretzel, washed it down with the protein smoothie that tasted suspiciously (and gloriously) like a Jack in the Box milkshake, then dialed her personal trainer and told her she was taking the next rest of her life off.

* * *

How come Gracie felt so much older at forty-one than she had at forty? She surmised it was because forty-one is closer to sixty than to twenty. Gracie remembered twenty well, as though she had been sitting in a creative writing class at UCLA just last week, but she had trouble imagining what sixty could be like. Sure, Gracie had seen pictures of Gloria Steinem, but Gracie didn't have Gloria's impressive genetics and style and more impressive sense of indignation. Gracie would have to creep into old age with her shortish legs and chronic sense of doom.

Doom. Perhaps it was postpartum depression run amok, but doom had been a shadow of her every waking moment for the last few years. Doom would greet her quietly at daybreak, seeping into her consciousness like the fog draped over Santa Monica on most mornings. Doom would wake with her, nestled comfortably in her head, assuring her gently that all would end in catastrophe. Doom had been her companion since shortly after the birth of her child, when Gracie realized that, after wanting a baby for so long, she had made a huge mistake in actually creating one. If a woman who has all the advantages finds the world a scary place, what hope does a seven-pound baby have?

Besides which, in Gracie's view, a forty-one-year-old broad with an almost-four-year-old is not a pretty picture. So why take so long to make a baby? The first answer is that Gracie forgot. Gracie was into her thirties before she and Kenny got serious about having a family. Her friends were starting to have babies, friends who once had careers and now had husbands, or friends who still had careers and wanted the added stress of motherhood. One of her friends at the time, Victoria, a former trial lawyer who now worked overtime at her children's private school (for nothing), was first pregnant at thirty-five. Gracie had experienced one of those maddening Oprah 'aha!' moments. Gracie thought, *Damn, of course, I knew I was forgetting something.*

That something was children.

Gracie called Kenny on the way home from Vicki's house to tell him that they needed to make a baby, and soon. The reports were out, the news was in: At the age of thirty-five, a woman's fertility drops precipitously. It was time to get on the stick. So to speak.

Three and a half years later, after six months with no luck and almost three years of assistance, with mixed results and her (un)fair share of miscarriages, Kenny and Gracie finally had their baby. What they didn't have was their marriage.

Gracie dropped Jaden at her class (avoiding Sharon Adler's piercing stare like a dose of smallpox) and drove to Starbucks and sat with her hands wrapped around a Venti something and pondered her next move. Gracie knew something about spirituality, a smattering about I Ching, a bit about the flexibility of the universe. And so, Gracie wondered what lesson the last thirteen, fourteen years could provide her.

Gracie actually wondered why she wasn't more present, more upset about her impending divorce. She felt as though she were in a fog, as though she were living out someone else's story line. Maybe Gracie felt like she deserved unhappiness in her life. Or maybe Gracie felt like she deserved more happiness. Either way, the fateful (cell) phone call from Kenny had been a signal to her.

That maybe, for good or bad, her life was about to begin.

★   ★   ★

A man sat down two tables from Gracie's, carrying a laptop and a latte in a ceramic mug. He wore glasses. He had a cap of thinning hair. He was in that male netherworld in terms of age and looks, somewhere between forty and fifty, and neither attractive nor unattractive. Gracie looked at him, stared really, and wondered what it would be like for her to start dating. Gracie hadn't exercised her 'dating muscle,' hadn't sent any mating signals out to men, except for that one spinning class with that one spinning instructor. But her signal got crossed with every other sweating, angry-at-her-husband female in the class. The signal hadn't been picked up.

Gracie decided to try out her somewhat rusty signal on this unsuspecting writer-type. He looked unhappy enough to actually respond; Gracie had sized him up pretty quickly. She suspected he wrote hour dramas. Or, more likely, had written hour dramas, a format being overrun by the less-pricey reality shows. He had a condominium in Santa Monica and drove a late-model Volvo. He voted Independent but thought Democrat and shopped at Whole Foods. He masturbated five times a week to DIRECTV porn but didn't feel good about it.

There. He finally looked up at her. Gracie smiled, cocking her head in a friendly, unthreatening manner. Did she look like a Labrador retriever? Gracie suspected she did. But this was only a run-through. A rehearsal. This was not her life.

The middle-aged writer adjusted his glasses and looked down. Gracie was suspended in midcock. Her smile hardened and had become painful, an emblem of humiliation. She let her eyes drift upward, toward the ceiling. Gracie was now smiling at the ceiling. Gracie prayed for a bolt of lightning to hit her between the eyes.

How could Gracie not even merit a smile out

of a middle-aged, out-of-work writer?

Gracie dropped her rictus grin and tried to not pinch her lips together, as the vertical wrinkles surrounding them had recently reached critical mass.

This is not my life, she thought to herself. I am not trying to pick up men at Starbucks.

A young woman walked in. 'Young' to Gracie meant anyone from three years old to three days after she was born; a subset of the population which included a lot of people. Far too many people for her liking. This particular form of infant looked to be in her twenties, but then most people look to be in their twenties to Gracie. What is it her father used to say? 'Growing old is not for sissies.' Maybe for men. For women, it's more like 'Growing middle-aged is not for sissies.'

So back to this girl. This fetus, really. She was all of about twentyone, judging by the angle of her backside jut. Gracie's backside no longer jutted — it leaned. And there she was, Gracie thought, look at her, how cute she is. Jesus. Keep me from vomiting. The girl danced over to the counter, and what was that? A yoga mat curled under her supple arm. How lovely. Really. Spectacular. Couldn't be happier for her. And a ponytail in her hair. And look at how much hair she has, and so shiny. And so hers. Isn't that wonderful.

And look at Mr. Frumpy. Look at him. Paying nary any attention to his laptop. And yet, moments ago, whatever cable TV Movie-of-the-Week crap was on it was so important to him.

Look at him, fascinated with the mat-bearing bimbo. Absolutely fascinated. Couldn't be happier for the both of them. Maybe they'll get married and have five thousand kids. But early, not like Gracie. Not too late, like Gracie.

Gracie watched the girl as she ordered her drink and waited. Her eyes skipped over Gracie's way for a mere nanosecond. Gracie was sure her existence rated not a blip on this girl's radar screen. And then Gracie remembered what another friend had mentioned to her; this friend been walking down Rodeo Drive and she'd just turned thirty-seven, and she realized everything she knew about herself before that moment was over with. Everything she'd taken for granted was gone.

Not one man looked at her.

Not a suit, not a construction worker, not a driver, not a young man, not an old one.

A moment ago, this woman had long, thick, blond hair, full lips, almond eyes, a lush body. And youth. Now, she still possessed all the physical attributes. But not Youth. Without Youth, she had nothing. Nothing but a rich husband who took long suspicious trips to Las Vegas and three beautiful kids.

And an ironclad pre-nup.

Which yanked Gracie to her next subject. Gracie was a woman on the verge of divorce, and she needed to get a lawyer. Joan had given her a Xeroxed list of divorce lawyers with fierce reputations and fiercer billing schedules.

Gracie decided to leave Starbucks for the warmer climes of her green-but-not-too-green

84

kitchen, where she stood little chance of further humiliation.

WIFE NUMBER TWO

Is married to a famous, and famously sexual, musician. Theirs is a happy marriage, partly because she procures his concubines while he's on the road, after putting them through a vigorous workout herself.

He recently went back on the road to pay for her jewelry.

4

If I Had a (Divorce) Lawyer

Gracie had a theory: Forty in L.A. is like fifty anywhere else — a single woman over fifty in New York can't get a date. In L.A., lop ten years off that number. A fifty-year-old woman in New York gets her first face-lift; in L.A., the number is forty. A fifty-year-old woman in New York can still carry an air of viability; in L.A., a woman after forty is no longer viable except to her children, and sometimes, if they are old enough for driver's licenses, not even then. Factor in the 'single' dimension and the effect is mathematically analogous to standing in a hall of mirrors.

Gracie was staring down the barrel at this future: She was a woman over forty years old in a city in which even if she had a face-lift and dieted her way back down to Mary-Kate proportions and published eighteen best-selling children's books, Gracie was still a person who would never have another date in her life.

Neither, apparently, would Gracie have a divorce lawyer.

First on her list was Mr. Maxwell Havens, Esq., lawyer to such luminaries as Jack Welch and Tom Cruise, nemesis to such luminaries as Michael D. Eisner and Bruce Willis. And friends with all of them. Known for having a chauffeur-driven Rolls and dressing like a dandy. Did time in prison for petty theft when he was a teenager. Tired of petty theft when he became acquainted with divorce law, a license to steal big money.

Gracie punched the numbers quickly, before she could back out, and also as a result of too much caffeine.

'Havens and Sussman?'

Gracie wondered why the receptionist posed the name of the firm as a question — was it a question where she was working? If so, hadn't someone answered the question by now?

'I need to talk to Maxwell Havens.'

'Hold, please.'

Gracie was switched over to an assistant.

'Maxwell Havens calling. This is Gina.'

A confusing way to answer a phone, but Gracie was familiar with the ploy — 'always appear to be on the move.'

'Hello,' Gracie said, slightly nervous though Gina had a calming voice. 'My name is Gracie Pollock. I would like to speak to Mr. Havens.'

'Your name?'

'Gracie Pollock.'

There was a pause.

'Gracie Pollock?' Gina asked.

Gracie got nervous. Was she supposed to still be using Kenny's last name? What were the rules of divorce for the Starter Wife? She would look it up on Google right after this phone call.

'For the last nine years — until Tuesday night,' as Gracie settled the question in her head.

The girl put Gracie on hold. The hairs on the

back of Gracie's neck, which was the only place she hadn't lost hair after the birth of her child, stood up. Gracie didn't know why, all she knew was that this particular 'hold' was weighted with portentousness. This 'hold' was a bad one. Why did she feel this way? Sure, Gracie was not in the habit of calling lawyer's offices. She barely knew any lawyers — except for the ubiquitous entertainment attorneys who argued with themselves over their competing clients' interests and considered the term 'conflict of interest' a quaint throwback, and who skied more than they worked and skied while they worked and considered skiing to be work. Gracie was about to hang up when a man came on the line.

'Gracie,' he said, 'how are you, sweetheart?'

Ah, yes, Gracie thought, the familiar over-familiar greeting, as the word 'sweetheart' rang in her ears, as though Gracie and this stranger were not only close friends but perhaps had had children with each other.

'My life sucks,' Gracie replied, 'who may I ask — '

'Maxwell. Maxwell Havens here,' the man replied. Still with the syrup in his voice.

The hairs at the back of Gracie's neck had given up standing and were now performing cartwheels.

'I'm so glad you called,' he continued.

'Have we met?' Gracie asked.

'No, no — but I'm a good friend of Kenny's.'

Aha! thought Gracie. She knew now that she couldn't trust Maxwell Havens — no one was a 'good friend' of Kenny's. Men in L.A. didn't have 'good friends,' they had commerce.

This little factoid made Gracie crave Maxwell Havens in her life and divorce even more. She searched her brain for some clue of what he looked like — late fifties, early sixties, in good shape (what with all that skiing). Gracie found herself daydreaming of making a love connection with someone who was old enough to be her father. Who was she kidding? If her father had been a teen groom.

'Which is why I can't represent you,' Maxwell said.

'What? You know that's why I'm calling?'

'I'm assuming — you're still getting a divorce, correct?'

Gracie's stomach lurched in the same way it did the time she accidentally cut a motorist off in traffic and he waved a handgun at her. Why would someone wave a handgun at a woman driving a Volvo with an I ♥ TINY MIRACLES PRESCHOOL license-plate holder? Seemed sort of beside the point, no? And what would have happened had the angry young man in the painter's cap shot her? Kenny would have dined out on that story for months. He would have made a wonderful widower — a dream widower. His wife cut down in the prime of her life (cough) while her young child sat in her booster seat, watching cartoons on the car's television screen. Gracie suddenly felt inferior; what was she doing exposing her child to television even in a motorized vehicle? She, who had been raised by parents who eschewed television completely. Her father claimed that watching

TV would turn her brains into oatmeal. Gracie caved in to peer pressure — all the Wives Of had televisions in their cars. Gracie had just purchased the Volvo last year, and when the dealer said she might need a DVD screen in the back — for those long trips to Disneyland, Gelsons, and the three miles to school — well, she meekly agreed.

'How did you — '

'Know you're getting a divorce?'

Why did men feel the right to finish a woman's thought? Well, maybe certain men.

Most men.

Gracie hated that behavior. But then, Gracie would never have to deal with that kind of behavior again, now would she? Because she'd never again be dating and/or married to another man, unless — unless a massive earthquake swallowed up all the young women in Southern California.

'No, how did you get to be such a fuckhead?'

There was a pause. Not many people called Maxwell Havens a fuckhead and lived to tell the story. There were rumors about his ties to the mob, and not like the nice mob, either.

He cleared his throat of his unpracticed response. 'I can't represent you, Mrs. Pollock. Your husband and I have already discussed your impending divorce. The fact is, I may be representing him.'

Gracie now felt the same excruciating, shooting pain in her head that she felt when the woman who ran Jaden's preschool called to ask her to chair their auction dinner.

'You can't represent me because you *may* represent my husband?'

'That's right,' said Maxwell Havens, Fuckhead-at-Law. 'And I've read your pre-nup. Kenny certainly plans ahead, doesn't he.' He sounded serene and in control. Degrading her had helped him recover from her juvenile name-calling.

It occurred to Gracie that the Fuckhead-at-Law knew about her impending divorce before she did; this guy probably knew that she was a lousy lay before she herself knew. Gracie wondered what else he knew — like, who Kenny had sent the one hundred roses to. But she needed to get off the phone. She wondered if a person could actually die of humiliation.

'Damn him,' Gracie whispered.

'I think you'll find this to be true of all the top divorce attorneys in L.A.,' he continued. 'He's met with every one. Kenny's a very thorough person. It's one of those qualities I respect most about him.'

Gracie hung up.

She looked at her list of attorneys. She knew that what the Fuckhead-at-Law said was absolutely right — Kenny had met with each and every one so that Gracie would not be able to procure any of them.

Her life was beginning to look like Pay-Per-View. But Kenny had already started the fight, long before Gracie even knew there was a ring.

★   ★   ★

A week later, Gracie learned that Kenny had indeed hired Maxwell Havens. She finally found an attorney in a cardboard office in the Wilshire Corridor who'd claimed that he could help her keep the one material thing she desperately wanted from the marriage. The Brown House. The house they lived in when Jaden was born. The house where she'd been most happy. Gracie would make a deal with Kenny — she would forfeit future spousal support if Kenny would buy that house for her and Jaden.

Gracie met her attorney-to-be — a chubby, bearded man with the pale, doughy skin of an infant — at the Starbucks in Brentwood on San Vicente, a different one, thankfully, than the one in which she'd spied the middle-aged writer who wouldn't look her way if she were standing, stark naked, spraying whipped cream on her nipples and singing 'The Star-Spangled Banner' (but not the second verse).

Is there anything as cruel as Los Angeles in springtime? Gracie thought not.

Gracie drove south from their (her? his?) house on Rockingham Avenue toward Brentwood Central, home of self-indulgent mothers and their overindulged children. And vice versa, ad infinitum.

Gracie wondered at how she had come to live on a street where a three-year-old, five-million-dollar mansion was considered a tear-down. It didn't seem that long ago that she was living in an apartment around the corner from Canter's in the Fairfax district, where everywhere she was surrounded by young people with no money and enough talent to anticipate bright futures. Most of her friends from that era had succeeded reasonably well, including Joan. Some were writers, some musicians. A couple had become teachers. Gracie had become someone's wife.

Gracie had, of late, romanticized the simplicity of her old life. There were three rooms in her apartment, the minirefrigerator containing two essentials: cheap cranberry juice and expensive vodka (for entertaining). She remembered fondly the bed and the flannel sheets she'd bought on her own — a naughty indulgence when one had only sixty dollars in the bank. She smiled at the thought of the fifty-dollar desk with her father's old computer, the printer that printed one page a minute, the furniture from Ikea. Her fourteen-inch television set. A carport.

Most Americans were upwardly mobile, wanting more, more, more — bigger cars, vast lawns, sky-high mansions. Gracie had become downwardly mobile. She'd stare at tiny houses buffeting her daughter's favorite Santa Monica park: houses with a hose and a sprinkler from Target instead of an irrigation system, homes where a father's bellow was the intercom, homes barely bigger than her living room, where the only art on the walls was something conceived in a second-grade classroom. She would imagine herself living there. And then, her mind would drift back to her early days with her husband.

When Gracie moved in with Kenny, she could hardly contain her excitement. It's true, his home was a modest affair — two bedrooms, one and a half baths, a quarter of an acre. The outside was brown from its foundation to its roof, which is why they'd called it, in a burst of imagination, 'The Brown House,' and why Kenny had sworn he'd sell the house every week or so. But the truth was, Kenny wasn't home so much in the last five or six years. The Brown House had become more of a favored boutique hotel to him: he knew where to get food; he knew where his favorite towels were.

But Gracie had loved that house — it was just the right size for their small family. The lush backyard boasted a canopy of oak trees which curved protectively over her daughter's wooden swing set. When Jaden was a tiny baby, Gracie had purchased the old-fashioned swing set on a whim, setting it up in the middle of the backyard. She'd put Jaden on the baby swing, holding her tight, and push her back and forth and back and forth until her baby would sleep. The moments so sweet she could literally taste them, like biting into a yellow cake with vanilla frosting.

Gracie hadn't wanted a big house; she hadn't wanted the burden of more space to take care of, more 'things' to worry about. She had been friendly with showbiz people with huge houses. And it was always the showbiz people who had the biggest houses, houses that ranged from 10,000 to you've-got-to-be-shitting-me square feet; six, seven, eight bedrooms (not counting the maid's); twelve bathrooms, foyers, decks, huge swimming pools, lap pools, indoor swimming pools for those bitingly cold Southern California afternoons, a panic room (for the wife?).

Kenny continued griping about being a prisoner in this 'shit-brown house.' Every time they'd have dinner at someone's larger, fancier, staffed-to-the-gills house — and they only had dinner with people who had fancy houses — he'd come home in a funk, complaining about how 'poor' he felt in his place.

Maybe it was fear of real estate — 'acrephobia,' Gracie called it. Gracie was supposed to be trying to find that perfect acre lot replete with McMansion and sycamore trees which had been planted yesterday, rather than forty years ago. Why was it that everything in Southern California had to be new, including the wives? What was wrong with an old house, an old tree, a worn bench, creaky floors, a lined face, gray hairs that sprang up like wiry jack-in-the-boxes? If she had searched long enough inside her psyche, Gracie might have come to another conclusion, different from the fact that in a world where New = God, she preferred Used = Comfort. She would have come to the conclusion that she was fearful of losing that last vestige of herself. She was fearful of losing whatever evidence there was that she was an individual, a fully formed human being with opinions and furrows and a soft tush. The Brown House had become her.

Finally Gracie had given in. She'd called a Realtor by the name of Jameson Rosenau who seemed to appear everywhere, from bus benches to the pages of the *L.A. Times* realty section to the postcards she continually found in her mailbox. He looked handsome in his photographs, but in person he was Lilliputian — from his doll feet to his wee hands, all of five feet and spare change. He stood military-style, chest out, chin high, teeny hand just about ready to salute his new client. 'I can get you a millsky for this place, I'm not kidding,' he said, smiling up at Gracie.

Gracie raced back into the house to find her purse and recover her bearings.

★　★　★

Gracie and Kenny moved into the house on Rockingham three months after that fateful trip with Jameson Rosenau. The house had five bedrooms, a guesthouse, a large pool, a cabana, a tennis court, and a long driveway that would be difficult to navigate without the aid of a car and driver.

The house was big, it was grand, it was extravagant.

Gracie hated it. Kenny, on the other hand, loved it, and pirouetted from room to room, a thick, graceless ballerina.

'We'll throw tons of dinner parties!' he exclaimed.

Gracie just nodded.

'We'll have people over to play tennis every weekend!'

Gracie nodded. She had never picked up a tennis racket in her life.

'We can have people stay in the guesthouse. Important people.' Kenny was on a roll. 'People from New York!'

'I have relatives in New York,' Gracie said, perking up. Kenny didn't respond.

'Jaden's room is downstairs and on the other side of the house,' she heard herself pleading. 'I won't be able to hear her at night.' The thought of her baby so far away panicked her.

'That's what they have monitors for,' Kenny said. 'C'mon, honey, this is what I've always wanted, what I've worked so hard for. Why can't you be happy for me?'

Gracie had thought about this. Why couldn't she be happy for him? Why couldn't she be happy? What was wrong with her? Didn't everyone want a house with a pool and a tennis court? Weren't they living the American Dream?

'It's beautiful,' she said, glaring at the chandelier above their heads as he stooped over her and hugged her.

'I can't wait to have people over,' he said. 'Hey, you can brush up on your tennis — no excuses!'

Gracie was secretly suspicious of all 'rich kid' sports — tennis, horseback riding, swimming outside of a community pool — she found solace in cleaving to her 'raised in borderline poverty' status. Living in a multimillion-dollar spec house in Brentwood would make it harder for Gracie to maintain her 'waiting for the revolution' stance.

The Rockingham house was supposed to be Modern Spanish, but it veered more into Modern Office Building with Spanish moldings. Everything about it was new, down to the week-old grass on the front lawn. Her first twenty-four hours in the house felt like an episode of *Rich Folks' Survivor*. On her first night in the McMansion — Kenny was out of town attending a premiere in New York (with all the Important People) — Gracie had not mastered the ne plus ultra, expensive alarm system. The system went off eight times in a span of two hours, driving Gracie out of her mind and her bed. She wound up begging the befuddled security guards walking down her driveway to gun her down as she ambled blearily, wearing the flannel pajamas she only wore when Kenny was out of town.

'Never get rich,' she warned the security guards, 'they'll force you to get a security system.' She never used the security system again. The dirty little secret of the wealthiest enclaves is that no one knows how to use their elaborate security systems (and everyone has ten-pound dogs).

Everything that could go wrong in the house did from the electrical system to the technologically advanced dishwasher to every one of the six toilets. The lighting system itself was so complex that on some nights Gracie was driven to tears, wondering how to get a lamp on so she could read. Outside security lights would come on for no reason. And forget the entertainment system. Gracie could never get any one of their eight television sets to work off of the fancy ten-pound remotes. If she managed to turn on a TV, the volume refused to budge. Worse were the times she could never get it off again.

The first week, Gracie wandered the halls, wondering how she would keep such a massive place clean. Her housekeeper, Ana, the one who'd been with them since Jaden was born, had taken one look at the house and almost fainted.

'You need more people, missus,' Ana said.

'No kidding,' Gracie replied. 'You know anyone?'

Thus, the house became a Rockingham El Salvador. Ana and her two sisters came to work, keeping the 8,000-square-foot-house spick-and-span, babysitting Jaden, cooking in case Kenny's friends dropped by for dinner or a Saturday-afternoon tennis game. These should have been the good old days, the salad days.

So why did Gracie feel so wilted?

'You need to find something to do,' Kenny said one morning as he dressed for work. 'I have a purpose, I have something that makes me happy — my job — you need to find a purpose.'

'I have Jaden,' Gracie said.

'And we're scheduled to have another,' Kenny said. 'As soon as she turns two, we'll start trying.'

Gracie shook her head. She hadn't forgotten. Kenny always wanted two; so had she. But lately, the news was getting to her. If terrorism wouldn't wipe them out, the environment was on the verge of collapse. And then there were all the shots she'd have to endure . . .

'What about all your boards?' Kenny said. 'You know, a lot of women find fulfillment raising money for charity.'

Gracie nodded. She was thinking about all the drinking she'd seen at ladies' luncheons. The rumors about Vicodin abuse; some of the women's best friends had names like Percocet or his cousin Percodan.

'I think I should go back to writing,' Gracie said. 'I really liked writing children's books.'

'Is there a market for that?' Kenny asked.

Gracie shrugged. She had no idea. She didn't examine her needs in terms of market value. She wondered when she would have time to write, anyway. There were so many petty obligations encroaching on her free time. It was the cosmic joke about having money: The more money you had, the more things you had, the more things you had to take care of, the more you worry about them, the less time you have for the important things, the unhappier you are.

Rich = Unhappy seemed to be Gracie's equation.

★   ★   ★

The one good thing to come out of El McMansion was that Gracie met Will. Will had been an up-and-coming designer — he'd worked hand in hand with the legendary designer Maria Paul — and was said to have completed most of her latest jobs, including Jackie Onassis's last apartment. Will walked into the house on Rockingham and said, 'I need a chair. Fast.' Gracie sat him down.

'Now, tell me what happened, and don't leave out a thing,' he said breathlessly.

'What do you mean, what happened?' Gracie asked.

'Water, I'll need some water.' Will waved his arm.

100

'We moved all our furniture in — '

'Stop,' Will said. He got up to leave.

'Where're you going?' Gracie said.

'I can't take this job. I'm sorry,' Will said. 'Forget the Aquafina, I need air . . . '

Gracie followed him out. 'Why can't you take this job?'

'We're incompatible,' he snipped.

'We're not getting married.'

'I can't work with you,' he said. 'Now, how do I get to Sunset from here?'

Gracie grabbed his sleeve. He looked at her hand as though it were a rattlesnake or, worse, a bad manicure.

'Look, Liberace,' Gracie said, 'I am in no mood to play Siegfried to your Roy. The least you could do is give me advice.'

Will looked at her and smiled. Gracie noted that his teeth were crooked — a rare treat in a homosexual man. The moment marked the beginning of a beautiful and somewhat complicated friendship, complicated by the fact that Gracie was paying Will for his companionship. She had sworn she'd never be one of those Hollywood wives who paid for friendship — whose best friends were their Pilates instructors, personal trainers, interior decorators. But she grew to love Will; she loved that he told her the truth — that basically she had no taste. She loved that she could complain to him. She loved that he shared his secrets, where to get highlights, where to find the best spa on the Baja Peninsula, where to get black-market Phenfen.

Theirs was a true friendship, paid in full at the end of each month.

★ ★ ★

The Wife Of was a full-time job; some women (and men) were better at it than others. Gracie and Will, during an extended shopping trip for a turn-of-the-century light fixture, argued over who was the most celebrated Wife Of, the one who turned her wife status into not just a Trade but a Calling.

The rules were stringent: The woman had to be able to warrant her own single picture in a weekly magazine, her own mention in Liz Smith or on Page Six, she had to count A-level celebrities as close friends, and she could not have had notoriety (or a real job) prior to her marriage.

One name kept popping up: Trudi Styler, married to Sting. What does she do? Hard to tell. 'And who cares?' as Will pointed out. 'We all know her name. We all know her face. And she's friends with Nicole Kidman.'

'And she seems to be aging backward,' Gracie agreed.

In the Pollock social circle, Gracie had met three types of Wives Of, who had two all-important components in common: None of them held actual jobs and, in a world where such things were of utmost import, they had all Landed the Whale.

There was the InStyle Blonde — which could have been a color unto itself. This type of woman

102

could be married to a producer who had won an Academy Award once upon a time and was on his third marriage. This wife could have been a cover model, save for the overbite (which could be corrected) and brief pit stop into porn (which could not). One could see her photo as one of Fifty Best Dressed in *Harper's Bazaar,* or wearing animal print in the back of the *Hollywood Reporter.* She would have two children and three nannies; she would know where to get Mexican Quaaludes and how many she could take with a vodka martini. She was a living, breathing 'Vagenda' — a woman with an agenda. Kenny admired the InStyle Blonde; Kenny did his best to turn Gracie into an InStyle Blonde.

The only problem with the InStyle Blonde?

Eventually, she would be an embarrassment.

Then there was The Perfect Match. Gracie would call her The Perfect Match because damned if her skirt didn't match her jacket didn't match her shoes didn't match her purse didn't match her sun-glasses didn't match her nail polish (fingers and toes) didn't match her agent husband's polo shirt didn't match her children's dresses didn't match their sandals didn't match their hair accessories.

Gracie would stare at this type in the same kind of wonder and awe usually reserved for Michelangelo's *David* or Angelina Jolie's Everything. 'Where did this creature come from?' Gracie would think upon running into The Perfect Match at a two-year-old's birthday party, immediately preceding 'Where the hell is the bar?'

Eventually she would be a crushing bore.

Then there was The Earnest Activist. Gracie actually felt a kinship with this type, as The Earnest Activist didn't give a rat's ass about appearance, nay, she didn't know from *Vogue,* and the only *People* she knew were the ones fighting the Contras in Central America. She had wrinkles and furrows and an expanding waist-band and gray hair sprouting in places that could have been easily waxed, if she so deigned. But she deigned not. She was Warrior Woman, sent here with a rich, cowed husband (and, perhaps, a trust fund) so she could save the rest of us from our SUVs, our cigarettes, our annoying habit of going off-topic if the subject of the Rain Forest popped up.

Kenny didn't particularly like The Earnest Activist, but Gracie liked them best of all. At least they cared about something besides the weekend numbers. But still, after going to Air Quality meeting after Lead Poisoning meeting after Save the Sea Anemone meeting, she found she could not keep up her anger. Gracie would leave each meeting vowing to write her congressman, hoping to make that phone call that would make a difference, but feeling in her heart that she was ineffectual, a dilettante in the environmental movement. So she wrote checks. A lot of checks.

Eventually, The Earnest Activist would leave her husband. For a female golfer.

★   ★   ★

Gracie drove up San Vicente Boulevard toward Brentwood in her Volvo with the now nonworking DVD player and entered a different world. As much as Sunset Boulevard defined the whole of Los Angeles, it was San Vicente which defined the West Side.

Turning up Ocean Avenue, curving onto San Vicente, Gracie would watch in awe as that parade of joggers would commence; it didn't matter what time of day one would be driving up the boulevard, there was always someone running along the grassy median dividing the street, dotted evenly by vintage coral trees.

The joggers were uniform in their athletic contours; the men's legs were a jumble of muscles lit up by the combination of sweat and the sun's rays. The men were older than twenty-five, younger than fifty, and all could have qualified for a *Men's Health* magazine cover — a magazine Kenny pored over each month for clues to the perfect six-pack or secret ways to cut carbs from an already carbless diet. Gracie, meanwhile, pored over the cover.

And then there were the women. Why were all of them twenty-five and under with glossy ponytails and light tans, bouncing along with nary a breath taken? There was no sweat, there was no effort, there seemed to be no hurry.

Ah, the glory of youth, Gracie thought. May they all rot in hell.

★　★　★

105

The infant-faced attorney was shaking his head and making the kind of clicking sound with his tongue that Gracie could barely tolerate from her own mother when she was alive, much less a round-headed stranger with milk foam gracing his thin upper lip.

'You have a pre-nup?' he whined.

'I told you I have a pre-nup,' Gracie said, 'but I think I can convince Kenny to buy back our old house for me and my daughter. It's all I want.'

'What motivation does he possibly have to buy it for you?' the attorney whined again.

Gracie was happy to not be paying him by the hour. The consultation was free. Perhaps this was a bad sign.

'Our child?' Gracie said.

The man's face lit up. 'A child!' he acknowledged. 'Very good. That means child support.'

'All I want is that house.'

'Nonsense. You need child support and spousal support. Only one child?'

'We have one child.'

He looked at her. He seemed sorely disappointed.

'It would have been nice to have two children,' he said.

'I'm pretty sure we have just the one,' Gracie replied, on the edge of impatience.

'Okay,' he said, sighing deeply. 'So, you've been married ten years.'

'Almost ten years.'

The man paled; he looked like a blanched almond.

'Almost?'

'Yes. We would have been married ten years in April.'

He shook his head, very slowly. Then he closed his eyes, put his face toward the ceiling, and let out a low, soft moan.

'What's wrong?' Gracie thought it might be heartburn.

'I can't help you.' He put his hands together, as though praying.

'Why not?'

'You haven't been married ten years. Ten is the magic number. Ten is when it all begins.'

'Nine years is a long time,' Gracie said. 'Have you ever been married nine years? To a studio executive? It's like riding a whale!'

'Ten is the Holy Grail, the three-point shot, the Hail Mary. Without Ten (he'd said it as though the word were capitalized) you got bubkes.'

Grace pondered this news for a second. 'Can I get my old house for bupkes?'

He just looked at her. All expression had left his face, along with his interest in her divorce case.

'I can't help you,' he repeated his mantra.

Gracie left, gathering up her things with as much pride as a pre-menopausal reject could muster.

She wished she hadn't paid for the man's coffee.

She took the long way, driving home on windy Sunset Boulevard. There were no sidewalks, and therefore no joggers to mock her in her sedentary state.

★ ★ ★

Saturday marked the first weekend since Gracie had been dumped by Kenny. Instead of celebrating with a Divorce Cocktail — a fountain of pink lemonade martinis and enough Xanax to soothe Norman Mailer in his prime — Gracie found herself at Qiana Nabler's two-year-old daughter's birthday party. Qiana was married to a producer with the body of a sumo and the personality of a crack addict, infamous for the fact that when he ran a major studio, he bilked the Japanese investors out of hundreds of millions of dollars. Perhaps that explained why he and his new wife — Qiana, an InStyle Blonde, was the third in a long line of tall, blond, buxom Mrs. Nablers — lived in a mansion in Beverly Hills, close enough to the Beverly Hills Hotel to order room service. Gracie had known Qiana when she was just plain Donna, before the personal lifestyle/high colonic guru. Qiana had a daughter, Lala Tuala Bell, who had, unfortunately, inherited all of her father's looks to go along with her mother's unfortunate choice of names.

Why Gracie was at the party was a good question. Yes, she had a young daughter; yes, she could be charmed by Qiana's southern hospitality, despite the ever-present yoga tights; and yes, she had no other good place to go. And though she was on her way to becoming the Starter

108

Wife, she figured it was too soon for everyone in L.A. to have received the fax.

So she found herself at a child's birthday party with valet parking, champagne cocktails, fake snow, fake psychics, and a real elephant.

Qiana greeted her with the same squeal as she greeted the other two hundred guests. 'Namaste, cookie,' she said to Gracie, bowing with her hands clasped in prayer. 'I honor your courage!'

Gracie took a half step back, as she always did when greeted by overwhelming insincerity.

'Nama — ' She stopped herself. 'What's this about courage?'

'Cookie, I'm so sorry to hear about your little, you know . . . ' Qiana looked at Jaden and whispered, 'Divorce thingie.'

Gracie was surprised, to say the least; it'd been a mere four days. Obviously, pending divorces were headline news in her neck of the woods.

'It's hit the circuit.' Qiana seemed to have read her mind. 'Have a nice time. Kenny should be here lickety-split.'

Jaden looked up at Gracie. 'Daddy's going to be here?'

Gracie watched as Qiana greeted another guest, a studio marketing executive who, Gracie knew, didn't have any children. In West Los Angeles, children's birthday parties had become just another excuse to network and climb, children or no children. Gracie wondered why anyone who didn't have to be subjected to chicken fingers would choose to.

Jaden tugged at her mother's sleeve. 'Where's Daddy? Let's find Daddy.'

Gracie stood there, sandaled feet screwed into the ground, Jaden's sweaty hand in hers, pulling her toward the party and away from her nearest escape, her dear, dear Volvo.

Her husband was coming to the party. The question was, Why? Gracie had to but look around to get her answer. Here was Reese Witherspoon bent over a toddler, there was the writer who'd won the Oscar last year, and farther out, Gracie saw the raison d'être, Kenny's boss, Lou Manahan. Lou was in his early sixties, had the laid-back, easygoing manner of a lifelong surfer, which he was, and dressed like a college student, which he had never been. Lou was famous for being a high school dropout, perhaps the most successful high school dropout on the West Coast. Lou was divorced, a couple, three, four times — it'd been hard to keep up, even for Gracie — and he had good relationships with all of his exes. He'd never had any children until his third (or was it fourth?) wife, who waited until after their divorce to get pregnant by him. As a result, he was often seen at these gatherings with a rambunctious three-year-old boy, Topper. Gracie had always enjoyed Lou's company; he was one of the few people of power in town who not only knew Gracie by name, without being prompted, but looked her in the eye when they spoke.

The truth is, Gracie always felt a little bit of a good old-fashioned stir when Lou was in the room.

She sucked in her stomach, patting the puffy area above her C-section scar, vowing to get hold of a plastic surgeon the first chance she had (which could be this very party), and made her way over to Lou.

'Gracie.' Lou smiled as he saw her coming. 'I'm just thinking about my new book. You're a writer, you could help me with some of the particulars.' Gracie found herself smiling back, basking in his crow's-feet. In a town where men were lining up on Rodeo Drive for collagen shots and Botox, Lou was a masculine throwback.

'Once upon a time,' Gracie corrected him. 'And that was just children's books.' Gracie was unaware up until now that Lou had any literary aspirations.

'Well, this isn't a real book. I'm just standing here, looking out at this thing we're calling, for the lack of a better word, a 'party.' You know, when I was younger, a party involved a trunk full of vodka, a mountain of coke, and girls a coupla decades older than these trinkets.'

'So, what's the book that's not a book?' Gracie asked. She noticed she was breathing again; when she'd heard Kenny's name, she must have stopped. Would paramedics have to follow her around for the next year or so, just in case Kenny Pollock was in the vicinity?

'We'll call it *Hollywood Translations*,' Lou said. 'It's like Berlitz. When you get to Hollywood, you're going to need to learn the language.'

'Example?' Gracie asked. Jaden had finally let go of her hand and had sat in front of a raggedy Elmo, who was busily blowing animal balloons. Gracie recognized him from Jaden's first birthday party. Elmo had demanded cash for his services rather than the agreed-upon check. Worse, he demanded the cash while maintaining his high-pitched Elmo voice. 'Elmo wants cash,' he'd kept repeating. 'Elmo's on crack,' Gracie had told Kenny.

'I'm so excited!' Lou said.

'New project?' Gracie automatically inquired.

'No, no — you know how everyone here always says, 'I'm so excited!''

''Excited' is the most overused adjective in L.A., second only to 'genius,'' Gracie replied.

'Exactly,' Lou said. 'So, translation: 'I have no fucking idea what I'm talking about!''

'Got it. What about 'Cute picture!'?'

'Translation: 'Who's gonna get canned for this piece of shit?''

'How about 'Congratulations on your new production deal'?' Gracie liked this game.

''Loser. Couldn't get a real job, huh?''

''I couldn't be happier for you,'' Gracie said.

''I hate your stinking guts.'' Lou looked up. 'I think I see your husband'?'

'That's an easy one,' Gracie said. ''Your dick is showing.''

Lou looked at her. 'What'd you say?'

Gracie smiled. 'You know, 'Your dick is showing.''

Lou maintained that quizzical look on his face. 'Kenny is here, Gracie,' he said.

Gracie's face fell; Lou was actually trying to tell her Kenny had entered the party.

'I'm sorry — I thought — ' She didn't go on, thinking better of it. How could she explain?

Lou smiled. 'Nah. Makes sense, if you think about it.'

Gracie turned to see her daughter, Jaden, running toward Kenny — and she thought about the fact that she hadn't really been watching her daughter. She'd been too excited about Lou talking to her. She wondered what that meant.

Probably nothing. Just a man paying attention to her.

'Hey, hey, Lou.' Kenny walked up to them with Jaden in his arms. 'I just saw the dailies on *Blue Bayou*. Fantastic, I'm not kidding.'

Lou looked at Gracie. 'Translation?'

'Hey, Gracie,' Kenny said, kissing her on the cheek and interrupting her insult.

' "Who said this woman could act?" ' Gracie replied to Lou.

'I'm sorry?' Kenny said, though he wasn't.

'I don't think it quite hits the nail on the head,' Lou said to Gracie. 'It's more direct. Try this: 'The dailies are great' equals 'Get me a director's list, because we've got to fire this hack immediately.' '

'Agreed, but then you are the master,' Gracie said. She was enjoying their secret language for the moment.

Kenny stood there, his smirky grin frozen, unable to move before he understood the game Gracie and Lou were playing. 'I'm just the ghostwriter,' she said.

'It's nothing,' Lou finally said to Kenny. 'We're just having a little fun in the sun. I'm sure the dailies are terrific.'

'They are,' he said. Gracie detected a rise in

Kenny's temperature. He tugged at his shirt, which was sticking to his chest. 'Can you hold her a sec?' he said, handing Jaden off to Gracie. And then he turned and was gone, heading for the nearest A-lister.

Lou and Gracie stood there for a moment in silence, watching Kenny go after Reese Witherspoon with the speed and trajectory of a heat-seeking ass-kisser.

'He'll learn,' Lou said to Gracie, as though answering a question she hadn't dared ask.

'We're getting a divorce,' Gracie replied.

'About time,' he said.

'I don't want it,' Gracie said. 'He does.'

'Of course,' Lou said, looking at Gracie. 'You're not going to get him on the cover of *Us Magazine*.'

Gracie looked away, ashamed. She knew what Lou said was true; for Kenny, press was everything, and that's the one thing his wife couldn't acquire for him: press. Gracie could put together a dinner party, she could write the thank-you notes, send the flowers, remind him of important birthdays, and buy the gifts. And wonder of wonders, she could carry on a conversation.

But she could not get him on the cover of *Us*.

Lou placed his roughened hand on her shoulder. 'Who'm I going to talk to at these things?' he said.

Gracie looked back at him without turning her shoulder. She didn't want him to remove that hand. 'What do you mean?' she asked. 'Am I dying or something?'

114

'You'll see,' he said. 'You'll see what happens. You'll come to a couple more of these parties, people will invite you, they'll want to keep the doors open for a while in case you're not really getting divorced and then they'll figure out the truth, that you're not getting back together, and then the invites will dwindle and pretty soon I'll be at another one of these overblown picnics and I'll be talking to myself.'

'That's my future?' Gracie asked. 'As The Former Wife Of?' She didn't know whether to laugh or to cry, to celebrate or grieve. She didn't know whether he was being helpful or cruel. Or both.

'Count on it,' he said.

Gracie didn't know what to say. She watched the party, the people, the servers, the animal balloons, the boob jobs and tank tops and collagened lips.

'Lucky girl,' Lou said.

'Me?' Gracie said. 'I'm about to be excommunicated.'

'You're getting out,' he replied. 'I never have.'

She looked at him.

'You're free,' he said.

★   ★   ★

Lou Manahan regretted being honest with Gracie. What was there to gain by him telling her that her life in Hollywood was over? Finished. Done.

He drove into the flats of Beverly Hills, where he'd recently purchased a home for him and his

115

kid. The kid who was asleep in the backseat. Pacifier stuck in his mouth. These were Lou's favorite times. Just him and the kid. No radio, no cell phone, no noise, nothing.

He hadn't been trying to hurt Gracie. The words had just popped out of his mouth like bombs landing on a soft target. The look on her face. But didn't she know? he thought. Didn't she know that her stock had dropped to less than the daytime hostess at The Ivy? Hadn't she seen what happened to other wives? Wives who traded on their husbands' names until the day he walked out with a secretary/actress/nanny? Lou was nothing if not honest, which in L.A. was about as rare a bird as sincerity. He looked into his rearview mirror, looked at the little head that was lolling to the side of his child seat.

Lou made a note to call Gracie. He'd take her out to dinner. He'd make it all better for her.

★ ★ ★

Later that day, Gracie put Jaden down for a nap, then drove into Beverly Hills, listening to two women talk about food on NPR and wondering when exactly she had stopped listening to music on the radio. She switched stations for a few moments, then turned the thing off altogether when she realized she'd been listening to what was considered an 'oldies' station, the one that played all the hits of the eighties.

'I've become the Prince-listening version of my mother,' Gracie lamented as she turned into the garage at Neiman Marcus. She remembered how her mother loved to listen to songs from the sixties on the radio, well into the seventies. She had vowed never to be stuck in a time warp, the way her mother had been — wearing red lipstick (fifties), saying things like 'jazzy' (sixties).

At least, Gracie thought, as she parked the Volvo between two black BMW SUVs, I've given up shoulder pads and the hope to someday date Michael Jackson.

★　★　★

Gracie knew it was wrong. She knew it was wrong and yet there she was, standing before the Loree Rodkin jewelry case on the ground floor of the Beverly Hills Neiman Marcus. She was wearing heavy sunglasses (very Jackie O, very *Vogue*-sanctioned) and a scarf tied around her head — the only scarf she owned — a Hermès giveaway at some charity event. Gracie was going for the 'chic widow' look to disguise herself, should she run into anyone she knew, but somehow had ended up with the 'post-surgery' look. Other shoppers looked at her curiously, wondering if it was a face-lift, brow-lift, eye-lift, or abusive husband that had her wrapped in the cheapest of last fall's Hermès 'To the Races' Collection.

But Gracie didn't care. She was too caught up in a mixture of guilt and glee and fear and the sight of the most beautiful pink diamond earrings she'd ever seen.

Or maybe just the only pink diamond earrings she'd ever seen.

A saleslady appeared, not at all put off by Gracie's odd appearance. In fact, the young, knowing woman sporting a chic black chignon seemed to be buoyed by the scarf/sunglasses getup.

'You see something you like?' the woman asked, with one of those indistinguishable accents so often heard behind sales counters in Beverly Hills.

Gracie giggled. Gracie rarely giggled these days — not even with Jaden, who could be counted on for a giggle even when headline news became overwhelming.

Gracie continued giggling and couldn't speak. She jabbed her finger at those earrings, gesturing like an actor playing a mentally challenged mute.

'Ah, yes,' the woman said, 'these are beautiful, no?'

And she took them out of the case, holding one in each hand like tiny, brilliant headlights.

'Be more gorgeous,' Gracie said to the earrings; she'd found her voice.

'Try them on.' The woman pushed the stones into Gracie's hands.

Gracie, in a fit of courage that ranked right up there with the time she saved Billy Novak from drowning in their blow-up pool in second grade, loosened her scarf and slipped it onto her neckline.

But the glasses remained.

She held up the earrings, one to each lobe.

'Go ahead. Try them on,' the saleslady said.

'I don't need to,' Gracie said. 'Wrap 'em up. Please.'

'Are they a gift?' the saleslady asked.

'Yes,' Gracie said. 'A birthday gift.'

'She must be a wonderful person, to deserve such a luxury.'

'She's the best,' Gracie assured her.

Gracie didn't ask how much they cost. She didn't care. She placed the American Express on the counter and made the sign of the cross over it to symbolize her last purchase on the card, a purchase she wouldn't have dared to make if she were still married.

She walked out, clutching the orange Neiman Marcus bag to her chest, into the late-afternoon sunshine.

5

This Is Why I Hate Morning Phone Calls

Gracie awakened to a phone ringing, an unusual event given that Kenny had moved out. At first she felt she was dreaming, the sound seemed so foreign, so interred in the past. She opened her eyes slowly, focusing on her sleeping child who now shared her bed, her back toward her, her hair a pale web of knots. The phone rang again, jolting Gracie into consciousness. She had the same feeling in her stomach she'd had since Kenny told her he wanted a divorce — a gnawing, as though she was starving — but she wasn't starving, she wasn't even hungry. How could she be when all she did in her spare time was eat? She knew what the feeling was: emptiness. And she knew if she was going to get over their impending divorce, she would have to fill it.

Gracie finally answered the phone, knowing immediately who was on the other end when she heard the breathing. Unfortunately it wasn't a sexual prank, it was Kenny. He was jogging on the treadmill and 'running' his morning calls. Gracie thought about how nothing, really, had changed for him. His life was the same. Except that she was no longer in it.

'Hello?' Gracie said. She tried to make her voice sound clear, which was rough going at this hour. She had read an article recently that informed the reader that even our voices age, because of wear and tear on the voice box. Gracie thought this was information she didn't really need. Even our voices age? Is there nothing we can do? Is nothing sacred?

'Gracie?' Kenny breathed, then coughed. He was using the speakerphone.

'Yes,' said Gracie.

'I wanted to talk to you,' Kenny said.

He wants me back, Gracie thought, *he wants me back, but it's too late, it's just too late because . . .*

'Olivier and I are engaged?' Gracie asked.

'What?' Kenny said. 'I can't hear you.' In the background, Gracie heard the incessant whir of the treadmill, his Jurassic feet pounding the wide rubber strip. Beyond the din of the treadmill, Gracie could make out actors repeating lines. Kenny was watching dailies, scenes from a current production.

'Nothing,' Gracie said. 'I'm just lying here with Jaden. It's seven-thirty and she hasn't even stirred.' Gracie kissed Jaden, her lips sinking into her daughter's cashmere cheek. Since Kenny left, Jaden had been crawling into bed with Gracie at night, as though sensing her mother had empty spaces that needed to be filled, starting with Kenny's side of the bed. Post-split-up, Jaden had become more like a friend than a daughter: holding her hand for long periods of time, patting her head while Gracie bathed her, exhibiting a sudden willingness to share her favorite red jelly beans. What is it, Gracie thought, about a mother's sadness that turns children into compatriots?

'Maybe it's all the cough syrup I've been feeding her,' Gracie joked to Kenny.

'Listen,' Kenny said, 'I've been thinking . . . hold on.'

Gracie waited, watching the timer on her phone. After one minute and fifty-two seconds, Kenny came back on the line.

'Where was I?' Kenny said.

'I've been thinking,' Gracie replied.

'You have?' Kenny asked. 'Me, too. What have you been thinking about?'

'No,' Gracie said. 'You said 'I've been thinking.''

'Good,' Kenny said. 'We're riding the same wave. I like that.'

'Kenny,' Gracie said, 'try to avoid the surfing metaphors. You don't surf.'

'Diaz surfs, Grazer surfs. I'm thinking of taking it up,' Kenny said. 'Listen, I think we should try to avoid running into each other, don't you?'

Gracie took a moment. Running into each other? When had they . . . ?

'The birthday party,' Kenny said, 'I mean, wasn't that just too awkward, I felt embarrassed — '

'You shouldn't feel embarrassed,' Gracie said. For all of Kenny's ego, and there was a lot of it to go around, he never failed to feel embarrassed about something.

'No,' Kenny said, 'not for me. Listen, I just want you to know, as a friend . . . '

Did he just say 'as a friend'? Gracie wondered.

' . . . people were talking,' Kenny puffed.

Gracie realized he'd felt embarrassed for her. That *she* should be embarrassed.

'Kenny, I've known Qiana for years, before she even got married, before the name, nose, the boobs, the yoga, the yoga instructor, the fake pregnancy, the surrogate pregnancy — '

'I'm just saying, people are talking, and it's not me they're talking about.'

Gracie felt her face flush; she knew she was turning purple. 'You have a lot of nerve,' she said, ignoring the early-morning old-voice-box gravel in her voice. 'So much nerve, in fact, there's little room left for brain!'

'Look, Gracie,' Kenny said calmly, 'if we're going to be buds, I have to be honest with you. Paula thinks that — '

'Who's Paula?' Gracie demanded. She ignored the fact that he used the word 'bud' in a sentence for anything other than a discussion on roses.

'My psychotherapist. She's very spiritual. She's like a high priestess of the Kabbalah. Anyway, she thinks that the problem with our relationship is that I could never be honest with you — '

'You have a psycho therapist?' Gracie asked, cleaving the term into two words. Kenny had never gone to a therapist. Kenny, ever the Neanderthal, thought therapy, much like Broadway, was for women and homosexuals.

'Every time I'd say 'Honey, maybe you should try dressing differently,' or 'Babe, I think you'd look great with more highlights,' you'd ignore me,' Kenny panted. 'And remember the time I wanted you to call Rupert Murdoch's wife?'

'You don't know Rupert Murdoch!' Gracie screamed like a wild animal. Jaden finally let out a groan.

'You have got to stop leading with your ego,' Kenny said.

Gracie made a choking sound.

'Why couldn't you have just called and invited them to our house for dinner? Would that have been so hard?' Kenny asked.

'Kenny! They have no idea who we are!' Gracie said.

'Paula said the wives in Hollywood determine social standing, wives are the connective tissue. All I'm saying is that you could have done more to help my career,' Kenny said. 'Now, I'm going to have my assistant call you and tell you what I'm doing this weekend so we avoid running into each other. Off the top of my head I have a brunch meeting at the Bel Air on Saturday morning, a screening at Lou's on Saturday night, and I think someone's getting married on Sunday.'

Gracie was rendered speechless for a moment. 'Who are you?' she finally asked. She realized he hadn't even stopped running, the weight of his feet punishing the treadmill even as he had the nerve to claim that everyone was talking about her, feeling sorry for her. Poor Gracie, future overage Former Wife Of.

'Listen,' Kenny said, 'we couldn't make it work married, but maybe we can make it work divorced.'

'That's beautiful, that's poetry,' Gracie said. If sarcasm were water, he'd have drowned.

'Thank you,' Kenny said with pride. 'I don't want to take all the credit. Paula told me how to say it.'

'As long as we don't run into each other,' Gracie said.

'As long as we don't run into each other,' Kenny agreed. 'I'm glad you see this my way.'

'Hey, Kenny,' Gracie said, 'I've found someone.'

She was pleased to hear the clop-clop-clop of his Adidas come to a sudden halt.

'Anyone I know?' Kenny asked, feigning emotional detachment.

'No one in the business,' Gracie said.

'Oh. Like a, what, a fireman? Construction workers?' Kenny asked.

'You wouldn't know him, he's in . . . ' Gracie looked around — Jaden turned her head toward her, her pacifier stuck in her mouth, ruining her bite, but in the cutest way. 'He's in the . . . rubber business,' Gracie said. 'So I wasn't going to be around this weekend anyway. Jaden and I are heading out . . . '

She gulped. 'On his jet.'

'He's got a jet?' Kenny asked. She noticed his studio-pres bearing had lost some of its grandeur.

'A small one,' Gracie said. 'Not like a 747 or

BBJ, like a G-something. It's a little embarrassing, you know, I'm not used to that sort of thing . . . '

Twist that knife, sister, she thought to herself.

'A G-5?' Kenny asked, his voice an octave higher. It sounded like someone was squeezing Kenny's shaven manhood.

'Have to run,' Gracie said. 'And Kenny? Thanks for being so honest with me.'

⋆ ⋆ ⋆

'This is why I hate morning phone calls,' Joan said. 'Anything that rings between the hours of twelve midnight and ten A.M. is decidedly off-limits. Oh, *God!* I *hate* this guy!'

'Turn off the news, Joan!' Gracie yelled. She could always tell when Joan had the news on. She would scream 'Mothertwister!' or some such tangled epithet in the middle of a sentence. It was headline-induced Tourette's.

'Why do I even watch?' Joan asked. 'Why?'

'Can we get back to our earlier conversation?'

'Kenny the Pig,' Joan said, 'is going to die of a heart attack before the age of forty-nine.'

Joan liked to put curses on people who crossed her or her friends; her mother's people, who crawled out from some swamp in Louisiana, claimed to have 'powers.' Gracie thought it was safer not to question her assertion.

'How could I have lied like that?' Gracie said. 'I mean, how lame. Why didn't I just say George Clooney thinks elastic waistbands on women are sexy?'

'I love me some George,' Joan sighed.

Gracie sighed as well. Didn't everyone her age love George?

'Okay, here's the thing,' Joan said. 'Lying is never the right thing to do — unless it's for the greater good, and in this case there was a greater good — that of grinding Kenny into the ground, at least temporarily.'

'What if I have to lie again?' Gracie asked. 'What if he asks me about the mystery man again?'

'Lie until you can't tell the truth anymore,' Joan said. 'You can't be the only honest person in this town.'

'It won't backfire?' Gracie asked. She seldom lied; she wasn't sure what the ramifications were.

'How could it backfire?' Joan asked. 'You're making up a person. There's no one to Google. There's no name to check out. You were specific yet vague.'

'I have to tell you, Joan,' Gracie admitted, 'it felt really good to sucker-punch Kenny. Lying about having another man was like instant Prozac.'

Then she thought for a moment. 'Maybe it felt too good.'

'There's no such thing as feeling too good,' Joan said. 'That's where you run into trouble. Now, have you seen the news this morning? I'm going to need me a Bloody Mary.'

★ ★ ★

Kenny, driven, Gracie believed, by the intense curiosity one has when one's ex is screwing someone else, called a couple more times during the week, and each time Gracie lived in fear that he was going to ask to meet her nonexistent but very rich and successful beau. With each phone call he dropped hints belying his need to know, and each time Gracie had to build upon her initial, feeble lie until she had constructed a man so perfect, so worthy, so desirable that she was sure that not only did this man not exist, but he could never exist.

'What does he do again?' Kenny would ask.

'He's . . . his family is in . . . the rubber business,' she'd say, 'but he's looking into other ventures.'

'Film?' Kenny asked.

'Well, maybe, sort of,' Gracie said. 'I'm not sure. And frankly, I'm discouraging it.' To her credit, Gracie would cross her fingers and toes.

'How much money does he have?' Kenny finally came to the real question — the question keeping him up at night.

'You know, I haven't asked,' Gracie said.

'Fifty mil? A hundred mil?' Kenny asked.

'Oh, that's not even in the range,' Gracie said. She thought thirty or forty mil sounded reasonable enough.

'A billion? The guy's a billionaire?!' Kenny's voice went to a pitch heard mainly by feral dogs.

Whoops, Gracie thought. She knew that now Kenny would be researching the Forbes list for the Rubber Man. 'I didn't say that,' Gracie said. 'I have to get Jaden to school.'

'If the guy's into the film business, we should talk,' Kenny said. 'I could help him.'

'I told you, I'm discouraging that particular trajectory,' Gracie said with proper gravity.

'Has Jaden met him?' Kenny asked.

'Have to run,' Gracie replied airily.

★ ★ ★

'I think you're being mean,' Cricket said. 'But I guess it serves him right.

'You can't tell anyone,' Gracie repeated.

'Gracie, you're going to have to find a guy, because he's going to find out,' Will said. 'And won't you feel like a Silly Sally.'

'I don't really care,' Gracie said. 'I'm just having Mad Divorcée Fun.'

'You'll care when he tells the story to his friends,' Will said. 'We have to find you someone. Someone who fits the perfect-man mold. And then you can have a short, nasty breakup. And no one will be the wiser.'

'I can't wait! Where should we find him?' Cricket asked. 'Sharon Stone found her boyfriend in the produce section of Ralph's. Melons are very sensual.'

'What's this 'we'? I have to find a guy,' Gracie said, 'not you. Me. You're married.'

'He's going to leave me, isn't he,' Cricket said. 'Jorge is going to leave me.' Cricket suffered from extreme empathy syndrome. If her friend is getting a divorce, she's getting a divorce; if her friend has strep, she develops a sore throat; if someone in China has a hangnail, Cricket can't get through the day.

'Next subject,' said Will.

★ ★ ★

Will had a plan of attack; he was nothing if not thorough. It was not easy for a close-to-forty-one-year-old woman to find a man in L.A., so Will said that they would have to think outside the box. Because inside the box, apparently, there existed only smooth-skinned lasses and laddies and their sponsors.

Will and Gracie went to a seminar given by a woman who called herself Dr. Melanie, the Relationship Diva. After two hours, having spent twenty dollars and scarfed down three dough-nuts and a cup of bad coffee (how hard was it to get good coffee in L.A.?), Gracie found out she was to be 'cherished' in a relationship. Gracie would have to find a man who worshiped her for the goddess she was, and she could not settle for anything less.

Gracie came out of it figuring this was possible, if one still believed in unicorns and magic fairies and a fellow named Santa.

Will came out of it with a lunch date on Thursday, a dinner date on Saturday, and an invitation for a weekend in Santa Barbara.

Later, they tried a dog park. Difficult when one has an ancient miniature dachshund, Helen, who was at best indifferent to other dogs, and at worst would chase and attack the giant ones.

Gracie met a few nice people, who happened

to be women over forty, looking for that same elusive bachelor with the yellow Lab, deep voice, and muscular forearms.

Will got three phone numbers and a lead on where to find a cockapoodle.

Finally, their third excursion to find a man (and at this point, any man would do — they had given up their narrow thirty-six to fifty-six focus and now were willing to entertain any and all above the age of consent to still breathing) landed them at the early-morning mass at St. Stephen's Church on Sepulveda. Will had heard through the grapevine that many cute straight men gathered there for God's wisdom (how he had heard this through the Gay Grapevine, Gracie was reluctant to ask). In addition, word was that the pastor was in the midst of a divorce. Gracie was opposed to using the church to further her own agenda until Will pointed out that God loves all his children and wants them to be happy, including Gracie.

She had to agree with that logic.

When she picked up Will that morning, she realized the error of her ways. Will had stayed up all night at a transvestite birthday party in West Hollywood celebrating 'Miss Pretty Mae Dawson's' Fiftieth and was not fit to step out into daylight without a dose of Maybelline and dark shades.

Gracie sat side by side with Will in a pew in the middle of a large, modern church. Gracie was dressed discreetly in pale colors and pearls, Will was dressed in black and wearing huge sunglasses that made him look like a young

Carol Channing. Worse, he would fall asleep intermittently and snore while the surprisingly cute pastor with the six o'clock anchor's tenor spoke about various challenges facing mankind, including the church's need to raise money to remodel their bathrooms.

Gracie, finding inspiration in the stained-glass windows and fine acoustics, found herself thinking about the challenges facing womankind. In particular, her own womankind.

Will rested his snoring head on her shoulder, and it stayed there throughout the sermon.

Gracie met several lovely couples and their wonderful children.

Will got the pastor's number.

★   ★   ★

Gracie had a Coors Light in one hand, her telephone in the other, as she talked on a conference call with Will and Cricket. The last time she'd been on a conference call with friends was sometime in the middle ages, like the 1980s. But desperate times call for desperate uses of technology.

'Can we get back to that thinking-outside-the-box concept?' Gracie asked. 'The only man I've met in the last couple weeks is you, Will, and I already know you and you're gay.'

'Alas, it's all true,' Will said. 'But I'm fresh out of ideas. My muse is taking a hiatus.'

'Cricket,' Gracie asked, 'you got anything for me?'

'A rabbi at George Junior's school,' Cricket

said. 'He's fat and his teeth aren't clean, but he's very nice.'

'I'm not Jewish,' Gracie said.

'You know, you really should think about it,' Cricket said. 'You could do a mini-conversion. It would take, like, ten days and a red string. Look at Madonna, I mean Esther.'

Gracie just sighed. She found herself sighing a lot these days. Maybe she wasn't sighing so much as wheezing, which scared her and convinced her she would die of lung cancer before she ever put Kenny in his grave.

'So, are we just going to give up?' Gracie asked. 'Is that it?'

'I wouldn't call it giving up,' Will said. 'I'd call it more like a vacation from Desperation-ville. Look, if you want, I can get you a gay decoy. But it would cost you hair and makeup. For him.'

Gracie hung up the phone. Things were bad, she thought, when the homosexual crowd was giving up on your sex life.

WIFE NUMBER THREE

Married to a baby producer. He brought something special home from the London set for her.
Herpes.

6

Moving On Out

In the last few weeks, Gracie, fully excommed, realized her life had changed in both subtle and drastic ways:

SUBTLE

1. She was able to open a mailbox without ten invitations to charity events dropping on her toes.

2. She was able to let the Romanian lady who blow-dried her hair go; Gracie had no reason to blow-dry her hair anymore. And she had too much pride to blow-dry it just to pick up Jaden from school with straight locks. Also, it was obvious the Romanian lady pitied her; she would prod her with ways to win Kenny back. 'You sleep with him more. Americans no make the sexy enough.' Gracie was pretty sure Kenny wouldn't come running back if she threw herself at him three times a day; he was on to better (read: younger) things.

3. Her answering machine at home no longer registered forty-five calls. It usually registered five, and three of those were from AT&T Wireless, seeking new customers.

4. Restaurants around town suddenly had no reservations open Friday at eight o'clock. But they could fit her in at four forty-five. On a Monday.

5. Jaden's List of No-No Words had been expanded. Gracie and Jaden had come up with a list of words that were considered off-limits. There were four of them: 'stupid,' 'hate,' 'dumb,' and 'dumb-ass.' Jaden would ask before she said any of these words: 'Mommy, may I say 'stupid'?' And Gracie would consider the request and the context, then give her daughter an answer. The List of No-No Words was now up to eight and counting. In addition to the aforementioned, there was also 'shit,' 'f-word,' 'a-word,' and 'butt' (Jaden, consumed with guilt over calling her best friend a butt, had added that one). Unfortunately, these were the only words Mommy had used in the last month and could fathom using in the near future. A vocabulary that had earned Gracie a 680 on her verbal SAT had diminished considerably. Two more no-no words and she'd be able to record an entire rap album. She was planning on calling it *Angry White Bitch*.

DRASTIC

1. Re Number Three, above. Except for the steady stream of invitees calling to say that, unfortunately, they would no longer be able to attend Gracie's forty-first birthday party as planned, because: (a) they had an important business meeting and/or operation, (b) they realized they thought the date was for last year, and are therefore unavailable, and (c) their bichon frise had been run over three weeks ago.

2. Gracie had been summarily dismissed from the Stevie Norber book club. Stevie was The Wife Of a semi-producer who had held the club in her home in Cheviot Hills every month for the last few years and had never let anyone else choose a book. Gracie was relieved to be exempt from reading yet one more novel about southern belles and their cancer scares.

3. She stayed home most nights. Except for those few times when Will, Cricket, or Joan pried her away from reality television.

4. Reality television: She had no idea.

5. Staying home = staying in bed except when absolutely necessary, like house on fire or child needs a ride to the hospital.

6. Remember the 'pulling the pin' thing? Gracie had exploded; she looked like she'd swallowed a grooming grenade. She'd canceled all of her maintenance appointments. Her hair was turning brown and wiry, her nails were splitting, and her body had exhaled. It had been holding back for years, and now . . . it was spreading.

7. The final blow: Gracie was going to have to move. Kenny the Pig missed El McMansion. Gracie could hear Maxwell Havens's smile stretch across his face as he told her the news.

★　★　★

Gracie had called Joan after she realized she was going to have to move out right away. When they'd sold the Brown House and bought the McMonstrosity, Kenny had not volunteered to put Gracie's name on the deed, and Gracie had not insisted on it. After all, it was Kenny's money, not Gracie's, which was buying the McMonster. And for now, Kenny did not see the point of buying the Brown House for Gracie when he didn't have to. Gracie would have to find somewhere else to settle down.

Joan muttered something about cutting off Kenny's balls with a blunt bowie knife and then muttered something about him not having any so why bother and then demanded that Gracie spend the weekend with her in Malibu, which Gracie took her up on after one additional sigh and two seconds of deliberation.

Gracie packed Jaden and her miniature dachshund, Helen, in her Volvo and drove north all of eight miles to Malibu. They arrived at the security gate to the Malibu Colony, where Joan lived with Pappy in their second home, when she wasn't hiding out in their Beverly Hills estate.

The Colony was both famous and infamous. This half-mile strip of coast housed some of the most celebrated faces in modern history, and the hundred or so houses behind the white security gates were on arguably the most expensive beachfront property in California and, therefore, the world.

And yet, Gracie said to herself, after her name was checked off the security guard's list and she entered the gates, turning left onto the private road, 'My God, these houses are close together.'

So close together, it was impossible to breathe in one house and not cough up carbon dioxide next door. The Malibu Colony homes, which would sell for upwards of five million, were right on top of each other. They were mere inches apart. It's like the most expensive ghetto in the world, Gracie thought.

In this most exclusive and expensive of enclaves, one had to pick one's neighbors very carefully.

Gracie hadn't been to the Colony in a couple of years. She and Kenny had spent a Fourth of July weekend there, and Gracie was promptly overwhelmed by the proximity of twin challenges: ocean sports and movie stars. She

138

couldn't look up from her reading without seeing a wetsuit, surfboard, kayak, or famous face.

They hadn't been back since.

Gracie drove over the speed bumps, amazed at the number of construction trucks lining the row of houses. There were more trucks than Mercedeses or BMWs, more construction workers than tenants.

She parked in front of the house at the southeast end of the Colony, a seventies wood building consisting of two large triangulated structures abutting the public beach. She noted the Latino families on the other side of the chain-link (topped with barbed-wire) fence, illegally grilling something that smelled both exotic and comfortingly familiar, its scent mixing sublimely with the sea air.

'We're here, Jaden,' Gracie said, 'we're at the beach.'

Jaden awakened from her nap in her booster seat and stretched her arms. Helen barked, sticking her tongue out of her tiny cage. They got out of the car and Gracie took another deep breath — the air felt good to her — and she felt as though it was the first true breath she'd taken since her husband broke up with her via the latest technology.

'Getcher butts in here!' she heard Joan yell through the intercom after she pressed the doorbell. 'Mommy,' Jaden said, reproachful. 'No-no word.'

Gracie replied, 'I'll talk to Aunt Joanie about the language.'

She grabbed Jaden and made her way past the

guesthouse and outdoor shower and up a row of wooden stairs into the main house. The house was a mint green color, a color one could get away with only on the beach; there would be no excuse otherwise. The front door was open; Gracie and Jaden stepped inside. The interior was entirely white with bleached floors; the effect was at once soothing and stimulating. There were floor-to-ceiling windows which on one side faced the public beach, on the other the Colony beach, where the fence divided 'us' from 'them.' The view on clear days followed the Pacific all the way to Catalina. Maybe it was worth it, Gracie thought as she looked out toward the narrowest crescent of island, to marry a rich guy with bowel issues and a hearing aid.

'You like my shack?' Joan asked as she rushed down from the upstairs bedroom to meet them. She had spent a year remodeling the place after buying it when the original owner passed away, and it was obvious she was proud of the outcome.

'It's a pigsty,' Gracie said. 'How can you live like this?'

'The beach!' Jaden said, standing at the picture window. 'Mucha aguita!'

'Then you don't want to stay here?' Joan asked innocently.

Gracie looked at her. 'What do you mean?' she asked.

'La playa!' Jaden yelled.

'Pappy's heart is set on staying in the south of France this summer,' Joan said. 'Now, you know I hate the French, but I do love my Grand Crus.'

'You don't hate the French,' Gracie said. 'When you were young — ' Joan raised an eyebrow. 'Young-er! You'd date anything with a French accent, even a fake one.'

'I want to go to the beach,' Jaden said.

'Even a French poodle, *mais oui*,' Joan said. 'But I told Pappy I hate the French, just so he doesn't think he's doing me a big favor. Anyway, we'll be staying at the Du Cap for three weeks, and then renting a villa.'

Gracie whistled. 'Du Cap' was French for 'cash only.'

'Mama, can we go out on the beach?' Jaden was now pulling down Gracie's overused Juicy sweats.

'Do you have sunscreen on?' Gracie asked.

'No,' Jaden said solemnly. 'I'm a little kid. You forgot to put it on me.'

'A hat and sunscreen,' Joan said. 'You don't want to look like Auntie Joanie when you get to be old, do you?'

Jaden studied Joan's face, then shook her head emphatically.

Gracie and Joan laughed. Joan was a natural redhead with a ton of freckles and the kind of fine Irish skin that didn't age well. Which was enough of an argument to marry someone with cataracts.

'That's okay, honey, I married old. He'll always be more wrinkled than me,' Joan said.

'Are you serious about the house?' Gracie asked.

'Serious as my last peel,' Joan said. 'You need a house, we need someone to keep an eye on it. Pappy can't stand the thought of renting to strangers. He doesn't like people knowing he has a special-needs toilet.'

'But you could get thirty thousand a month for this place.'

'Fifty thousand,' Joan corrected her. 'Over three months it would amount to a seventeen-karat Tiffany tennis bracelet or a condo in the Valley, but hey, who's counting?'

Gracie took a moment, then shook her head. 'The special-needs toilet sounds captivating, but I can't take it.'

Joan looked at her. 'Okay, I'll say it. I'm worried about you.'

'What?' Gracie asked. 'Now you're sounding like someone's mother.'

Joan looked at Jaden. 'Honey, have you seen the deck? I need you to select the right sand toys for me. I picked them up at Sav-on, but I don't know if they're any good. It's been a long time since Auntie Joan dug a hole in the sand.'

Jaden nodded, her eyes alerted to any sign of neon-colored sand toys as Joan walked her out onto the front, beachside, glass-enclosed deck.

Joan walked back a moment later.

'Now, cut the shit,' she said. 'You need rehab.'

'Rehab is thirty days and involves calm, sweet-talking drug counseling types,' Gracie replied. 'And sometimes you get to sleep with the other rehabitués.'

'Speaking of sleeping, you're not, and you're not taking care of yourself.' Joan lifted a lock of Gracie's hair. Gracie pulled it back, realizing she had forgotten the last time she'd combed her hair. She found herself pulling in her stomach — it had to be obvious that she'd gained ten, maybe twelve pounds (maybe a little more?) over the last few weeks. Her favorite pants when she was a size four now only fit over her head.

'And I'd bet my husband's golf club collection you haven't shaved your legs in three weeks.'

'Why would I need to shave my legs?' Gracie said. 'Doesn't that imply someone would be seeing them?'

'How about under your arms?' Joan asked.

'Okay, okay, maybe I have a little . . . problem,' Gracie acknowledged.

'And your eyebrows look like two dead caterpillars,' Joan said. 'You know, the first thing to go when someone's clinically depressed is body hair.'

'I thought it was personal hygiene.' Gracie knew she had taken a shower in the last few days, she would swear it. Except that she wasn't sure what day it had been.

'I'm not saying you smell great, either,' Joan said. 'Here in Malibu you will find three things: fresh air, a beach to walk on, and the feel of the sun on your skin. You will rediscover the pleasure of life.'

'And I don't have to pay fifty thousand dollars a month for that privilege.'

'Consider it your ninety-day rehab program,'

143

Joan said. 'At the end of ninety days, I predict you will be a new person. Just don't look for a bookstore in town because there aren't any. And you'll need a special courier for the *New York Times*. I'm not saying Malibu is civilized, just beautiful.'

Gracie looked at her friend. 'I love you, you know that?'

'You say that to all your sponsors,' Joan said. 'Who knows, you may even find a . . . *man*.' She bugged out her eyes and wiggled her fingers around her face.

Gracie made a buzzing sound. 'No, thank you,' she said. 'Haven't I suffered enough?'

'For a man? Never!' Joan said. 'Now, you'll need an extra set of keys, and be careful to lock up, even during the daytime. There's more construction than living going on in the Colony, so you never know who's around, watching the place. One of the neighbors had her necklace and a Bulgari watch stolen recently. Of course, she'd left them on her kitchen counter when her Pilates teacher came over.'

'Crime in the 90265?' Gracie said. 'Horrors!'

Joan waved her hand at her as she made her way to the deck where Jaden had picked out a shovel, a pail, and a rake. 'Let's throw some sunscreen on this kid and get down to the beach before she throws a snit fit.'

Gracie sniffed under her arms to make sure her personal hygiene had met FDA standards and followed her friend outside.

THE FLYER SAID:

Nothing to Do This Saturday?
Going-Away/Birthday Party for Me!
Hubby Wants the House Back!
Let's Give Him Something to Complain
  About!
502 Rockingham Avenue, Brentwood
Saturday, May 21st, 2004, 7:30

It wasn't verse, but it got the point across: Gracie was having a going-away party at Kenny's oversized, energy-sucking McManor with Will, Cricket, and Joan — and two hundred strangers. Gracie had printed up flyers and strewn them around various neighborhoods, from Ocean Park to Montana Avenue. She wanted to have a party, but she knew that most of her old 'friends' wouldn't attend — they wouldn't dare risk offending Kenny. Now that she was no longer going to be a Wife Of, people in her previous, insulated life were no longer interested in her. A Wife Of could lend her name to a charity opening, a Wife Of could help get a job, a Wife Of could write a check. An ex-comm Starter Wife with less than ten years of marriage and a pre-nup was a civilian with no husband credentials and not enough money to warrant a phone call.

Gracie, no longer interested in the people who were no longer interested in her, invited two sets of people: her few, true friends and people she didn't know. Ana picked Jaden up for an overnight stay at her home in Inglewood, where

145

Jaden could play with Ana's grandchildren and her three dogs and eat tamales and yell in Spanish and stay up late and participate in the kind of giddy, liberated house-filled-with-kids noise that was not normally found in Brentwood.

Around eight o'clock, people started showing up. First her three friends, then a steady stream of new faces — UCLA students, hipsters, divorced people, older people on a budget, sullen teenagers, baristas with tongue and eyebrow piercings from Starbucks, several homeless people, couples with young babies, lonely writer types, blue-collar types, non-English-speaking types. Gracie was determined to throw a blow-out party to celebrate her new life and, incidentally, to leave the house a wreck for Kenny the Pig.

Gracie ordered enough pizza from Jacopo's to cover over two hundred people and enough beer to cover spring break in St. Petersburg, Florida. Kenny's stereo was set to decibels that would register with the space shuttle, and the older folks argued with the younger ones whether to play a little Frank Sinatra or more Jack White. Joan, who arrived without Pappy (he was, as usual, tucked in and asleep by eight-thirty), was getting her freak on with a boy who'd probably became legal just that morning. One could maybe slide a piece of paper between them as they danced in the living room. Cricket had come with her husband, Jorge, a normally decent man who was now wearing a cap on his head with beer cans lining the top.

Gracie had just set down her fifth or sixth

extra-cheese pizza when she saw Cricket standing alone in a corner, watching her straitlaced husband playing irresponsible frat boy.

'Are you okay?' she asked Cricket. 'You look a little shell-shocked.'

Cricket grabbed her arm. 'Gracie, someone peed on the Chesterfield, I'm not kidding.'

She was talking about the antique couch in the library. Kenny's favorite couch to pretend to read on. 'So, he'll stand,' Gracie said, looking over toward the couch she'd purchased after much deliberation. How much time had she deliberated over that couch? How could she get that time back?

'You don't know who any of these people are, do you?' Cricket said in accusation.

Gracie looked around. 'Sure I do.' She pointed in some general direction. 'That girl works at the Starbucks on Montana, he's that masseur at Whole Foods on San Vicente, she's a checker there, I'm pretty sure those three guys are in Sigma Chi — '

'And what about that woman?' Cricket asked.

She pointed to a figure; it was hard to tell whether the figure belonged to a woman, man, or bear. Gracie surmised it was a woman. The figure wore a hood and clutched a shopping bag to her chest. She appeared to not have bathed in this millennium.

'Don't know her.'

'She's homeless!' Cricket said. 'She could have germs. She could have some sort of . . . pox!' Cricket had gone through a germaphobe stage

147

that coincided with her claustrophobic stage, just missing her agoraphobic stage.

'I doubt she has pox,' Gracie said, peering at the woman closely. 'Probably more like TB.'

'I have to get Jorge out of here,' Cricket said. 'He's making a fool out of himself.'

'He looks like he's having fun,' Gracie said. Jorge was lying on the floor now while two frat boys attempted to pour beer in his mouth through a funnel connected to a tube held high in their hands. He seemed to be choking and laughing at the same time.

'How are you two, by the way?' Gracie asked. She hadn't thought of asking Cricket about her marriage in a while, consumed as she was with the demise of her own. The thought occurred to her, though, that she always believed Cricket and Jorge would be the first to divorce in her group. Cricket had been convinced Jorge was cheating on her since the day they walked down the aisle.

'He's cheating on me,' Cricket said.

'Cricket,' Gracie said. 'How do you know? Where's the proof? Where's the WMD?'

Jorge flipped his body around and promptly threw up on the floor.

'He's two years younger than I am, he's successful, he's handsome,' Cricket said. 'Of course he's cheating on me.'

Jorge was all of those things. The man throwing up on Gracie's living room floor — er, Kenny's living room floor — had four television shows on the air in addition to a pilot's license and a body fat count of 4.2 percent. He was an overachiever's overachiever.

148

Waves of 'Go, Jorge!' filled the air. Gracie smiled and clapped her hands; she hadn't had this much fun since the four days she had off in the hospital after her C-section.

'He's doing a military hospital show now,' Cricket said. 'Filled with real nurses!' she exclaimed. 'I can't compete with a nurse. They have those uniforms! And they like helping strangers!'

'I know, it's sick,' Gracie said. 'Cricket, you've got to stop this.' But she was in no mood to manage someone else's personal crisis. 'You've never caught him in any lies. As far as I know, he's never even looked at another woman.'

'That's his MO, Gracie,' Cricket said. 'They all have one. I mean, how did you find out about Kenny?'

'How did I find out about Kenny what?' Gracie asked.

'Nothing!' Cricket yelped.

Gracie grabbed her by the shoulders. 'Tell me, or I'll spill your guts all over this room.'

'Really?' Cricket asked.

'No, God, of course not.' Gracie took a deep breath. 'I could never hurt you. So who is it? An actress?'

'No, no,' Cricket said.

'A model?' Gracie asked. 'Typical. A young, stupid model. Of course I should have known — '

'No, not really a model.'

'Then what?'

'She's more like a . . . a . . . what's the word?' Cricket paused as Gracie wondered whether to

149

strangle her. Who would pause at a moment like this?

'International superstar,' Cricket finally sputtered.

'That's two words,' Gracie replied coolly.

'Britney Spears,' Cricket said.

Gracie looked at her, wondering when the joke would land. It didn't. 'I'm burning the house down,' she said.

'He's cheating on me,' Cricket said, looking at Jorge, who had passed out cheek-down in his own vomit.

★　★　★

Gracie wrapped herself up in her comforter and curled up into a forty-one-year-old, flat-assed, freckle-handed ball and whimpered like a beaten dog while the party raged on to epic proportions.

Will finally found her around two o'clock in the morning. He fell onto the bed next to her and patted her hair. As he was drunk beyond repair, his 'patting' was on the verge of 'slapping.'

'Why so glum?' he asked.

'A thought just came to me,' Gracie said. 'Britney Spears is a home-wrecker.'

'But love, love, love her grace and artistry,' Will replied, performing a Britney move with his hands and head. 'By the way, I'm pretty sure a garage mechanic named Manfredo just proposed to me. This is the best damn house-wrecking party I've ever been to.'

'Did you know about Kenny and Britney?' Gracie asked.

'Oh, please,' Will said. 'She wants to act, of course she's going to date the head of a studio. Even if he does iron his jeans.'

'He's going to be in *Us Magazine*, just like Lou said,' Gracie wailed.

'Do you think you'll be in the catfight section?' Will said. 'That would be fab! It would really help my career. Do try!'

Gracie hit him on the arm.

'See, you're feeling better already. You're already rolling fags,' Will said. 'Now, come on, it's after two, your future hangover called. It wants your head.'

He helped her up and grabbed her around the waist.

'You're never going to cheat on me, are you, Will?' Gracie asked, looking up at her friend. 'You're not going to decorate for Kenny again, right?'

'Never, I couldn't work for Britney,' Will said, his hand to his chest. 'I'd faint at the first mention of the word 'doily.''

A moment later, they were tripping into the living room, where the wide-screen television set had been turned on.

'Who turned on MTV?' Gracie yelled.

Britney Spears herself was singing and rolling over the bodies of several oiled-up dancers on Kenny's big-screen flat TV, a recent and completely necessary purchase. Gracie threw a beer bottle at the screen.

The party mania paused briefly.

'Look at that,' Will said. 'I had no idea you could shatter a flat-screen.'

151

7

June Gloom

The day they left the McMansion, Jaden and Gracie played their final game of 'What Do I Love?' in Jaden's spacious bedroom with the story of Black Beauty played out in an elaborate watercolor mural on three of the four walls. Kenny had wanted Cinderella; it was basically the only fight Gracie had won regarding the house.

'What do I love?' Gracie asked as she finished packing Jaden's Hello Kitty suitcase. She wiped her cheek before she looked up at her daughter. Leaving the McFright, though she'd never considered it 'home,' was much more difficult than she'd imagined.

Jaden looked up at her mother. She had already dressed herself for the beach: pink flip-flops on her feet, an orange bathing suit, tiny neon sunglasses. Gracie didn't have the heart to tell her there was no sun at the beach. June gloom had set in; it was sixty-four degrees in Malibu.

'I love your eyes,' Gracie said, looking at the most beautiful face in the world. 'I love your nose, I love your fingers, I love your toes.'

'That's four, Mommy,' Jaden replied, her lower lip poking out. 'We're only supposed to do three. That's our rule.'

'I can't help it,' Gracie replied. 'How can I help it?'

When Jaden was about three months old, Gracie invented the 'What Do I Love?' game. Baby Jaden would look at her and smile as Gracie would ask 'What do I love?' and then would tap gently on her cheeks, her nose, her tummy. As Jaden grew, Gracie used the game as a touchstone to secure their relationship and to understand what Jaden was caring about now, today.

Gracie could tell whether her daughter was angry or sad, or needed more attention through her answers.

'Okay, what do I love?' Jaden said, satisfied. 'What do I love? I love your mouth, I love Ana, I love Mommy's new earrings.'

The kid loved her nanny and she loved jewelry. Jaden definitely needed more attention. Gracie laughed out loud, the reverberation so foreign to her that she was almost surprised.

★   ★   ★

Living in the Malibu Colony for a few days brought out the modern primatologist in Gracie. She quickly became the Jane Goodall of the Beach-Bimbos-and-Bentleys set, making mental notes of the more blatant attributes and behaviors of the residents:

Parking spots are more important than food, air, or water.

Brag even when seemingly unnecessary. For

example, claim that someone offered you twenty-six million for your house, as opposed to the true inflated number, fourteen million.

Stare at every car that drives by. Analyze the driver and passenger for signs of fame.

Leave your dog shit to the Fates.

This last trait would have stuck in Gracie's craw if she knew what a craw was: Rich people don't pick up their dog poop. The day after she moved into the Malibu Colony, Gracie had walked around the back of her Volvo carrying two bags filled with groceries and had landed a Michael Kors sandal directly on top of a warm pile of dog excrement. She let out a yelp as she felt her foot slide into what seemed to be an endless Black Hole of Poo. The yelp was followed by a five-minute stream of well-chosen expletives befitting such a momentous occasion.

As luck would have it, #250, on the end of the Colony cul-de-sac, was the first house to go to if one had a dog that needed to relieve itself. Gracie would watch in wonder as various neighbors would walk their dogs, most of whom were the official Malibu cur, the yellow Lab, to the end of her driveway to deposit the remains of last night's Dog Chow, or more likely, filet mignon. There was a small trash can at the end of the street, specifically for depositing dog poop, which no one used.

After sidestepping several more of Fido's gifts, Gracie decided to take action.

First, she bought a pooper scooper and put it within sight of all who would be walking in front of the house. Then she put out a sign, a picture

154

of a dog squatting with a slash through it. Then she wrote up a memo to all her neighbors alerting them to the fact that Joan's driveway was not in fact a dumping ground.

And finally, when none of that seemed to work, she became a poop detective, hiding behind her doorway or the bushes or her Volvo station wagon, jumping out when an offender made an appearance.

She didn't have to wait long. A few doors down there was an odd couple — he was much older and was pushed around in a wheelchair by his driver, who also tooled him around in a Mercedes limousine; she deigned to drive herself around in a convertible baby-blue Cadillac. She was Viking tall, wore frosted pink lipstick, and was fond of unitards. He wore baggy shorts with pale, stick legs and a permanent scowl and had made his fortune in slot machines.

Gracie knew she'd have trouble with them her first day in Malibu; she was walking Jaden in a stroller when the Cadillac came careening down the street, not breaking for the speed bumps, barely missing little Helen, who was tethered to a leash next to Jaden.

Gracie ran and screamed after the Cadillac, which was forced to slow down for a moving van. 'Are you crazy? You almost hit us!'

To which the woman replied, 'I've got good aim!'

Gracie was not a big fan of this couple. She called them the Shits. Until she learned their real names, which seemed punishment enough: Monique and Harry Boner, late of Reno,

Nevada. As far as she could tell, from her little communication thus far with the neighbors, there weren't a lot of fans on their side of the fence. The Shits, er, Boners, had made plenty of enemies in the Malibu Colony. Gracie would have to stand in line.

'Who is that woman in the Cadillac?' Gracie asked an unsuspecting Colony security officer, tooling around in the ubiquitous white pickup. The man just rolled his eyes.

'Number 226.'

All the houses were numbered.

'Is she crazy?' Gracie asked. 'I'm surprised she didn't kill us.'

'Oh, there's time.' He grinned. He had one gold tooth, which added glamour to his otherwise bland demeanor.

'So, they're the bad neighbors.'

'Oh yes, ma'am,' he said.

Days later, Gracie was poised to strike. She was hidden on one side of the Volvo station wagon as Jaden rode her tricycle in the driveway, watching with a burgeoning sensation of righteous anger as dog after dog spewed out of 226 — big, furry, loud dogs bumping into each other like so many pinballs in a pachinko machine.

They looked like a good argument against inbreeding.

The big balls of fur were tumbling toward her house. The dogs knew where to go; they'd probably been dumping here their whole furry, oversized, stupid lives.

And out came Madame wearing palazzo

156

pants, a crazy cap of bleached blond froth held down by a silver headband, both items of which should have been placed in an eighties time capsule. In the morning light, Gracie could see she wasn't as young as she'd thought. She was probably in her forties, like, er, Gracie (gulp), in which case the woman did not have youth on her side as an excuse for her bad behavior.

For some reason, this just made Gracie angrier.

After all, this woman had almost turned her hot dog, Helen, into a shredded meat sandwich.

'Tiffany!' the woman sang. 'Cartier!'

Gracie didn't know why the woman was calling out the names of jewelry establishments until she realized the woman was calling her dogs.

'Gucci! Prada!'

Gracie crouched down behind the Volvo as the woman walked toward the fence with the barbed wire on top, separating the Colony from the unwashed masses on the public beach. She watched as the woman spread her arms, holding some sort of baton with a cup at the end, a throwing gizmo to use with tennis balls.

Gracie watched as the dogs crapped, peed, dug holes in the dirt where the asphalt ended, peed some more and matched that act with more crap.

The woman made not one move toward the pooper-scooper, threw not one glance at the mini-trashcan, traipsed not one inch toward the plastic bags hanging on the fence (with a sign, 'for your convenience').

Gracie was so taken aback by the chutzpah on display that she almost forgot to put her anger into her presentation. Finally, panting as though she was having an anxiety attack or being forced to sit through a screening of a Ben Affleck comedy, Gracie stood on her wobbly legs and shouted, 'I see you!' Jaden looked up at Gracie, curious. The yell was somewhat garbled; the rise in adrenaline had flattened her diaphragm.

The woman made a lazy, lackadaisical turn, as though not surprised by this sudden turn of events; it was probably habit for her to be chastised by neighbors, Gracie thought.

She looked at Gracie and smiled.

Gracie marched toward her as Jaden watched, her arms swinging up at her sides. 'Your dogs are — they're pooping all over the place!' Gracie didn't like how that came out. 'Poop' had less impact than 'shit' or 'crap' even. She made a mental note for future reference. There was a reason, after all, that swear words were as popular as they were. Jaden would just have to understand.

The woman looked at her dogs, who had gathered around her like furry soldiers with friendly faces. They'd even come toward Gracie, slobbering and full of the dumb, happy energy that dogs with a lot of hair often seem to have. 'C'mon, Pumpkins,' the woman said to her dogs, 'time for your manicures!'

She started walking away, followed by her slew of fur.

'Hey!' Gracie yelled. 'You can't just walk away from me! You've got to clean up this mess!'

'Sorry!' the woman said in a singsong voice, her hips swaying back and forth in her palazzo pants as she sauntered back to her home.

'You look ridiculous in those pants!' Gracie shouted. Her diaphragm had finally inflated. 'And that headband should be in a Billy Joel video!'

Jaden rode her tricycle over and watched the dogs roll toward their home as Gracie slapped her hands together and proceeded to clean up with her brand-new, never-used pooper-scooper.

★   ★   ★

The Malibu Colony is located west of the Malibu Pier, directly next to the Malibu Lagoon, at the end of the Malibu Creek. The creek dissects world-famous Surfrider Beach, where one can spy the ghost of Gidgets past, and where sewage runoff makes the waters at Surfrider Beach poisonous and the mussels that live there inedible. It is a place, as Will said, 'Where the effluent meets the affluent.' It's a wonder that the surfers Gracie would watch every morning when she got up before six (because divorce evidently causes insomnia) didn't have three eyeballs and two heads, like the tender, amphibious creatures that populated polluted waterways.

But the view was sensational.

Gracie would come downstairs in the early morning before Jaden awoke, make a pot of coffee, and look at the antidepressants that her therapist prescribed (as did her friends), then put them back in a kitchen drawer, to be taken out and stared at again the next day. What was it Will had said to her? 'Happiness comes from inside. A pill.'

Gracie would gaze out the kitchen window, which looked directly out onto Surfrider Beach, where she could see on clear days from lifeguard tower 2 all the way to the Palos Verdes Peninsula. And she'd count her blessings, the same ones, every morning: (1) She had great eyesight (since the LASIK). (2) Her daughter was healthy (this usually came first). (3) She had a wealthy friend (who offered her an eight-million-dollar beach house for the summer). There sometimes was the fourth one: good teeth and excellent gums. Sometimes, when Gracie was feeling particularly needy, she'd count that last one as two.

So even though Gracie would never have another date in her life; even though there were numerous people she had considered if not friends then friendly, who would never condescend to speak to her again; even though her hands were freckled despite numerous attempts at bleaching gels and sunscreen; and even though Kenny was threatening to sue her for damages to his prized McRidiculous house (Something about vomit spots on the antique rug. Apparently, Jorge had eaten berry cobbler earlier in the day. And also, there was the matter of the shattered flat-screen), there was no denying she was one of the lucky ones. At least through the prime real estate months of Memorial Day through Labor Day.

Gracie took time with her coffee — she would

have only two cups a day — soaked in soy milk (for calcium, the only thing less attractive than the word 'dowager' was 'hump'). She'd measure out the coffee after grinding it herself. She'd pour exactly four cups of water in, and not a drop more, leaving two cups for Joan's housekeeper, who'd come in every other day around nine. And then she'd stand in front of the kitchen window, the venerated view in the house, and watch.

She was beginning to pick up the regular rhythms of Malibu life. She recognized certain surfers as they walked barefoot down the sandy path through the Malibu Lagoon from the parking lot next to Pacific Coast Highway — the older, balding ones with the emerging guts who got there before dawn, before they headed to their real jobs. She imagined some of them were dentists, others teachers, a few definitely had blue-collar bodies. They all seemed married. They'd smile as they stretched in their tight black wetsuits, pulling the zippers on their backs up to their necks as they bent over at the waist, their feet planted in front of their surfboards. Inevitably they'd get down on their hands and knees, waxing their boards in the same circular motion, steadily, methodically. Then they'd hoist their boards and stand at the shore, pointing and debating, Gracie imagined, as to whether the waves were good, whether the water was cold (it was always cold), whether they'd have fun or not (they'd always have fun).

Finally they'd slip onto their boards and paddle to the waves about fifty yards out. They'd sit for a time and take turns catching the usual two- or three-foot waves. The amount of sitting versus surfing was dependent on how many surfers were bobbing up and down in the gray water.

Forty-five minutes to an hour later, they'd come out, wet and shivering, with blue lips, whipping the water from what was left of their hair. Maybe they'd high-five each other or shake their heads at the lost wave, the broken leash line, the youthful aggros who were encroaching on their turf. But they would always be smiling.

Watching them almost made Gracie want to surf. Then she remembered that surfing was a water sport. She didn't particularly like getting wet. Then there was the fact that she wasn't a good swimmer.

Why was it never easy for her?

Gracie poured her half cup of coffee with her half cup of soy milk and prepared for her usual pre-kid, surf-sand-and-sea respite. She and Jaden had lain in bed together last night, watching *The Princess Diaries* until late. Gracie had actually cried at the end, a bad sign for her mental health.

Gracie looked out toward the beach, her eyes resting momentarily on the surf shack to the east of the access path to Surfrider Beach, a haphazard construction of large rocks, old wooden planks, and palm tree leaves, decorated by half a century of graffiti and decades' worth of beer bottles and condom wrappers. Why, Gidget herself was probably deflowered in this very stronghold of Malibu surf culture. Recently

162

Gracie had taken note of the modern category of tenants — the vagrants with their cigarettes and stolen iPods, the gang members with their shaved heads and large bottles of orange soda (and only orange soda) and twelve-packs; the tough, beautiful surfer dudes with their full-body tats and their full-bodied girlfriends.

The surf shack was quiet. No bodies, no movement.

Gracie's eyes drifted toward lifeguard tower 2, which was closed up until about eight, when she'd see the silver pickup truck drive onto the beach. The lifeguard with the sun-reddened skin and sun-bleached hair all over his body would get out and trudge through the sand to his tower, where he'd sit until evening.

Gracie thought he had a pretty good gig; then she remembered that occasionally he'd have to go in the water and save people from drowning. This seemed like a lot of effort for a woman who had to wear 45 sunblock all over her body just to walk into the kitchen.

Gracie noticed a lone figure lying on the beach between her house and the lifeguard tower, about twenty feet from the chain-link Colony fence with the barbed wire on top of it. A thick, dark green blanket was covering the figure, so she could not tell whether it was a woman or man, though she figured by the length of whatever was under the blanket, it looked to be a man.

She also presumed by the rapid, rhythmic jerking motion taking place under the blanket that the figure must be male. Gracie's eyes widened and she performed a screwball-comedy spit take, her scientifically combined coffee cascading onto the floor. She didn't like having to share her morning respite with a public masturbator.

'Jesus!' Gracie said. 'He's going to hurt himself!'

His movements were getting stronger, gaining speed. Gracie wanted to look away, but couldn't. The pull of watching someone, even someone who was covered up, sexually satisfying themselves was too compelling.

Gracie felt inclined, as a good citizen, to put an end to the debauchery. She started knocking on the window, thinking that might get his attention; he might realize that, yes, there was a house mere yards from his 'activities,' and yes, there might be people living in that house.

The movement did not abate. Gracie wondered if the man was trying to kill himself by masturbating to death. She wondered if she should call the Malibu sheriff (there were no police in Malibu); she wondered if she should call an ambulance — and given her heart rate, she wondered if it should be for the homeless guy or her.

Then suddenly the movement stopped. The figure under the blanket was still as a stone.

And then the man popped up, the blanket dropping to the sand. Gracie jumped back, spilling the rest of her coffee on the bleached-wood floor.

'Shit,' she said, but her eyes remained fastened to the man unfolding his long body in front of

164

her. He was well over six feet, with a loopy question mark of a bod, and a haystack of blond hair.

And he was in his tighty whities.

He didn't appear to be dirty or particularly destitute. He started to dress, taking his time, as though he were in his sitting room off the master bedroom. He put on a dark blue blazer and topped off the outfit with the ubiquitous iPod and headphones, found on every homeless man Gracie had seen this side of the Malibu city limits. He bundled up his blanket and headed for the path leading through the lagoon, up to Malibu Creek and the Pacific Coast Highway. Gracie presumed he was going to get his morning coffee at the Starbucks at Cross Creek; she was angered by the fact that his morning coffee wouldn't be interrupted by the sight of galloping self-satisfaction.

Gracie poured herself another cup and wondered what treasures the rest of the day would bring.

She also wondered how it was that a homeless man could have a better (and considerably more self-sufficient) sex life than she.

8

Malibu Literary Life and the Demi Problem

Gracie, anxious to combine exploration with the semblance of being a good mom, had walked Jaden across Pacific Coast Highway to the Malibu Library, where they attended a storybook reading session for young children. Jaden was taken with the young, hip librarian in the Malcolm X glasses, and Gracie took advantage of her crush to hit the stacks. There was an entire section dealing with the history of Malibu. Gracie applied for a library card and took out several books on the Chumash Indians, who had claimed Malibu as home for four thousand years. An older librarian confided to Gracie that 'Malibu' was actually Chumash for 'sick land,' although the books maintained it meant 'water which sounds loudly.'

The Chumash put a whole new spin on Gracie's outlook on Malibu. By all accounts, these people were the Cindy Crawfords of American Indians — tall, attractive, smart, and well-adjusted. They were sophisticated artisans; their colorful, bold cave drawings were mainly abstract rather than figurative. They built canoes out of planks for as many as twelve people, rather than the more simplified hollowed-out tree trunk. They lived a relatively sophisticated existence, replete with uncomplicated divorce proceedings and the regular practice of abortion. Theirs was a privileged life filled with natural abundance and peace and shell money. These 'chosen people' weren't all that different from the current inhabitants, except they wore moccasins instead of Uggs and hunted deer instead of the latest iPod, and Christianity would not have a prayer of wiping out the current population.

Knowledge of local history had a soothing effect on Gracie's state of mind. The decimation of an entire culture cheered her up, making her problems seem, well, irrelevant.

★　★　★

Gracie adjusted to her newly-single-with-child life by staying up late and taking long baths and supplementing her history education with fashion magazines. One evening, while reading the latest issue of the *Star* to Jaden, she realized she was exactly the same age as one Ms. Demi Moore. She found this bit of information useful in several ways: (1) Demi Moore with her preternaturally glossy black mane and superhero thighs never looked better. (2) Demi Moore seemed happier single than married (at least, according to reliable sources quoted in the *Star* and the *Enquirer*). (3) Demi Moore was in the throes of a love affair with a teenager — a Boylita, if you will.

The third tidbit of Demi-information blew Gracie off course. As much as Gracie was interested in dating, she was terrified of having sex with anyone under thirty-five. She was afraid of the shock value of the endeavor; what would a boy in his twenties have to say about falling knees? What would he say about the flaps of skin bowing to Enemy Number One, Gravity, layered over her elbows? Elbows should not have layers. And was it just yesterday morning that she glanced in the mirror and noticed a sparkling new phenomenon: upper-arm dimples?

Gracie didn't want to be entangled in sheets with a smooth, hairless body. She would, however, be willing to make him a hot chocolate. Was she any less of a feminist because she didn't want to have sex with a boy whose first musical memory was 'Mmm Bop'? Who didn't have the vaguest notion who Walter Cronkite was or that Vietnam was not only a destination spot for sex tours but a war?

No, Gracie was far more interested in the men-over-forty demographic. If she could find a man over forty. In her travels through Los Angeles, she could divide them into categories: Married with Kids, Divorced with Kids, Not Married and Unavailable, and Gay. Within the category Divorced with Kids, there was a subcategory, which covered the 90 percent of men she'd found: only interested in younger women.

★ ★ ★

In Malibu, Gracie had decided that though her new neighbors covered the spectrum of age demographics, from the babies in their Bugaboo strollers and sixty-dollar 98 percent Angel tie-dyed onesies to the lifers who'd lived in the Colony since the sixties, with their golf hats and Cadillac sedans. They had two things in common: They were bored, and they were rich. Gracie couldn't comment on the moviestar neighbors, for they hadn't moved in yet for the summer. But judging by the ones she believed lived there part-time, well, judging from movie posters and trailers, those people were at least busy.

Rich, bored people. Gracie, who was no longer rich and never bored, would find herself wondering what all these people in all these hundred or so houses did for a living.

Gracie would stop at the guardhouse at the mouth of the Malibu Colony on Malibu Road and interrogate the security guards, all of whom were minorities and/or immigrants. The disenfranchised were charged with protecting the mega-franchised — multimillionaires, and even a couple billionaires.

'C'mon, Lavender,' Gracie would say to the lady with the café au lait skin and blond cornrows, reading up on Thackeray for her English Lit class, 'I know you want to tell me what number 228 does all day.'

'Two twenty-eight?' Lavender would say. 'That's inherited. Mommy's money.'

Two twenty-eight belonged to the only cute, seemingly single guy Gracie had seen in the

Colony who was lingering in her thirty-five to one hundred and two target demographic. Gracie knew that in order to secure a date to Cross Creek's Coffee Bean and Tea Leaf or Nobu, she'd have to shed that vision of herself with a man who was around her age, around her level of interest in news events, or around her, period.

She had spied 228 while having breakfast one morning on her glass-encased deck. 228 was long, 228 was lean, 228 knew his way around a surfboard, and 228 may have smiled at her as he passed her house on the way to Third Point, in front of Surfrider Beach.

Or he may have been squinting; Gracie was at the point at which even a grimace could constitute a come-on. She was not above false or even nonexistent flattery.

'Mommy's money?' Gracie asked. She didn't like the sound of that. No good came out of inheritance in her opinion. Not that she'd ever get to experience the concept of 'inheritance.' She wondered if her daughter would, and what that would do to her, how that would warp her concept of the world.

And then Gracie decided that Kenny would probably marry his assistant after Britney dumped him, and the assistant would have five children, and Jaden would never have to worry about that warped thing.

Back to inheritance.

'Are you sure?' Gracie said. 'He drives an old Triumph. Plays eighties music. Seems kind of cool.' Why Gracie thought that driving an old

170

Triumph and playing eighties music seemed cool, she couldn't answer.

'Do you trust Lavender?' Lavender asked.

'I've known you all of a week and a half,' Gracie said. 'So yes, of course. I was always gullible. Ask my soon-to-be ex.'

'Stay away from 228,' Lavender said. 'Mommy's money, mommy issues.'

Gracie nodded, taking in her new best friend's sage advice. 'You're so lucky,' she said to Lavender. 'I wish I could be a lesbian.'

'With what I've seen in this town, you probably will be someday,' Lavender said. 'There's hope for you yet.'

Gracie crossed her fingers and waved her hand in the air and walked off.

★   ★   ★

Scarier than taking a midnight stroll through Fallujah with an American flag wrapped around one's shoulders was accompanying one's child to the kiddie park in the Cross Creek Shopping Center on a typically crowded Saturday morning.

Gracie had been pleased to find out there was a park across the highway from the Colony, and even more pleased to find out that it was adjacent to not one but two coffee establishments — Coffee Bean and Tea Leaf for their Iced Blendeds and Starbucks for their Grande Soy Lattes. But such a slice of heaven could only come at a price, and the price Gracie would have to pay was obvious to her the moment she happened on the park with Jaden in tow on a weekend morning.

Gracie hoisted Jaden out of her stroller, took one look around, and realized that she was back in high school — if her high school had been chock-full of model-tall blondes wearing Ugg boots and white tank tops and Juicys that never looked that good on anyone human. Yes, she knew these women (mothers, in fact!) were people. She knew intellectually that she and they were of the same species, but there was no proof of that fact at first glance. Or even second glance. Gracie spied one mother performing a hatred-inducing flip on the monkey bars and almost coughed up her perfectly good latte all over her daughter's curls.

Resigned to bystander status — Gracie would never be able to do any sort of flip anywhere anytime — she sat down on one of the wooden benches surrounding the small park, sipping her latte.

Gracie watched Jaden, with her curly blond hair and her bright blue eyes and her long legs, blending in with all the other towheaded, blue-eyed, long-legged children with an ease that Gracie had never experienced.

She didn't know whether to be proud or frightened.

★ ★ ★

Malibu was exactly twenty-five minutes from where Gracie had lived with Kenny in El McMansion. But it may as well have been

172

located in another dimension of time and space.

Gracie was quickly learning — from her travels in the 'bu, from the Cross Creek Shopping Center with John's Garden (for sandwiches with sprouts, drinks with sprouts, sprouts with sprouts) to the Psychic Bookstore (there was, like Joan had warned, no other kind) to Howdy's Mexican food across the street, from Starbucks to PC Greens on Pacific Coast Highway (PCH) for organic produce (and if one was very lucky, a glimpse of a shockingly laid-back Sir Anthony Hopkins) — that, as in all of her past love affairs, Malibu was not going to change for her, so she was going to have to change for Malibu.

Physically, Gracie was going to have to get back into some semblance of shape. In a moment of weakness (there were many throughout the day), Gracie pondered applying to *Extreme Makeover*, the television show that took normal people with ordinary features and appendages and made them into that girl on *Access Hollywood*. Even the men, who seemed to hate their 'man noses' and their Chia Pet hair, wound up looking like Leeza Gibbons.

Gracie had decided she was man enough — make that woman enough — to stand naked in front of a mirror and assess all of her recent damage.

There she was, in all her fifth-decade glory. Her shoulders were beginning to sag forward. Her breasts were still fine. They would be fine ten years after her death. Silicone never dies. But the bottom of her navel seemed to be drooping.

And the area below her navel and above her C-section scar (for lack of a better word, her 'abdomen') looked like something she'd seen on the beach when her mother and her aunties would gather in their two-pieces. This was her mother's stomach. Except her mother had had three children, not one.

Her legs still looked nice and smooth from the front. Gracie breathed a sigh of relief, her first breath in the last three minutes. Her toes, thankfully, were perfect, each one a pale gem. Men always complimented Gracie on her feet. It occurred to Gracie that perhaps she had only dated freaks.

Feeling brave, buoyed by the sight of her beautiful feet (wait — were those wrinkles on her toes? When did that degradation occur?), she turned her back to the mirror and looked over her shoulder. Her fist flew to her mouth, stifling a scream.

'Mommy?!' she heard Jaden outside the door. 'Are you breaking down?'

'Mommy's fine!' Gracie yelled.

'Was it a monster?' Jaden said. She was trying to open the handle. 'Mommy, you know I'm not scared of monsters.'

Gracie wrapped herself in her towel and opened the door. 'Jaden, honey,' she said, crouching down to look her daughter in the eye. 'Worse than a monster. Mommy saw her butt.'

Her daughter looked at her sideways. 'Can I see it?'

'No,' Gracie said. 'I'm putting it away in a safe place.'

Jaden's eyes shot around. 'Let's put it under my bed!'

'Great idea,' Gracie said. 'But first I need it to go shopping. Mommy's will has weakened and Mommy needs to get Ugg boots.'

Jaden wrinkled her nose. 'I don't like that sound.'

'They're called Ugg boots,' Gracie said, 'because they're ugly and they're boots. And Mommy needs to get a pair. We're living in Malibu now, Jaden. It's the law.'

9

It's a (Homeless) Man's World

Six twenty-eight A.M. Samuel Jonas Knight was greeted by the kind of view that shows up regularly on postcards and travel posters but rarely makes an appearance in real life. Except a life like his.

The sun had begun to cast its spell on the ocean, shooting the first morning rays across the dark waters of Malibu. He never tired of the view. Each morning he would look out, and whether he was tired or anxious or angry, he could stand in the sand and look out and instantly his mood would lift.

He had been swimming this ocean from this very spot for almost eight years; standing in front of #68 at low tide, he had trouble remembering a missed day. He was seldom sick, an amazing feat given the level of bacteria he'd read about in the waters of Malibu. He'd heard the tale of the Malibu surfer enduring that flesh-eating bacteria at a local hospital; there were more than a few stories about the strain of hepatitis you don't get from sex or needles; there was the rumor of a mysterious brain tumor found in a fellow early-morning swimmer.

Nothing in the water, save for a few dolphins, had ever touched him. He unwrapped his towel and let it drape on the railing above the stairs leading to the beach. He took off his T-shirt, an artifact from a Surfrider Foundation celebration given on the beach; immediately his skin chilled, goose bumps rising in formation, like tiny soldiers, in response to the chill. The curly salt-and-pepper hair adorning his wide chest stood on end. Without looking, he slipped off his well-worn huaraches, a throwback to an era in his life he had almost succeeded in forgetting. All that was left on his body were his orange shorts, the color of a lifeguard's buoy. He tightened the drawstring around his waist, which was tanned a deep brown all year long. He patted his stomach, which was lean and bulky at the same time — a strong torso which enabled him to work long hours if need be, to lift heavy objects, to fix what needed fixing.

He ran his fingers through the thickness of his black hair and down around his mustache, scraping his beard, then took a final look at the water before walking in and plunging.

The yellow Labrador that had been sitting beside Sam now serenaded him with his barks before he, too, finally dove in and followed, as though chasing a human ball.

★　★　★

7:00 PM. There were two things Gracie could count on at this time of the evening, when the skies turned and daylight exploded in a symphony of color. Three things, if one counted her feeling of inadequacy in not being able to capture adequately the disappearance of the sun into the rocky, ragged cliffs of Point Dume. As she watched the sunset, she often thought Van Gogh would have painted the scene perfectly, with the grays and blues and oranges and purples, the brilliant cusp melting slowly on the horizon. Peaceful and violent at once.

But then she comforted herself with the notion that she had both ears, was not in love with a prostitute (yet), and with any luck would probably not die penniless.

The two things she could count on were the sunset. And the stout, dark-haired, bearded man. The bearded man made his way through the path to Surfrider Beach every day around this time. He was large and lumbered rather than walked, as though every step were a test and he had to use brute strength to reach his destination, the old telephone pole just this side of lifeguard tower 2. His gait reminded Gracie of heavyweight champions as they lunged down the stairs into the ring, driving heavily forward.

The bearded man would stop at the pole, facing the gray, dreary, beautiful Pacific. She wondered if it looked the same to him as it did to her — like a woman who lets herself go but can still bring pleasure.

He would suddenly drop to his knees. And bring his thick hands together in prayer. Gracie couldn't see them well but imagined his hands to be hardened by work and an unforgiving life. His clothes were worn; what was left of his hair a confusion.

She would watch him for long moments as she

stirred something in a pot or talked on the phone. Or listened to Jaden singing to herself. Or did nothing at all. She wondered about this man, but mostly she wondered at how a stranger, someone whom she had never met at all, could bring her such solace.

WIFE NUMBER FOUR

Is married to a film director known for his soft romantic comedies. She was surprised to come home one day to him wearing not only her La Perla lingerie and her best Manolos but a blond wig she'd saved from a Halloween party.

She and 'Marilyn' go out to lunch several times a week.

10

A Sea Change

'You know what makes the Malibu Colony so weird?' Will said. 'It's the only place in the world where you walk into the back of your house. Up is down, down is up — it's all backwards.'

Gracie stared at him.

'Oh my God,' Will said as he fanned his face with his hand. 'You would not believe what just happened to me. Seriously, this is life-changing.'

Will had just walked into the house, wearing oversize sunglasses and a scarf Isadora Duncan would have been honored to have broken her neck with. He and Cricket had demanded that Gracie go with them to Nobu, Malibu's raw fish answer to Spago, for dinner. Will had heard that Suge Knight was recently spotted there. Much like Patty Hearst, he had a thing for the gangsta set.

'Did you take a 'straight' pill?' Gracie asked, regarding his obsession with all things hip-hop.

Will twisted his small, turned-up nose. 'Eww. Bad picture. Change the channel.' He sat down with a flourish on Joan's soft white overstuffed couch. Will tended to do everything with a flourish. Gracie wondered for a moment what he was like in bed — was he always this dramatic?

180

She wiped the vision from her head with a mental squeegee.

'Why is it that every couch in Malibu looks like something out of *The Cat in the Hat*? It's Shabby Chic Purgatory,' Will said, looking at her accusingly. 'Where all the overstuffed couches go to die.'

'You're just jealous of anyone who makes more money at the same profession as you,' Gracie replied.

'Of course,' Will said, 'there's not enough to go around, I don't care what anyone says, gazillionaires with bad taste do not grow on trees.'

'You were about to tell me about your life-changing experience? Or would you rather I slip into a coma while you rant at other successful designers.'

'I was at Cross Creek, innocently picking up an Ice Blended and I saw' — he put his hand to his chest — 'Pamela Anderson Lee Anderson . . . Lee Anderson Pamela.'

'No!' Gracie said, more excited than she meant to be. What was it about blond, bosomy celebrities? Could we not get enough? 'How did she look?'

'In a word: You would hate her!' Will said.

'I knew it!' Gracie said, sitting down next to Will and getting swallowed by a man-eating pillow. 'Go on,' she said as she offered him a bowl of M&Ms.

Will grabbed at them with his soft, childlike hand. 'Cocoa butter tan. Not a stitch of makeup. And judging by her Juicys, full-on commando. I heard she waxes from here to Uranus.'

'If she's single and out there, I should just retire my vagina.' Gracie asked, 'How old do you think she is?'

'I don't know,' Will said. 'Should we cut her open and count the rings?'

'Where is Cricket?' Gracie asked, realizing that the third member of The Coven had not shown up, even though she had driven with Will.

'Oh,' Will said, 'I left her outside, crying. Question: Why do you people get married?'

'Hey,' Gracie said, 'you people will be able to get married someday.'

'Never,' Will said. 'I'm praying to the Gay Gods for that constitutional amendment. Why should we suffer like the rest of you? You will never see this girl before a minister reciting 'love is patient, love is kind,' et cetera, ad nauseous.'

Will was not a romantic; he even broke down the word one day for Gracie's edification. ''Roman' and 'tic,'' he said to Gracie. 'One is an ancient Italian, the other is an insect that gives you Lyme disease. I want neither in my life, thank you.'

They were about to get up from the couch (this took awhile — sitting on the couch was like skiing in four feet of powder) when Will looked down at Gracie's feet.

'What are those?' he demanded, pointing.

Gracie looked at her new Ugg boots. 'The Pamela wears them,' she protested.

'I'm not going out with you if you wear those,' he said. 'They're an abomination. You look like an albino Inuit, if there is such a thing. Which there shouldn't be.'

'I'm trying to fit in!' Gracie said. 'I have to have Uggs! People here practically sleep in them; infants wear them, grandmothers wear them. They're the official footwear of the city of Malibu!'

But Will would not budge, so Gracie trudged upstairs and put on a pair of flat-soled metallic sandals.

'Much better,' he said as they walked outside. 'I thought I lost you there for a moment.'

★　★　★

Gracie sat at a round table on the patio outside Nobu with Will and Cricket. Between sobs and passion-fruit martinis, Cricket laid out the map to her marriage, starting with her wedding day, when she knew something was hideously wrong because a crow had landed on the roof of her car that morning and pecked at her windshield, and ending with that very morning, when Cricket and Jorge, who had finally engaged in battle, had fought until three A.M.

'What was the fight about?' Gracie asked, though she already knew and didn't want to know more.

'Married people always fight about three things,' Will said. 'It's money, sex, or sex and money.'

'Sex. Jorge wants more sex, and I just want to nap,' Cricket said. She turned to Gracie. 'You look so beautiful, by the way. What is going on? You never looked this good.'

183

Gracie shook her head. 'I'd like more sex. Or any sex. I'm getting less sex than I did in the last year of my marriage.'

'Negative integers. Interesting,' Will commented. 'There's got to be someone in the Colony who fits the Gracie: A-Time-of-Crisis profile.'

'What profile would that be?' Gracie asked.

'Male,' Will said. 'Human.'

'Just male?' Gracie asked. 'Not even hetero?'

'Picky, picky, missy miss,' Will said. 'Most married men tend to turn out gayish anyway after about ten years.'

'Jorge would be a great gay man.' Cricket perked up. 'He likes shoes. And clean nails.'

'Well,' Gracie said to Will, 'I have to confess, Mother Superior-to-me, I did do a little research.'

'And?' asked Will, his highlighted eyebrows hitting new heights.

Gracie had become close with several guards at the front gate, especially her favorite, Lavender. Somehow the guards knew she didn't belong there — it could have been her earlier lack of Uggs and the confidence that comes from having a body that could withstand a thong in direct sunlight. She knew they didn't belong there, either. Gracie believed that people who were not invited to the party tend to recognize one another.

Gracie had strolled over with Jaden one morning after an outing at the park, stopping as she regularly did to talk to Lavender, who was now halfway through *Pride and Prejudice* for her

184

Women's Studies class.

'Whattaya got for me this morning?' Gracie usually asked Lavender. To which Lavender would always say, 'I got nothing.'

This morning was a little different in that Gracie had been doing 'directed' research on the Colony. She'd been walking Jaden up and down the private street, studying each house and every car, looking for clues to their inhabitants. Were they male or female, were they single or a couple or a family, summer tenants or landowners? For the first week or so, the only other life form Gracie noticed was 228 and what seemed like a few thousand friendly construction workers and gardeners, who eyed her curiously but not covetously, the new (middle-aged) girl on the block, as she walked past with Jaden in a stroller.

Then in the last week, which marked the first week in June, there'd been a sea change of activity — black Mercedeses with expensive rims instead of pickup trucks on steroids, Toyota Land Cruisers instead of forklifts. Gracie walked out her door and saw Tom Cruise instead of the telephone repairman; on her bike, she ran into Harrison Ford instead of the plumber.

The workingman had been replaced by the public man.

Gracie had decided to make a game out of her personal dilemma as she spent the summer drying out from the hangover of her marriage. She would perform a scientific study in which she herself would be both control group and guinea pig: Could a woman over a certain age in Los Angeles be able to find a (reasonable) date?

185

And to that end, she had made a list. Will had told her she needed to be 'proactive' in her quest for, if not a new relationship, than a new conversation over a cup of coffee. Gracie agreed, even though she did not see the need to use the term 'proactive.' (Why is that a word, anyway? Was 'active' not a 'proactive' word?)

Will told her she was getting offtrack, and she needed to get herself off her ass and go out and lasso a man, preferably a surfer with great abs, no work ethic, and a strong desire to screw anything short of a flagpole.

Back to her 'secret' list: Gracie had taken mental notes of the information she'd compiled of the people living in the enclosed neighborhood. She viewed the Colony as her very own petri dish.

Gracie took the list out of her notebook, which she took to carrying around like Harriet the Spy without the concerned parents (unless one counted Will and Cricket), looking both ways for oncoming eyes before she began to read it to Lavender.

'One forty-six: double lot, one and a half story, bread-mold green [Gracie didn't know any other way to put it] exterior — '

Lavender was looking at her over her black-rimmed glasses, her chin on her chest, her mouth open; she appeared to be having a Whoopi Goldberg white-people-are-plumb-crazy moment.

'Mercedes 250SL in the driveway, no other cars present except from nine to four, presumably a housekeeper — '

'You have got to be kidding me,' Lavender said.

'You know everything that goes on around here. I'm just trying to narrow down the field,' Gracie said. 'I have to attack this like a scientist.'

Lavender shook her head. 'I could get fired.'

'For telling me if there's a single male living on the premises?' Gracie asked.

'They'd fire me for less,' Lavender said.

Gracie shut her notebook. 'Okay, fine, here's what we're going to do.' She was determined not to let her hard work go to waste. 'I'll call out a number, you give me a two-word assessment. Then I'll let you get back to your book.'

Lavender leaned back and crossed her arms over her ample chest. She had recently dyed her hair a strawberry color; Gracie admired her courage.

She cleared her throat. 'So, as I was saying, number 146?'

'Married,' Lavender said.

'That's only one word, but an important one.' Gracie scratched that number off the list. 'Number 148? White clapboard with blue trim. Funny mailbox.'

'Cute. Female,' Lavender said, looking at her closely. Smirking.

'Scratch that, we'll come back to that one in a few years.' Gracie looked down her list. 'Number 172? Gray stone building. One car, as far as I can tell — '

'Old man.'

'How old?'

'Old, like wheelchair-and-portable-oxygen-tank old. That's his nurse's car.'

Gracie crossed Wheelchair/Oxygen Tank Man off her list. 'Ah, 176?'

'Models.'

'178?'

'Have you actually seen him?'

'186.'

'Happily married movie star.'

'218?'

'Hookers. Drugs.'

Gracie shook her head. 'I'm running out of houses here.'

Lavender looked at her. '152.' Then she turned her back to Gracie and started reading again.

'One fifty-two?' Gracie asked. 'Who is 152?'

'Moved in two days ago. Summer rental. Now, I got work to do here,' Lavender replied, her nose fixed in her book.

11

Working for the Man

Lavender Jackson lived in a neat one-bedroom apartment on South La Cienega in Inglewood, a mile and a half from the Forum, where the Lakers once played. The area, all black when she was growing up, had become mostly Latino. She was fine with that, except for the music thing on the weekends. But then she mostly worked on the weekends. If she happened to be home at night on a Saturday, she could count on her downstairs neighbors, the Abuelas, to be celebrating something — a birthday, a graduation, a haircut. These people celebrated at the drop of a sombrero, Lavender joked, though she knew she was envious.

Lavender was alone, no family since her grandmother passed away over five years ago. Her grandmother, Lady Eva, raised her from a baby. Lavender knew her mother when she'd come by for her disability checks — disabled from what, she did not know. Her grandmother only would hand over the checks and tell her daughter, Tamia-Mama (Lavender used to call her), that she would pray for her in church, like she always did. Her mother would run over to Lavender, almost knocking the child over, smother her with sloppy kisses and heavy cologne. Lavender didn't know the name of the cologne, but she'd smelled it in a red bottle at Thrifty's. When Tamia-Mama disappeared from her life completely, Lavender paced the perfume aisle at that drugstore in the basketball shoes Lady Eva forbade her to wear inside the house, unwrapping the bottles, spraying her wrist with the samples.

The red bottle. All she had left was a scent; she had long since forgotten the name. Lavender had taken a couple of psych courses at Dominguez Hills — she had something that the textbooks called repression. She'd repressed that name.

Lavender remembered the day Tamia-Mama stopped coming. She remembered the checks piling up — the gray-green welfare checks, the light pink disability ones. Lady Eva never spent a dime of her mother's money. The checks withered in her kitchen drawer before Lady Eva finally accepted what she could not prove and sat down to call the authorities to tell them her daughter would no longer be needing those checks.

Lavender did not stand out at her local elementary school. Lots of kids were being raised by their grandparents; it was a sign of the times, as Granny E used to say, long before Prince said the words.

'Sign of the times,' her grandmother would say when an eleven-year-old boy got mowed down at the corner on his bicycle. Just another drive-by. 'Why,' Lavender asked Lady Eva, 'do they always get the ones who looked to be on the way out?'

'Sign of the times,' her grandmother said during the riots. Granny E had lived through the first round, the Watts riots. She'd seen the bodies, dead from policemen's bullets. Nothing surprised her. Not anger, not hate, not despair. During the Rodney King riots, she prayed for the white truck driver that got his head bashed in not far from their apartment house.

Lavender learned quickly. She learned to keep a low profile. She was a generally shy child, so this was not particularly hard for her to do. Keep to yourself, don't engage, don't get involved in other people's business.

As Lavender got older, though, she released herself from fear of her neighbors, from expectations of her grandmother, from repression of her sexuality. And her laugh, the one her grandmother said she was born with but seldom laid claim to after her mother left, the laugh that was a vessel for her soul, made a return.

She was in her twenties then. She had been a virgin until she was twenty-three. What a ridiculous waste of time, Lavender thought.

Still in her early twenties, she'd signed up with a security company and found herself a night job manning the Malibu Colony guard station. The work suited her. She liked her coworkers; there was camaraderie. They all got shit pay for shit work, nobody was aching to get ahead, no one was climbing over the next guy for more hours, easier shifts. There was a silent agreement between the guards that in the scheme of things, they had it pretty good. Except on Fourth of July

191

weekend, when all hell would break loose. She'd been there almost ten years.

A car drove up as Lavender was halfway through chapter 3. Number 152.

'Hello there,' he said, this older man with the small kid in the backseat. Lavender hadn't noticed the kid before. She wondered if he was married and not wearing a ring, or maybe just separated. She wondered what assessment Gracie, the Amateur Sociologist, would have of this man.

'Hello,' Lavender said, as she wheeled her chair back from the desk and took two steps toward him.

'You have a package for 152? Manahan?' he said. The kid in the backseat started blowing raspberries.

Lavender turned to look through the stack of FedEx and UPS packages that had come in that morning.

'Nothing here, sorry,' she said.

'That's okay,' Manahan replied. 'Saves me the trouble of opening it.'

Lavender waved back to him as he drove off, his arm sticking out the side of his brand-new Jaguar. He seemed like a nice man, she thought, a decent man, the kind of man who would make sure to hire valet parking if he had a party on July Fourth.

WIFE NUMBER FIVE

Walked into her famous TV action star husband's Las Vegas hotel room years ago wearing little more than high heels; he had ordered a voluptuous redhead.

They'll be celebrating their thirtieth wedding anniversary this November.

12

A Hairy Encounter

On the fateful morning that Gracie swore that this would be the day she would meet 152, her future husband, or at least future stalking victim, she saw hair on her face. She did not notice the six o'clock sun angling menacingly toward her as she splashed water on her face, humming, ignorant of the ensuing horror. Then she had the audacity to glance into her bathroom mirror. Nature's cruelty was never more apparent: Gracie was growing a beard. She had found fine blond hairs not only in their usual nesting place over the shallow vertical lines dividing her mouth into a hundred sections. These she had grown accustomed to. But this was different. Tiny dark hairs had taken root under her chin. When had this happened? All she could think about were ancient women in babushkas sprouting wild hairs out of their chins, women she had known in her very own family when she was a child. Women who had names like Bushka and Malnif. This would not do for a modern widow, er, divorcée, living on the most expensive real estate in the nation — even if it wasn't her real estate — even if she couldn't get inside the gate with what she had in her checking account (what savings account?). All plans were scratched for the pareo she had purchased at a price usually reserved for elective surgery; foiled were her hopes for the pink flip-flops that showed off her new pedicure in a color named after Sarah Jessica Parker. She could not walk down the beach with fur on her face; she'd have to bikiniwax her whole body, furry forehead to hirsute toe.

Why did God make women more hairy as they aged? Gracie wondered. Did He/She know that there was no one at home to keep us warm so we needed to manufacture our own coats?

Kenny's words came back to her at the oddest times, mostly when her self-esteem could be found near the bottom of the ocean, along with all the old paint cans.

'You just don't seem to fit in,' Kenny had said to Gracie years ago, when they'd come back from a dinner party populated by fabulous people with a penchant for mixing narcotics with French Bordeaux. 'I don't think you make enough of an effort,' he'd said. On the way home, Gracie had been making fun of the women at the party; she could not judge the men, as they didn't talk to her as much as look through her.

The women — with their sleek blond locks, courtesy of Fekkai; taller-than-thou height, courtesy of genetics and Manolos; great big white teeth, courtesy of cosmetic dentistry; cheekbones courtesy of Lasky Clinic — seemed to be speaking in a foreign language. They knew the home number of the 'lady' at Hermès New York, they had tubs of the London brand of perfume that was all the rage, they had the dates of the trunk shows at Neiman Marcus on their PalmPilots, they knew what day to get what purse at Louis Vuitton and how to skip the wait list, they knew what shade of pink to wear during what season on their toes. Gracie grew up knowing she wasn't cool, but she had no idea there was an actual language barrier.

And she was squatting up against the wrong side of the style barricade.

The women were nice enough, so nice that Gracie felt kind of bad making fun of them — *kind* of bad, but not bad enough. She could no longer get Kenny on her side, though. They were supposed to be a team, she and her husband, but it turned out he was running offense for the other side. Kenny had changed. He admired these women; they looked good, they fit in.

Gracie, who had avoided all manner of sorority in college, would have to join Kappa Alpha Wife Of.

Gracie took what Kenny had said seriously. She attended dinner parties and studied the bearing, habits, and rituals of the Wives Of in attendance. She literally took notes. Several times a night she'd sneak into a bathroom and scribble observations: 'Patchett: salesgirl at Barneys,' 'Dr. Vogel: Botox/collagen — no bruises,' 'Playpen: Toes, Outdoor Sex: Hands.'

And Gracie, the cynical student, learned. She began changing herself, one body part at a time, starting with her head. She started dying her hair. She added extensions. Then the Turkish lady tortured — er, rather, blow-dried — her curly, frizzy hair into submission twice a week (complaining the whole time about how hard Gracie's hair was to blow-dry compared to, say, the locks originating from Mrs. John Travolta's scalp). Gracie likened the experience to being one of the extras in *Midnight Express*. She moved on to her eyebrows: Gracie arrived fifteen minutes early for the Eyebrow Queen and was shocked to see a line around the block; the Eyebrow Queen had not only double-booked like a fire-marshal-infuriating premiere, she'd quadrillion-booked.

Gracie visited the Beverly Hills dermatologist reportedly behind Madonna's preternaturally youthful appearance and Demi's sudden metamorphosis into a forty-year-old teenager, but then fainted at the sight of a needle coming toward her forehead. Sedated on Valium, Gracie finally took shots of collagen in her upper lip (nothing like going to a plastic surgeon to find out how many, many things are wrong with your appearance), which proved to be more painful than cutting one's finger off with a rubber knife and not nearly as festive. But she was not to be deterred. At the urging of a doctor who hadn't met a face he didn't want to change, Gracie was on the verge of getting cheekbone implants when she happened on an article about the Wildenstein woman in New York and realized the very same phenomenon was happening all around her — the town was becoming Wildensteined.

The body came next. Gracie went on a Kenny-sponsored mission to lose those stubborn eight to ten pounds around her hips and thighs. She went to the Diet Guru — again, in Beverly Hills, so at least she could say the architects of her transformation would be geographically desirable. The Diet Guru, a woman who wore either black and vertical stripes or both, recommended that Gracie drink her 'exclusive' name-brand tea and eat only pink grapefruit for a one-week cleanse. Gracie was cleansed all right; the only thing that didn't make it out of her body was a Burger King Whopper she had eaten in 1982. After one particularly onerous bout on the master toilet, Gracie was fearful she had lost a major organ. She wondered if it were possible to have disgorged a liver.

Still Gracie was not deterred. She tried the Zone, Atkins, South Beach — any diet, in fact, that was sponsored by someone who once had a medical degree but hadn't practiced medicine in twenty years.

Gracie started working out; to augment the slow rate of weight loss, she chose to exercise. She joined a gym that was more like a bar — Sports Club, Los Angeles. She got a writer-director-trainer. She tried the treadmill, she tried the elliptical (why?), she tried the exercise bike, she tried the StairMaster, she tried the one with the giant steps, she tried the rowing thing. There were 368 different ways to sweat in this gym, but the most surefire method was to walk into the women's locker room, where Gracie would be surrounded by women halfway out of their knickers, standing around like Victoria's Secret models on a coke break.

Gracie had emerged, like a butterfly from a cocoon, with a new face, a new body. And the same old personality.

All she had left of her painful, hard-won transformation was her character.

And a few errant hairs on her chin.

★ ★ ★

Sam Knight hadn't been able to get to the water right away that morning. Mrs. Kennicot, who lived in #191, had tripped over a warped plank of wood in her old floor when she got up for a drink of water in the middle of the night. Sam had been on his hands and knees early, sanding the warped spot down to a smooth finish. Mrs. Kennicot hired him for various odd jobs — moving furniture, building a chest of drawers, snaking a plugged toilet. Before they met, he used to watch her, eighty years old and still swimming in the lagoon every morning, oblivious to the chill or the pollution. She inspired him, and later they became friendly; unusual for strangers, more unusual for an old lady and a homeless man. She was the first to hire him in the Colony. He felt beholden to her in more ways than he could articulate; she'd fed him when he was hungry, she paid him for a job well done, and even though she'd been widowed, even though she'd watched her husband sink into the morass of Alzheimer's, she made Sam believe that while life was not just, it was pretty good. Better than the alternative. And so he did his best to keep her safe — sanding down warped planks was just part of it.

The Kennicots' house was on the 'street side' of the Colony, next to their faded tennis court with the deeply cracked surface, where no one had played since their grown sons had moved away. Behind the house, there was an overgrown trail, hidden from view. Sam became aware of the trail when he grew tired of sleeping in the open, on the beach. He had been comforted by the sound of the ocean at night, but he could feel the eyes on him. Not just of the residents of the Colony, but the unseen, those who slept in the bushes along the pathway leading to Surfrider Beach.

He discovered the trail on a hot day, searching for a cool spot to eat a sandwich he'd found tossed in a garbage pail festooned with the numbers of a local radio station. To him, the trail was serene; in reality, it was moderately untraversed. He set up shop there for his first night, and from his vantage point he could see the lights of the houses along the street side of the Colony. He could watch a family eat dinner, enjoying their interactions without imposing. From here, sitting on his rolled-up sleeping bag, he had watched Mrs. Kennicot wheel Mr. Kennicot to the table, wiping his mouth between bites. Discussing that which was no longer understood. Holding a hand and laughing, alone, at a memory. The trail became his home. All who passed there, whether or not they saw the navy blue blanket folded neatly under the bush, the long pieces of cardboard ripped every other week from refrigerator boxes, the

200

Tupperware bowl tucked away for washing, knew that they were walking through someone's home.

Occasionally Sam was forced to defend his prime territory, much as a man in one of the fancier living quarters in the parallel world, both literally and figuratively, would defend entrance to his home. Sam didn't consider himself a violent man, a consideration that would have been laughed at by both his compatriots and his superiors. He had given up his Purple Heart; the Silver Star had been stolen long ago. He wasn't sad to see it go, though it had been his only possession of worth; its only value to him was that he could have sold it for a sandwich at John's Garden, a cup of coffee, clean socks for the winter months. Despite his protests that he was a peace-loving man, he would not tolerate an incursion into his space.

There was this one, who all the guys knew. The story was this creep had come off a bus from Ohio after doing time for assault. He was younger, he reeked of alcohol and poor hygiene, he had a smirk on his face and an attitude to go with it, and Sam knew from other acquaintances that this one stole. All the guys knew who stole. People who have nothing material to speak of are sensitive to this type of behavior; the lawless don't take criminal behavior lightly.

A missing pair of Adidas, someone's head-phones — the men who 'lived' in Malibu, around the Colony, were very specific about their belongings. You didn't need to see Hog's name scratched into an iPod (taken from a surfer's backpack, of course) to know it was his, and so it was with Sam's blue blanket and army-issue sleeping bag. And so it was with Sam's books.

Eight-thirty in the morning, Sam had come back from a swim. Even before he saw, walking down the trail and brushing back the branches with his outstretched hand, he knew. Everything was gone. No blanket. No sleeping bag. Not one damn book.

He went looking for the guy with the smirk. It didn't take long to find him, huddled under the surf shack, empty bottle of cheap amber liquid by his feet, passed out under the familiar sleeping bag, snoring like an old dog.

Sam knew better, but he picked the young man up by his hair and threw him onto the sand. The guy was airborne before he was awake. He got to his feet, and Sam squared off before him, waiting for the first punch. Sam never unleashed the first punch. He was a last-punch kind of guy.

He didn't have to wait long. The man aimed at Sam's stomach and landed surprisingly hard. Sam bent over and noticed a glint of something, a knife in the man's hand, winking, approaching . . .

Sam flicked the knife out of his hand and broke his wrist, the snap scaring off a flock of pelicans that had been watching, a curious, winged band of spectators.

The man screamed and went to his knees, cradling his hand. Sam calmly collected his belongings; the books were out of their bag, moist and sandy, and his sleeping bag would never smell the same. But Sam knew he wouldn't have to deal with this one again.

Except when he turned up dead a couple weeks later, and Sam, along with the myriad of other homeless, was questioned and released.

Sam combed his hair back and took a swig of water and headed to the beach access next to #184. He had overslept; he had been dreaming in memory. He wondered what that meant as he opened the gate to the beach.

13

Saved

The next-door neighbor, an elegant older woman with an old California name, arms wrapped in gold bangles and a full glass of amber liquid in her hand every evening, had regaled Gracie with stories about the Malibu before the railroad, before Pacific Coast Highway, before movie stars. Before all of this, there had been May Rindge, a feisty widow whose family had owned all twenty-six miles of Malibu. She'd kept out government officials and trespassers by hiring armed guards and dynamiting highway construction attempts. Finally May had exhausted her fortune and was forced to rent out plots of coastal land to entertainers. And thus the Colony was born. In 1926, the woman told her, her bangles serenading her as they slid down her arm, the first white surfer had ridden his first wave at what was then Malibu Ranch.

Gracie looked out from her deck and saw every day what was worth protecting.

Her neighbor had often invited Gracie to use her kayak anytime she wanted, as long as she put it back under the house when she was done with it. Gracie was heartened by the neighborly gesture but had never taken the woman up on her offer. Frankly, kayaks scared Gracie. Was it natural, she wondered, for a human being to kayak? And why were they called kayaks? Did the word mean 'compact drowning tool'? Gracie had never actually been in a kayak, and had no idea how to maneuver the thing into the water, much less how to actually bring it back to shore.

But after studying the display of kayakers streaming down the Pacific from Point Dume every morning, wrapped in their life vests and sporting bright baseball caps, Gracie had the unfortunate idea that kayaking looked easy. She reminded herself that tennis looked easy, too, when Agassi played; Christ, gymnastics looked easy when she went to Cirque du Soleil. She had pulled her back out trying to touch her toes after a particularly inspiring performance by a Chinese tumbler.

Jaden had taken up residence with Kenny (i.e., Ana and her sisters) for the weekend and so was not around to act as her mother's natural deterrent. And Gracie had come up with a plan to try one new thing in her life every day (a plan devised twenty minutes ago over coffee). So Gracie decided that she would learn to kayak.

Wearing a baseball cap with the title of one of Kenny's movies across the bill, she dragged the green plastic ten-foot flotation device out from under her neighbor's house and pulled it down to the beach to an area she thought looked most inviting to someone who was completely unskilled and ignorant of this fact.

She pulled the kayak to the shore break and got in, holding the oar in both hands. She was wearing a T-shirt over her bathing suit, recalling the days when, as a chubby preadolescent, she lived in the T-shirt-over-bathing-suit look over the long hot inner-city summers at the public swimming pool.

It wasn't her best look, as she remembered. Her father's long white T-shirts would stick to her protruding belly, accentuating what she hoped would be eliminated. Why, she thought, had no one warned her?

But no matter. Here she was, sitting in a kayak on the beach feeling the spray in her face, the wind in her hair — why, Gracie was practically the female Kelly Slater!

Except that she was marooned. The water was moving away from the kayak. She had not even set foot in the ocean and already she was stranded. She got out and pushed the kayak forward toward the surf. And got in again. The water merely teased the bottom of the kayak. There was not enough pressure to pull her in.

She got out again, pushed the kayak farther in, and, in a feat of human physicality she'd not experienced since sex with a javelin thrower in her freshman year of college, she jumped in the kayak at the same time the water rose, buoying the contraption. Then she grabbed her oar and did some sort of waving thing with it in the water, hoping she looked like the professional she knew she could be, and actually *moved forward*. She was *kayaking!* She was an *athlete!* She was One with Nature!

After twenty exhilarating seconds, a wave suddenly rose in front of the kayak. Gracie, in a panic, turned sideways instead of moving straight into the oncoming charge of water. In that moment, she deeply regretted the fact that she had neglected to ask her neighbor about a life jacket because she'd been too ashamed to admit she needed one.

She was no longer an athlete! She was drowning! This was two new things in life that she had accomplished in one day!

A second wave followed the first rush of water, knocking her from the kayak and unscrewing the oar from her clenched hands. She thought this was totally unnecessary on the part of Mother Nature, to leave her without any hope of surviving, a mere thirty feet from a lineup of the most expensive beach houses on the planet. She would only be a footnote to her death. She could just see the news headline: 'Forty-ish Woman Drowns in Front of Celebrity Homes.'

She thought about Jaden. She thought about what dead bodies look like after they drown. Closed casket, she hoped. No sense in scaring the child.

And as she was sinking down in the water, gulping salty liquid rather than the preferred oxygen, she thought about Kenny. She wondered how he would feel, knowing he'd left Gracie and then she'd drowned in front of the Malibu Colony. Would he feel shame? Remorse? Anguish at how he broke up with her, and for whom?

The answer came fast. Kenny would dine out on Gracie's death for months. Even if Britney left him after a few weeks, women would be flocking to him forever. Everyone in town loved a widower!

Gracie couldn't leave on those terms. She made a decision to live. She was not going to be the one to bring Kenny that level of happiness.

Her feet touched the sandy bottom and she pushed up, propelling herself through the water, spinning upwards. Feeling her lungs exploding, she reached up with her arms. Then her head was above the water for a moment, and she made the most of it. She *screamed*!

Another wave went over her head and she was forced under again. She feared the worst was going to happen, no matter how strong her motivation to live in order to make Kenny unhappy. And then she felt something tug at her T-shirt sleeve.

That something grabbed her around the waist, pulling her to the surface. Gracie had a split second to look down, registering the tanned, bulky forearm circling her waist. It made her think of baseball, those professional players with forearms like Popeye, great for hitting balls out of the park. And encircling waists.

Gracie finally broke the surface. She coughed and spat water, trying to get out some semblance of a thank-you (having not let her manners go along with her pride), and then leaned back into what felt like a wall of human sinew as she was pulled closer to shore. Once this human wall found his bearings in the sand, he picked her up as though she weighed as little as Helen the dachshund and held her tight against his chest as he walked onto the dry sand. Gracie's arms were curved around his neck; they couldn't be pried from him with a crowbar.

Gracie had met men when she was younger in several ways: in a college class, a popular bar, standing in line at a restaurant. She had never met a man while drowning. As this particular man set her down on the dry sand and hovered over her, she wondered why she'd never tried it before.

She wiped the salt water from her face and peered up at him, her eyes half closed, keeping her knees together and her legs bent to the side to appear sexy yet demure, like a newspaper hosiery ad.

He stood with his legs apart, his arms crossed over his chest, watching her with the kind of attention, Gracie thought, a doctor gives to a patient who's trying to kill herself.

Gracie noticed several things about him at once. He was tall; he was built; he was tan; he had a strong jawline and wide-set dark eyes, my God, he had great hair; and he was in her demographic.

And there was no wedding ring.

Gracie felt like one of them should speak, since obviously they were going to be married. After all, they had practically had sex. Being saved was the closest she'd been to a man since she chased the masturbator off the beach a couple weeks ago.

'Thuidnk yduo,' she said. She realized she hadn't spat all of the water out of her mouth. She coughed again.

He looked at her, cocking his head slightly to one side. He seemed to be taking his time, assessing her with a sort of detached amusement. His eyes weren't exactly warm, but they weren't cold, either. He reminded Gracie of a younger Clint Eastwood. Standing before her was the classic reluctant hero. Maybe he wasn't used to seeing soaking wet divorcées starting a new life by baptizing themselves from the inside out.

A moment passed. Clint (her pet name for him) turned back to look at the ocean. Gracie wondered if he was planning his escape. Was she so scary that she could frighten off a man with abnormally strong forearms and a torso like a brick wall? She pictured Kenny in his bathing suit, Kenny who worked out every morning but was never quite able to leave the sheen of the upper-middle-class boyhood behind. There would always be a fine, soft layer above the muscles nurtured by the latest protein drink and a personal trainer named Gunnar. Kenny had a nice body, there was no doubt, but the man Gracie was staring at could eat him for breakfast, stationary bike and all.

Gracie shuddered. Maybe her new boyfriend even ate bread!

'Thank you, I mean,' Gracie said, trying to amend her earlier communication breach. And then, 'Oh, no, no — the kayak!' She had lost the kayak and the oar. So much for making friends with the neighbors.

Clint hadn't moved; he was standing, still as a rock, now looking out at the ocean. Then he turned and started walking toward the water, slowly, then picking up speed. Suddenly he dove in, leaving Gracie in her lingerie-model position, wondering who the hell had just saved her life. And confident that she had just met the most attractive man she'd ever seen without the help of artificial light.

'Would it have killed you to get a name?' she said to herself as she got up, brushing sand from her bottom and watching him as he swam with long, strong strokes away from the potential disaster scene. Her life.

Gracie turned and ran to the house; she'd have to get dried and dressed and talk to Lavender.

Gracie knew she had found 152.

★ ★ ★

Gracie wasted an entire hour before she finally biked down to the guard station to see Lavender. First of all, she felt as nervous as she would for a first date — what could she change into that would be casual enough for a drop-in visit and yet pretty enough to be attractive to the age/geography-appropriate man who had saved her life?

She thought about the proverb 'Once you save a life, it is yours to keep.' She wondered if her mystery man, 152, knew the proverb. She wondered if he was thinking about it when he stood there, watching her with what she realized now was a sort of practiced wariness.

She wondered if he would have looked at her with those eyes if she were Pam Anderson.

You can see why she changed her clothes about twenty times.

Then to the gift. What kind of gift should she bring him? Wine? Great idea. Unless he was an alcoholic — and might he think the same of her for bringing a bottle of red to his house on a hot afternoon. How about food? When was the last time she baked? And what if he didn't eat sugar or flour or — like those people who were sprouting up in Northern California — what if he didn't eat anything cooked, period?

Oh my God, Gracie suddenly thought, what if he doesn't speak English? After all, Gracie couldn't be one hundred percent sure that he'd understood her when she thanked him. What if he was embarrassed that he couldn't speak English?

Gracie was at a loss. And was no closer to being dressed and ready to bike down to see Lavender than when she started.

Finally she decided to throw caution (and her future dating life) to the wind; she would bring him a book. A simple book. Her favorite one, the one she never tired of reading, F. Scott Fitzgerald's *The Great Gatsby*.

Even if he didn't speak English, he would have surely heard of Fitzgerald. And he would think her worldly and intelligent.

Or a freak, Gracie thought, as she pulled on her never-worn pareo and a tank top, blocking out her fear of flabby upper arms with the vain hope that her ten-thousand-dollar breasts would be a viable distraction.

★　★　★

Lavender was not there. At the moment that Gracie needed her most, Lavender had taken a sick day. Gracie bit her lip and wondered if she should consult the current security guard. He was a younger white man with a heavy accent and the kind of look on his face that said he was an engineer in his mother country and here he was working for peanuts as a security guard of all things.

Gracie decided not to ask him about 152.

But she did spend the next forty-five minutes biking up and down the half-mile stretch of Malibu Colony, back and forth and back and forth, F. Scott's beauty of a novel safely strapped into the basket between her handlebars. Forty minutes into her endless loop, she saw a new Jaguar drive up to #152 and park in front. Her heart started beating faster immediately. Sweat droplets formed under her arms. She wished she'd worn a white top. She wished she was ten pounds skinnier. She wished she were ten years younger. She wished she'd find that lotion that would finally, finally, get rid of the wrinkles on her hands (why were her hands so much bonier than the rest of her body?).

She wished she could change many things except one: her newfound valor. Perhaps coming so close to death (okay, maybe not so, so close to death) — anyway, coming so close to almost drowning had changed her. Gracie had never been that most brave of souls when it came to the outside, physical world; she had no desire to climb a mountain using ropes and pulleys, none at all to scuba-dive in a shark tank, nothing at all registered in her as excitement in regard to jumping out of an airplane over the desert.

But she had never been afraid of confrontation.

And this factor of her personality, combined with the adrenaline rush of her morning activities, spurred her along as she rode up to the Jaguar, spinning her wheels soundlessly, with her feet stuck out at the sides, then raising one leg over the bike to settle both feet on the ground, stopping the bike directly in front of #152. And just as Clint stopped the car and got out, Gracie grabbed the book and turned to greet him and heard, 'Well, goddamn, look who's here.'

Gracie's eyes had to refocus, for whom she was standing in front of was not Clint, the man who saved her life and as a result owed her his, but Lou, the man for whom Kenny worked. Lou Manahan was #152.

Gracie stood for a moment, frozen smile on her lips, hands frozen around a paperback edition of F. Scott's masterpiece, voice box seized up, knees locked.

Lou came toward her and gave her a bear hug, which, frankly, went a long way to helping her thaw. The hug felt like a strange hybrid of fatherly touch and 'old friend' touch mixed with a subtle patina of 'you're divorced, let's have sex' touch.

True, an alarm went off somewhere south of her belly button (did she even have sex organs anymore? And were they called organs?), but Gracie didn't trust her own instincts. Weren't they the instincts that had her marry Kenny in

214

the first place? The instincts that let her down when she first spied that (*MOTHERF-CKING*) earring in his left ear? The instincts that told her that the rapturous Clint was #152, not the old-enough-to-be-your-father-if-your-father-were-a-teenager-when-you-were-conceived Lou?

Lou was standing, smiling at her, the deep wrinkles around his green-gray eyes at once inviting and off-putting. 'You staying in the Colony, Gracie?' he asked.

It seemed like a simple enough question — unless you were Gracie and felt the need to nervously overexplain in charged situations.

'I am, on the far south side, but only temporarily. I mean, a few months, sort of like marriage rehab. I'm not paying rent, the house belongs to a friend of mine. It's good to have rich friends, right?' she asked, looking at him, hoping that her expression could convey her thoughts better than anything coming out of her mouth.

Lou nodded, thoughtfully. Thankfully he seemed distracted. 'What's that you got there?' he asked.

Gracie looked at her hand; she'd forgotten about the book. 'Just some . . . reading material.'

He took it from her outstretched hand. 'That's for Clint,' she wanted to say. 'Clint, you know, the man I thought was waiting here for me.'

'Much better than what I have waiting for me this weekend.' He glanced toward his briefcase.

Gracie nodded. Everyone complained about reading scripts over the weekend, but she was surprised and pleased that Lou still bothered reading. Usually men of his station left that thankless task to underlings. Kenny claimed he only read certain pages of a script: the first page, page 10, and pages 30, 60, 90, and the last, 120.

Why had she been married to such a bozo?

'You want to have dinner tomorrow night?' Lou asked.

Gracie just looked at him. 'I usually have dinner every night,' she said.

'Great. How about a little Italian. I prefer the Italian to the sushi.'

Kenny's boss was asking her out. Where was The Coven at a moment like this? What were the ramifications? Where would they live once they were married? Would Lou fire Kenny after their wedding? Would the kids bunk up together or have separate bedrooms? And since when was Gracie such catnip for men?

'Okay,' she said.

'Saturday night. I'll pick you up. After all, I know where you live. Temporarily. During your marriage rehab.'

He smiled his famously charming smile and handed her back her F. Scott and headed into his house. Number 152.

14

Britney Spears Has Kidnapped My Daughter

Britney Spears had moved into Kenny's house. Gracie had learned this from her daughter when Kenny's assistant dropped her off in Malibu after spending the weekend at what was now her father's home.

Gracie knew that something (more) was rotten in the State of Kenny when Jaden showed up wearing a tight pink T-shirt with the words PORN STAR on it, tied and knotted up under her rib cage, and tiny pink shorts that looked like they had come from Barbie's closet. Gracie chewed through her knuckle to keep from screaming as Jaden jumped from the assistant's VW Bug, bounding toward her mother, looking not unlike a midget hooker, which, according to her Internet spam, was easily attainable and at low prices.

Moreover, Jaden smelled like cologne — a sweet vanilla tincture, appropriate for pop stars like Britney or Ricky Martin or even that Justin Timberlake guy, but not, dear God, her three-year-old daughter.

Gracie hugged her daughter and kissed her cheek, then looked at her upturned face.

Oh my God, thought Gracie, was that lip gloss?

Gracie immediately looked at her daughter's nails, and yes, they, too, were pink.

'Mommy, we had so much fun!' Jaden said. 'We went to Disneyland and we went on the rides and we didn't even have to stand in line — '

'You went to Disneyland?' Gracie had been meaning to take Jaden to Disneyland again. She'd taken her once. Jaden had screamed throughout the entire Small World ride and then had thrown up her hot dog lunch. *This experience is yours for ninety-eight dollars (not counting gas) and three hours in bumper-to-bumper traffic!*

'And I got twelve whole stuffed animals!' Jaden exclaimed. Gracie looked at Jaden's pink and white overnight case, bursting at the seams.

'And we got a man-cure and we went to a nightclub!' Jaden said.

Gracie thought she must have made a mistake. You know, kids . . .

'Nightclub?' Gracie asked. 'I don't think you mean nightclub, honey.'

'Oh, yes, Mommy. That's what Daddy and Britney called it,' she said. 'They let me stay up late.'

Now, she was looking at Gracie with accusing eyes. Her mood had suddenly changed. It was Hate Mommy Time.

'Britney says I'm the prettiest girl in the whole world,' she said, twirling. Gracie's mind went to the film starring a prepubescent Brooke Shields,

218

Pretty Baby. 'Do you think I'm the prettiest girl in the whole world, Mommy?' she asked, twirling, twirling.

Kenny and Britney Spears are turning my baby, Gracie thought, blood of my blood, flesh of my flesh, into a child prostitute.

'I think you're beautiful inside and out,' Gracie said.

Jaden gave her a look which, translated from the three-year-old-ese, said: That isn't good enough.

'Britney says I can go to her concerts anytime I want,' Jaden said. 'She says she'll even bring me up onstage. I can be one of her dancers!'

Gracie could not keep Kenny from dating Britney Spears — the lure of young skin and an *Us Magazine* cover were too great — but she could keep him from turning her lovely, smart daughter into a stripper.

Couldn't she?

'Honey, you're the smartest little girl I know,' Gracie said, her voice straining. Her daughter finally stopped twirling and landed in a heap on the ground, her legs splayed in front of her. 'See, there is more to life than beauty. There's intelligence, kindness — '

'Britney is so pretty, huh, Mommy?' Jaden looked up at her mother.

'She is. She's definitely pretty. If you like that sort of thing. I personally prefer, like, Sophia Loren, Gina Lollobrigida, Mommy prefers classic, ageless beauty.'

'She's almost my age, Mommy!' Jaden said. 'She said she's gonna be my new best friend! She moved in and everything!'

Gracie knew that God had big, big plans for her, based on this conversation. He/She would never let Gracie suffer through this for no apparent reason.

'I'm glad you like her, Jaden,' Gracie said. 'I'm sure she's a very nice person. Where, exactly, did she move into?'

'You know, your old room. With Daddy. You don't need it anymore, right, Mommy? Daddy says you want Daddy to be happy. I want you to meet her, Mommy,' Jaden said.

'I would like nothing more, except maybe a root canal . . . without Novocain.'

'I learned about canals,' Jaden said. 'What's No-Caine?'

'Oh, honey,' Gracie said, wrapping her arms around her daughter and holding her against her chest. 'It's just something Mommy needs every once in a while for her heart.'

'Mommy, I think you're beautiful,' Jaden said.

Gracie smiled. Jaden was her daughter, probably the only child she'd ever have. Of course she would never turn her back on her mother. Of course she would never really prefer Britney over Mommy, except for short periods of time. And that would wear off, at least until the next twenty-year-old child came along in Kenny's life.

She knew Jaden would never abandon her mother, the woman who knew her true heart. What was it Gracie's father had told her years ago? 'Love expands,' he said. 'Love doesn't subtract.'

'But not like new-beautiful,' Jaden said, stroking Gracie's cheek. 'Like old-beautiful.'

'Jaden, have Daddy and Britney told you what vodka is?' Gracie asked. Her daughter shook her head.

'Good,' Gracie said, and she got up to make herself a drink. Sure, eleven A.M. was a little early for a screwdriver, but when the going gets tough, the tough get tipsy.

★   ★   ★

How does one have dinner with her ex-husband's boss, Gracie wondered, as Saturday night loomed ever closer.

'You don't,' Will said. 'Isn't he, like, a hundred years old?'

'He's barely into his sixties,' Gracie said. 'And you can't deny he's still sexy. You're just mad at him because he didn't hire you to redo his house.'

'He is so Tom Jones, don't you think, with just a sprinkling of Jack Nicholson?' Cricket said.

Cricket and Will were soaking in the sun outside the deck on the beach side of the house, though there wasn't any sand to rest their chairs on. They were actually sitting on the steps leading to the beach. The tide was high, and Joan's beachfront house had become, instead, a boat.

'How much does it cost to rent this house?' Will asked. 'This is like an episode of *Gilligan's Island*, seriously.'

'Can we talk about important things?' Gracie

said, as all three of them lifted their feet on cue as a wave splashed over them.

Earlier, they had been sitting a few houses down, on the dry beach in front of the Boners, until their housekeeper had trotted down the stairs and, while apologizing profusely in Spanish, informed them that this beach was private and they'd have to move. Gracie said she wasn't aware of any private beaches in California — the entire coastline was in fact public — but the maid was obviously in fear of losing her job. And so, grumbling, they moved their beach towels and chairs a few feet north, and made camp in front of the neighbor who, according to Lavender, preferred hookers to conversation.

The hooker-preferring neighbor came out on his deck a moment later, followed by a girl in the smallest bikini possible, with doll thighs and the biggest tits of anyone Gracie had ever seen. Gracie would have listened closer to what he was saying (yelling), but she was waiting for the girl to tip over the railing headfirst onto the beach. Even now she couldn't recall the girl's hair color; when boobs are that big, hair color is superfluous. Everything else is superfluous.

The gist of his emoting was that this beach was private and you can't sit in front of my house and it's private here and don't you read the signs and my beach is a private beach and I'll call the security guards, and on and on and on and so forth . . .

Will stared at him, the stare of the gay and perpetually bored with heterosexual men who have obvious sexual hang-ups. Cricket just giggled hysterically.

Gracie, tired of having to move, said, 'Get security.'

The man huffed and walked away.

A few minutes later, Lavender came walking down the beach, wearing her regulation dark khakis and short-sleeved white shirt, her badge and forehead shining in the midday sun.

Gracie rose to greet her, immediately sorry that she was the cause of Lavender's long trek. 'Are you here to arrest me?' she asked.

'This guy has a major stick up his behind,' Lavender said, waving and smiling toward the man now standing, hands on his hips, on his deck.

'Well, doesn't that young lady get paid to work it out for him?' Will asked, taking a long sip of iced tea.

'I have to ask the question,' Lavender said.

'Please don't,' said Gracie. 'We've already moved once, for the Boners.'

'He's just going to keep calling me out here and I'm gonna have to keep coming out and pretending to chastise you until you finally leave,' Lavender replied. 'Now, you know it's too hot for my liking and it's too hot for me to be taking a walk.'

'What're you reading?' Gracie asked.

'Science fiction,' Lavender said. 'This black woman author. There's a test next Thursday.'

'Cool,' Gracie said. 'Okay, I don't want you to have to walk down here anymore. We'll leave.'

Lavender nodded her thanks and waved again

to the man who hadn't moved from the deck, and turned and walked back up the beach. The man walked into his house. He would probably not even come out for the rest of the afternoon, Gracie thought. She had never even seen him on his deck before.

Cricket and Gracie started gathering up their towels and chairs and drinks and magazines when they noticed that Will was no longer standing next to them.

They looked up to see Will standing on a boulder with his back toward them, facing the man's deck, swaying side to side, peeing on #228's chaise lounges.

⋆ ⋆ ⋆

Gracie had been nervous about getting ready for her 'date' with Lou Manahan. She shouldn't have been, really — she'd known him for over ten years. They'd shared meals and laughs and compared cold, hard appraisals of the people they ran into every day. In a town where friendship meant little and love meant less, they were a rarity: two people who couldn't help each other who enjoyed each other's company anyway.

Well, that's not actually true, Gracie thought. Lou was Kenny's boss; of course it had mattered to her to make a good impression on Lou.

But now she found herself analyzing. What would Lou like to see her in? What item of clothing made her look taller? Skinnier? Voluptuous? At all, perish the thought, classy? She didn't even want to think of all the women Lou had dated; there was a list as long as the metropolitan phone book, minus all the dental offices and legal services. In the last three decades, Lou had dated only the most ravishing women in the world: Ali MacGraw and Dyan Cannon in the seventies, Farrah Fawcett and Jacqueline Bisset in the eighties, Madonna and a postop Courtney Love (but only once) in the nineties.

His most recent fling — the one Gracie had only heard about through the Hollywood grapevine because Lou was never one to kiss and tell — had been with Demi Moore. The only girls Gracie had ever seen him with had one thing in common, and it was enough: extraordinary beauty.

What Gracie was looking at when she looked in the mirror could be extraordinary (as in, 'What extraordinarily wrinkled elbows you have,' or 'How extraordinary that your three-year-old C-section scar still looks like an old bicycle tire'), but not necessarily associated with 'beauty.' At most, Gracie believed, she could be associated with extraordinary stability and pleasantness.

She reminded herself that she was a fine-looking woman with many attributes. And besides, Will was right, why was she nervous when, really, she was going on a date with someone who was old enough to have voted for McGovern?

Unless he voted for Nixon, Gracie thought as the doorbell rang. Then she would really have problems.

WIFE NUMBER SIX

Is a scientist. She likes to mix just the right amount of vodka with Mexican Quaaludes before she goes out dancing with her child's swim instructor.

She trusts him. He knows mouth-to-mouth.

15

Planning Your Own Funeral

Lou Manahan was so often called the King of Hollywood in the media that people had taken simply to calling him 'King' or 'El Rey' or 'Your Highness.' Honestly, he didn't know whether to be embarrassed or pleased. If he'd had a mother, he would have believed his mother wouldn't have raised him to take pride in false flattery. Sure, he could feel a little pride in his accomplishments. Lou, who hadn't even graduated from high school, who joined the Marines at seventeen lying about his age just so he could catch a ride to the front lines, where he could shoot a gun — and it was *legal*!

And then he became the prince in an urban fairy tale. He had taken some shrapnel, caught a train from Pendleton back to Brooklyn, and was riding in a taxi, sharing it with some older fancy guy who said, after a minor conversation about the sorry state of the world, that he saw in Lou what he himself had when he was young. The guy had been in World War II, the last good war, a tail gunner. They wound up being friends. More than friends, really, the man was like Lou's father. And he got Lou work in a mailroom at the biggest agency in New York, made him wear a suit and tie, taught him to control his mouth but not his mind.

He taught Lou to keep coiled, like a snake, to pounce only when absolutely necessary, to talk softly and move quietly; to read up on all the ancient methods of war, to incorporate them into his thoughts and actions, and then to forget them, as though they never existed.

Lou still kept the old man, now living in an old folks' home on Long Island, on payroll.

Lou poured himself a scotch rocks and walked out onto his deck and looked out at the immense stretch of water and thought about how people always complained that 'things have changed, the business has changed,' and that it was true. In came the accountants, and gone were the perks. Lucky for Lou, he had lived through the best of it. He'd had a string of hits, both commercial and critical, while he was at Paramount in the late seventies and early eighties that had yet to be duplicated by any other studio, and now, working for himself, he had proven to be both a good studio chief and a great producer. He had experienced it all: the money, the girls, the magazine covers, the notoriety. He was known as a drinker in a sober world, a smoker in a nonsmoker's universe, a slut in a place where people talked only about sex.

But as he grew older, and as he had experienced not one but two heart attacks (which were quickly downplayed in the press as gastric episodes), he was thinking about something bigger than his rep, bigger than his movies: he was thinking about his life; he was thinking about his legacy.

He was thinking about if anyone would give a shit if he died.

It was a thought that was with him when he went to sleep, that was beside him when he woke up. Would anyone care if he died?

He'd been to too many funerals. People's cell phones playing TV theme songs during the eulogy, agents making pay-or-play deals while genuflecting in front of the casket, actors complaining about the dead son of a bitch while his widow cried crocodile tears and wondered when she could get back to her boyfriend, the contractor.

He had become that thing that he loathed in others: Lou had become jaded. And nothing brought it out in him like a Hollywood funeral. The older he was, the more funerals he'd gone to, the more obsessed he became.

And that's why he was planning his own funeral. The difference being, he would hold his funeral while he was still alive. And he would attend; he would be a guest at his own funeral.

Lou knew that if he were in a healthy relationship (besides the one he had, intermittently, with his toddler son), he wouldn't have these thoughts. Having himself 'die,' only to be wearing a disguise and sitting in the third row at his funeral, listening in on the action. He knew that there was one thing that could cure his fevered mind, and that was love. Lou was nothing if not a romantic. He had been married three times — four if you count the fact he'd married his third wife twice.

Which is why he asked Gracie out to dinner.

Normally she wasn't his type, even as he slid into, let's call it, older age. She was attractive but not beautiful; she was older than he preferred by a decade. But she had a sharp wit, she was unbowed by the dullards in this town, and most important, she understood him. Gracie saw through his ladies' man reputation, his press clippings, his successes and failures and saw what he really was — just a pretty good guy who got lucky, damned lucky. And made the most of it.

Lou walked back inside to the bar, having finished his scotch. He poured himself another, enjoying the crackle of the ice, as he always did, when the scotch filled the glass halfway. Were it not for that sound, he doubted he would ever take a drink.

He looked at himself in the mirror over the bar.

'How'd you get so old?' he wondered. It was a question he'd been asking himself a lot lately.

*   *   *

Good start: Lou had arrived exactly on time at Gracie's house. Gracie had forgotten that there are occasions when a man is on time. Bumpy start: Gracie's date with the boss faltered when the Italian place was packed; Lou's assistant had forgotten to make a reservation, and the maître d' was not interested in appearing interested in the movie business or those successful in the movie business, so Gracie suggested they skip it altogether and try their luck at Nobu, where she had seen many a recognizable face. She convinced Lou they had cooked items on the menu, but Lou wasn't so sure. He wasn't a fan of fish in the first place, much less a fan of fish in the raw.

Gracie heard Will's voice in her head, saying this was a sign she should definitely date a younger man. Younger men aren't afraid of sushi.

She made a note to date a younger man, should any become available, say, before she died.

Ah, what bounty! The pretty Asian hostess at Nobu gave Lou a table just because he was Lou, which he seemed to appreciate. Gracie could tell he was relaxing. Didn't everyone like being recognized?

'Watch. Pretty soon,' Gracie told him as they were led to their patio table, 'you'll be making this your very own *Cheers*.'

'Not unless they change the menu,' Lou growled.

Gracie liked a growl on a man. She just didn't realize it until now. Kenny never growled, she thought. Mostly he whined.

They sat across from each other and Gracie assessed Lou while he ordered their drinks — a Cosmo for her, an Asahi beer for him. She liked that he was a beer kind of guy; she felt it was a more manly choice than sake. She watched his face move, his tan, the slight gray stubble, the full head of hair. Ready smile. Lou looked like a candidate for a Viagra ad.

Gracie was disturbed that she'd had this thought; she wondered if he was taking Viagra.

She wondered if he needed to take Viagra. She'd heard that Viagra sometimes gave men hard-ons that would last for hours. She glanced toward the space between his legs, veering sideways at an odd angle. She'd also heard, through the Hollywood cock-vine, that Lou was the proud owner of a penis the size of a bowling pin. She didn't know whether to be enticed or frightened, but Gracie couldn't get rid of this thought throughout a string of questions he threw at her.

Finally he said, 'You seem distracted.'

Strrriiike, Gracie thought.

'And,' Lou added, 'you seem to be looking at my zipper. Even more than I'm accustomed to. If you're not planning on tailoring my pants, would you like to ask me something?'

'Are those khakis?' Gracie asked.

'Yes, they're what we on Earth call khakis,' Lou said, leaning in. 'I'll take them off and you can hold them if you like.'

'I'm sorry,' Gracie said. 'It's just a little odd, dating my husband's boss. My husband's boss who usually dates . . . younger, famous, under-fed, overpaid girls.'

'Not in the last six months,' Lou said.

'Four!' Gracie replied. 'Or have you forgotten Demi?'

'Demi's not younger than you,' he said. 'She doesn't count.'

'Anyone who can bounce a coin off her ass is younger,' said Gracie. 'Those thighs alone lop five years off her age. The abs are another decade. In fact, if you work your way through her face and body, her age will be somewhere in the negative numbers.'

'Gracie,' he said. Gracie liked hearing her name come out of his mouth. Or was it just that she hadn't heard a man, besides Will, a card-carrying homosexual, say her name lately? 'This is just dinner between friends, a friendly dinner,' Lou said, not meaning it at all, but sounding as though he did. 'It doesn't have to be a date.' He had practiced sounding sincere for so long that sometimes he surprised himself by actually seeming sincere.

'I know, you're right, I know.' Gracie exhaled, grateful for Lou's sincere response. She found herself wishing her husband had been more like him. 'And besides, Kenny the Pig's not really my husband anymore.'

'Let's drink to that,' Lou said, just as their drinks arrived.

'Did you know he's dating Britney Spears?' Gracie asked.

Lou raised an eyebrow. 'I'm not sure whether to laugh or weep,' he said dryly, then took a mouthful of beer. 'He'll be making the newsstand any day now.'

'Bless his heart. Let's check out the Malibu newsstand,' Gracie said, suddenly excited. 'After our friendly dinner.'

★　★　★

Gracie felt somewhere near the region of relaxation about halfway through the dinner. She had gulped down her first drink (something she did when she was nervous and out of control and thinking bad thoughts about Lou's Viagrated penis) and sipped her way through her second and had eaten little and was convinced that she had expended five pounds through a combination of nerves and liquid diet.

And then she saw them come into the restaurant.

Gracie's hand shot out toward Lou's forearm to steady herself, although she was already seated. She'd grabbed him in the middle of a funny story about his third (fourth?) wife and her obsession with remodeling houses and coming home to find her giving the contractor a very personal bit of instruction about her own infrastructure —

'Gracie?' Lou asked. 'Are you all right? You just ruined the punch line. But I've been telling that story since 1985, don't worry — '

'It's them!' Gracie squeaked.

Lou looked at Gracie, and for a moment Gracie saw something in his eyes that made her forget who was now walking toward them — one of them loping like an eager, oversized dog, the other taking mincing, pigeon-toed steps, her hair covering half of her famous face.

The light in Lou's eyes had expired. Where had his life gone? What was wrong with him?

Suddenly Gracie felt a need to take care of Lou. Enough of the small talk, Gracie thought, what is going on in your life, Lou Manahan? What's the problem? Talk to me.

But by that time, Kenny and Britney had already made it to the table.

'Lou!' Kenny said, giving Lou a heavy pat on

the shoulder. 'Look at this! Gracie! Lou! It's like old home week!'

Gracie leaned over so far to escape his friendly pat, she was practically hugging the floor.

'This is great, how you guys doin'?' Kenny asked. He sounded more like a frat buddy than an ex-husband. Not only was he not worthy husband material, Gracie thought, he was not worthy ex-husband material.

'We guys are good, Kenny,' Gracie said.

'Hey, you're not talking about me, are you?' Kenny asked. 'Nah — I'm not worthy!' he concluded, smiling. Gracie was amused at his assessment and wished for the day it would be accurate.

'Are you going to introduce us?' Lou asked. Britney had been standing behind Kenny during this exchange, hiding her surprisingly small frame behind his surprisingly large one. The move reminded Gracie of Jaden, the way she was when she walked into a room and didn't know anyone.

'Oh, yeah, hey,' Kenny said, 'this is Britney. Britney Spears.'

She peeked out from behind Kenny, holding onto a corner of his shirt.

'Thanks for specifying,' Gracie said as she shook Britney's soft, childlike hand. 'Nice to meet you.'

'You, too,' she said.

Lou shook her hand as well, smiled. Gracie concluded he wasn't all that interested. At that moment, she thought she might marry Lou Manahan.

'Thanks for being so nice to Jaden,' Gracie said.

'Oh, I love Jaden!' Britney replied, suddenly animated.

'Britney loves Jaden!' Kenny parroted. 'You should see those two together.'

'We have so much fun,' Britney said, now holding Kenny's hand (Look, Ma, no wedding ring!) and looking up — way up — at him with her Bambi eyes.

Gracie just smiled. She kept smiling until they walked off and sat down half a restaurant away.

'You can drop it now,' Lou said. 'It's safe, they'll never see the scowl.'

Gracie dropped the smile, almost audibly. 'Oh, I love Jaden!' she mimicked Britney with a high-pitched nasal voice.

Lou started laughing. And didn't stop. Tears were coming from his eyes, his stomach heaved up and down.

'What's so funny?' Gracie slurred/demanded.

'Your ex-husband is dating Britney Spears,' he said. 'She could be your daughter's stepmother!'

'That's funny?' Gracie asked. 'That's so not funny!'

'Of course it is!' Lou said, choking. 'It's just one fucked-up crazy life!'

Gracie started to laugh along with him. They were still laughing when they left the restaurant.

★　★　★

Lou and Gracie were rounding the corner into the Malibu Colony, past the guard gate and toward Joan's house, when they collided with the bicyclist. Lou had been looking at Gracie for a split second, watching her for a reaction to one of the stories he kept handy for dates with attractive women of above-average intelligence when he hit something — or, more accurately, felt something hit the front end of his new Jaguar. Whoever or whatever it was seemed to appear out of nowhere to fling themselves at his car.

Gracie had screamed, and Lou joked that another punch line had been ruined.

Secretly his heart was beating through his chest. He was thankful that even though he'd had a few beers, he couldn't have been driving over ten, fifteen miles an hour. He was hoping against hope that he hadn't hit a kid.

But as soon as it had happened, the person he'd hit — a man in his late forties or early fifties? wearing orange shorts and a beat-up T-shirt, looking like Harrison Ford — popped up, and without even glancing at the man who ran into him, rode off toward the guard gate and into the night.

Lou, breathing hard, looked at Gracie. 'The nerve of some people,' he joked. 'I ran into the guy, and he won't even say hello.'

Gracie, her eyes wide, her hands glued to the dash, just shook her head.

'You have any idea who that was?' he asked.

'I don't have a name,' Gracie said, 'but he saved my life.'

'Geez,' Lou said. 'That's kind of a tough act to follow.'

He rolled down the Colony toward her house, as slow as his car would allow, barely making it over the speed bumps. When he stopped in front of #250, he looked at Gracie. 'Look at me. Do you think I could save your life?' he asked.

'Not a chance,' Gracie said, looking at him. 'But if you're lucky I could save yours.'

Lou shook his head as he got back into his car after walking her to her front door. 'How,' he asked himself, 'could a woman be that smart?'

16

Nerves

The Queen of Bad Timing, Gracie thought to herself as she paced the kitchen, bent on wearing a groove into the bleached wood floor. Lou had almost killed the man she was going to marry — or at least meet, in the next few months. On the other hand, maybe it was kismet, running into him like that, his hands windmilling toward the sky as Lou's Jaguar knocked him from his bike. Maybe it was good that he had seen her with another man, another successful man, maybe he would think she was . . . desirable!

Was Gracie Pollock desirable? she asked herself. Lou seemed to find her desirable. Although he'd chastely kissed her cheek when he dropped her off, she distinctly felt the possibility of a diversionary tactic. He was kissing her cheek to keep her off-guard in the event his lips would someday land on hers in the not-too-distant future. She knew Lou had been in the Marines — didn't everyone know Lou had been in the Marines? He was the only Hollywood player ever to wear a uniform that didn't have any connection to a religious school; he was the only Hollywood player who had good old-fashioned guts.

Which brought Gracie back to the idea of age.

Lou had close to twenty years on Gracie. Yes, as Will had so helpfully pointed out, he could be her father — if her father was sexy and drove a Jaguar and dated movie stars and was just past his teens when she'd been born. Gracie couldn't imagine her own father being so cool. Besides, there were benefits to Lou's age, Gracie thought. Didn't everyone say that age brought wisdom, security, experience — attributes which Kenny seemed to be doing swimmingly without. On the other hand, Gracie could see age as being a detriment. What if she tired of Tony Bennett? Would she run screaming at the first sight of Old Butt? And what about death? Of course a younger man would generally be around longer than an older man, but was this necessarily a good thing? Could Death, in addition to diamonds, be a girl's best friend? And besides, Gracie thought, beggars can't be choosers. And although she wasn't exactly begging for it, she was asking more than she'd been asked.

Or was she? Hadn't Lou asked her out? And didn't she lock eyes with Clint, the man who saved her life, just as he tumbled out of sight, swallowed up by the front end of Lou's new Jaguar?

If she was desirable, when did that happen? And what could she do to preserve her newfound desirability? Or should she just accept that she was man-nip in a beach cover-up?

Gracie looked out her kitchen window and watched the moon reflected in the night's black waters and wished she had a man's arms wrapped around her waist, the two of them looking in the same direction, surrendered to the moment. She closed her eyes and imagined who that man would be.

★　★　★

Crazy fucking rich people, Sam thought to himself, as he shook off his encounter with the front end of a Jaguar. He could've been killed, minding his own business, biking to Sav-on for a bottle of that antidiarrhea medicine Mrs. Kennicot needed. The Jag had come out of nowhere. The driver, some older guy, wasn't even looking at him when Sam rolled over the front of the car. Just before impact, before he went flying, Sam could see that he was talking to the woman at his side. But she, she was looking at Sam; their eyes had met as he flew forward. It's funny, Sam thought, the images people remember right before a traumatic event. He remembered bits and pieces — laughter, cigarette smoke, a friendly blow on the back. Then boom. One rocket (apparently), the jeep flies up in the air (apparently), three weeks in army hospital in a coma (apparently), and all you can remember are the seconds before impact. The life-changing event is not worth remembering, according to the human brain. It's what came before that matters.

Sam locked his bike outside Sav-on, limped past the guys sleeping on benches, past the empties — generic vodka bottles — decorating the ground. His ribs hurt, his legs were on shaky ground, his bike was screwed up — the chain, which was never perfect (the bike was old when he 'got' it), was now totally bent out of shape — but nothing was going to keep him from getting that bottle of medicine to Mrs. Kennicot. He was late as it was.

★ ★ ★

How many times, Gracie thought, do I have to walk back and forth on this stretch of beach? She'd been up at six that morning, quite the feat considering she'd had two drinks more than her usual (which was no drinks) the night before. She'd awakened with a feeling of determination — she would find her mystery man once and for all, and put an end to the cycle of anticipation, self-flagellation, and eating boat-loads of processed sugar.

Jaden had spent a good forty-five minutes with her, digging holes in the sand while Mom meandered back and forth in front of the opening leading onto the beach, which the tenants on the land-side houses used. But then Ana, who was driving Jaden back to Kenny's place, had arrived and flagged them down; she spent a good amount of time chastising Gracie for providing only dry cereal and a juice box for Jaden while she went on her wild-goose chase searching for a good-looking phantom.

Finally Gracie sat down in the sand and let the water, which was moving toward high tide (she'd taken to reading the tide charts in the newspaper) tickle her feet. She closed her eyes and let the sun seep into her skin, pretending to be unafraid of wrinkles, sunspots, sunburn, and sagging. Was there nothing she feared?

'Trying to drown yourself again?' she heard a man ask as she felt a shadow edge across the upper half of her body.

'No,' she said without opening her eyes. She realized she was afraid of something: actual intimacy. She took a deep breath and opened her eyes. 'But if I have to in order to track you down, I'm willing to do it.'

He was looking down at her, his expression opaque. Was there any way of reaching this man? What did a girl have to do? Gracie was never a big fan of the strong, silent type. Kenny was more like the weak, loud type. Maybe that's what she liked.

'Did you run into my friend's car last night on purpose?' she asked.

'No,' he said, looking up at the water, then down again at her. 'I prefer to fling myself at a Mercedes or a BMW — Jaguar drivers seldom go fast enough for my liking.'

Humor! Gracie thought, Eureka! We have progress!

'See, they tend to be a little older,' he continued.

Not just humor, Gracie thought. Biting Humor!

Why did I say that? Sam thought.

'Are you going in?' Gracie asked. His Labrador came up to Gracie and sat beside her. She reached over and scratched the dog's ear while trying to keep from hitting herself on the head for asking *such a stupid question.*

243

'No, I brought a towel because I like to lay out for a few hours, work on my tan,' he said.

'Oh, me, too,' Gracie replied, showing off her white arms. She kind of liked that he wouldn't give her an inch after such a lame comment.

'I would invite you in,' he said, tilting his head toward the ocean, 'but after our little meeting last night, I think I bruised a rib. I can't guarantee your safety.'

'I think you should sue us,' Gracie said. 'It's obvious we were playing a dangerous little game of Jaguar tag.'

'I'm talking to lawyers. My lawyers are talking to lawyers. We'll get back to you,' he replied.

Gracie noticed he hadn't sat down yet. 'Do you ever sit down?' she asked.

'It's not my best skill,' he said.

'Oh, I'm really good at it, look,' she said, opening her arms to show off her sitting prowess.

''Ah, but a Man's reach should exceed his grasp . . . or what's a Heaven for?'' he said.

'Oh, that's terrible,' Gracie said, 'you're showing off. Nobody knows quotes anymore.'

'Some of us have time to read. When we're working on our tans,' he said.

'Some of us are impressed,' she said.

'Some of us should be.' He smiled.

Gracie smiled. They were smiling at each other. Now, Gracie thought, willing him to make a move. Take the next step, she thought. I can't take the next step, I'm a girl — well, not a girl exactly, maybe an old girl. Anyway, ask me out!

'I'm going in,' he said. And he walked off toward the water. Gracie jumped off the sand

244

like she'd been stuck in the ass by a crab —

'Wrong answer!' she yelled as he dove into the water. The Labrador started barking. 'Tell him that's not what he was supposed to say!' she said to the dog, who ignored her and chased his master down the beach.

Then she realized the dog had tags; the tags would tell her where this man lived. Gracie ran after the dog, full-force, sand spinning in the air under her feet. She felt like a movie heroine, chasing down her boyfriend before he left for the war. But no, Gracie thought as she heaved, her lungs betraying her. I'm a forty-one-year-old woman chasing after a dog because I'm trying to get information on a man who dared talk to me.

She slowed down and bent her body at the waist, resting her hands on her knees. She was busy coughing up mucus when a familiar presence made itself known by licking her hair.

'Well, hello,' she said to the dog, who had dropped a tennis ball at her feet. 'Hello, hello,' she said as she reached down for his tags. 'Your name is Baxter, and you live in . . . number 191.'

She looked into the dog's eyes, which were pleading with her to throw the ball.

'Okay, Baxter,' Gracie said, tossing the tennis ball, soaked with dog spit. 'It's the least this girl can do,' she told him as he ignored her and ran for the ball.

* * *

Swim, Sam thought as he knifed through the cold, murky water, his strokes even and strong, his body stubbornly ignoring the residual pain of his accident. Swim, swim, swim. Just keep swimming. How could he have flirted so boldly? It was as though he'd exercised a muscle he'd forgotten he had — and he wasn't sure how he felt about it. Mostly he found it painful. Part of him enjoyed flirting with a member of the opposite sex, sure — how often did a homeless man get the chance to do that? But there was pain, pain in being reminded how much time had passed, how much had been lost. No girlfriends, no wives, no children, no home. What kind of life had he led? His encounter with this woman reminded him that he was not an island. That he was a man, merely a man, just flesh and blood, muscle and bone. Oh, shit, would he even know what to do with a woman? How long had it been? He closed his eyes. Swim, keep swimming. Do not stop swimming.

Why was she so interested? he thought suddenly. Because she was definitely interested, that he was sure of. She'd been waiting for him; she'd even stated it as fact. She was a new face; did she think he was a homeowner? Did she think he rented? He almost smiled. A few years ago, he'd had one close encounter with the ex-wife of a famous actor. Sam knew who the man was because when it was raining in Malibu, the college kids working the counter would let him sleep in the local movie theater. He'd seen a couple of the famous movie star's pictures, respected his tough-guy acting stance. The woman had brought up his name as if to impress Sam, but the truth was, he wasn't impressed.

Acting seemed to him to be a girl's job. She'd brought it up once, then twice, then never again when she could discern no reaction. Other than that, they barely talked. The sex was wham, bam, thank-you ma'am, and Sam was grateful for that. Less painful that way, all gravy. The woman had known about him, knew he was some kind of handyman. Maybe she even knew he didn't have a proper home. But she didn't care. There was no exchange of ideas, no discussions. Certainly no flirting.

But this woman, this one, wanted more, Sam thought, she wanted more than a onetime encounter. He could look into her eyes and sense her decency, he heard sweetness in her voice. And need. She wanted a relationship. And eventually she would want the truth. All of it. 'Why?' He could see her asking him, her eyes wide and bewildered. 'Why don't you have a home?' And what could he tell her? That he tried? That he moved home after his second tour of duty? That he went back to college? That he was desperate to fit in? That the professors who called him and his buddies baby-killers made him ill with anger? That there was not one war he could win, including the one with his family? They hated him for leaving and they made him suffer when he returned. His problem wasn't drugs, it wasn't mental instability. His problem was the human race.

He'd have to avoid this woman, he thought. Neither of them were up for the truth. She just didn't know it yet.

A former tennis pro, married the eighty-year-old billionaire mogul after he impregnated her; later, she bore him a baby girl. When they broke up a few months later, she sued for over $300,000 in monthly support; the billionaire went through the trash of a younger billionaire and got his DNA off a piece of dental floss.

The DNA matched that of the baby girl; he's still paying child support.

17

Independence Day

How many times can a person walk back and forth in front of a house until someone notices? Gracie thought. Not long after her meeting of the minds with Baxter, Gracie had donned new tennis shoes and her most fetching smile and had walked Helen and Jaden, in her stroller, down the Colony past #191 so many times that Helen had finally sat down in the middle of the street, refusing to budge. Gracie had to carry her back to the house, pushing the stroller with one hand.

Number 191, on the land side of the Colony, spanned two lots. On half the double lot stood the house, the other half appeared to be a faded tennis court. Any net that had been there had been taken down long ago. Grass popped up inside cracks drawn like a child's scrawl all over the court. She wondered when anyone had last played there. Not for decades, perhaps.

The house was old and modest — perhaps one of the original homes built in the Colony. It was a one-story wood structure with white paint that was peeling off in places. Gracie had stood and stared at #191 until Jaden finally screamed for her to keep pushing; she wondered why she, who was sensitive to wallflowers of all stripes, human and otherwise, hadn't noticed the place before.

For all its lack of gloss, she found it charming. And it heightened her interest in Baxter's low-key master.

★ ★ ★

'Relationship Question number 2,489. When does flirting become something more serious?' Gracie asked. 'When does it cross the line?'

'If you have to ask, you haven't done it yet,' Will said. His eyes were closed, his pug nose pointed toward the sun.

'I flirted boldly,' Gracie said. 'I flirted until it was uncomfortable.'

'Flirting is always uncomfortable. Are you planning on sleeping with this man?' Will asked. 'If you are, it may be important to get a name. This isn't the eighties.'

Will was joining Gracie and Cricket at Joan's house to celebrate the Fourth of July — which to Malibu is what Bastille Day is to Paris. Gracie had awakened that morning to find yellow tape strewn across the fire lane in back of her house where everyone parked and no one was supposed to.

She'd stopped Lavender that morning as her security pickup truck made its turn, skirting the fire lane. 'What's with the yellow ribbon?' Gracie asked.

'Parties,' Lavender said, 'up and down the Colony — we don't want people parking here — we'll get fined.'

Gracie just nodded her head.

'It's the Fourth of July,' Lavender said. 'Hot dogs, corn on the cob, beer — Gracie, where have you been?'

'Of course it's the Fourth of July,' Gracie said, looking down the road. Here was a catering truck, there a party rental truck she'd seen at the house she shared with Kenny. Already she could see valet stations were being set up.

'Oh, shit, it's the Fourth of July,' Gracie said. 'I should have people over, right?'

'There's going to be fireworks,' Lavender said. 'Just like they have every year. Didn't you get your notice?'

'You already sound tired, Lavender,' Gracie said.

'You have no idea,' Lavender said. She tugged on a pack of cigarettes in her breast pocket. 'You check out number 152 yet?'

Gracie, her mind somewhere else, took a second to respond. '152?' Gracie asked. 'Yeah. Turns out I know number 152. For a number of years.'

'So?' Lavender asked.

'So,' Gracie said. 'So, I'm not sure.'

'So, it's your funeral,' Lavender laughed, and waved as she drove on.

Gracie ran back into her house to call Will and Cricket — it couldn't be the Fourth of July without them.

★   ★   ★

Lavender drove slowly down the Colony, toward the north end, the knot in her stomach growing

251

as it always did this time of year, this section of the Colony. She would always try to talk herself down, tell herself to relax. She would chide her nervousness, the way her voice caught in her throat, the way her heart beat faster.

'It's just one family,' Lavender repeated to herself. 'One out of fifty. Come on now.'

She rounded the dead end of the Colony, in front of the fence, which was padlocked. She didn't see the car. Good news, she thought. Good, good news. Maybe the kid wasn't going to be here this summer. Maybe the family had sent him away. He was probably in Europe. Somewhere in France — where was it where rich people went in the summer? The south of France.

She exhaled her anxiety. Here she was, a grown woman, afraid of a sixteen-year-old. Her grandmother would've chided her. She could hear her voice in her head, Granny E — 'Child, what are you afraid of? A boy, he's jus' a boy,' she would've said.

'He almost had me fired, Granny E,' Lavender would say.

' 'Almost' doesn't get it,' Granny Eva would reply. 'Ain't nothin' 'almost' — it is or it ain't.'

Actually, Lavender thought, Granny E would've used 'isn't' — she wasn't the 'ain't' type.

But the rest of it, Lavender knew she had right.

Just at that moment she saw the car. A black Range Rover with trademark tinted windows bore down on her, emerging out of nowhere, like

Death itself. Big piece of steel flying over speed bumps like they were gum wrappers. And then at the last split second, the wheels spinning, the smell of rubber burning. The sound of laughter. 'Ha-ha,' she could hear him. She could feel him thinking — Ha-ha, did you see the look on her face? Scared the bitch half to death.

Ha-ha.

Lavender continued down the road, her hands shaking at the wheel, saying a silent prayer that the day would pass quickly.

★   ★   ★

Lou was planning on spending the Fourth of July by himself — difficult to do on the most crowded stretch of beach in California during the most popular national holiday. He had rented in the Colony during the summer for years — always the same house and always at higher prices — and he knew the score. People he didn't know would be all over his deck, drunk, loud, from morning until all hours of the next morning. People he *did* know would be all over his deck, drunk, loud, from morning until all hours of the next morning. He was fucked either way, but for his plans, the Fourth of July mayhem would figure in perfectly.

Since his date with her, Lou had been thinking that if there were one person, one civilian, besides his psychiatrist, that he should tell about his plans, it was Gracie. He knew he shouldn't tell anyone on the outside, really. There was the unwritten law that if you tell one person a secret, that person will of course tell one person, and so on and so forth. But he felt as though she would understand his compulsion — maybe even forgive him. Was that what he was looking for? Lou thought. Forgiveness?

His child was away in Europe, on a boat trip outside of Greece with his ex-wife. He couldn't tell his ex-wife — she never had much of a sense of humor — and besides, she would use the information against him — for more money or threaten to cut off joint custody. His child and his ex-wife were unreachable for the next week or so — all he needed was three days to pull this off. They would never find out.

He had told his psychiatrist about his fantasy. 'I want to die,' Lou said.

'You need antidepressants,' the doctor had told him, reaching for his pen and his pad. 'Don't sweat it. Everybody's on 'em.' Then he pointed at Lou. 'And don't worry, the way they make 'em these days, they don't interfere with your hard-on. Thank God, right?'

'No, no,' Lou said, 'I don't really want to die. I want to have a funeral. I want to be . . . a participant . . . at my own funeral. An observer, if you will.' The doctor looked at him. 'I have to see what people really think of me.'

'What do you care what people think of you?' the doctor asked. 'It's none of your business. You're over sixty years old, for Christ's sake. I keep telling you that.'

'I don't know. It's an obsession. I've been in Hollywood too long. I've been to every bris, every bar mitzvah, every graduation, every engagement party, every wedding, every funeral.'

'So wait until your kid hits thirteen.'

'No,' Lou said. 'There's something about death that brings out the truth in people. I went to a guy's funeral last year — '

'Lonnie's?'

'No.'

'Murray's?'

'No, no — anyway, this guy was beloved — '

'Gordon's.'

'Yes, Gordon's,' Lou said. 'And you know Gordon. Everybody loved Gordo. Oh, the stories they told, up there on that podium. What a dear friend, what a wonderful husband, loving father, expert storyteller, consummate professional.'

The doctor nodded.

'But I'm sitting in the pews, I'm down there with the people, waiting my turn to kiss the ring of the dead guy' — Lou leaned forward — 'and all I'm hearing is shit. There's no muffled tears, no choked-back emotion. I'm just hearing shit. 'What do you think of Eisner's chances?' 'I gotta get out early — you going to the Lakers today?' 'This guy should have died before he made that last picture.''

Lou sat back again. 'Shit like that.'

'And?' the doctor asked. 'What do you expect? It's a Hollywood funeral. I keep telling you, people here would run over their own mothers for a two-picture deal. You're over sixty years old, Lou. You've got to grow up.'

Lou looked down at his hands. His elbows were on his knees. He felt suddenly vulnerable, a feeling he wasn't used to and usually squelched with a quarter bottle of Seagram's finest.

'I gotta know how it's going to go down,' Lou finally said. 'I have to know. Who's going to be taking off to see the Lakers? Who's going to go after my studio? Who's going to say I was a stupid sack of shit?'

Lou wondered why he was tearing up. Maybe he really was depressed. Maybe he needed one of those pills that wouldn't mess with his hard-on.

'You already know all the answers.'

'You don't understand,' Lou said. 'You know I never had a family — '

'You do now.'

'Barely.'

'You have a child,' the doctor pointed out.

Lou thought about his kid. The kid he thought he never wanted. How could he have been so stupid? How much time had he wasted avoiding women who wanted children with him? How many abortions had he had a hand in? He rubbed his face. He didn't want to even think about it. He hadn't even seen his own child being born. He had denied fatherhood up to the day the doctor called him with the facts, that this boy had his DNA. That Lou had a son.

What a son of a bitch he was.

'He'll never know,' Lou said. 'Besides, he's too young to understand.'

The doctor just shook his head. 'You are the ultimate malignant narcissist. And I've seen 'em all. So that's saying something.'

Lou smiled. 'So, what do you think I should wear?' he asked, leaning his body back against the couch, his arms sweeping outward.

★ ★ ★

The partying started at 9:01 in the morning. Gracie and Will were out on the deck, awaiting Cricket's arrival. Cricket was packing her three kids and a nanny to haul over to the Colony; Jorge was busy filming a show that week in New York. Gracie and Will lay on chaise longues while Jaden played in her plastic tub as Ana sprayed her with water from the hose. Ana had told Gracie a week ago, in no uncertain terms, that she was going to babysit Jaden today. Gracie was convinced that Ana thought Gracie would lose Jaden to the crowds.

Will and Gracie looked at each other as Mexican wedding music suddenly started to blast from underneath the deck.

'What is that sound?' Will asked.

'I believe it's ranchera music,' Gracie replied. 'Ana?'

Ana nodded.

'Please make it stop,' Will said. 'Cinderella needs her beauty rest.' He patted his chest and closed his eyes.

Gracie shrugged and walked down the steps to the beach. The house was up on thirty-year-old pylons covered in noxious black tar. The shade underneath the house was a magnet for all kinds of interesting life forms — men posing half nude for *International Male* magazine, women in neon bikinis posing topless for *Muscle & Fitness*, couples making out, kids playing with cigarettes. And now, several Latino families out to enjoy the Fourth of July, celebrating Independence Day

257

with a boom box and a cooler full of Coronas.

Gracie stood there for a moment, wondering if she had the heart (or guts) to inform her 'guests' that they were sort of, really, absolutely trespassing. Their boldly colored blankets with Pepsi and Coors logos were spread out. The kids were already making use of the large pieces of driftwood jutting out of the ground at various angles, half buried in sand and rocks. Babies were already piling sand into their gaping, precious mouths, the grown-ups were sitting back on the palms of their hands, taking in the surf and the first beer of the day with equal enthusiasm.

Gracie took one look and they took one look at her, and there was a crucial moment, a moment when all manner of decisions were made. Then Gracie waved and smiled, and the families all waved and smiled back, and then she walked right back up the stairs.

'No luck?' Will asked.

'They said they're very sorry, and they'll turn it down,' Gracie lied.

'I can see that,' Will replied, his voice loud over the ranchera music. Ana was now dancing with Jaden on the deck. 'I want you to rest up. According to Internet estimates, there are fifteen parties between here and the twenties.' (The 'twenties' being the houses at the other end of the Colony.)

'Do you think he'll be at one of these parties?' Gracie asked, expertly changing the subject.

'Every person in Los Angeles is going to be in the Colony. Of course he will,' Will said. 'Now work on your tan. Everyone looks better with a little color.'

Gracie, with her paper-white skin, situated herself back under an umbrella watching while Jaden and Ana spun to the beat of the boom box and laughed.

Finally Will and Gracie leaned back in their chaise longues and closed their eyes in an attempt to rest up for the big day.

★   ★   ★

There was nothing that could have prepared Gracie for her first official Fourth of July in Malibu — not Vietnam, not Iraq, not the Fred Segal Annual Sale.

Everywhere she looked were bodies: in her driveway, under her house, outside her kitchen windows, south toward the pier, north into the sun. And every house in the Colony seemed to be hosting its own Fourth of July party. Each house vibrated and groaned as scores of people streamed out onto the beach. Music clashed with music clashed with dogs and parrots and forced laughter.

Gracie was miserable.

Gracie, Will, and Cricket had worked their way down from the north end of the Colony, as per Will's instructions. Will had jotted a map of the Colony down on a napkin — Leo lived just north of the Colony, then Sting, then the head of UTA, then Beyoncé, who was renting (and had forgotten or neglected to order valet), and on and on and on. As they walked north along the sand, skipping the houses from the hundreds through the eighties (Will had spied too many children), Gracie experienced a sense of vertigo — she realized she was already claustrophobic — even walking along the beach in the open air. Just the thought of attending five parties in a row sent her into a tailspin.

But Will was not to be denied. Dressed in khaki shorts and a linen shirt, with leather flip-flops gracing his waxed feet, he was in his best homo-couture. His black and gray sunglasses, the latest in a string of design triumphs from Marc Jacobs, set off his new array of carefully devised highlights. He declared himself homo-fabulous.

Gracie, according to Will, was less divine. After he expressed fear and then anguish over her choice of last year's Juicy sweats and a long-sleeved dull gray T-shirt, Will had flown through her closet and insisted on a bathing suit/sarong combination that Gracie felt made her look like a woman on the prowl for a third husband. Will made it clear that this was the look he was after and the look she should embrace.

'But I've only been married once, and I'm not on the prowl,' Gracie said.

'Then what are you doing, Ms. Boldly Flirtatious?' Will asked.

Cricket walked in, sweating profusely as she carried two small children and a sack of sand toys, followed by her nanny toting a third small child and a beach umbrella. 'I can't park in the fire lane! They threatened to two me!'

'But I have plenty of parking out there,' Gracie said.

'No, you don't,' Cricket said. 'There's five cars, a valet, and a giant bouncie in your driveway. I parked outside the gates and walked.'

Welcome to Malibu on the Fourth of July. Good luck getting a parking space.

FIRST PARTY

Leo's house. At least Will was pretty sure it was Leo's house. It may not have been Leo's house at all — in fact, there was no proof it was Leo's house. There were no pictures displayed, no Gisele sightings, no evidence, in fact, that anyone actually lived there. Because there was no furniture — no tables, no chairs, no couches, no TVs, no rugs, no nothing.

What there was, Gracie ruefully noted, was an abundance of excessively beautiful, excessively young people.

'This is ridiculous,' Gracie said to Will. 'People like this don't exist outside of Versace ads.'

She was watching a girl, fifteen, sixteen, float from one end of the deck to the other, beckoned toward an open-air bar and the promise of illicit, fruit-flavored vodka. She was wearing a bikini over a body for which clothes were an unnecessary burden.

'Oh, but they do, as you can see,' Will said. 'I call them 'The Blanks.''

He watched eagerly as a young man with blond hair and tawny skin, seen all the better

261

with an open-to-the-waist shirt and jeans that accented the kind of package that had been opened many, many times, walked by.

'Hello, Jon Voight,' Will said, waving a bottle of Neutrogena. 'I do sunscreen!'

Gracie shuddered at the reference to *Midnight Cowboy*.

'And the Blanks are?' she asked.

'Look at the expressions,' Will said. 'It's not Botox, it's that heady mixture of youth and stupidity.'

'Maybe it's disinterest.'

'Trust me, these people aren't 'Spellers,'' Will said.

'That's it. What's the point of me staying here?' Gracie said.

They took off, the median age of the party dropping two decades the moment they walked off the deck.

SECOND PARTY

'What's that smell?' Will said, beating at the smoky air in front of his face.

'It's called marijuana,' Gracie coughed. A bearded man was thrashing bongo drums in a living room covered from floor to ceiling with what Will claimed were East Asian textiles.

'How retro. You know, this could be like the Swan of houses,' Will said, looking around. 'Look at the bones.'

Gracie looked around. She felt as though she were in a sequence from *Helter Skelter*. The women lying on the low couches could be stand-ins for Squeaky Fromme et al.

'Leave?' Gracie asked.

'Too late. Cricket has been indoctrinated,' Will said.

Cricket was in a corner, about to share a joint with a man who could have been a Cheech or a Chong (Gracie couldn't remember the difference).

THIRD PARTY (after dragging Cricket from the second party and the clutches of Cheech/Chong)

Very many famous people in a too-small venue. Gracie bumped into Barbra Streisand. Will had a conversation with Michelle Pfeiffer. Cricket, stoned, asked Jim Carrey to marry her. Mel Gibson clutched a Diet Coke and scowled at the water.

'I'm the only person I don't recognize here,' Gracie said.

'I know, isn't it divine?' Will said. 'Michelle's so animated, it's like she's on beta-blockers.'

'Do you know her?'

'Of course not,' Will said. 'But look at her. She's so ethereal, like Cate Blanchett from *Lord of the Rings*. If she had a penis, I'd be married.'

Matthew McConaughey squeezed by, pinching Gracie's butt as he passed.

'Oh my God,' Gracie said. 'I'm in love.'

'You're so easy,' Will said. 'That was arbitrary harassment.'

'What's your point?' Gracie asked. 'I'm forty-one and a gorgeous man just pinched my butt. I can die now.'

'I hear he's hung like Wilbur,' Will said.

'Wilbur?' Gracie asked.

'The horse, you idiot,' Will said. 'What is happening to the world of cultural reference?'

★　★　★

Two parties later, and finally they had made it to friendly territory. Number 152. Lou's house. Gracie didn't recognize his house from the beach — the architecture was obscured by people in various forms of dress and undress lying on the expansive deck.

By this time Gracie was nearly in tears. She didn't know if she could fight her way back home, and she was thankful for the respite. 'I'm not strong enough,' she said to Will as they walked up Lou's steps, past the bodies, whimpering as he stroked her hair.

But Will, feeling a little brave and a lot more drunk, was eager to attend more parties, so he left her to her own devices.

'Will you be okay?' he asked.

'I think so,' she said. Then, 'What happened to Cricket?'

Will looked around. 'Oh, shit. I think I lost her at the A-list party.'

He blew her a kiss and teetered off. Gracie walked onto Lou's deck and crossed over to the open door leading to his living room.

‘Lou?’ she asked, placing one foot gingerly in front of the other.

‘Lou?’ she continued as she looked around his living room, passing the kitchen. As loud as it was outside, the place was quiet. A tomb.

‘Lou?’ she asked again.

She looked at the stairs leading to what she imagined were the upstairs bedrooms. She looked around again and decided that they were friends, it was okay, he wouldn't mind if she went looking for him.

She walked up the stairs and into the master bedroom. It opened up onto a balcony. The view was magnificent, better than Joan's (of course, she wouldn't tell her). The bed was neatly made. Several books were on a side table. Gracie walked onto the balcony and sank into the view.

‘Gracie,’ Lou said. He was standing behind her.

Gracie turned to see him and immediately felt ashamed. What was she doing, standing here, walking through his house as though she owned it? As though she owned him?

‘I don't mind,’ Lou said, as though reading her mind. ‘You were looking for me?’

‘Honestly, I was looking for somewhere to rest before I went on to my place,’ Gracie said. ‘Even when I get there, I know I'm going to be greeted by mobs. You didn't tell me how scary Fourth of July in Malibu is.’

‘You didn't ask,’ Lou said.

Gracie stared at him. The way he was looking

out at the water. Did she smell scotch on his breath? Did she even know what scotch smelled like? How could she be forty-one and not know what scotch smelled like?

'Are you okay?' she asked.

'Hey, I had a good time the other night,' Lou said. 'A really good time. How come you didn't marry me instead of that knucklehead?'

'First of all, you didn't ask. And second, you're talking about your number two guy,' Gracie chided. 'Your right-hand man.'

'Ah, he's a piece of shit,' Lou said, 'but he's my piece of shit, I guess.'

'I better be going — ' Gracie said. She wasn't even sure why she was standing there.

'No,' Lou said, grabbing her arm and then just as quickly letting it go. 'I need to talk to you.'

Gracie looked at him.

'Sit down,' Lou said. Then, sensing her hesitation, 'Please.'

She sat on one of the no doubt very expensive but highly uncomfortable wrought-iron chairs on his balcony.

'Am I getting a little color?' she asked, looking down at her arms.

'You know what you look like in that getup?' Lou asked. 'I was looking at you and I just realized. You look like my fourth wife.'

'Really?' Gracie asked. 'Because I was really going for the third-wife look.'

'Well, you missed it,' Lou said. 'Listen, Gracie, I have something to tell you. But I don't want to tell you unless you can guarantee me that you'll

266

keep it a secret.' He looked her straight in the eye.

'Oh, my God,' Gracie said. 'You're gay.'

Lou smiled, but he said, 'It's not a joke.'

'Let me think,' Gracie said. 'To be honest, I'm not entirely sure that I'm trustworthy.'

She sat there and thought for a moment. Could she be trusted with a secret? A highly secret secret?

'Go ahead,' Gracie finally said, 'shoot.'

'Are you sure?' Lou asked. 'Because I feel like I want to tell you, but it's a burden, what I have to say.'

'Then why tell me?'

'Good question,' Lou said. 'Here's the sad part. You're the only person who will understand.'

Gracie leaned back. So here it was. He was going to level with her, tell her the reason for the shadow behind his eyes. Was she ready for it? Here was real intimacy, something she hadn't experienced with her husband since . . .

'I'm going to kill myself,' Lou said.

Gracie gasped. And then she sprang up and started hitting him. 'You idiot!' she screamed. 'You stupid, stupid, dumb, stupid — '

'Stop!' Lou said, grabbing her flailing arms. 'Gracie, stop!'

'You have everything to live for!' Gracie yelled. 'You have a child, you have, you have . . . a really nice car, and the women — Lou, think of all the women you haven't slept with yet! Think of them, for God's sakes, Lou!'

'I'm not really going to kill myself!' Lou

said, grabbing her from behind, his arms wrapped around her back, pinning her arms to her sides.

'I'm going to kill you!' Gracie yelled. 'Why are you screwing with me?! I'm emotionally vulnerable!'

She started struggling again —

'No fucking kidding,' Lou said. He was still holding on to her. The pleasure of feeling a man's arms wrapped around her was not lost on Gracie, even if it was solely to keep her from hurting him.

'Are you ready to listen to me?' he asked, still holding on to her.

Gracie just nodded. He started to let go. 'Just . . . don't let go,' she said.

Lou kept his arms wrapped around her. 'Okay, you're calm now, right?'

Gracie nodded again.

'I'm going to kill myself' — he squeezed her as she struggled again — 'but I'm not going to kill myself.'

'What do you mean?' Gracie asked.

'Gracie, it's like this.' Lou looked at her. 'I have this fantasy. It's something I've thought about for a long time. I want to go to my own funeral.'

Gracie shook her head, disgusted.

'You're sick,' Gracie said. 'You need help. I hear the new antidepressants don't mess with your, you know — '

'I'm not depressed,' he said. 'I'm obsessed. For the last couple years, I've been to more funerals, and I got to thinking about my own, and you know what? I want to be there.'

'But you would be there . . . at your own funeral,' Gracie said. 'Lou, how is it possible that you're this sick? You're supposed to be the rock!'

Lou shook his head. 'I just . . . want to experience it,' he said, 'and then, a couple days later, I resurface. It becomes one of the great Hollywood stories. But now I know who my real friends are.'

Gracie looked at him. Lonely, lonely Lou.

'Real friends?' Gracie asked. 'You know how many real friends I have? Three. And that's a lot. You don't need to do this. I'll save you the trouble. I'll tell you right now how many real friends you have.' She made a zero with her thumb and forefinger. 'You want real friends? Live somewhere in Ohio.'

'You're my friend,' Lou said.

'How can I be your friend, Lou?' Gracie looked at him. 'I don't even know you.'

Lou let go of her and looked out at the water.

'Can I talk you out of this?' she asked.

Lou just stared at the water. 'Did you ever see *A Star Is Born*?'

'The first, the second, or the third?' Gracie asked.

'I'm old. I'm talking the first or the second.'

'Good, because frankly, not a big fan of Barbra Streisand's hair in the third,' Gracie said. 'That Orphan Annie thing. Not attractive.'

'That's how I'm going to do it. I'm going into the water tonight. I'll leave my clothes on the beach, a note.'

'I'm begging you, Lou,' Gracie said. 'You don't need to do this. Please, for my sake, for your child's sake, please don't.'

Suddenly Lou pointed. 'Hey, did you see that? A dolphin. Dolphins are good luck.'

18

Do You Feel Fireworks?

Despite everything she'd been through in the last couple of months, Gracie had never felt so depressed as she did when she left Lou's house. And it wasn't because she thought every single female in sight had a better body than she had, although that would have been enough.

Lou, the one man in the world that she took for being a sane, well-adjusted, upstanding serial monogamist, was just as nutty as the rest of them. That he was willing to create an elaborate hoax by faking his own death so he could attend his own funeral, all the while taking notes on his so-called friends, proved beyond a reasonable doubt that he was damaged goods. Lou was just another tragic figure from the Land of Broken Toys.

Gracie meandered down the beach, much like Jaden did when she didn't want to go home but had no choice in the matter. Was there anything Gracie could do? She'd tried to reason with him. She'd tried yelling at him. She'd pointed out the damage he could be doing to his son.

She'd even informed him, in serious tones, that this endeavor was an incredible turnoff. That she had been this close to sleeping with him. Yes, maybe it wasn't the ultimate threat

271

— she was not a supermodel; her vagina was not a weapon of mass destruction. But still, she had felt that flicker of something. Was it anticipation? Before meeting the Unknown Suitor, she had forgotten that flicker — her flicker had flicked out.

Nothing could move him. And so she'd left. She hadn't touched him, she hadn't kissed his cheek. She'd left not only his physical being but also the promise of more with him. She was done.

This guy was cooked. And Gracie's track record with men was now officially 0-2.

A strange thought entered Gracie's mind as she passed the party at the Boners' and walked up the beach toward the Mexican wedding which had been at Joan's house. Are firefighters this wacko? What about those guys working construction? Where are the real men?

Another thought entered her mind. The number of men she knew presently and would sleep with had now officially been whittled down to one. And she was determined to sleep with him — before she found out that he, too, was just another wack job.

Otherwise she just might be forced to close up shop for the rest of her life.

★ ★ ★

Jaden skipped her nap that day. Who could blame her? Who could sleep seated front row center at the largest outdoor concert in town? Gracie, Jaden, and Cricket's kids stayed inside

272

for the rest of the day, avoiding the heat and listening to Raffi songs (when they could hear him) and watching *Finding Nemo* so many times that even the youngest children had memorized Bruce the Shark's lines. Cricket, who sounded increasingly 'relaxed' as the day went on, interrupted every twenty minutes or so to make sure that all three of her children were still breathing.

Finally, just as the sun went down, the fireworks started. The kids screamed and ran out on the deck and Gracie wrapped Jaden in a blanket and sat on a chaise, her daughter cradled in her arms, watching color after color explode above her head, then disappear into the black water.

Gracie forgot about her marriage; she forgot about her exhusband. She forgot about her future, about her past. All that existed was this moment. She and the warmth of her drowsy child and the delighted squeals of toddlers and the rhythm of the waves and the people huddled underneath her house and scattered out on the sand. And the explosions, each one more beautiful than the last.

'Okay, God,' Gracie said out loud (though who could hear her over the fireworks?). 'I think I've found it. This is happiness.'

★　★　★

Gracie waited until she had seen the last of the fireworks, the ultimate display of patriotism, red lights bleeding into white bleeding into blue.

People clapped and cheered, the loudest being the ones probably newest to this country, the families huddled under her house. And then, just like that, the festivities were over. As people gathered up their blankets and boom boxes, the last of their orange sodas, and their sleeping children and headed for the Surfrider exit, Gracie held her own sleeping child, opened the sliding glass door into the kitchen, bid farewell to Cricket's nanny and her children and Ana, who had decided to call it a night, and walked upstairs to Jaden's room.

Gracie was out of breath by the time she made it upstairs. Jaden was not a small child with featherweight bones. The fact was, she was deceptively heavy. She was made of sturdy stock — descendant as she was of people who worked fields long before they worked computers.

Gracie rolled Jaden onto her bed, took off her shoes, and draped her comforter over her body.

She had almost forgotten that by this time Lou would have killed himself.

*   *   *

Sam knew better. He knew it was a fool's errand. It must have been the fireworks or the smell of the day — hot dogs, the ocean, sunscreen, bonfires.

Something about this particular Fourth of July brought out a sentiment he usually commandeered with little or no effort — nostalgia.

He was overcome by nostalgia. As he made his way through the July Fourth crowds negotiating

274

their way back to their Toyotas, Hondas, and Saturns, he wondered why.

Why was he feeling this way now, today?

Normally he could pass a mother holding on to a sleeping child, or guiding a toddler by the hand from the beach, without so much as a glance. Their lives had no bearing on his. He had so little in common with the common folk he did not recognize the usual parameters of everyday life. This is my son. This is my daughter. This is my mother. My father. My sister.

He had a sister. She was his first love. His eyes would track her, his mother had told him, from the time he was born. He would only smile for her. His first laugh was at the sight of her face. He loved no one else as much and never would.

His mother told him that she told his sister, his only sibling, to remember his love — because it was the greatest love she had ever witnessed. To remember the love of her little brother — because no one would ever love her as much in her lifetime.

His mother.

As it turns out, it wasn't much true. His sister had found a husband, had two daughters of her own — or were they sons? Sam couldn't remember. There were none of the standard markers that normal people used to define their relationships — no cards, no phone calls. No 'I'll see you soon.' No 'I'll come up during Christmas.' Nothing.

★ ★ ★

275

And it was his fault. All of it.

He had started doing drugs in high school. His parents had sent him to boarding school in a desperate attempt to separate him from the booming drug scene in San Francisco's Haight-Ashbury. But it was a tactic as tardy as it was ill conceived. There were more drugs in boarding school than even on the streets of the Castro. And they were within spitting distance — here was an ounce of coke he could score off his roommate, there was the new thrill — heroin — introduced to him by his TA.

Then his father died. But big deal, Sam thought at the time — he hardly knew his father. It's that 'old family' shit — everyone getting by on traditions and gestures and not dealing with reality. Your son is on drugs, deal with it. Your daughter is about to enter an abusive marriage to get out of the house, deal with it.

The war. Did he sign up for it out of spite, or was it reverence for his father's military background? Sam couldn't decide, still.

He hadn't figured it all out. He didn't know what he was doing. Sam had gotten his ass fried a million ways to Sunday, and he still didn't know what he was doing.

He was fifty-three years old, and he didn't have a clue.

His mother must be close to eighty, Sam thought. If she was still alive.

And then, as he walked through the entryway, opening the chain-link fence with his key, he was seized by a thought: Surely his mother would have forgiven him by now.

He walked onto the Colony, bustling with Mercedeses and SUVs, filling up with men, women, and children heading home to Del Air, to Brentwood, to Beverly Hills. He avoided eye contact. He walked swiftly and quietly. He knew this feeling, he found comfort in its familiarity. He felt like a man about to commit a crime.

I have to kiss that woman, Sam thought. He was thinking of nothing but her mouth.

★　★　★

Gracie had put Jaden to bed and was downstairs in her kitchen when she heard the doorbell ring. How she heard it was a mystery, even to her — but it showed her how quickly a crowd could dissipate, how swift the ending could be to a chaotic day.

She figured it must be Will — parties were winding down and surely he had either found his Prince Charming or given up.

Gracie padded down the stairs in her bare feet, anxious for the day's postmortem, in which Will would dissect each party, from the partyers to the libations to the homes themselves.

Gracie opened the door, a smile already alighting on her face. She was ready to laugh.

The porch light fell upon the person standing in front of her in such a way that it formed a halo effect. All she could make out was the outline of a tall, imposing figure with thick, wavy hair — her eyes focused, separating light from dark, and within moments colors formed: the orange shorts, a white shirt.

This was not her homo friend with his blondish hair and linen.

Images dashed through Gracie's head — most of them developed from too many afternoons walking on the treadmill and watching Oprah. Would he drag her by the hair and rape her in the living room? Would he chop her body up and toss her fingers into the blender?

How could she have been so stupid as to flirt with a complete stranger? Even if he had, for argument's sake, saved her wretched life. Just so he could murder her in her best friend's living room while her child slept upstairs!

'Hello,' he said.

Gracie's hand had been frozen to the side of the door; she'd been standing just as she had when she opened it. Right then, she decided she was no good in an ominous situation. She should really move to a neighborhood where nothing bad could ever befall her, where no one masturbated on the beach under her window, where seals did not turn up dead on the sand, where shaved-head gang members didn't gather at four o'clock in the morning.

She would plan to move to the cheap streets.

'Are you all right?' he asked. He rocked back on his heels.

'I'm fine,' Gracie croaked. 'I'm just . . . can I help you?'

She straightened her spine. She didn't want her posture to scream 'victim.' Crime victims had bad posture — this much she'd learned from afternoon television.

'My friend should be here any second,' Gracie

continued in a blur of words. 'He's a black belt in . . . oh, God, what's the name of that thing where you . . . '

She made a stance with her knees bent and her hands, fingers together, angled up.

He reached forward with his hands, wrapping his fingers around hers in a move that was both gentle and charged.

Gracie stopped breathing. She was still standing with her knees bent, one leg forward, as though she were about to pounce. But he had his hands around hers. Her mind had stopped computing.

She was really, really not good in ominous situations.

And then, still holding her hands, he took one step forward. And let go of her hands and wrapped his around her face. And kissed her.

Her hands went limp at her sides. Her knees buckled like a schoolgirl in a melodramatic 1930s movie. He was literally holding her up by her jaw.

The kiss lasted almost as long as the last presidential address to the country, Gracie thought, but with more substance.

And Gracie hadn't stopped thinking the whole time.

This was what was going on in her mind:

'Oh, my GOD! He's going to strangle me! No, he's kissing me! We're . . . kissing? Oh, my GODGODGODGOD, what a kiss, holy shit, this is some kiss, oh, JESUS, it's like unbelievable, who kisses like this? This mouth — it's so warm and soft and it's like the best pashmina, but not the illegal kind from whatever that country is with all the mountains — ooh, I love that beard — I love that beard — why have I never had a man with a beard? — oh, no, I'm going to have that beard-face thing — that red face — my face will be all burned up by the beard, but damn, this is good — this is an epic moment in my life — there's barely any tongue, I love that — I don't like a lot of tongue, frankly — there's no sloppiness whatsoever, I mean Kenny was always kind of sloppy, who cares about Kenny — oh, God, I hope he doesn't want to sleep with me — I have to lose weight — maybe with the lights off that's okay. But my inner thighs ... What if he has AIDS? He doesn't have AIDS, of course, he doesn't have AIDS. Does he have AIDS? No! But still, should I use a condom? Of course I should use a condom — don't you watch Oprah — I don't have any condoms — God, I hope he has a condom — oh God, I hope he doesn't have a condom, if he has a condom that means he's EXPECTING me to sleep with him — and screw him, I'm not easy — '

The kiss ended in a draw. His hands were still on her face, and whether he knew it or not, his hands were the only thing between Gracie's body and the floor. They were warm and strong and calloused and they could have held her up forever, as far as Gracie was concerned.

His face was on hers, her cheek to his. She could feel his breath. She assumed he could feel hers, but she wasn't entirely sure she was breathing again.

She found her voice in a triumphant return to earth.

'I've had a C-section,' she said.

He didn't respond. He had her up now, against the door. His face to hers.

'So there's this scar. And my belly.' She tried to look down, grimacing toward her stomach as though it were an old friend who had recently let her down.

She sighed. 'I didn't shave today. I can't get into that whole waxing thing, it's just not me.'

SHUT UP, Gracie thought to herself. FOR THE LOVE OF GOD, WOMAN, SHUT THE HELL UP!

'I'm getting gray hair, and if you want to know the truth, I haven't slept with anyone in — '

Oh, Jesus, Gracie thought, he's doing that thing, that thing he did when he carried her out of the water, and lifted her up like she was Cleopatra and he was her slave — no, better yet, like that Lina Wertmüller film that Gracie thought Madonna and her cute husband completely screwed up but where her biceps looked amazing. But somehow scary, and yet she's still fabulous, which is, of course, the mark of a great star. He picked her up like that Italian guy, like Marcello Mastroianni, and brought her inside the house, and somehow, Gracie was able to lift one limp, lifeless hand up to indicate 'stairs' and 'up' — and then he was holding her in his arms as he walked up the stairs, taking two at a time, not one, and Gracie became afraid, suddenly, for his health — after all, she was not Jaden's size. We're talking some weight here. I mean, I'm not a candidate for that new stomach surgery that the singer did — and she looks so great, but she always did have a beautiful face, let's be real, Gracie thought, but I could lose, like, fifteen, twelve, seven pounds.

Gracie wondered why she always seemed to be revising everything, even life. Was this the burden of a frustrated writer?

He kicked open a door lightly (Gracie slightly worried about the scuff he would leave and how she would explain it to Joan) and carried her to the bed and set her down and looked at her. Gracie watched him looking at her and defined that look: He was looking at Gracie like she was a juicy piece of rib eye and he hadn't eaten in weeks. But he was taking his time, enjoying that moment before you actually stick your fork in. That scintilla of anticipation — breathing in the aroma of the meat, appreciating its thickness, the cut, the color, he was appreciating the whole package. All the senses are alive in the penultimate, keyed up for the climactic moment.

In other words, it was not a good time to hear the words 'Gracie? Come out, come out, wherever you are!'

Followed by footsteps.

'Gracie?' Will was saying. 'Are you playing hide-and-go-seek? Who sleeps at this hour?'

And then she heard him trip on the stairs.

'Blast!' she heard him say. 'What a stupid place for stairs!'

Gracie looked at Clint (still her pet name for him) and he looked at her. She had no idea what to say, no idea what to do. She couldn't stay there, and she couldn't leave.

And then he smiled. His teeth were white but not that scary, bonded white, and the corners of his eyes were accented by a fan of wrinkles —

'Wow,' she said, 'what a smile you have.'

He kissed her just as Will knocked on the door and peered in —

'Gracie?' he asked.

Gracie sat up on her elbows and looked over her shoulder while Clint stood by the bed.

She couldn't help but notice all systems were go in his orange shorts.

Neither could Will as his eyes adjusted to the dark.

'Oh, *madre mia!*' Will said cheerily. 'Did I interrupt something?'

'Not yet,' Gracie said, 'but you could wait five minutes and come back. It could be even more interesting.'

'Hi, there,' Will said, looking Clint up and down and resting his eyes momentarily on the orange shorts. 'I'm Will, and I'll be your annoying intruder for the night.'

Clint shook his hand. Gracie could tell that Will was impressed by the whole package. He had to be — even Clint's handshake belonged to that species of man who belonged on those old Marlboro bill-boards she'd loved as a child.

'And you are?' Will asked, flashing his most ingratiating, space-between-his-front-teeth smile, the one most often reserved for potential clients.

'Sam,' the man said. 'Sam Knight.'

'Like the Round Table or the hours between seven and mid-night?' Will asked. 'Actually 'seven' would be more like 'evening' — but then 'Sam Evening' wouldn't be a good name, now, would it?'

Gracie could tell Will's excitement meter was off the charts; he could hardly keep his voice within a normal octave.

'Will,' Gracie admonished.

'I know, I know, but don't you understand? It's just too good, the whole thing, I have to know,' Will said.

'He's drunk,' Gracie said, turning to the man whose name was to be deciphered. 'You don't have to answer him. Sam. Sam Knight.'

'Or, Sam Night?' Will asked. 'And yes, I am drunk.'

'It's like the Round Table,' Sam said, crossing his arms over his waist, but not because he felt defensive. He was trying not to reach out for Gracie. He knotted himself up to keep from grabbing her.

'Sam Knight,' Gracie said. 'I like it.'

'It's like a fairy tale,' Will said, 'except the princess is going through a nasty divorce with a big fat loser who's dating Britney Spears and living in the Colony.'

'It's a Malibu fairy tale,' Gracie said.

Sam stood there, and Will stood there, and Gracie remained lying back on her elbows. For a moment the pause in the room became pregnant.

And then suddenly Will said, 'Well, it was nice meeting you, Mr. Knight.'

'Sam's fine. Or just Knight,' Sam said, shaking Will's outstretched hand again.

'A thought just popped into my head,' Will said, looking Sam up and down. 'A knight requires a sizable lance — '

'I don't want you driving,' Gracie said.

'I have no intention of getting behind the wheel,' Will said. 'I know what all these people have been doing in Malibu. You couldn't force me to be out on PCH. Even though I know you'd like it . . . '

And now Sam was escorting Will out the door as he blathered on —

'And don't worry about Cricket,' Will said. 'Miss Parents Magazine is downstairs, passed out on the couch.'

And Sam closed the door.

He turned back to Gracie, who was about to apologize for her friend —

Sam moved toward her, put his finger on her mouth with as little weight as needed, and then he kissed her again.

'When you're right, you're right,' Gracie said as she came up for air and rolled on top of him and kissed him as though she had never kissed before in her life, had never lived before this moment.

★ ★ ★

Gracie had heard, and believed, that life was made up of moments. She had believed this primarily after giving birth (being cut open) to Jaden. She could think of so many moments as a mother that made up her life — so many that they crowded out earlier moments — losing her virginity, getting married, the first time she had a book published.

But her first kiss with Sam would definitely make it into the top five.

The top five being:

- Jaden's first smile, which happened to be at Gracie's breast.
- Jaden's first laugh.
- Jaden's first step.
- The first time Jaden said 'Mama.'
- The first time Sam and Gracie kissed.

'But did you sleep with him?' Will asked, first thing in the morning. 'Did you do the deed? Did you make the beast with two backs?'

'I didn't,' Gracie said as she scooted around the kitchen, making coffee and generally floating somewhere two feet above the ground.

'*Quel horror!* I don't understand,' Will said. 'As a gay man, your foot is always on the accelerator.'

'I liked it,' Gracie said. 'I don't think either of us were prepared for the first kiss, much less the feature presentation.'

'Strange,' Will said. 'I will never understand the Way of the Breeder.'

'Well, thank God you don't need to,' Gracie said.

Cricket walked into the kitchen, holding her head as though it were a vase that had been thrown on the floor —

'Since when does pot give you a hangover?' Cricket asked.

'Since it's mixed with five shots of tequila and a tab of Ecstasy,' Will replied.

'I don't do drugs!' Cricket said. 'Please don't tell my children!'

'Cricket, your kids can barely talk,' Will said.

Cricket looked at him, squinting her eyes against the bright sunlight. 'The sun wants to kill me,' she said, pointing toward the kitchen windows.

'If you're going to be an over-forty single mother, you're going to have to get used to these kinds of things,' Will said. 'Hangovers, drug talks with your three-year-old . . . '

'Who says you're going to be a single mom?' Gracie asked. 'What have you done?'

'You didn't tell her?' Cricket asked Will.

Will shook his head as he went to take coffee mugs down from a cabinet. 'Number one, it's too personal, and I thought you should be the one to say something, and number two, it totally slipped my mind. How did that happen?'

'You're off your game,' Gracie said.

'It's all because I saw Brad Pitt last night,' Will admitted. 'I'm off-kilter. My systems are down — it's like I'm a fuse box — I saw his face, and BOOM! No more lights on in the house!'

'Did I see him?' Cricket asked.

'Not in the sense that your eyes could focus,' Will said. 'But you bumped into him and he said 'Excuse me,' and you said, I'm para-phrasing, 'Watch it, pretty boy' — '

Cricket covered her mouth with her hand and squealed. 'I was rude to Brad Pitt?'

'She was rude to Brad Pitt?' Gracie asked.

'It was one of the proudest moments of my life — I'll probably flash on it in my dying hours. It

287

was that important.'

Cricket sat down on the floor and put her head in her hands.

'Can we talk about this 'single mother' insanity?' Gracie said. 'I need to know what's going on.'

'What's going on is that Jorge and I are getting a divorce,' Cricket announced. 'That's why I was out all night, drinking and being rude to movie stars.' And then she burst into tears, wiping her nose with the back of her sleeve.

'Are those my pajamas?' Gracie asked.

'Well, they're not mine,' Will said. 'I don't believe in flannel as concept or actuality.'

'Cricket, you don't have to get divorced just because I'm getting divorced,' Gracie said, ignoring Will's harangue against her beloved, defenseless flannel.

'It's not about you. I can't take the deception anymore,' Cricket said.

'Jorge does not cheat on you,' Gracie said.

'Not now,' Cricket said, 'but someday!'

Will started pouring the coffee. 'Far be it from me to say, but do you really believe in preemptive divorce? Isn't that like not having sex so you don't have sex?'

'This is crazy,' Gracie said. 'Seriously, Cricket, you're scaring me.'

'You wouldn't understand,' Cricket said. 'You were never really happy with Kenny — it's not like you lost your best friend.'

'But I *was* happy with Kenny,' Gracie said.

Her friends looked at her.

'Well, I thought I was. For a while,' Gracie

said. 'Early on. The first few years.' She looked at them. 'Days?'

Will yawned and shook his head.

'Hours?' Gracie amended. Always revising.

'Digging a hole you can stumble into?' Will asked.

'The truth is, we were good together,' Gracie said. 'We were like a well-oiled machine.'

'That's so exciting!' Will said. 'Please, God, let me be a part of a well-oiled machine someday!'

'Jorge is younger than me,' Cricket suddenly said.

'So far so good,' Gracie said.

'He has more energy than I do, he has . . . needs,' Cricket said.

'Go on,' Will said. 'But let me sit down and get a clearer picture.' Will had always had a mini-crush on Jorge, the kind that only homosexual men have for straight men — rare, fleeting, but impactful.

He sat down on a Shabby Chic chair, put his feet up on the glass coffee table, and closed his eyes, with his hands at his temple.

'Ready,' he said.

'He wants sex,' Cricket said. 'A lot. Sometimes twice a day.'

Gracie grabbed her heart and moaned.

Will stood up and applauded. 'Finally, a straight man who speaks Homo.' And then sat down.

'It's not funny,' Cricket said. 'I can't keep up with him. I have three kids under four and a half years. It's impossible — Gracie, you understand.'

'You must get a divorce,' Gracie said. 'There's

no other way. It's a deal-breaker.'

Cricket looked at her, her long, beautiful face sinking.

'Really?'

'No!' Gracie said. 'But maybe you can rent him out to friends?'

'Does he masturbate?' Will asked. His eyes were closed again.

Cricket wrinkled her unwrinkled forehead. 'I don't know,' she said. 'I've never actually seen him . . . '

Will jumped up. 'I'm a genius!' he yelled.

Gracie looked at him. 'Yes, yes. The Madame Curie of decorators.'

'Not a bad moniker for a drag queen,' he said, 'but wait — one patient at a time.'

He walked over to Cricket and placed his hand on her forehead in a dramatic manner, as though he were a healer and she that poor little girl onstage with braces around her legs.

'Repeat after me,' he said. 'Masturbation . . . '

'What? I can't — ' Cricket replied.

'Do it!' he yelled. 'Masturbation!'

'Masturbation!' Cricket yelled back.

'Is the key!' Will yelled again. Gracie was thankful Jaden had not awakened yet.

'Is the key!' Cricket yelled.

'To hap-piness!' Will yelled, accenting the second and third syllables so that the word came out like 'ha-*penis*!'

Cricket repeated the phrase, syllable for syllable. And finally, her face broke into a smile.

'My God, Professor Higgins,' Gracie said, 'I think she's got it.'

'Do you really think it'll work?' Cricket said.

'Not only will it work,' Will said, 'you may never actually have to have sex again.'

'Liar!' she said. Her face was beaming. Gracie was fearful she would burst into tears again — but this time, tears of happiness.

'Swear!' he yelled back.

'We don't own any porn,' Cricket said apologetically.

'Do I have to draw you a map?' Will said. 'Run. Drop by your local adult video store and pick up, I don't know, something cheesy — *Girls Gone Wild* or something.'

'What am I doing?' Cricket said, suddenly up on her feet. 'I've got work to do — I've got a husband on a steep learning curve.'

'Steep but swift,' Will said.

Cricket smiled and kissed Will all over his face. 'Please,' Will said, pushing her away. 'I don't even like my mother kissing me.'

'Thank you, thank you, thank you,' Cricket called as she ran out the door, clutching her purse and smoky clothes to her chest.

Gracie looked at Will after she'd gone.

'Do you think I'll ever get those pajamas back?' Gracie asked.

'No,' Will said, shaking his head. 'But please, if you're planning on getting laid by men with unusually symbolic names for the rest of your life, you will never settle for flannel again.'

'But they're Oprah's favorite,' Gracie said.

'So save them for when you sleep with Oprah.'

Gracie thought for a moment, sipping her coffee, which tasted especially good since her sexual awakening the night before. How, she thought, did groping affect one's taste buds? Is this why teenagers ate so much?

She looked at Will.

'Do you think you could have saved my marriage to Kenny?' she asked.

'Honey, your marriage was doomed from day one,' Will said. 'That's what you get for marrying a man who insists on displaying his high school baseball trophies in the living room.'

Gracie nodded, a little sad.

'I bet he used to wear his collars up, right?' Will asked, flipping his collar up so the lapel hit his cheeks.

'Just all the time,' Gracie said.

'Oh, honey, you are so much better off without him,' Will said. 'Just stick to this Sam person. At least until I know his particulars.'

At that moment, the front door opened. Will and Gracie looked at each other.

'She's bringing back the pajamas,' Gracie said.

'I'm throwing myself in front of her body — ' Will said, getting up.

Instead, standing in front of them was Joan, lugging two Louis Vuitton suitcases. (Gracie, after ten years, had learned to recognize the logo. But only after ten years.)

Her sunglasses were on top of her head. She looked thin. Her face was pale behind the clusters of freckles. Her hair had seen better days.

'Joan!' Will yelled. 'Thank God!'

He ran over to her, lifting her up and spinning her around.

'Joan?' Gracie asked. 'You look like you've seen a ghost.'

'Gracie,' Joan said in an unfamiliar, quivering voice. Joan didn't quiver, Gracie thought. Joan proclaimed.

'Lou,' she said.

Again with the quiver.

WIFE NUMBER EIGHT

Found out that her television-network-chief husband was cheating on her with a supermodel one morning. Who told her?
   Page Six.

19

Death of the King

Gracie had totally forgotten about Lou's imminent planned demise. And who could blame her? She was a middle-aged woman who only just recorded the best make-out session of her life the night before.

'Gracie?' Joan asked. 'Did you hear me? Are you okay?'

'He's dead,' Gracie said.

'Drowned,' Joan said. 'Last night. He left his clothes right out on the beach — and walked into the water, and . . . '

She groped for a chair and sat down.

'Not the new Prada sandals, I hope,' Will said.

'Shut up, Will,' Joan said. 'Don't you have any respect at all?'

'I'm not good at tragedy,' he admitted. 'I'm more like a . . . fair-weather boy.'

Gracie stood there, unable to comfort Joan or admonish Will. She didn't know what to do — Lou had placed her in a terrible position — should she tell them that Lou was alive? That rumors of his demise were premature and greatly exaggerated?

Instead, Gracie said, 'I just can't believe it.'

'Do you think he killed himself?' Joan asked. 'Why would he kill himself?'

'Too much young pussy?' Will asked.

Gracie and Joan looked at him.

'Is this really a time to be joking?' Joan asked.

'Eight o'clock in the morning?' Will asked, looking at his watch.

That comment made Joan smile.

'I knew I could get you,' Will said. 'Tragedy is comedy plus twenty minutes. Or the inverse.'

'I'm pretty sure it's the inverse,' Gracie said.

'You knew him well, right, Gracie?' Joan asked.

'She not only knew him,' Will said, 'she went on a date with him last weekend.'

'Not a date,' Gracie corrected. 'Just a friendly dinner.'

'Friendly with tongue served on the side,' Will said.

'No tongue,' Gracie corrected. 'Not even a real kiss. Just here.' She pointed to her cheek.

Joan was staring at her.

'How did you know?' she asked Gracie. 'How did you know he was dead?'

Gracie stammered. 'It wasn't very difficult,' she replied. 'First of all, you look like someone ran over your dog, if you had one.'

Joan nodded, not following her windy trail of logic.

'Secondly,' Gracie said, 'the way you said his name. I'm very intuitive. You know that.'

'No, you're not,' said Will.

'No, you're not,' Joan said. 'You seem very calm about his death. Are you all right? Are you on something?' She turned to Will. 'Did you give her something?'

'Do I look like a dealer?' Will asked, looking from Joan to Gracie. 'I couldn't hang out on corners — too drafty.' He looked at Joan. 'Gracie came *this* close,' he said, pinching his forefinger and thumb together, 'to getting laid last night.'

Joan screamed and clapped her hands. 'Who?!' she demanded.

'Get this,' Will said, 'his name is — '

'Not for public consumption! Yet!' Gracie said, turning to Joan. 'What happened to France? What happened to the Du Cap and boatloads of Haut-Brion?'

Joan looked at her. 'You're never going to believe this,' she said.

'Hold on,' Will said, 'I have to check myself. I may just be on gossip overload. It's never happened before, but . . . ' He stood there for a moment, thinking. Finally he said, 'Okay, I think I can handle it.'

'It's Pappy,' Joan said.

'Not Pappy!' Will yelled. 'Dear God, please don't take our Pappy! Where will we stay on the weekends?'

'He's not dead,' Joan said. 'Unfortunately.'

'I don't like the sound of that,' Gracie said.

'He wants a divorce,' Joan said.

'Grampa wants a divorce?!' Will asked.

Joan just shook her head. 'He met someone.'

Will and Gracie exchanged a look that lasted not more than one-tenth of a second but was overflowing with opinions of a particularly cynical bearing.

'Oh, honey,' Gracie said, going to Joan and wrapping her arms around her shoulders.

296

'Who knew? Pappy is a chick magnet,' Will said.

'Someone older,' Joan said, choking.

'How much older?' Gracie asked.

'She's seventy,' Joan said. 'How'm I supposed to compete with that?'

Joan cried soft tears as Gracie held her and admonished Will with a look so severe it would have stopped Genghis Khan in his tracks.

Will zipped his lip but appeared dangerously close to exploding.

'Will,' Gracie said, 'you can probably go now. I'll handle everything from here.'

Will nodded his relief. 'Thank you,' he said, mouthing the words.

Gracie thought she heard him guffaw at twenty paces.

★   ★   ★

Gracie walked Joan upstairs and then went down to make her a cup of tea, which she brought back upstairs on a platter, with a couple pieces of toast and jam.

Joan was all tucked in by the time Gracie had made it back upstairs, her body turned toward the picture window.

'Bird shit is good luck, right?' Joan asked. 'That's what I've heard.'

Gracie looked at the window, streaked at the top with white and green bird poop stalactites.

'So why don't I feel very lucky?' Joan asked.

She turned back to face Gracie, who was still thinking about whether bird shit could be construed as good luck.

'I think it's good luck if it's on your shoulder,' Gracie said in conclusion.

'Ah,' Joan said. 'I guess I am lucky. I have you, don't I?'

Gracie sat down. 'Eat,' she said.

'One step at a time,' Joan said. 'The first step is I can stand to look at food without throwing up.'

Gracie nodded. She understood. 'The divorce diet,' she said. 'I don't know why someone hasn't written a book.'

'It's much better than South Beach,' Joan said. 'But maybe not as lasting as the Zone.'

They sat for a moment. Joan slid her hand over to Gracie's and held it.

'Distract me. Tell me about him,' Joan said. 'Your mystery man.'

'It's not important,' Gracie said. And then she smiled. 'Except that I think I'm in love.'

'Madly?' Joan asked.

'Mama's got it bad,' Gracie admitted.

'When can I meet him?'

'He seems a little shy.'

'Bullshit,' Joan said. 'I'm going to have a dinner party and he's going to come because you're going to tell him I'm despondent over my spouse *ancien*, and he needs to entertain me.'

'That seems like a tall order for anyone,' Gracie said.

'This Saturday,' Joan said. 'I need to be cheered up.'

Gracie smiled. And nodded. 'I'll tell him. After all, he handled Will under difficult, semi-naked circumstances. He can handle anything.'

'Where does he live?' Joan asked.

'In the Colony,' Gracie said.

'Ooh,' Joan said. 'He has money.'

Gracie shrugged.

'What does he do?' Joan asked. 'Besides making out with lonely divorcées?'

'Isn't that enough?' Gracie asked. 'What's with all the questions?'

'I have to know who my daughter's going to marry.'

'I don't know what he does for a living.'

'I'll bet it's something unusual — like that man who used to live here who made shoe boxes for a living. The guy was a gazillionaire. Shoe boxes!' Joan exclaimed. 'You know, he always took up more than his share of parking spaces.'

'Not a great trait,' Gracie agreed.

Joan thought about it, then looked at Gracie. 'Leave it to me, I'll find out everything.'

'You won't scare him off?' Gracie asked. 'I really want to keep him, Mommy.'

'I won't scare him off,' Joan said. 'Just make sure he eats meat. I'll put some steaks on the grill, which won't be my grill after the summer. We'll have some wine, we'll have a great time.'

Joan loved to plan a party, even under dire circumstances.

'All right, all right,' Gracie said. 'I'll tell him today.'

They watched as a triangle of pelicans flew past, diving like feathered kamikazes in the water in front of the house.

'Who told you?' Gracie asked nonchalantly.

'Who told you about Lou?'

'Lavender at the gate,' Joan said. 'She was pretty upset.'

Joan smoothed the sheet over her body. Her throat made a gargling sound. She looked up at Gracie, the sheen of tears in her eyes.

'They found his body this morning,' she said.

★　★　★

Gracie flew, flew on her bike to see Lavender. She didn't remember running down the stairs and spinning out the front door; she didn't even remember jumping on her bike.

'Lou, Lou, Lou,' Gracie murmured to herself. And then, louder, until she was screaming — 'Lou! LOU!'

She soared over the speed bumps and turned the corner toward the security gate, narrowly missing a black Range Rover that seemed to speed up as they closed in on each other.

Gracie slowed down and let the Range Rover pass. She tried to catch her breath and started hiccupping instead. Gracie made a mental note, scoring her reaction: 'Handling bad news — C-minus at best.'

She got off the bike, left it by the side of the road, on its side, the wheels spinning. She walked toward the security quarters, a small white structure, just big enough for two people with pleasant personalities, three people if one happened to bring enough food for all of them.

'Lavender!' Gracie called out. 'Lavender!' She

was leaning against the outside wall.

Lavender was directing someone in a red Ferrari on the other side of the white structure, holding a clipboard in her hand.

Lavender turned and looked at her.

Her eyes were pink underneath the black-rimmed glasses. Her light cocoa skin was ashen. This gave the effect of making her look blond all over.

She waved the car past without looking back, then walked around the structure, meeting Gracie at the back.

They looked at each other.

'Is it true?' Gracie whispered. Then, 'It can't be true.'

Lavender just looked at her, the wrinkles in her forehead showing the sense of stress and anguish.

Gracie grabbed her by her arms, jerking her body.

'Lavender, it's not true.'

'He's dead,' Lavender said. She sighed and Gracie could feel the rattle in her chest.

'Not Lou,' Gracie said. 'It's someone else.' Her head shook back and forth, the word 'NO' repeating itself inside her brain. NO NO NO NO NO NO!

'Number 152,' Lavender said. 'Lou Manahan. He drowned.'

Gracie's hand went to her mouth; she felt her face pull back into a grimace. She bit down so hard she cried out —

Lavender grabbed her as Gracie's knees buckled beneath her.

'I got you,' Lavender said, 'I got you, I got you.'

Gracie cried into her shirtsleeve, tears streaming down Lavender's arm. Gracie held on to Lavender as she bent over her, guiding her slowly to the ground, the loving act of a good mother.

Gracie's eyes closed. 'Did you see a body?'

'What?' Lavender asked.

'Did you see a body?' Gracie opened her eyes. 'Are you sure it was him, Lavender? Are you sure?' She was looking up at her, her vision glazed and foggy.

'Gracie.'

'It was an accident!' Gracie yelled, pulling back. 'He didn't mean to kill himself — he didn't want to kill himself. It was just a stupid — '

Lavender's eyes were tracking her, watching her, listening.

Gracie stopped. She threw up her hands and looked up to the overcast sky.

'I hate you,' she screamed and shook her fist at a sky seldom filled with dread. 'I hate you!'

Lavender stood there with her, oblivious to the cars piling up in front of the security station until the first several started honking their horns in a cacophonous opus.

⋆　⋆　⋆

Gracie walked her bike back to Joan's house and left it in the driveway, bereft of the energy it would take to pull it over the doorway.

She dragged her body up the stairs to the front

door and willed her way to the couch and was grateful for its overstuffed cushions and the ridiculous number of pillows because now she needed the comfort of ridiculously expensive, ridiculously comfortable furnishings.

She became aware of her breath, jagged as a patient in an emphysema ward.

So this is what it feels like, Gracie thought. *This is what tragedy feels like.*

Shortly after sadness and disbelief came anger, the second-cousin emotion. And with anger came energy.

A half hour later, Gracie found herself in the kitchen filling a blender with ice cubes and frozen strawberries and vodka from an old bottle in the freezer.

Yes, it was still morning. But Gracie needed a drink — just not a stiff one. Stiff drinks scared her. She didn't like the taste of hard liquor — she'd never been a scotch rocks kind of girl. A daiquiri would fill the bill nicely, even under these circumstances.

She wondered if it seemed pussy of her, having a daiquiri when she should have been waving a bottle of Jack Daniel's around. 'Geez,' she could hear herself say to others, 'I was so despondent I made myself a pitcher of strawberry daiquiris.'

Also, she wondered if vodka was in fact the proper liquor to make daiquiris with.

Either way, she decided that no one had to know; and after all, Lou might actually find it funny.

She turned on the blender and stood in her

favorite spot in the kitchen from which she could see everything — Palos Verdes, Catalina Island, post-adolescent surfer musculature molded from too many days on the beach and too few days working —

And . . . the familiar green blanket. The familiar frantic yet surprisingly rhythmical pop-pop-pop underneath.

'Oh, for crying out loud!' Gracie said. 'That is so inappropriate!'

She opened the kitchen window — a fancy, expensive window from Germany which, like all the other fancy, expensive windows from Germany in the house, served only one purpose fine — to look through. Otherwise, it was impossible to open, and would leak whenever there was rainfall.

She opened it barely two inches, with much effort — 'Have you no shame?!' she yelled at the offending figure under the blanket, wondering why she had chosen words appropriate for a Catholic school nun annoyed at a rambunctious student.

There was not a moment lost in the vigorous activity taking place.

'Have you no decency?!' she yelled, continuing on her Catholic school rampage.

No response. If anything, the tempo had stepped up a bit.

Gracie shook her head.

'What's your goddamned secret?!' she finally screamed before shutting the instrument-of-Satan German window.

Married to a famous action-movie producer with an exciting, masculine style. She reluctantly agreed not to have children, because he wanted to have all of her attention. Ten years into the marriage, after it was too late for her to bear children, he impregnated another woman.

He never acknowledged his illegitimate son, who also became a famous action-movie producer with an exciting, masculine style.

20

The King is Laid to Rest

'Slow news day,' Will commented as Gracie tracked news of Lou's death throughout the day. CNN, all the local channels, even the major networks and their major anchors had all mentioned his untimely demise. Gracie was particularly impressed with the saddened expressions gracing Katie Couric's and Diane Sawyer's gorgeous mugs. They appeared to have lost their best friend, not a studio head whom they had never met and would not know if they bumped into him on Madison Avenue.

'He was important,' Gracie said.

'Yes,' Will said. 'Without Lou, we wouldn't have had the sixth *Godzilla*.'

Will was still pissed off that Lou had not hired him to decorate his ski house in Sun Valley — even death would not protect him from Will's surly comments. Never cross a decorator with attitude.

And they all had attitude.

Gracie turned off the television set. She was obsessing over the news. Obsessing over the facts. Would they explain what had happened? Could they explain what had gone wrong? Surely he had hit his head, Gracie thought. Maybe it was one of those sandbanks that haunted surfers,

306

turning them from bronzed gods into pale quadriplegics with one bad dive. The sandbanks would have been well hidden beneath the dark water, especially with the fireworks going off overhead. That must be it, Gracie thought, he dove in and hit his head and never recovered.

Lou didn't want to die. He had everything to live for.

If Lou had wanted to check out so badly, Gracie thought, what was the point for the rest of us? Was it like that poem Gracie had loved when she was in high school — the one about the handsome man with all the money who shoots himself in the head one day? Gracie loved that poem, not for its artistic merit, hell no, but because it made her feel good about herself — that even the beautiful people had bad days.

Thoughts like these brought her comfort when she had to read about Gwyneth Paltrow's career, husband, mother, new baby, diet.

During the morning, Gracie had noted all the snippets in the news coverage that Lou would appreciate — and all those that would have made him cringe.

Every headline mentioned him being the King of Hollywood. Lou would have loved that (even though he had pretended to find the label annoying). There were many movie stars who agreed to be interviewed on camera: George Clooney, Tom Cruise, Julia Roberts. Lou, the son of, literally, no one, would have appreciated seeing their faces — knowing they had to get up at 4:30 A.M. for the New York feed.

At the same time, he would have noted who

had declined to be interviewed — or worse, who had simply dialed in their thoughts and remembrances — Catherine Zeta-Jones ('I knew her when she had one last name!' Lou would growl), Brad Pitt and Jennifer Aniston ('Stop them before they procreate!' Lou would yell).

And what about the 'no comment' from the bubbly movie star he'd dated a decade ago? Surely Lou would have had something to say about that.

Joan came downstairs, finally, still wrapped up in her down quilt.

'Anything on the news?' she asked.

'No,' Gracie said. 'Not counting CNN, ABC, NBC, FOX, BET, Nickelodeon, and I'm betting the Playboy Channel as well.'

'Wow,' Joan said. 'Impressive.'

'Maybe it's even on the Tennis Channel,' Gracie said. 'I haven't checked.'

'Ooh,' Will said, grabbing the remote and turning on the TV. 'Let's turn on the Korean channel — I want to see them talk about Lou in Korean.'

Joan sat down in her overstuffed chair as Will flipped through channels. 'I wish he were still alive,' she said, sounding wistful.

Gracie shook her head and rubbed her face with her hands. 'I know, I know. It's crazy.'

'Because then I could've dated him,' Joan continued.

Gracie looked at her.

'I mean, when you were done with him,' Joan clarified.

'It wasn't a date,' Gracie said. 'I was way out

of all his demographics — age, weight, height — '

'Okay, enough about dating dead guys,' Will said. 'I have to take Gracie shopping. I've looked through her closet — there's no fabulous, sexy, King of Hollywood-appropriate funeral frock to be seen.'

'I told you, I'm not even sure I'll be invited to the funeral,' Gracie said.

'Of course you're invited,' Will said.

'I might not be — after all, Kenny worked for him. I'm leaving it up to Kenny. And he won't be comfortable with me there.'

'Honey,' Will said, putting his hand on her shoulder, 'I already put it out on the Gay Network. Not only are you going, you're seated in primo territory.'

Gracie surprised herself by crying. 'Thank you,' she sniffed. 'That is so sweet.'

'Sweet, nothing,' Will said. 'I'll just need a play-by-play later,' he continued. 'This is the hottest ticket in town. It's like when The Artist Formerly Known As Prince did his comeback tour, but without the music. I got you front row center.'

'That is the most jaded thing I have ever heard,' Gracie said. 'Even from you.'

'So you're not going to attend?' he asked.

'You pushed her too far this time,' Joan said, shaking her head. 'Even Gracie has her limits.'

Gracie looked at Will, serious. 'Not in the wrong dress, I'm not.'

'That's my girl!' Joan said, clapping her hands together.

Funerals. The idea of attending a funeral inevitably made Gracie think of her father's. But she could not, for the life of her, remember that day. She remembered the day her mother showed up on her apartment doorstep, she remembered what her face looked like. Who is this old woman on my doorstep? Gracie had thought as she'd climbed the stairs. Who is she waiting for? She didn't recognize her own mother until she stood and fell into Gracie's arms and told her that her father was dead. Grief had sent her mother into a state of disrepair.

Gracie remembered the day her mother called two weeks later to tell her she was heading back to Seattle, as though she'd just settled into Los Angeles six months ago rather than twenty-five years ago. She remembered cleaning out her father's closet and drawers and ashtrays because her mother could not move from the couch. But she could not remember the day of her father's funeral.

★ ★ ★

She and Will drove Will's brand-new black Prius (which he claimed was Liberal Gay catnip) and parked in the lot outside Forest Lawn on the east side of Hollywood. Will had been able to reserve a spot based on a promise extracted from him that he would give someone's assistant free advice on the design of his condo's dining room.

It was a heavy price to pay, pimping out his art

for a ticket to a funeral, but fortunately Will was unburdened by such ethical and other qualms in general.

As soon as she left the car, Gracie started to observe as though she were using Lou's senses, watching for what he would have looked for, hearing what he would have been listening for. Feeling what he would have felt.

They walked past the news vans and news cameras and news anchors (de rigueur for celeb sightings — they'd camp out at funerals as easily as camping out at the newsstand in Malibu) to the funeral home and paced themselves, moving up the steps to the front doors while taking in as much information as possible, but for separate reasons. Will hunted gossip — under his black, reflective Marc Jacobs, his mind was working like a FOX News video cam, picking up a Leo appearance here, a Farrah spotting (girlfriend, early 1973) there, an Aniston tear — his concentration was so complete, he would, for the first time since they'd met, not utter a word.

Gracie and Will found their seats — not front row center as Will had promised, but no matter. They squeezed into the third row, where they had ample access to all visual and oratory ejaculation.

At least that's how Will put it, when he finally spoke, in a hushed voice.

Her first sense of the funeral was that it was surprisingly subdued. There were no Armani-suited agents at the doors, greeting people as though it were a premiere instead of a memorial service. To a man (and woman), all heads were bowed at 45-degree angles. The sounds that she heard were murmurs, the hum of people offering support under difficult circumstances.

There was no mention of basketball scores, or 'the numbers' (what the new releases had made the night before), or 'the overnights' (television ratings), or whether Eisner was keeping his job.

Gracie tried to put her finger on the feeling she was experiencing, past the sadness, past the shock. And then there it was, emerging fully formed and rare and gorgeous:

Respect.

Jesus Christ, Gracie thought, *people are actually here to pay their respects. They actually care. They care that Lou's dead. They are experiencing his loss. They are in the moment. They are not onto the next big thing, the coming news flash, tomorrow's Peter Bart column.*

'Holy shit,' Gracie actually said out loud. If she could have, she would have grabbed at the air and shoved the ill-chosen words back down her throat.

Several people turned to look at her. She bowed her head, burrowing into Will's shoulder. 'Keep it down,' Will whispered, 'some people are trying to mourn and others are trying to watch them do it.'

The only commotion damaging the proceedings occurred at that moment, thankfully distracting those who were offended by Gracie's blue commentary. She didn't have to turn her head to see whose voice had shattered the sanctity of the moment — she'd lived with that voice for over a quarter of her life.

312

'Hey, how ya doin',' she heard Kenny stage-whisper to someone in the back. Kenny was not the master of the soft whisper; in fact, his attempt at whispering was louder than a normal person's unaltered voice. 'The dailies look great,' he continued in his stage whisper.

Gracie smiled. Somewhere, Lou was screaming 'Bullshit!'

Will looked back, then whispered into Gracie's ear, 'So ridiculous.' He jeered, 'Together, they make half a person.'

Kenny walked past Gracie and Will's row, arm in elbow with his girlfriend, Britney. His was the only head that was cocked at an angle that signaled pride rather than sorrow or regret. Gracie was pleasantly surprised to see that even young Britney knew how to angle her chin at a funeral. Her face was downcast, her shoulders forward in her black cocktail dress, as though she knew that her famous body could be a distraction, even under the circumstances.

For a moment, Gracie wondered what it was like to have a body like that. Before she squeegeed her mind of the superficial thought. There would be plenty of time for superficial thoughts after the funeral.

She added that one to the Post-it in her head.

Kenny and his new wife, Britney (not really his new wife, but Gracie was trying it on as an exercise in masochism), sat in the middle of the front row, two rows directly in front of Will and Gracie.

Gracie had forgotten how tall Kenny was, how much space he took up. She found herself staring at the back of Kenny's head as the people in the second row teeter-tottered their heads back and forth, determined to find a comfortable angle from which they could view the proceedings.

Gracie didn't bother for a better angle; she liked looking at the back of Kenny's head, where she could observe the effects of time without interruption. What she saw lifted her mood, as though unexpectedly finding a Sara Lee cake inside her freezer. Kenny was going bald. He had a hair halo around a tiny circle of white skin she hadn't noticed before — but why would she? She'd never sat behind him, in all the years they were married.

As though Kenny was beckoned by the power of Gracie's eyes boring into the back of his (BALDING!) head, he turned.

Gracie jumped slightly, afraid that he was reading her mind, and then willing him to. *You're going bald!* Gracie thought as hard as she could, as she forced a polite smile, which she knew more resembled a grimace or the look a baby gets on his face when he's passing gas. *Hey, Baldy! Hey, nice air-conditioning system you've got up there! What, no more hair?! You've got your own solar panel!*

And then, Kenny winked.

He WINKED! As his mentor, the man who had plucked Kenny from obscurity and set him on the road to riches and $12-million homes with security systems that can't be figured out, and that frikkin' stupid Mercedes with the electrical system that goes on the fritz the moment you hit the 101 Freeway, and the golf lessons at the country club that set you back a cool $100,000, and the tennis court that keeps cracking, and the chef who charges $120 for tuna salad, and on and on, ad infinitum, et cetera.

Lou had given Kenny everything he'd ever wanted. And here he was, WINKING at Lou's funeral as though it were a Dodgers game.

Gracie's jaw had not recovered from dropping to the ground before Kenny whipped his (HAIR-LACKING! FOLLICLE-CHALLENGED!) head back into place.

The first speaker was someone Gracie did not recognize. From the back, Gracie could see her blunt-cut silver-gray hair, the ramrod-straight back ('What exactly is a ramrod?' Will asked when Gracie talked about the woman later, during their postmortem postmortem), and then, as she turned and approached the podium, Gracie noticed, as did everyone else, the striking blue eyes, the proud lift to the chin. The wrinkles. And in her spotted hands (did this woman's bravery know no bounds?) she was holding what appeared to be a letter.

Gracie felt that she looked like someone who was a better person than everyone else in the building. She looked like someone who cared about herself but not to the extent that she neglected the rest of the world.

'Wow, no work' is what Will whispered, drawing a circle in the air around his face. 'Has she no shame?'

Gracie pinched him as the woman cleared her

throat and began to speak. She imagined this woman to be an aunt. Too young to be Lou's mother, Gracie thought — and hadn't Lou's mother died when he was a child?

'Hello,' the woman said, her voice clear and strong. Gracie imagined a tennis racket in her right hand, beating the crap out of Martina Navratilova in some country club game. 'My name is Claire Lawrence Olsen. I can't imagine that any of you would have heard of me, but I was married to Lou when he was eighteen. And I was seventeen.'

Claire was Lou's first wife. Lou had a first wife? Gracie remembered the second, third, and fourth, but no one had ever mentioned the first.

'You all knew Lou much later in life,' Claire said, 'but I can tell you this — from what I've learned in these last, sad days, he hadn't changed much.'

She went on to describe how she met Lou by accident outside a movie theater in Brooklyn, and how he strode up to her and asked her what she thought of her new husband. She went out with him twice afterward, supervised, and he had already written her a letter, trying to convince her to marry him; her parents were not keen on having their only daughter marry an orphan with a Jewish last name and no prospects.

'I wanted to share this remembrance I've kept in a drawer at home through my last two marriages,' Claire said. 'And no, I'm not a serial divorcée — unfortunately, now, I've outlived all three of my husbands. With that record, I doubt I'll be getting married again soon.'

The audience responded, laughing.

'At least that's what Lou used to tell me,' she continued.

She put a handkerchief to her eyes and nose and dabbed at the burgeoning wetness. And then she opened the letter she'd been holding, smoothing down the triple folded pages on the top of the podium.

She began.

''My dearest Claire . . . ''

Noises simmered through the building. Gracie recognized the noises because she herself was making them — distinct sniffling, the crinkly sounds of Kleenexes being freed from their wrappings.

''You say you don't know me, so I'm going to tell you everything you need to know about Lou Manning.''

Claire looked up, peering above her blue-rimmed reading glasses. 'Lou used to be Lou Manning, before he became Lou Manahan.'

She continued. ''I'm five foot eight inches tall.'' Claire smiled. So did everyone else. Everyone knew Lou wasn't over five seven, if that.

''Okay, on a good day, I'm five foot eight inches tall. But I believe every day is a good day, don't you, my darling Claire?' '

She went on.

''So, I didn't graduate high school. Your parents have, duly, told you this again and again. I don't deny it. This much is true. School wasn't for me. I wanted to do something else with my life. So I joined the Marines. What an

317

experience. What a bunch of guys. If you don't marry me, Claire, at least promise me that you'll marry a fellow Marine. That way, I know you'll be safe. I know that someone will always have your back.''

Claire had to clear her throat. Her handkerchief was doing double duty.

''I'm going to be something one day, Claire. I'm going to be big — not middle management, not just a guy who wears a suit and tie and hikes it to work every day, hating every minute. I'm going to be big in something I love.''

She paused. And looked up. And smiled. How could he have been so prescient? The question was on the minds of everyone attending the service.

Claire looked down and continued. ''And I want to take you along with me, on this wonderful ride,'' the young Lou had said. ''Claire, at the very least, I'll be the husband you'll remember fondly. You'll never regret a moment with me.''

Claire cleared her throat for the umpteenth time.

''My heart is yours, Lou Manning.'

'And then he added,' Claire said, ''You have until the 18th to make up your mind.''

Everyone in the room howled. The young Lou was not so different from the older one — both were famous for their ultimatums, their time constraints, their willingness to drop any deal, no matter how important, if specific parameters were not met.

Claire looked up. 'We did get married. But I

did not share Lou's courage. It was I who left Lou, not the other way around. He always had faith in himself, and I wish I had shared that faith. I wish I had stuck by him.'

She paused. 'I will, like many of you, love him forever. Death changes nothing.'

She folded up the pieces of paper as she must have done time and time again over the years. Time and time again over the last few days. And then she slowly walked down the stairs and back to her seat. And no one said a word. It would be the first and last time the people in this room were in agreement.

The rabbi approached the podium. He bent the microphone down toward his face. 'And now, Kenny Pollock, Lou's protégé and close friend, will speak.'

Gracie looked at Will, who widened his eyes, looking not unlike her husband's new girlfriend, Britney, when faced with a tough question like, 'Is global warming really caused by increases in carbon dioxide levels as a result of human activity?' or 'What goes in a shoe?'

Kenny solemnly approached the podium, bending the microphone to a straight, vertical position. Gracie caught the flicker of a smirk washing over Kenny's face — he was always so proud of his height. He couldn't even hide it under the circumstances. She wondered if others were aware of the tiny manipulation of his features. Looking around, she concluded they were still caught up in Claire's eulogy. As she should have been. But how could she help it? She was staring at a man she had spent over a decade with — and wondering WHY.

'Lou Manahan was more than a mentor to me,' Kenny proclaimed. 'He was my friend.'

'Good start,' Will said. 'That must have taken the better part of a day.'

Gracie elbowed him in the ribs and realized that there was a thick swath of material covering his midsection. She looked at Will, questioning.

'Are you wearing a girdle?' she whispered.

'Shhh,' he said. 'Have you no respect?'

Gracie brought her hand to her mouth to suppress a giggle. Of course Will was wearing a girdle. His recent complaints about his sprouting love handles had reached epic proportions.

Kenny went on, detailing the course of his life with Lou. Talking about where he was when he first met Lou, what he was doing when Lou hired him, the movies he had developed and produced under Lou's aegis.

Kenny seemed very comfortable up on that podium, Gracie thought. Probably because he was talking not really about Lou but of his favorite subject: himself.

Twenty minutes later, when Kenny had finished selling his latest lineup of potential blockbusters, he stepped down from the podium and the rabbi once again tilted the microphone toward his face. Will leaned over to Gracie and whispered, 'My God, you missed a bullet. You're like that stewardess who fell a mile out of a plane and survived by eating pine needles. Remember her, she was, like, Swedish or something? And gorgeous, by the way. You're so lucky you're on the divorce-trail.'

Gracie paused on the steps with Will as they left the funeral. She watched as the old movie stars left, their spouses or caretakers holding them gingerly at the elbows, riding the balance between merely assisting and making them seem decrepit. She watched as the ex-girlfriends filed out, their eyes ablaze with tears and mascara. She watched as Kenny passed her, walking out with Britney, breaking his usual stride so the photographers could achieve ample coverage.

Gracie knew she'd be seeing her ex, finally, on that cover of *Us*.

But she also knew this: Lou Manahan would have been very happy. Little of the cynicism she'd associated with Hollywood funerals had been found within those four walls. There's the irony, Gracie thought, Lou's death would have brought him closure.

'Goddamned idiot,' she said out loud. Will gave her a look as he escorted her down the stairs, as though she herself were one of those fragile movie stars.

WIFE NUMBER TEN

Keeps her hip-hop artist husband medicated on a rotating cocktail of Vicodin, Xanax, Prozac, Percodan, and Ritalin. She slips the pills into his morning wheatgrass-and-flaxseed smoothie.

People comment on his calm demeanor.

21

Words Are Better Than Pictures

Gracie swung into the gate at the Malibu Colony and waited for the slim wood barricade to rise. Usually she was just motioned on through, as by this time, though she was not officially a resident, she was a recognizable face. But today Tariq, one of the guards, the one who was probably a ballplayer in high school or college, what with his tall, lanky form, waved her down with a languid reach of his arm —

'Got something for ya,' he said, waving a white envelope in her car window.

Gracie took it from him, forcing a small smile. From what she knew from high school physics (which was little), she felt that this effort took about one million gigawatts of energy. She was amazed she could pull off even the smallest nicety.

She peered through her thick sunglasses at the envelope in her hand.

'It came for you a couple days ago,' Tariq continued in his slightly southern, singsong voice. 'I think it fell through the cracks here, what with all the hoopla, et cetera.'

Gracie just stared at the envelope.

'Sorry 'bout that,' he said, the thick gold cross around his neck dropping close to her car window.

She waved at him as he raised the wood barricade and drove on, the envelope weighing heavy now on her lap.

'Gracie, #250,' in a fifth grader's scrawl, was all that was written on the outside of the envelope. She didn't know Lou's handwriting, but she knew it was his.

★   ★   ★

Joan must have been walking on the beach when Gracie arrived at the house. She was grateful for this time alone, because she needed it — any more social interaction, even with a best friend, would be courting emotional disaster. Gracie slid to the kitchen, opened the refrigerator, got out the bottle of white wine she knew would already be opened (thanks, Joan!), and poured herself a glass and thanked God she wasn't an alcoholic.

Yet.

Then she sat down on the couch and placed the envelope on the coffee table and took a good, hard look at it. She stared at it as though she could reach the words telepathically.

Having failed that, she set her wine down and tore open the envelope with the fervor of someone expecting a much-needed check.

There were several pieces of paper.

She immediately went to the end. To the part that said, 'Love, Lou.'

His handwriting was atrocious. Gracie found

herself chastising him for not taking more time, or being less drunk when he wrote it. She found herself chastising him for being dead.

"Gracie," it began.

"You're going to think I'm crazy."

'You're right, Lou,' Gracie said out loud. 'I do think you're crazy.'

"I had this all planned out, as you know," Lou continued, "but there was only one hitch to the plan when I really sat down and thought about it."

Gracie took a deep breath.

"And that was," he wrote, "I had devised a symphonic, poetic ending to my life. I had written, as it were, an ending that would bring an audience to its knees. And yet I wasn't going to be taking advantage of it."

Gracie started crying.

"Don't start crying," Lou wrote.

'Fuck you,' Gracie said. 'Fuck you, Lou. I'll cry if I fucking want to.'

She wanted to state her case in words that Lou would understand and respond to. She didn't like anyone, even a dead man, controlling her emotional states.

"I've done everything I've ever wanted in life," Lou wrote. "I've traveled the world, I've lived in the greatest houses, driven the greatest cars, dated the greatest women (don't start, Gracie!)," Lou wrote. "I've even done the one thing I said would never happen. I became a father."

Gracie could not have stopped the tears if a gale force wind had hit her square in the face.

"I love my son, Gracie, you know I do. But I barely get to see him — the lawyers have taken care of that — the more my ex-wife has him, the more money she gets. He'll be better off without the tug-of-war."

Gracie shook her head. How could someone so smart be so stupid?

"Forgive me, Gracie," Lou wrote on, "that is all I'm asking of you. Forgive me."

Gracie folded up the letter and placed it back in the envelope and then closed her eyes, her lids heavy with spent emotion. And she found herself back in time, holding hands with her mother at her father's funeral, staring off into space as the reverend eulogized the only man who had ever loved her unconditionally.

⋆   ⋆   ⋆

'You do realize we're still on for Friday?' Joan announced after Gracie had awakened from her brief grief-nap, sliding the envelope into the back of her skirt.

'Friday?' Gracie asked. She couldn't even remember what day it was today.

'Dinner,' Joan said. 'Remember, I'm making dinner for you and your beau. Do you think he knows anyone?'

Gracie shook her head. She hadn't thought of her one great kiss.

'Oh, honey,' Joan said, looking into Gracie's eyes. 'I'm sorry. Here I am, wondering what to serve . . . Was it that bad?'

Gracie nodded.

'Will told me all about it,' Joan said. 'He said Kenny concluded by trying to sell his fall slate.'

'He did.'

'Were you ever really married to that asshole?' Joan asked.

'I still am,' Gracie answered.

Joan put her arm around her. 'It's time for us to move on to our next mistakes, isn't it?'

Gracie just nodded. But she knew one thing: She did not want another mistake in her life. She wanted simplicity. She wanted normalcy. She wanted a life without a moving soap opera. She did not want a security code.

And she wanted to kiss Sam again.

★ ★ ★

Gracie ran into him, as she knew she would, the next morning in front of the street entrance to the beach. He was standing in his bright orange shorts, facing north toward Point Dume, which rose heroically through the fog; the Labrador was at his feet, making headway into a recalcitrant old tennis ball.

She could feel that he felt her presence, even though he didn't turn as she walked up to him.

He didn't flinch when she put her hand on his arm. He reached his hand across his chest and placed it over hers. The warmth of his skin shifted into her hands, up through her arms, into her body, into places which had been quarantined. He was so alive, this man. She could feel that every cell of his being was at the ready. He was fight-or-fight — the adrenaline response — personified.

But what was he fighting? Or fleeing from? She knew she should care, but she didn't. She was like a teenage girl who gets on the back of a motorcycle. She was exhilarated. She was happy.

Jesus Christ, she was horny.

He turned to face her and, once again, put his hands on her face and drew her mouth toward his.

Oh, that kiss, Gracie thought, there it is, again. That once-in-a-lifetime kiss is happening twice!

They separated, just as an older couple made their way past, pausing momentarily as they spied Sam and Gracie and the intimacy of their posture.

Gracie didn't care, she thought, let them look. Let them see what new love is like. Let them remember and take it home with them.

'Is this what I think it is?' Gracie said, admonishing herself even as the words became whole outside her subconscious. How could she be such a girl?

'Never mind!' she said, almost immediately. Why, she wondered, did she need a running narration, a commentary — why couldn't she just let things happen, mature, take shape without the burden of language?

Because she couldn't, that's why.

Sam was looking at her. She wondered if she confused him as much as she confused herself. He looked like a man who was confused about little. He looked like a man who knew his place in the world and was content with it — who made decisions and lived with them, and didn't second-guess every little thing. He looked confident and secure.

She wondered what the hell he saw in her.

'What do you think it is?' Sam asked. His head was bent toward hers. The crowns of their foreheads almost touching.

She could taste his breath, unencumbered by flavors — no coffee, no mint toothpaste. Just health.

That's what it is, Gracie thought, *finally putting a mental finger on the word that seemed to fit him most — unencumbered.*

How does one get to be unencumbered?

'Pure animal lust,' Gracie said, finally answering her Prince in Orange Shorts. 'And I'm okay with that.'

'You mean, you don't love me for my mind?' Sam looked at her, his eyes filled with feigned worry.

'I have enough mind,' Gracie said. 'What I need is a body.' She didn't really mean it, but it sounded clever enough. And right now, she needed someone to think she was clever.

'I can live with that,' Sam replied.

'A body with a heart,' she said as he kissed her again, reaching her in places where no man had ever been before. He was a hunter, she was the Heart of Darkness.

'Careful,' she said, as they paused for breath, 'you're going on an intrepid excavation.'

He laughed. God, she loved those crow's-feet that appeared at his eyes.

Even his wrinkles were masculine.

How would she ever survive this much passion? She would be a mere puddle when he got through with her. People would walk over her and say, 'Oh, there's Gracie Pollock — remember when she was a full human being? Before she had sex with that man who turned her into a mass of jelly?'

'Oh,' Gracie said, remembering that little thing called 'breathing.' 'I almost forgot. Are you available Friday night?'

Sam looked at her. Something passed quickly over his face, then disappeared into its recesses. What was it? she thought.

Oh my God, he's married, Gracie thought. He's married and he's kissing me — in front of old people!

I'm a slut, Gracie thought. *I'm a wayward slut and I'm going straight to hell.*

'I'm available,' Sam said, and then proceeded to wipe out any possible guilt the minx Gracie had about prying this innocent man from his wife and ten children by pressing his warm, full lips to her neck, thereby rendering her a quivering, helpless mess. She felt like that goo Jaden played with, the stuff that came in a plastic egg that stuck to carpets, even though it came with a piece of paper that proclaimed it 'nontoxic and easy to clean!'

Why did they lie? Gracie thought, those mendacious, heartless goo manufacturers?

'I'm going in,' Sam said, finally breaking from their last, earth-shattering kiss. He touched her cheek with his hand and then turned and walked off toward the water, followed by the dog, leaving her shattered remains behind.

Why am I so dramatic? Gracie asked herself. *It certainly doesn't serve me well,* she thought as she watched Mr. Unencumbered dive over the waves.

And then she thought of Lou, diving over those same waves. Her mind spun forward — what were his final moments like? What was he feeling when he walked in? When he dove? When he chose not to take another breath?

She wiped away the one tear she would allow herself that day.

It was soon followed by others. Her effort was mocked. Her tear ducts were staging a mutiny against her mind. Why was she always being betrayed by her body?

'Screw it,' Gracie said to the wind, as she sat in the sand and cried.

22

My First Date in How Many Years

How does a guy my age get ready for a date? Sam Knight thought. At least he thought he was getting ready for a date. The woman had asked him to dinner. A dinner party. A group of people. Why had he said yes? Had he said yes?

Sam walked to the security gate to have a talk with Lavender. He needed to know particulars. What to wear, what to talk about. He hadn't had a conversation about anything substantial with a person for a long time. Mrs. Kennicot, she only commented on the weather, which was always the same, or the temperature of the water, which, like the weather, seldom changed. The Pacific was always cold, the coast was always temperate. Some days started out foggier than others. Other than that, she would ask him things: Can you fix the faucet on the bathroom sink? Can you grout that tile? The old station wagon's making a funny noise. What's that funny noise?

Occasionally, he would talk to the men who gathered on the outskirts of the Starbucks hoping for a free coffee, some change. But he was a snob, he was the first to admit it. He wasn't on his own because of alcohol, drugs, because of money issues. He had chosen this life. He preferred this life.

This woman was the first to make him question his choice.

Lavender would know what he should wear. He'd have to be discreet, though. He didn't want her or anyone else knowing he had a date. He knew the guards — they were like a ready-made family. J.D. was the patriarch, the all-knowing, all-seeing father figure. Tariq was the younger brother, the easygoing one who sometimes made mistakes. Lavender was the sister, smart, hypervigilant. He didn't want her thinking he was taking advantage — he knew some people probably already thought that — thought that he was taking advantage of the Kennicots. Which is why he never moved in with them, even when Mrs. Kennicot asked every other week or so, until she didn't anymore.

Lavender was bent over a book, as usual, when there weren't poor people to kick off the beach, or someone driving an Escalade looking for a party.

'Excuse me, Lavender,' he said. 'What've you got there?' She smiled but didn't bother looking up. They had known each other for as long as she'd been there.

'You are so cute,' she said. 'I got homework. More homework.' But he could tell she wasn't complaining. Books were her escape from the four-wall syndrome, whether it was here, the security shed, or her one-bedroom apartment in Inglewood.

She looked up, peering at him over her glasses.

'I have a question for you,' he said. He was rubbing the side of the door. Why was he so nervous? One small step toward 'the normal life' and he had become a jumble of tics.

'Shoot,' she said, looking at him. Waiting.

'I have to get a pair of pants,' he said. 'I have some money saved up. I can buy 'em.'

Lavender smiled. She shook her head. She always did that when she was delighted. 'You're buying a pair of pants,' she said, looking at his shorts. 'Will wonders never cease?'

'Here's the problem,' he said. 'Where do I go? And what kind do I buy when I get there?'

She looked at him. 'What's it for?'

'Personal,' he said.

'Ah,' she replied, smiling widely, the spaces between her teeth mocking him. She looked like a cartoon character.

'Okay, then,' she said. 'I'm assuming it's not formal.'

Formal. Just the word sent shivers down his spine. He shook his head, emphatically. Still rubbing the doorway with his thumb.

'And not too casual,' she said.

He nodded.

'Dockers,' she said. 'And you might want to get yourself a shirt, too, while you're at it.'

Sam looked at his shirt. He had three like it — all short-sleeved T-shirts. One gray, one white, one gray and white. One of them was a Surfrider benefit giveaway. The other two had been given to him by Mrs. Kennicot, when she'd tired of the logos.

'Any idea what kind of shirt goes with these 'Dockers'?'

'Boy, you got to figure out some things on your own,' Lavender said. 'Do I look like a personal stylist?'

'What's that?' Sam said.

But Lavender was lost to him. She was facing away from him now, and though he could not see her face, he could feel her mouth curve down, her eyebrows pinching together. Her mood had shifted. Something about the way her shoulders rose beneath her crisp white uniform shirt. Her fingers tapping the pages of her book.

A large black car was turning into the Colony. Lavender was half standing, half sitting as it suddenly sped up and whipped past —

Lavender leaped up, raising the wooden barrier just in time.

Sam caught the half-opened window, the shock of black hair with bleached tips. The black sunglasses. The smirk. The sound of laughter coming from all sides.

When Lavender sat back down, Sam could feel she was vibrating.

'Assholes,' he said, clearing his throat. He wished he could sound more articulate, for her sake. He wished he could put together a string of words that would make it all better for her. That would put an end to the humiliation he knew she was feeling. He brought his hand forward, as if to touch her shoulder, to undo the knot that he saw form in front of his eyes.

'Just kids,' Lavender said, staring at the pages

of her book. 'That's all. Just kids.'

Sam walked off, toward Mrs. Kennicot's. It was only when he got halfway there that he realized he'd been clenching his fists.

23

Dinner With Friends and Lover

7:20 P.M.: Gracie standing, dress on over pants, looking in the mirror.

7:22 P.M.: Gracie standing, T-shirt on, nothing underneath, looking in the mirror.

7:24 P.M.: Gracie standing, naked, looking in the mirror, razor in her hand.

7:25 P.M.: Joan yelling at Gracie to get the hell downstairs and help her with setting the table.

7:30 P.M.: Table is set. Joan is looking at Gracie and shaking her head.

★ ★ ★

'What are you wearing?' Joan asked.

Gracie looked down at herself. 'I saw Kate Hudson wearing a long T-shirt over pants.'

'That's Kate Hudson. She's a child. Now go upstairs and put on a proper dress.'

Which is how Gracie wound up wearing one of Joan's Diane von Furstenberg wrap dresses, one with forgiving fabric and design.

Gracie made a mental note to write a letter to Diane, thanking her if she got laid that night.

By 7:45, most of the guests had arrived — the guests being Will, Cricket, and Jorge. Joan was serving Mojitos, the Cuban drink, which was being billed as the new Cosmopolitan.

Prince Charming the Unencumbered had still not arrived.

Gracie was already on her second Mojito — a sort of Mojito-drinking record for her, as she had never had one before. She was grateful that Jaden, sleeping over at Daddy's house, would not be a witness to her bender.

'Maybe he didn't get the time right?' Cricket asked.

'Why are you smiling so much?' Will asked Cricket.

'Those *Girls Gone Wild* tapes,' Cricket whispered. 'They've changed our lives.'

Jorge just grinned and held up his Mojito.

'I should be a masturbation agent,' Will said. 'But how would I collect my ten percent?'

'Can you bring me up to speed?' Joan asked. 'Because I'm going to need my own help, now that Pappy's gone.'

'Oh, Pappy,' Will cried, 'we hardly knew ye.'

There was a knock at the door, which was slightly open. Gracie and Joan pushed each other as they vied to be the first at the door.

'He's my date,' Gracie hissed.

'My invite,' Joan hissed back. 'And my house — at least for the time being!'

Joan was there first, being more slim, agile,

and faster on her feet. Gracie held herself back, aided by the iron grip of Will's hand on her shoulder.

'Indifferent!' Will whispered in her ear. 'You need to appear aloof and indifferent! Think Jackie O in her heyday!'

'Right,' Gracie said. 'How do I do that?'

'Look at me and laugh,' Will said, sitting her down. 'Tilt your head back while you do it.'

Gracie tried, she really did. She had her head back at a dizzying angle and was laughing gaily when she felt Joan and Sam step into the room.

'That's enough,' Will said. 'You're going to hurt yourself. You look like Jackie Oh-No!'

Gracie stood up and looked over to where Joan and Sam were standing. Joan had a curious look on her face. Gracie couldn't quite place it — her expression looked halfway between disturbed and fascinated.

Sam was in a white collared shirt with the sleeves rolled up to his elbows and slightly slouchy khaki pants. He looked like someone who would be very comfortable throwing a football around on an expansive patch of Hyannisport lawn.

And he was holding a bouquet of daisies in his hand, wrapped neatly in a green napkin.

'Sorry I'm late,' he said to Gracie. Sam hated being late. If only she'd known how many times he'd combed his hair, how he'd agonized over what kind of flowers to bring. He hoped that Mrs. Walsh at 218A would forgive him; he'd picked the best ones he could find in her yard. He'd make it up to her somehow. 'I brought these for the hostess — '

'Thank you, I'll put them in water,' Joan said lightly. Her voice sounded about an octave higher than normal. As she passed Gracie, she tilted her head toward the kitchen, in a conspiratorial manner.

Gracie smiled at Sam, who looked very alone without his flowers. 'Will, can you get Sam a Mojito?'

'Love to,' Will said as he put his arm in Sam's and steered his intractable body toward the bar, where Cricket and Jorge were staring into each other's eyes like sophomores on a first date.

If Joan's kitchen had had a door, she would have closed it. As it was doorless, she made do with whispering.

'How do you know him, exactly?' Joan asked. The color of her freckles intensified as she spoke.

'Are you angry?' Gracie asked. 'What is this about?'

'No, no,' Joan said. 'He just looks so familiar to me, I'm trying to place him.'

'I met him on the beach,' Gracie said, measuring her words, recalling events as they unfurled slowly in her Mojito-fied brain. 'He takes a swim every morning. And he's got a dog!'

She said that last part too loudly. She wondered why she should be excited about him having a dog, as though that proved he was a more worthy human being than a dogless person.

'Well, he's ridiculously handsome,' Joan said finally. 'If he's not gay or married or both, you, my young friend, have hit the take-me-I'm-yours jackpot.'

Gracie smiled, giddy. 'I know,' she said. 'Maybe there is a God.'

'I know I've met him before,' Joan said softly, almost to herself, as she poured dressing on the salad.

★　★　★

Cricket, caught up in the first blush of Mojito, was regaling the table with a story about her new life with Jorge, Post-Masturbatory Age. 'So, we're lying on the bed at his mother's house in Palm Springs, you know, we sometimes spend the weekend there, and he's got one hand on my boob (Will covered his ears at this) and with the other, he's, you know, whacking away. He was watching . . . 'Girls Gone Wild in . . . Baja'?'

'The sequel?' Will asked.

Cricket pinched Jorge's cheek. He turned crimson and poured himself some wine.

'Anyway,' she blearily continued, 'I'm reading the *Enquirer* or *Star* while he's 'busy' . . . I forget what I was reading . . . so his mother opens the door — I don't think she knocked — ' She turned to Jorge. 'Did she knock?'

Jorge shrugged. 'I don't think she knocked,' he said.

'She's not a knocker. She opens the door, and sees us — imagine it, now, I'm lying on the bed, fully clothed, except my top's open, I've got the *Enquirer* covering my face, Jorge's hand is on my breast (Will screams), and he's almost done — '

Gracie looked sideways toward Sam, who was following the story. She couldn't read his face. Was he enjoying it? Did she want him to enjoy it?

Emboldened first by rum, and now by the Argentinian red, she slid her hand over to his knee, praying that he would take it.

He did.

'And she goes, 'Excuse me!' and jumps out the door — '

Jorge nodded. 'I think she jumped.'

'That's fascinating, Cricket, really — ' Joan said.

'I'd like a bit more detail,' Will said. 'But delete the bare breast. This is a mixed crowd.'

'I'm not finished,' Cricket said. 'So, later on she says to him, 'Is Cricket a good wife? Is she taking care of you?' '

Everyone laughed. Partially because it proved to be a funny story, but mostly because Cricket so needed them to.

'You know what, Cricket?' Joan said when the laughter died down. 'I think I liked it better when you were miserable. Right now, your successful love life is more than I can handle.'

'You're a true friend,' Cricket said, a bit slurred. 'True friends are those to whom you can freely express your jealousy and hatred.'

'Here, here,' Joan said, and she raised her glass. She threw back the rest of her wine. 'Anyone need anything?' she asked, as she stood. 'I'm going to get my cigarettes.'

Sam stood up as Joan left the table, and stayed standing until she disappeared up the stairs. He had stood for practically half the dinner — when

Cricket went to the bathroom, when Gracie had to grab the salt and pepper, when Joan had forgotten the bread, which had been burning in the oven.

Will looked over at him. 'You're like Sean Connery meets Emily Post. Love that standing thing.'

Sam shrugged and smiled. 'It's been beaten into me, I guess.'

'Some people are civilized,' Gracie said to Will as she stood to take her plate to the kitchen, Sam jumping up to help her with her chair.

'Not in the wilds of Malibu,' Will retorted.

Gracie slipped into the kitchen and scraped her plate into the wastebasket below the sink. The steak had been delicious, but she hadn't eaten more than three bites. The drinks had made her giddy, and Sam's presence had rendered her completely satiated. She remembered this feeling from long ago and savored it — the feeling that she was falling in . . . if not love, then infatuation. And she would happily settle for infatuation. Infatuation, she thought, gave you a glow, put energy in your step, made you forget that you were dumped by your husband the minute your upper lip disappeared . . .

Gracie pressed her thinning upper lip toward her nose, catching her reflection in the kitchen window. Then she saw, outside in the twilight, the familiar green blanket, the remarkable rhythm.

'Is there no escape?' Gracie said. 'Our entertainment has arrived!' she shouted, turning her head toward the living room.

Joan and Will, followed by Sam (Cricket and Jorge were busy making out at the table), encircled Gracie as she pointed to the beach.

'Oh, dear,' Will said, his hand sliding to the side of his cheek like a queer interpretation of Jack Benny. 'He's going to hurt somebody.'

'Disgusting!' Joan said. 'Right outside my window! Doesn't he realize people live here?'

'He's been performing every morning,' Gracie said. 'I've talked to the lifeguards, I've called the sheriff. Apparently, it's impossible to arrest someone for covert masturbation.'

She sighed, watching him. 'I guess he's extending his hours.'

'He's the 7-Eleven of self-stimulators,' Will said.

'He's ruining breakfast *and* dinner!' Joan said, leaning farther out for a closer look.

Sam watched intently for a moment, as though committing the act to memory, then looked away. Gracie saw something flash across his eyes, and then just as quickly extinguish.

Joan tried to open the German window, to no avail. Then she banged her fist on it. But the windows were soundproof — and her fists were no competition for the crashing of the waves.

'I think I just hurt myself,' she said, cradling her hand. Sam took Joan's hand and turned it over in his and rubbed it gently between his thumb and forefinger.

Joan stared at him, and then looked over at Gracie, her eyebrows dancing.

'Is that better?' he said as he handed Joan her

limp hand back. She just nodded, looking up at him with her mouth ajar, as though she'd had a stroke. Gracie moved closer to Sam and put her arm around his waist, marking her territory. Just in case.

'Oh, honey, he does massage?' Will asked Gracie. 'I have this knot in my shoulder,' he said, turning his back to Sam and pointing.

Sam placed both his hands on Will's shoulder. Gracie could see his large hands squeezing, tightening, holding, releasing, as Will groaned and sighed. 'You have no idea how stressful it is, taking care of all the Hollywood wives. I'm actually twelve years old, but look at me. I look twenty-seven.'

Soon, Jorge and Cricket were lined up, eager to experience Sam's 'magic hands.'

Gracie was the last one in line, just as the sky was darkening outside. The others were dispersing to different areas throughout the house. Cricket and Jorge had made themselves cozy on the living room couch. Joan was sitting across from them. Will made himself comfortable on the armrest, his head resting on Joan's shoulder.

'Come with me,' Sam whispered in Gracie's ear. Gracie literally shuddered in anticipation as he took her hand and led her outside.

The moon, so big and white, could not help but cast its spell over anyone who looked its way. Gracie had never understood the pull of a full moon until just that instant.

Sam sat down on a chaise longue and motioned for her to sit directly in front of him, with her back to him. She slipped her dress up and put one leg over the chair, and sat down. The chaise fabric was damp, but her desire overrode discomfort.

'What do you think of my friends?' she asked.

Sam didn't answer. He knew Gracie didn't need him to, that she was still a little nervous, making conversation. Instead, he took his finger and drew a line slowly along the side of her neck, down to her shoulder, then up again toward her earlobe. And then he did the same on the other side of her neck, pressing lightly and then increasingly hard. Her mind told her he was just sizing up the knots in her muscles. Her body told her something else. Those two would have to get their stories straight at some point.

Sam put one hand on the side of her head and tilted her face toward the sky and gently worked on the side of her neck with his free hand as he held her head in the other. She sighed as she slipped into the moment, one that moved as slowly as she wanted. One that approached with patience.

One that she hoped wouldn't last too damn long, as she really wanted to kiss him again.

She put her hand on his and turned to face him, pushing her lips onto his mouth. She felt like a martial artist in the sport of love, a black belt in kissing.

'Dessert!' Joan cried.

Gracie looked up to see Will, Cricket, Jorge, and Joan staring at them.

'You like apple tart à la mode or plain?' Joan asked, holding up a dessert plate.

'Come on,' Will said. 'It smells heavenly, come

on, come on, come on.' He walked out onto the deck and grabbed Gracie by the arm, hauling her up from the chaise.

'What has gotten into you?' Gracie asked.

'You love dessert,' Will said. 'I know you. Especially anything with apples.'

'You love apples,' Cricket said, her eyes wide. Jorge stood next to her, nodding frantically.

Gracie narrowed her eyes at them. 'I don't know what you guys are up to — '

'Up to?' Joan asked. 'We just want to eat!'

Sam stood up and followed Gracie into the kitchen.

'Gracie,' Sam said, 'I'm tired. Maybe we can continue this another time.'

Gracie looked at Sam. It was the first time she'd heard him saying her name. Or maybe she just hadn't been paying attention. His body had been too heavy a distraction.

Joan nodded and smiled, too sweetly for the Joan that Gracie knew. 'Oh, that's a shame. You sure you don't want any dessert?' she asked.

'Joan,' Sam said, 'I'm afraid I couldn't eat another bite if I tried. Thank you for your hospitality.'

He nodded to Will, who gave him a little wave, and to Cricket and Jorge, and then walked out of the kitchen. Gracie followed him, but not before turning back to glare at her friends.

She grabbed Sam at the door. 'I'm sorry,' Gracie said. 'They're being overprotective, I think. You know, I'm going through a divorce.'

Sam took that moment because he thought it might be all that they'd have. And he kissed her again, running his hands through her hair, as though memorizing every curl with his fingertips.

'I'll see you tomorrow,' Gracie said, breathlessly. What was it about this man that turned her into mush?

Sam stepped outside and into the cool night air and Gracie watched him go, then closed the door. She stood there, her back pressed against the door, locked in Sam's imaginary embrace. Gracie closed her eyes.

When she opened them, Joan was standing in front of her, a look of concern shading her face.

'How well do you know Sam?' Joan asked.

'Joan,' Gracie said, putting her hands on her friend's shoulders, 'I know him well enough to fall in love.'

Gracie stared into Joan's eyes and knew that her friend was making a decision. She was silent for a moment.

'Great,' Joan finally said, and hugged Gracie. 'I'm happy for you.'

Will had joined them in the foyer. 'I think I'm going to skip dessert,' Gracie said. 'I swear, I'm floating on air. How did this happen to me?'

She kissed Joan and Will good night, and they watched her as she ascended the stairs. Joan looked over at Will. 'Goddamn,' she said. 'She *is* floating.'

WIFE NUMBER ELEVEN

Was somewhat uncontrollable. Husband is a powerful entertainment lawyer. She had three young children, she was a brunette, she had big (new) boobs, and she was a drunk who would throw herself at other men. Lots of other men. Her husband, an amateur photographer, was at his wit's end. Finally he snapped pictures of Mrs. Lush after a party, as she administered a blow job on a valet parker in her driveway. The husband put the film in a safe-deposit box. He threatened to show the kids, when they were old enough to understand.

She stopped drinking. They recently had a fourth child.

24

The Morning After

Gracie barely slept. How could she sleep when her entire nervous system was on high alert? She was giddy, overflowing with carnal expectation. She was fully awake and dressed by six o'clock in the morning. She set about trying to fill her time until the moment when she would see Sam again. She watched the news without focusing. She took an extra-long time to make the pot of coffee she didn't need. She meandered onto the deck and watched pelicans swoop down into the water. She observed a trio of dolphins arcing up over the waves.

And then it was six-fifteen.

Finally, she decided to go for a power walk up the beach. Gracie thought of waking Joan, who hadn't seen a sunrise since the 1980s. But she couldn't wait to get started on the day, so she walked down to the beach alone.

★   ★   ★

An hour later, Gracie found herself standing in front of #191, restlessly shifting her weight from foot to foot. She was wondering if it was too early. Would she wake Sam? It wasn't time for his morning swim quite yet. But Gracie could not wait any longer. She decided to surprise him. Finally she knocked. Then tousled her hair, shook the sand off her feet. And knocked again.

No one answered. Gracie knocked once more.

She thought she heard a voice calling out, the warbly sound of someone who is old and weak.

The door opened slowly. A very old woman in a housedress and slippers was standing there. The hairs on her head stood up like dandelion seeds; they looked as though they could be blown away by a soft wind.

'Sorry, sweetie,' the old woman said, squinting in the sun. 'I'm not too quick on my feet anymore.' She coughed.

Gracie shook her head to reassure the woman and also because she could not suppress her confusion. What was this old woman doing in Sam's house? Was she his mother? He hadn't mentioned a mother . . .

'I'm sorry, I'm just looking for Sam,' Gracie said, peeking her head inside. The furnishings looked old and threadbare and chic at the same time, as though trends had circled around through time and caught up again.

'Sam . . . Knight lives here, right?' Gracie found herself asking. The old lady looked as though she was having a flashback. Her eyes faded from the present and then returned.

'Oh, I've wanted him to move in, many times,' the lady smiled. 'But you know, he just refuses. He doesn't want favors. Such a nice boy.'

Gracie's mouth felt as though it were stuffed with sawdust. 'Where . . . does he live?' she asked, the words feeling dry and stiff, like tiny pieces of wood.

'Over there,' the lady said. 'Just beyond the tennis court.'

Gracie looked over to where the old lady was pointing. She saw . . . shrubs. Behind the shrubs was a thicket of overgrown trees.

'There?'

'Yes,' the old lady said, looking slightly perplexed. 'You can come through my kitchen, if you like. I'll open the back door. Sam usually just hops the fence. I don't recommend it. My boys had to get tetanus shots years ago because of that fence. I should probably have replaced it . . . ' Her words trailed off.

Gracie stared at the shrubbery.

'Come with me,' the old lady said, as she shuffled into the house. Gracie followed, her feet suddenly leaden.

'Do you have a problem with your plumbing?' the lady turned and asked her when they entered the kitchen, which faced the back of the Colony. Gracie could see through a dusty window the lineup of bushes and trees and not much else. Not anything else. Gracie looked at her.

'I don't mean to pry,' the lady said, looking at the expression on Gracie's face. 'Sam's wonderful with his hands, he's blessed. He can fix anything, that boy.'

Gracie nodded. He almost fixed me, she thought.

The old lady opened the ancient latch on the door. The door wheezed open. Gracie stepped outside.

'He's just down the trail,' the old lady said. 'But I doubt he's there right now. He takes his swim every morning, you know. He and Baxter.'

She waved to Gracie, and Gracie turned and put one foot forward, and then the other, and willed herself onward.

★   ★   ★

Grace walked slowly along the back edge of the land-side Malibu Colony homes, which cost half as much as their more tony beachside companions.

The trail was thin; two people would have trouble walking side by side. The Colony side was protected by a chicken-wire fence topped with rusty barbed wire. On the other side, there was overhanging brush, pockets of trash — soda cans, beer bottles, slashes of paper.

Gracie suddenly spied the glint of something that felt familiar to her, although she'd never seen it before.

She had to get on her hands and knees and crawl in like Jaden at ten months, unaware of dirt and insects and skinned knees and discomfort, thinking only of . . . discovery.

There was a clearing in the brush. A neat six-by-six patch, covered by cardboard sheets. In the corner was a blanket, folded neatly over a rolled-up sleeping bag. There was a stack of books piled in the opposite corner, along with several T-shirts. A pair of orange shorts. And one pair of Dockers. Gracie stepped inside, under the brush, and reached for the Dockers, smoothing the material beneath her fingers. She pushed them into her face and smelled Sam. Sadder still, she could even smell her own perfume from the night before.

Her heart didn't stop beating like she thought it should. Her breathing, ragged though it was, still struggled on.

She sat on that cardboard buried in the thicket, like a lost storybook character, and waited as tears began to roll down her cheeks. She had been made a fool of not once, not twice, but three times by men in the last few months. It had to be some kind of record.

At the very least, Gracie thought, *I should get a medal. What was the saying? Fool me once, shame on you. Fool me twice, shame on me.*

'Fool me three times,' Gracie said out loud. 'I give up.'

She stood up, clutching at her stomach, and suddenly threw up what she hadn't eaten the night before, right onto the trail.

As she wobbled toward the public beach, it occurred to her that Joan had tried to tell her the truth last night. But Gracie hadn't wanted to hear it.

She was rounding the trail as it collided with Surfrider Beach when she turned and saw, inside the Colony fence, the red light on top of the black-and-white casting an intermittent glow on the Millionaire Row of beach houses.

★ ★ ★

'Mr. Right is Mr. Homeless,' Joan said. 'I'm sorry.'

Gracie looked at her, eyes swollen and moist, then took another Kleenex from the box Joan was holding and blew her nose for the hundredth time. 'I knew something was up last night,' Gracie stuttered, 'but I thought you might just be jealous because I had a boyfriend who still uses a normal toilet.'

'I wish it weren't true, Gracie,' Joan said, putting her arm around her. 'Believe me. I would love to see you with the right man.'

Gracie burrowed into her friend's shoulder.

'That's not the only thing,' Joan said. Gracie looked up at her. Her face was so serious, Gracie drew in her stomach, physically girding herself against incoming.

'The rumor is,' Joan continued, 'he killed a man.'

A cry emitted from Gracie's lips. She pressed the back of her hand to her mouth.

'With his bare hands,' Joan said.

★ ★ ★

There wasn't enough soap on the planet to clean out Gracie's mouth.

'I can't believe I kissed him!' Gracie screamed as soap foamed up in her mouth. 'Did it have to be with his bare hands?!'

Gracie thought Joan must have hashed and rehashed the discovery of the night before with the whole gang before going to bed. *Why wouldn't they talk about it?* Gracie thought. Sam was interesting without the homeless/murderer factor — with it, he was practically *Time*'s Man of the Year.

'I let him massage my hand,' Joan pointed out. 'It's kind of sexy, really. The possibility of a handsome, refined psychotic in our midst.'

Gracie looked at Joan as a ray of hope emerged. 'It doesn't necessarily mean he's a bad person, right? People make mistakes.'

'Strangling someone is not a mistake,' Joan said. 'It's a life choice.'

'I'm such a loser,' Gracie said, looking at her lathered reflection in the mirror.

25

Man on the Run

'Any particular reason why the cops are looking for you?' Lavender asked Sam without looking up.

Sam shrugged and hoped the shrug conveyed a sense of conviction. But he knew Lavender was too smart to depend on gesture. 'I believe . . . alimony payments,' he said, smiling. 'I'm owed about twenty years.'

Lavender cocked an eyebrow. 'You were married?' she asked.

'Why? Don't you think I'm old enough?' Sam Knight asked, and then, 'So, what'd you tell 'em?' He looked off past Malibu Road, feigning disinterest as he focused on a spot somewhere above PCH.

'They showed me a picture of you in uniform,' Lavender said. 'I said they don't let ugly like that in here. We got regulations.'

Sam allowed a smile. He'd been chased by the cops before, wasn't the first time, wouldn't be the last. Happened all the time to people with his type of 'undeliverable as addressed' location. Only, there wasn't a reason he could think of this morning. Had he done something wrong? Or was this his past, catching up with him, like the stubborn child who eventually overtakes his father on the tennis court, the basketball court, in life.

'I told him I hadn't seen you,' Lavender said, forcing a casual tone as her eyes pored over her latest book, 'but if I did run into you, I'd turn you in.'

Sam looked at her. Lavender was smiling, her mouth closed in a quarter moon, turning the page.

Sam gave her a little wave and started to walk away.

'I'm graduating, you know,' Lavender said, soft as a passing cloud.

'What's that?' he asked, turning back. He wasn't sure he had heard her right.

Lavender pulled up her head, facing him. Color had risen in her cheeks. 'I'm graduating. I'm getting my AA — the degree, not the other thing.'

Sam hesitated for a moment — he was filled with the type of pride he would feel for a child. He put out his hand — which she accepted, breaching the awkward moment. They had never touched before. *Years*, Sam thought, as they stood facing each other. *Years, I've known her, and this is the first time I feel her skin.* Her hand felt dry and warm and pleasantly full, like a mother's hand should feel.

Lavender suddenly pulled him back with her arm, yanking him into the station. The sheriff's car was rolling up slowly, silently. Lavender motioned for Sam to crouch behind a tower of boxes haphazardly stacked, with labels like COLONY, 1997.

Sam saw Lavender touch her finger to her forehead and flip her hand out, a good-bye gesture to the men in the car.

'It's okay,' she said to him. He stood up.

'They said this was the last place you were reported seen,' she said, as though talking to the air. 'They said it was a personal matter.'

Sam just nodded. 'Could be, could be.'

'What'd you do?' Lavender asked, though he could tell she was afraid of any possible answer.

'I don't know,' he answered. And this time, he didn't.

She flipped a card over to him. 'I wanted you to . . . ' Lavender said, faltering. 'It's this thing. Next week — I know you probably can't make it, but, I figured, you know, we're friends . . . '

Sam was looking off toward the brake lights of the sheriff's car as it rounded the corner and sped onto Malibu Road.

It was only when he was walking away, toward Mrs. Kennicot's, when he looked at the card Lavender had given him.

It was a graduation announcement. Lavender had invited him to her graduation. Sometimes, Sam thought, you had to leave a little window open in your soul for the element of surprise.

★   ★   ★

Later in the afternoon, Joan was still in the kitchen, staring out the window, the sport of choice in a place where the view cost upwards of $1,000 a day.

'The masturbator,' Gracie said as she walked in. 'He's gone.'

She gestured toward the green blanket, lying there on the sand, between the house and the lifeguard station.

'Wow,' Joan said. 'Do you think Sam took care of him? That would make him some kind of hero.'

'There were cops inside the Colony,' Gracie said. 'I thought someone might be looking for him.'

'You are getting carried away,' Joan said to Gracie.

'You're the one who told me he may have killed a man,' Gracie replied.

'I was thinking about that,' Joan said. 'And two things: One, that was years ago, ancient history. And two, it's probably not even true. Suburban legend.'

She went to light a cigarette. Gracie remembered when Joan had quit, years before. It had taken a long time and a lot of accessories — NicoDerm patches, Nicorette gum, the works, to kick the habit. Gracie stared at her as she brought the lighter close to her face.

'What?' Joan said. 'You've never seen a cigarette?' She lit it and, with much effort, opened the German window, sticking the lit side out. 'Don't worry, never in front of the baby.'

But now Gracie was thinking about Sam. She wanted to approach the issue of her homeless, perhaps murderous boyfriend in a methodical, logical manner, taking into consideration every aspect of his being.

Mostly, she was curious to see if her need to have sex with him outweighed more practical considerations — like the fact that he may have killed someone.

Suddenly Gracie understood why the Son of Sam and that guy who terrorized Los Angeles in the early eighties (not Rick James, the other one) had more than their fair share of possible booty calls. She was fighting something primal — the brute caveman who clocked the pocket protector — caveman and dragged off his woman by the hair survived. Who was she to fight off thousands of years of biology and evolution?

Gracie grabbed a pen and a pad of paper.

'What are you doing?' Joan asked, taking a drag off her cigarette, then peering over at her. Gracie took note on her morning walks of just how many cigarette butts were left on the beach — it was a wonder to her that people came to one of the few places left on earth that had clean air and proceeded to light up.

'Deciding my future,' Gracie said.

Gracie consulted Joan on the benefits of dating a homeless man — one who may or may not be homicidal. They divided the major categories into home, work, play, family, with various subcategories for each.

Over coffee, they discussed Gracie's possible future and compared it to her past (with the horrible Kenny the Pig). Joan wrote:

A. HOME

a   Pro: Not underfoot. No early-morning comparisons of 'the numbers.' No searching the L.A. Times, New York Times, USA Today and Post for bad news about your friends. Very little complaint about the size of Scott Rudin's swimming pool as compared to yours. Not a lot of time spent on the Exercycle watching countless hours of Tivo'd Entertainment Tonight and Access Hollywood. Perhaps more interested in sex than in resting heart rate. Not big on fixtures. Could make own meals out of neighbor's trash. GREAT kisser.

b) Con: Tough living with homicidal maniac. Violence a key factor in marital happiness. Also . . . what does he eat? Would he sleep outside? Would he insist on showering from the hose? Who are his friends? Do they have teeth and are they clean enough to sit on furniture? Would have to hide all sharp objects (see: homicidal maniac, above). Would have to monitor daughter's use of the word 'homeless' (perhaps by substituting the word 'apple' for 'homeless,' as in 'why can't that 'apple' get a job like everyone else?').

c) Questions for Future Reference: Sports fan?

B. WORK

a Pro: Not a big upside here. However. Is available for babysitting. And sex. Doesn't have to entertain work 'friends.' Doesn't scream epithets into the phone in front of three-year-old when the script 'isn't right.'

b) Con: No visible means of support. Could get old.

C. PLAY

a Pro: Heavily available for all activities. Movies, theater, sex, long walks, and sex. Tennis not a major priority. Also, there's the matter of lots of sex.

b) Con: May not like enclosed spaces. Have to check.

D. FAMILY

a Pro: Not much of a problem with mother-in-law issues. Or any family issues, for that matter.

b) Con: Can't have homicidal maniac around three-year-old daughter. Tricky.

★ ★ ★

'All in all,' Joan said, taking a look at the list, 'I'd say it's a tough call. Care for a Bloody?'

'No,' Gracie said, 'I'm fine. The last time I had a drink in the morning was the last time I had a drink in the morning, if you get my meaning.'

'I think every day should be like a vacation, don't you?' Joan asked, without needing or expecting an answer. So Gracie didn't bother answering her back. She just stood and watched Joan take tomato juice from the refrigerator and vodka from the freezer and proceed to mix them in a tall, slim glass, all the while squelching the terror seizing up in her stomach. Gracie's stomach was the most dependable measure of her emotions. Though her stomach lately resembled a shopping bag more than a body part, she still trusted it like an old, seen-better-days friend.

Gracie's best friend was in the throes of a major problem; Joan was looking down the line at a future of morning Bloody Marys followed by mid-morning Tequila Sunrises followed by afternoon tugs on fat joints followed by bottles of Trader Joe's cheap but amiable Chilean reds topped off with a mountain of wet cigarettes piling up in a sink somewhere in the Hollywood Hills where once-glamorous actresses and writers go to retire.

'What is it?' Gracie whispered. She realized she'd been so caught up in her homeless boyfriend's antics that she'd forgotten about her friend's pain — the friend who had given her and her daughter a place to stay, the one who always made sure her needs were taken care of, the one who held her as she realized the love of her life ate out of trashcans and peed in alleys.

Only a true friend could tell you these things and live.

'Pappy called me,' Joan said. 'He definitely wants a divorce.' She tossed the cigarette into the sink before it was done, then lit another.

'I'm so sorry,' Gracie said, even though she wasn't so, so sorry — she never thought Pappy was right for Joan or anyone who could get around without need of orthopedic shoes.

'I know you think I never should have married him,' Joan said.

Gracie just looked at her. When did Joan start reading minds? This could be dangerous. Gracie chided herself not to get annoyed at Joan's more annoying tics. 'Of course I did. You married Barnaby Jones. I thought it was insane. I still do,' she said, building strength. 'In fact, you shouldn't even waste your time being sad, as far as I'm concerned.'

Instead of screaming at her, Joan nodded. 'That's the fucked-up thing about love,' she said, taking another long drag on the cigarette. 'It doesn't discriminate.'

Gracie stared at Joan, at the sadness of her posture, the languid, tragic way she stared out the window. In the muted light of the morning fog, she looked like an actress in the kind of French film that seemed important when you talked about it, but that really made no sense at all when you watched it.

Gracie found herself shaking her head with a

sense of wonder. 'Love has no taste,' she said. 'You're in love with your grandfather, and I'm in love with a guy whose idea of a job is squeegeeing windows.' Gracie mimicked being on the phone with her 'husband.' 'How's work going, honey?' she asked. 'Oh, yeah? Forty-three windows today? Wow!'

'Damned profound, huh?' Joan asked.

Gracie thought about this for a second. 'Friends Über Alles. C'mon,' She continued, pulling on Joan's sleeve. 'Let's go out on the deck and welcome the unwashed masses.'

Gracie jumped up and ran out on the deck, leaving Joan to contemplate her sudden vivacity. 'What's making you so fucking happy?' Joan called after her. 'Don't you know your life is a complete shambles?'

*   *   *

Gracie stood out on the deck, which abutted the fence dividing Surfrider from the Colony. The fence was as ridiculous a deterrent as a constitutional monarchy on a third-world island nation. First of all, it was made of rusted chicken wire which probably started showing the effects of nature and age soon after it was erected thirty years ago. Secondly, though there was barbed wire woven onto the top of the chicken wire, it was a deterrent without teeth. Because thirdly, there was four feet of fence, and anywhere from three to five feet of open space underneath, depending on the tides. Also, as if all this were not enough, the fence was not built past the low tide line. Anyone could walk *around* the fence, if they were not eager to bend down the five inches it would take to walk *under* it.

But what the fence did have was a sign. A simple sign, which read in big black block letters against a white backdrop: PRIVATE BEACH. DO NOT TRESPASS. And then, in fine print: TO THE MEAN HIGH TIDE LINE.

Well, Gracie had checked out the mean high tide line. She had asked J.D., the bulky, world-weary security chief at Malibu Colony, what the hell a mean high tide line was.

'You're trying to get me in trouble,' he'd said to her.

'I'm just curious,' Gracie'd said. She'd seen the news crews out by the fence from time to time. There was a class storm brewing — rich people did not want 'others' in front of their houses on their private beaches.

There was only one catch: The California coastline — all 1,100 miles of it, was public. There was no private beach in California.

Oopsies.

J.D. had taken a walk with Gracie along the beach and pointed out the mean high tide line.

The mean high tide line could be found in the spacious living rooms of most people living in the Colony. The mean high tide line could reach all the way to their plasma screen television sets, to the minor Picassos they deemed worthy of their second homes. The mean high tide line was definitely beyond the French chaises and $20,000 barbecue grills gracing the deck.

In other words, the hoi polloi could legally eat

out of their KFC family-sized tubs right at the dinner table, alongside the chateaubriand and Cristal.

For days after her conversation with J.D., Gracie had watched in earnest as people would walk up to the unassuming fence with the intimidating sign. She could predict their behavior, depending on what the person was wearing, what they were carrying, how many children they had, their ethnicity. She could do her own sociological study, based on people's reaction to what she regarded as an infamous sign, now that she questioned its legality.

American tourists — usually a mother bogged down by an enormous tote which held everything, Gracie surmised, from Handi Wipes to psychedelic Fruit Roll-Ups to pepper spray (this being Los Angeles, after all), a father toting a camera and a fat wallet in his waist purse, two prepubescent kids exposing their soft white bellies for the first time in a year to sunlight — would walk slowly up to the fence, their eyes never leaving the sign. They would read very, very carefully, then look up the beach, then reread, then look up the beach again, consult each other for a minute or two, read the sign again, take note of the people walking onto Surfrider from the Colony. Then, in a towering gesture of defeat, they would turn and walk away.

German tourists, tall, broad, tan, and violently blond, would try to read the sign, take note of the barbed wire, and then take pictures of Joan's, er, Pappy's house. They, too, would stay on the

Surfrider side of the beach.

Mexican families would barbecue and lay out their picnics on the other side of Joan's, er, Pappy's house, but generally they would ignore the damned sign if they felt like sticking their toes in the water or even fishing on the rich, pristine side of the beach (thus, and so, Fourth of July).

Surfers carrying their boards under their arms would just bend down far enough to get under the fence, chatting loudly. The sign wasn't their concern. The sign was there to keep the landlocked out.

Gracie and Joan stood at the foot of the deck nearest the sand, where Gracie could see the fence most easily. Just as she predicted, there was a family standing there, the father's face red from exertion and sun, the mother staring quizzically at the sign. Two kids. Gracie waved at the family, signaling that it was okay to make the seemingly verboten trek to the other side of the fence. They looked at her and smiled. They always did.

'You can't do that,' Joan said.

'I do it all the time,' Gracie replied. She grabbed the drink in Joan's hand and placed it on the outdoor table. 'Come on. It'll make you feel good,' she said to Joan.

For the rest of the afternoon, Joan and Gracie sat on their chaise longues waving in a steady stream of people who wished to continue their walks along the beach.

'You know how this feels?' Joan asked her as the sun set over Point Dume and the Great

Painter washed the sky with reds and oranges and purples.

'It feels like we just had a party,' she sighed. Gracie just nodded and watched as her friend bounced back inside the house.

26

Chili's Revenge

The Malibu Chili Cook-off is traditionally held on the hottest day of the year, no matter the actual date. The scent of twenty different types of chili mixes with the smells of perspiration and popcorn and the sounds of ten different thrill rides spinning and twirling and rising and dropping and kids screaming and parents yelling for their lost children, and generally speaking, it's the kind of thing that looks like great fun from a distance of about a quarter mile.

Which is where Gracie was, at the Malibu Colony security shack directly across the street from the fairgrounds.

Gracie and Lavender were staring at the jumble of rides that had risen overnight like neon sphinxes.

'They're gonna be coming now,' Lavender said, shaking her head. 'You know I got to drive here from Inglewood?'

Gracie nodded. She'd heard about the Inglewood drive before. Many times.

'Don't eat that chili,' Lavender warned. 'Nothing good comes out of that chili.'

'I hear it's pretty good.'

'Don't listen to me then,' Lavender said. 'You pay the piper one way or the other.' The clever positioning of her hands made it clear that payment would include either vomiting or having the runs.

But Gracie was lost to her, staring at the giant, lit-up Ferris wheel exuding both thrills and danger, and the promise of vomit. Gracie trusted the safety of thrill rides that were set up in less than twenty-four hours at outdoor fairgrounds about as much as she trusted a Hollywood agent to tell her she had something in her teeth.

'Jaden's never been on a Ferris wheel. I think she'll love it,' Gracie said. She was already planning on taking her daughter across the street in their little red wagon. Though she had issues with Malibu, there was something to enjoy about the village atmosphere — the multimillion-dollar-village atmosphere.

* * *

'Daddy's on a magazine,' Jaden announced as she walked in the front door. Kenny was right behind her. Gracie couldn't be certain, but it sounded as though Jaden had been coached. She had that 'child actor auditioning for a Burger King commercial' tenor in her voice.

'Is that right?' Gracie said. 'Will wonders and slow news days never cease.'

'It's really nothing,' Kenny said, in a way which virtually broadcast the opposite. 'It's just the cover of — '

'*Us?*' Gracie asked.

'Oh, so you saw it,' Kenny said, his left hand

stopping midway to the magazine tucked under his right arm.

'No,' Gracie smiled. 'Just a good guess. I was pretty sure it wasn't *The New Yorker*.'

Kenny, as oblivious to insult as a Jim Carrey movie, was off and running. He whipped the magazine from under his arm. 'It's a shot of us, you know, me and Britney — ' He looked up at her.

Gracie nodded, as though trying to communicate with a toddler. 'Somehow, I didn't think it was you and me.'

'I guess I'll just have to get used to it,' Kenny said. 'You know, all the paparazzi.' He sighed with all the skills of a Method actor and pushed his hair back. Jaden had gone up to her room. Gracie noticed she was back in her Jaden clothes — tennis shoes, a knee-length dress. No belly dynamics. Something had changed.

Kenny smoothed the magazine on the kitchen counter. 'I have other copies,' he said. 'You can have this one.'

Gracie looked at the magazine. 'Wow, really?' she asked. 'You would do that, for me?'

She went back to staring at the magazine as curiosity wrestled her powers of sarcastic detachment and won. She saw Britney, her brown eyes smiling in one direction even as her full mouth pouted in another. She was in black. A great deal of her skin was covered.

Gracie recognized the outfit — Britney had worn it to Lou's funeral.

What she didn't see was Kenny.

'Where are you?' Gracie finally asked, after

studying the photo for clues. She took heart in the fact that Britney was obviously wearing false eyelashes. Gracie had always had nice eyelashes. One point in Gracie's favor.

Maybe half a point.

On the other hand, if Gracie was wrong, and Britney's eyelashes weren't fake — Gracie could lose about five points. Comparing body parts with international superstars, even those who admit to lip-synching during live concerts, was a tough game for Gracie to be playing at this or any point in her life.

'I'm right there,' Kenny said, stabbing a finger into the cover.

Gracie looked to where his finger had dented the side of Britney's body. She wasn't above noticing that Kenny had gotten a tattoo around his ring finger.

But first traumas first.

'Kenny, I don't see it — '

'That's my hand,' Kenny said. 'You see? Inside her elbow. I was leading her down the stairs.' And then he said, in hushed tones, 'You know, at Lou's funeral.' He lowered his eyes.

Gracie looked at the picture again. Then looked up at him. And for the first time in years, she felt sorry for her soon-to-be ex.

'Kenny.'

'Also, you can see part of my face,' Kenny continued. 'At the edge here.'

He peered closely at the page, outlining the edge with his finger. 'And I'm mentioned inside — '

The cover story read: 'Britney's Secret Sorrow.'

Kenny grabbed the magazine and flipped open to a page which had been marked with a tiny neon-green Post-it Note. He handed her the magazine.

Gracie took a look and started reading out loud: ''Britney Spears endured heartache when her mentor, Lou Manahan of Durango Pictures, died suddenly in a terrible drowning accident. She's seen here leaving the Forest Lawn Mortuary with a friend.''

'Where does it mention you?' Gracie asked. She was almost desperate for Kenny to get some satisfaction.

'Well, it doesn't exactly mention me by name, that'll come later,' Kenny said. 'I'm the friend.'

'Oh,' Gracie said, putting the magazine back on the counter. 'Right, right.'

'I have to be careful where I go — you know, I'm being followed by paparazzi,' Kenny mentioned for the second time. Gracie actually saw his chest puff out.

She merely shrugged and raised her eyebrows and cocked her mouth to the side as if to say, 'Poor thing.'

'Hey, are you going to the Chili Cook-off today?'

'I was going to take Jaden there — '

'Because I'm going to take, you know . . . '

'Britney? Britney Spears is going to the Chili Cook-off?'

'She's in town for a few more days and then she's taking off on tour. She's, you know, just a small-town girl. She likes that sort of thing. We have to be careful of the, you know . . . '

Gracie nodded. 'Paparazzi.'

'Did I tell you they're following me?' Kenny asked. 'Oh, hey, I just want you to know, it's okay if you're going, too.'

'Thank you,' Gracie said, as she savored the bittersweet taste of sarcasm. Divorce had not made her a better person.

Maybe the next life-changing event would.

'Hey,' Kenny said. 'Are you taking that guy?'

Gracie went blank.

'You're not dating anymore?' Kenny asked.

'Oh no, we're dating. We've never stopped dating. It's pretty much nonstop dating here in the Malibu Colony.'

'Okay, maybe I'll see him there — what's his name?'

'Sam. Sam Knight.'

'Knight. Any relation to the Knight family? The rubber business is just part of it, right? That's a good business. Bronfman was in liquor, Anschutz in real estate. Marvin Davis was oil. The Sony guys were . . . Japanese, right? Maybe I should talk to him.'

'No,' Gracie said, blunt as a fist.

'I'm sure Britney wouldn't mind double-dating,' Kenny said, oblivious to the negative bent of Gracie's reaction. Perhaps, Gracie thought, his obliviousness was some sort of survival mechanism.

Perhaps Kenny was more evolved than Gracie.

'Over my old dead body,' Gracie said under her breath. Which proved the evolved theory.

Kenny was turning to leave. 'Oh, Kenny,'

Gracie said, 'I hear the chili at the Cook-off is great.'

Kenny flashed her a thumbs-up and went out the door.

★ ★ ★

'Twirly cups!' Jaden screamed, pointing at the oversized cups that spun around. Jaden and Gracie had been on the mini-roller coaster, the Ferris wheel, and some other ride that had no name but definitely had a purpose: to cause the rider to swear never to ride it again, as long as he or she lived.

Gracie didn't know this Jaden — the Jaden who was pulling her from ride to ride, from nausea to worse. Her Jaden was serious and wise and old beyond her years. Her Jaden would be able to do Gracie's taxes in a couple years. This Jaden was something else entirely. Had Britney had a (shudder) good influence on her overly serious daughter?

'It's the corn on the cob,' Joan said as she watched from the sidelines as Gracie hobbled and Jaden hopped out of the whiplash-inducing, innocently named Twirly Cups. Joan was the official Holder of Belongings — as she would no more get on a ride at the Malibu Chili Cook-off than agree to have her nails yanked out of her fingers with needle-nose pliers. 'Theory Number One on outdoor events: Wherever there's corn dogs, there's trouble,' Joan informed Gracie as she bent over, flipped her head between her knees, and heaved.

'Daddy!' Jaden suddenly screamed, and ran through the sun-stroked masses, slipping away from Joan and Gracie.

'Jaden!' Gracie gurgled. 'Jaden, come back here!'

'I'll go after her,' Joan said, diving into the fray. Gracie checked her balance and ran after them. *Carnivals*, Gracie thought, as she pushed through the red-faced maze. *The ultimate parental test.*

Gracie came upon a knot in the crowd that was impenetrable. People were hovering like bees in a hive, except they were holding their cameras aloft, up over their heads, their lenses fixing on the center of the human knot, the vortex of the fleshy tornado. Gracie jumped high enough along the periphery to catch the top of Joan's red head. Jaden had disappeared —

'Jaden!' Gracie yelled. Her voice came out raspy. Her throat was tightening; like screaming in a dream, she thought.

'JADEN!'

Jaden shot forward between the legs of one of the two bodyguards, hurling herself into Kenny's arms.

'It's my daughter, it's all right, Bo,' Kenny said to the bodyguard. The bodyguard put his hands up; his massive pinky ring, coated in diamonds, flickered. That's cool.

Standing next to Kenny was Britney, attacking the remainder of an ice cream sandwich. Gracie focused briefly on Britney; she looked as though she could have been in her living room, sitting on a plaid couch, sucking the liquefying vanilla ice cream from between two chocolate wafers. She seemed entirely unaware of the impact of her presence on the rest of humanity. Bo the Bodyguard started to push Gracie back into the crowd, his shoulders braced against her chest —

'Not without my daughter!' Gracie screamed, uttering the same words as Sally Field in the movie in which she displays her acting chops by trading in a nun's habit for a burka.

★ ★ ★

The crowd dispersed after they'd captured their pictures of Britney eating junk food, or at least witnessed enough junk-food debauchery to report back to family that evening over the dinner table.

Gracie was holding Jaden's hand while Kenny held the other one. It was a nice domestic tableau, had it been at all domestic.

'We have to go now, Jaden,' Gracie said, tugging at her child's arm; the child who attached herself to her mother like a limpet for months of preschool was not budging.

'I want to stay with Daddy,' Jaden said, brutally slashing at her mother's heart.

Britney had sent one of the bodyguards to get her a hot dog, and he had returned. She was off to the side, awaiting the handoff.

'Can I talk to you?' Kenny said, low.

Gracie looked at Kenny; his color was off. She couldn't tell whether Kenny really looked green, or if it was just the reflection of the sun mixing with the riot of primary colors of the carnival.

'You're sick,' she concluded.

'I can't be sick in front of Britney,' he said, his voice carrying a tenor of desperation around the edges.

Gracie looked at him with an expression of, well . . .

Joy?

'It's kind of a sensitive time in our relationship,' Kenny whispered.

'Well, what do you want me to do about it?' Gracie asked. How was she supposed to help him out of this one? She couldn't have his diarrhea for him, for God's sake.

'Can we go to your house?' Kenny whined. 'I don't think I'm going to last much longer.'

Britney came over with her hot dog. She smiled and ate, smiled and ate.

Gracie smiled back. 'So, listen, we've got to go — ' She tugged again at Jaden's arm.

And then she turned to Kenny. 'Kenny, were you going to finally fix that thing for me?'

'Right, right,' Kenny said. 'The, ah, thing in the sink . . . '

'It's called a faucet,' Joan offered.

'I'd better go do that right away,' Kenny said. '*Right* away.'

★ ★ ★

Kenny came out of the bathroom paler than Nicole Kidman in winter.

'Both openings?' Gracie asked, grinning. She couldn't help herself.

Kenny held on to the doorway. He tilted his

head in what appeared to be a nod.

'Wow,' said Joan, 'impressive.'

'Do you think I could . . . ' — Kenny was gulping air like a landed goldfish — 'stay here tonight?'

Gracie looked at Joan. Joan looked back at Gracie. They shrugged.

'On the couch,' Joan said.

'Brit's leaving for a twenty-city tour in a couple days,' Kenny explained. 'I didn't want to leave her with a bad impression.'

Gracie nodded, sympathetically.

And then she and Joan stumbled into the kitchen. Gracie laughed so hard she barked.

★　★　★

The digital clock contended the time was 3:32 A.M., but the white-blue light outside declared it to be closer to six. Since Joan had arrived back home, Gracie had been sleeping in the small downstairs bedroom, sometimes called the maid's room; it resembled a cave. She had been wide awake for twenty minutes, had rolled around for a good hour, hour and a half, before that. She finally rose and peered out the window facing Surfrider Beach. 'Hello, you,' Gracie said. The full moon, high above the house, cast a lantern glow over the whole of the beach. 'No wonder I can't sleep,' she said.

Suddenly, so faint she couldn't be sure of its veracity, she heard a muted tap-tap-tap at the window facing the entryway to the house. Gracie thought it was an animal sound at first — a

380

squirrel, perhaps the oversize raccoons that came down from the lagoon for their nightly repast in Joan's garbage cans. She raised the blinds.

On the other side of the tempered glass, Sam raised his hand.

Gracie jumped away from the window and fell backward, knocking over the side lamp. The light went on as the lamp rolled onto its side.

Gracie lay twisted on the floor, her heart pounding. She weighed her options as quickly as possible — tell him to leave at once or she'll call the police, tell him not tonight, or ask him to come in and see if he'd like something to drink or make out with.

Gracie chose the third option. She stood back up and went to the window and pulled the blinds up again.

No one was there.

Gracie put her hand sideways over her forehead, eliminating the glare from the streetlamps, and pressed her nose to the window. She could see no one.

Gracie mentally kicked herself. How could she have overreacted so, well, overreactedly? She had no evidence that Sam had done anything wrong — all he had done to her was bring her flowers, massage her back, kiss her wildly, and save her life.

'I'm an idiot,' Gracie said out loud. It wasn't the first time in her life, or even that week, that she'd had that thought.

And then she put her slippers on, tripped over the lamp once again, yanked the bedroom door open, and ran out.

Sam hated the reaction he'd seen on Gracie's face. He knew the origins of that expression too well — fear. She feared him. Not only did she not miss him like he'd missed her the last few days — she was afraid of him.

'Dumb, dumb, dumb, idiot,' Sam muttered to himself, as he kicked a rock with his sandaled foot. He knew what had set off the fear — he knew that she had found out the truth — probably from her friend, the redhead who stayed there with the old man.

He jumped the fence leading to Surfrider, the rusted barbed wire lining the top nothing but a minor nuisance as he skated over to the other side.

As he walked back to his 'den,' as he liked to call it when Mrs. Kennicot asked him where he made his home, he swore to himself that he would never make the same mistake again. It was folly for a man like him to get emotionally involved with a woman — any woman. Sam reminded himself that even Romeo and Juliet, the star-crossed lovers who had youth and idealism and healthy knees on their side, had wound up dead.

★ ★ ★

Gracie wasn't sure what she was doing as she moved her legs, but she knew she had that same feeling in her stomach as she did when she was a teenager and she would park in her boyfriend

Gorgeous Georgie's Mustang two blocks from her house to make out for what seemed like seconds but was really hours. The windows would be so thick with steam, droplets of water would form inside and roll from the top of the windshield down to the dashboard.

The tide was high. Of course the tide was high, Gracie thought — look at that frikkin' big round moon! Gracie cursed her luck and her sudden venture into the Land of the Impulsive. She waited for the waves to subside before she scooted under the fence, the edges of her nightgown dragging up saltwater and sand.

★ ★ ★

Sam had spread his blanket and rolled out his sleeping bag. He'd made a pillow of his clothes — the new Dockers were an especially prudent purchase — rolled up, they gave real support to his neck. He didn't feel like reading anything, which he often did to calm his mind, to reach out to the purity of the words after a day of contending with the outside world. He was thankful he didn't have access to a television set. He never, unlike the other guys, really wanted a Walkman, or whatever they were calling them now — iPods? He liked music, but he liked the sound of the ocean better. He'd grown up with the sound of waves lulling him to sleep; he would die, he hoped, hearing the same.

Sam got into his sleeping bag and lay back, his hands tucked under his head, and stared up, past the barbed wire, to the sky. The moon, at its most full, its most bright, had denuded the stars. No matter, he thought. He was content. The moon had hypnotized him; he was as vulnerable as a deer caught in the headlights of a pickup truck.

The hair on his arms suddenly stood on end. He had the sensation of being watched.

Sam had never used the switchblade he had taken from the guy who had stolen his gear. He actually hadn't even taken it from the guy — he'd found it on the very spot the man dropped it. The spot on which he'd snapped the man's wrist in half. He figured no one else wanted a part of it; seeing how it hadn't brought that particular guy much luck, no one else would touch it.

But it proved lucky enough for Sam. Sam didn't plan on using it as a weapon — in fact, since he'd been in the war, he didn't like the idea of weapons in general. But the knife had a sharp, thin blade — all he had in his pack were a couple old butter knives. This one could cut apples or rope — whatever he needed.

Whatever he needed.

He waited, unmoving. This was his training, after all; he'd been trained, for two whole years, to lie in wait for the enemy. To lie still, breathing shallow, paint on his face, camouflage on his body, his helmet covered in leaves. He'd lie there as tropical snakes slithered over his body, attracted by the warmth of his blood; he'd lie there as centipedes marched over his face.

He had no trouble lying still.

Twigs snapped. Footsteps were falling heavily,

haphazardly. The person was drunk or uncaring about disturbing his sanctuary.

The switchblade was open in his hand.

Three steps away.

Sam closed his eyes.

Two steps.

He slowed his breath.

One step.

He tightened his grip —

Sam sprang from his open sleeping bag and grabbed the offender around the neck, holding the blade to a pinpoint at the most vulnerable part of the carotid artery. If he pushed in one quarter inch, the man would die.

Except as his surge of adrenaline retreated, he realized that in his arms was not a man but a woman.

A woman wearing a damp nightgown.

Sam released her as quickly as he had grabbed her. The intensity of the moment, the realization of what he had almost done to her, brought tears to his eyes, eyes that had not shed water in twenty years.

That was a lie, Sam admonished himself. There was that old stray that got hit by a Mercedes on PCH. He had picked up her body from the highway, buried her in the back of the lagoon, and cried for days. He had hidden himself from everyone — Lavender, Mrs. Kennicot, everyone.

Sam had tracked that Mercedes, which hadn't bothered stopping after hitting the poor mutt, for weeks. When he'd finally seen the car, parked in a fire lane outside Nobu, he'd left a tidy souvenir in the form of a bashed-in windshield.

Lavender had mentioned something called a 'rage issue' to him once. He wondered if he had it, and if hc should keep it or get rid of it. Seemed to come in handy in his line of work.

Suddenly Sam grabbed at Gracie again to keep her from falling backward. Gracie had fainted.

'Oh, no,' Sam said, as he cradled her in his arms. 'No, no, no — '

Gracie was out — her eyes rolled back in her head.

Sam laid her down and placed his 'pillow' of clothes under her feet to bring blood back to her head. He put some water from his stash of bottles on one of his T-shirts and applied it to her face.

She really was very beautiful, he thought, as he drew the damp cloth across her cheek.

So serene. So quiet. So peaceful.

'What the — ' Gracie said, as her eyes flickered open. 'You tried to kill me!' she said as she wriggled away from his embrace.

'I'm sorry,' Sam said. He heard somewhere a long time ago that it was best for a man to just say 'Sorry' to a woman during moments like this. And repeat, ad infinitum. 'I'm sorry.'

'You're sorry?!' Gracie said. Now she was standing, on legs which were rebelling against the very thought — they trembled beneath her. *C'mon, you guys,* Gracie said to her legs, *give me a break —*

'I'm sorry,' Sam repeated. He was hoping the trick would work soon. 'Let me help you — '

He put his hand out to take hers — she slapped it away — and then her knees mutinied — and he caught her for the second time that night.

'I'm sorry,' he said once more. Sam doubted sincerely that he would ever get married again. He didn't know how long he could keep this up.

'Okay, okay,' Gracie said. She took a deep breath.

'I'm sorry,' Sam said.

'God, shut up,' Gracie said.

Sam smiled.

'What are you doing with that . . . thing . . . that switchblade — I mean, Jesus Christ, you could kill someone with that — ' The thought of the missing masturbator was not far from her mind.

'I use it to cut fruit,' he said as he snapped the blade back into place. Gracie watched him as he put it back under his sleeping bag. She looked dubious at best.

'Nice place you got here,' Gracie said, finally taking her eyes off the switchblade.

'It's a little drafty, but you can't beat the rent,' he said.

'So,' Gracie said, her hands pulling the nightgown around her in a sudden gesture of modesty. Sam wondered if she could be any cuter.

'Aren't you going to show me around?' she asked.

Sam looked at her. Was she mocking him? Why would she mock a homeless man? Was there anyone so cruel? And then he remembered something his father had told him — he remembered everything his father had told him because he hadn't spoken more than three sentences to him as a child — 'Sam,' he'd said, after a shouting match with his mother, 'remember, women are the meaner sex.'

Gracie looked back at him, her arms crossed across her chest, her chin thrust up, sweetly defiant. Sam thought he would have liked a picture of her then, in that moment, looking as dignified as she possibly could while wearing a soaking-wet nightgown.

'I'd like a tour,' she said.

Sam held out his hand. She accepted it.

He turned and took one step forward, toward the underbrush. 'This is the living room,' he said, extending his arm out.

'I like what you've done with it,' Gracie said. 'Was this always here?' She tugged at a branch.

'Yes,' he said. 'You've got a great eye.' He put his finger to his lips in a move feigning thoughtfulness. 'I wanted to keep the integrity of the original architecture,' he further explained.

Gracie nodded somberly. 'Wise choice.'

'And this is the library,' he said, pointing to his small stack of books, several of which, he reminded himself, had to be returned to the Malibu Library that very weekend.

He hated when people didn't return books on time. His list of pet peeves regarding the behavior of his fellow human beings was perhaps longer than other people's. He had been inspired once, by an especially egregious maneuver on the part of one such human being, to actually sit down and make a list of specific things that bothered him most about other people.

The list included: littering, talking loudly on cell phones, obnoxious children, obnoxious parents (he often saw both at the park at the Cross Creek Shopping Center), parking over the line, SUVs, Hummers, Hummer drivers, bad drivers, short drivers in huge cars, people with loud radios on the beach, people who smoked on the beach, people who screamed at their kids on the beach, people who drank on the beach, people who peed on the beach (there were more than a few of those, and not including the four-year-olds), men who wore thongs, women who wore thongs who should know better, crowds, any seat in the movie theater except the back row, bad movies, and finally, that surly kid at the Starbucks who poured his coffee only two-thirds full when it's supposed to be three-quarters full (according to the pretty, apple-shaped manager). Which may explain why he spent his nights sleeping in the bushes.

'Lovely,' Gracie said, picking up a book. Sam snapped to the present too late to distract her — 'Danielle Steel?' she asked, her eyebrow cocked, forming a virtual question mark.

Sam grabbed it back. 'I find her entertaining,' he said. He felt like a college student who left *Penthouse* magazine out on his coffee table, rather than *Portnoy's Complaint*, or whatever the hell college students were reading these days to impress their girlfriends.

Gracie put her hands up. 'Whatever you say,' she said. 'I'm here to snoop, not judge.'

Sam cleared his throat. 'Well, anyway, as you can see, I sleep — ' He looked at the sleeping bag. Suddenly he didn't find this ruse they were participating in amusing anymore. He was a grown man who had chosen to sleep outside for the last twenty years. He hadn't slept on a mattress in twenty years. Five sleeping bags. He'd gone through five — and that's because three had been stolen. He was a grown man whose sole possessions were worth less than — were worthless, period. He was a grown man who was able to take regular showers and use a proper toilet only because of an old lady's kindness. Sometimes, to be honest, Sam still crapped in the woods — much like the proverbial bear.

Shame was a powerful emotion, Sam was forced to admit. He was bewildered by the almost physical grip he felt, the tightening around his chest, the way his breath became labored and heavy.

Oh, fuck, he thought, I don't want to cry. I can't cry in front of her.

'You okay?' Gracie said. She put a hand on his arm. He knew she only meant to comfort him, but her light touch felt like a slap.

He pulled away, wiping his hand across his nose. He wished he'd taken a shower that day. He covered his head with his hands.

Gracie took a step back. 'You're right,' she said. 'It isn't funny.'

Sam just shook his head. Over and over, like a small child unwilling to accept a parent's reprimand.

'I'm sorry,' he said, repeating himself, for the last time.

Gracie backed away and found the trail in the moonlight. Close by, she heard an ambulance wail. She hoped Jaden would not be awakened.

27

Worst-Case Scenario

The wailing matched the tumult inside Sam's chest. He listened as the ambulance started up, and expected, as always, that the sound would build for a moment, and then, gradually, become more distant, locating that car that had, invariably, wrapped itself around a pole on Pacific Coast Highway.

Instead, the sound became louder. Sam's heart began pounding. Where would it end? he wondered. It felt as though they were chasing him.

He worried about Mrs. Kennicot. She had a nurse staying with her at night now. A tiny Filipino lady with a big sense of humor and more than a few missing teeth.

He stood.

The ambulance was rounding the corner into the Colony.

Sam was up over the fence before the ambulance made its next turn.

Taillights. He saw taillights. It wasn't Mrs. Kennicot. Not tonight. He scrolled quickly down the list of potential victims as he ran up the Colony street — there were several people in their sixties or seventies — all of whom were in great shape. Still playing tennis, walking the

Colony, taking the occasional jog down the beach. There was the semiretired business manager in his seventies who still rode his Harley on PCH at least twice a week.

He ran.

The ambulance had stopped at the north end of the Colony and the paramedics had already hit the pavement. Sam recognized the big black Range Rover parked at an angle halfway out of the garage.

The security truck still had its lights on.

Sam broke through the crowd that had begun to gather, in their pajamas, their robes, slippers, their carefully coiffed hair askew. They were attracted by the lights, the sounds, just as he was. It was the second time they'd heard an ambulance in the Colony within a month.

This kind of thing didn't happen here.

Sam didn't recognize Lavender at first, but he knew it would be her. She was on the ground, lying faceup. Her eyes were closed. She was not wearing the ubiquitous glasses. There was no smile.

The paramedics had begun working on her.

'I'm her friend,' Sam said, 'I'm her friend — ' He bent down next to her, next to Tariq, who was kneeling, holding his large gold cross in his hand, rocking back and forth —

They ignored him, continuing their work. Heartbeat. Blood pressure. Concussion. Signs of internal bleeding.

'Let's get her up — ' one paramedic said to the other. They were both young. Professional. Serious, like he had been. They hoisted her, carefully, gently, onto a gurney. One of the paramedics looked at Sam as he closed the back door to the ambulance. 'We'll have to airlift her out — ' he said.

Sam nodded. He knew what the young man was saying; these injuries were potentially serious. Life-threatening. Tariq stood next to him, crying now, great tears tumbling slowly down his face. The crowd parted silently and the ambulance roared away, leaping over the speed bumps.

'She's gonna need her glasses,' Tariq said. 'When she wakes up — how's she gonna see? How's she gonna read?'

Sam realized her glasses had been thrown from her face on impact.

'I'll find 'em,' he said. 'You just, don't worry.' He put his hand on Tariq's quaking shoulder.

A sheriff's car appeared where the ambulance had been. Sam kept his head down. He was looking at the Range Rover parked in the driveway. The car had hit her, it occurred to him — the car had hit her and kept going. The boy had parked the car after he'd hit a human being.

Something someone said to him once, in the jungle, reverberated through his brain. Death is too good for some motherfuckers, the man had said.

Sam was suddenly aware of the conversations murmured by departing residents. Words like 'accident,' 'drinking,' 'kids' wafted over to his ears as he searched the road for Lavender's glasses. He finally found them, in the decoratively arrayed olive bushes. He picked them up gingerly and lifted them to the night sky. He could see the moon clearly through the lenses. Not even a scratch. They were in perfect condition.

He walked off, quickly, away from the sheriff, who was heading into the house where the boy lived. He would drop the glasses off with Tariq.

And then he would take care of business.

★   ★   ★

Word was, not even an hour after the accident the kid had already gotten himself one of those world-class attorneys — the kind that rich people hire when they know they're guilty — shit, when the whole world knows they're guilty, but when they're planning on getting off, anyway, fuck the rest of you.

After the sheriff cleared out, Sam was hanging out at the guard shack, picking up bits and pieces of information. J.D. laid out the story for him: Lavender had been on nights, to accommodate her full load of morning classes. She was out in the truck, making the rounds. Nothing of note. Then Tariq had noticed, a little after four o'clock, that Range Rover come in, speeding through the gate as usual — from what he could tell, two, maybe three kids in the car. The usual suspect driving — the one with the black hair, sunglasses on, even at the blackest hour, skinny like a junkie. Laughing at the way people jumped when they saw him coming. J.D. couldn't tell, since the only TV he watched was the kind that told him what to invest in, but he heard the kid was dating some kind of TV actress. He'd also heard the kid had been in trouble through the years — rehab, brushes with the law. Nothing major.

Nothing like attempted murder.

'It was an accident,' J.D. said to Sam. Sam had a place in his heart for J.D. — the Zen master of security. J.D. had been a Marine. They shared their stories. 'The sheriff took down all the information.'

'Then why did the kid get a lawyer?' Sam asked.

J.D. just looked at him. 'I'm retiring in a year. That's all the information I've got for you. You want to ask me that question in twelve months plus twenty-four hours, I might have a different answer.'

'She's going to miss her graduation,' Sam said. He couldn't meet the man's eyes. Every time he thought of that graduation — the day she'd worked so hard for —

'Son, she's lucky she's alive,' J.D. said. He waved in a convertible Mercedes.

Sam was turning to leave, having been properly reprimanded, when J.D. called out to him.

'Cops got a bone to pick with you?' he asked. His tone was casual. Sam could tell he was concerned.

He looked at J.D.

'They came around here this morning. I told them nothing,' he continued. 'But a danger foreseen is half avoided.'

Sam knew better than to write the plan down. This kind of thing, you relegated to the recesses of your brain. You think. You dream. You prepare. You leave no evidence. No pieces of paper, no half-legible scrawls. No leading conversations (although he'd already had one or two with J.D., the only man on the planet who would never finger him). This would be easy for him. A piece of cake.

Sam was, in a way, happy to have the distraction. He was released from his obsession with Gracie, his obsession with possessing her — that womanly body, that throaty laugh. He was released from his obsession with sex. He was now only interested in one thing: revenge.

His plan was simple. He knew from experience that the best ones are — the more complicated the plan, the more likely failure would ensue.

In his mind, all was in order:

1. He would kidnap the boy.
2. He would force a confession out of him; he would tape it.
3. He would confront the boy's father with the confession.
4. He would extract enough money out of them to last Lavender a lifetime.

It was a simple plan. But not simple enough. For one thing, he didn't have a tape recorder.

Sometimes being possessionless had its down-side. He developed a different plan:

1. Find the boy.
2. Beat the living shit out of him.

★ ★ ★

Gracie had forgotten all about Kenny. She'd forgotten that he'd spent the night. She awakened a little late, given the events of the night before, and padded down to the kitchen to make coffee.

She was shocked into an alert state by sensory overload — the smell of eggs, the sizzle of bacon. The sound of toast popping up out of the toaster. Kenny was standing in the kitchen with an apron on, humming to himself.

After a moment, he felt her presence and turned to look at her —

'Coffee?' he asked.

'What are you doing?' Gracie asked, although she accepted the coffee. She took a sip. Damn, it was good. Who was this man and when did he learn to make coffee?

'I was hungry, I didn't feel like going to Marmalade,' Kenny replied. 'You know, I've had the paparazzi — '

'Chasing you,' Gracie said, 'I know.'

Kenny sighed. 'It's so hard for her, you have no idea,' he said, shaking his head.

Despite the taste of the coffee, the smell of bacon and eggs, Gracie was suddenly losing her appetite. Her brain was fighting her senses.

'You're going to have some, of course?' Kenny asked.

'Of course,' Gracie acquiesced. She had to think of her health, after all. She was a mother. She could not live on caffeine and candy corn alone. Though she had made a valiant attempt to.

She sat down and put a napkin on her lap and waited as Kenny served her.

He watched her as she ate. Gracie suddenly grew self-conscious.

'What?' she asked.

'You look good' was all he said.

Gracie's hand went automatically to her hair. 'Oh, no,' she said, 'my hair, it's too — and I've gained weight, you know, and — '

The doorbell rang.

'You're not great at taking compliments, you know that?' Kenny said, motioning for her to stay seated.

★   ★   ★

Sam was so relieved at being relieved of his obsession with having sex with Gracie that he actually found himself at her house, ringing the doorbell, wishing to apologize for his weird behavior the night before. And he knew she probably hadn't heard about Lavender. He felt strangely possessive that he should be the one to tell her. He had been deliberating for several moments on how to best express himself that he didn't notice that the door had opened and that there was a man standing in front of him.

399

'Hey,' the man said. He was tall, with a wide, loopy grin, clean-cut except for the wire earring. Sam had witnessed the earring stage on middle-aged men — the look ranked right up there with stringy, gray ponytails on men, as far as he was concerned. But the grin was engaging — the guy seemed nice enough.

A small girl with sleepy eyes, a mess of blond curls and a pink Cinderella nightgown suddenly poked her head under the man's arm. The man curved his arm around the girl and absentmindedly kissed the top of her head.

'Help you?' the man asked, looking up at Sam. Sam realized he hadn't spoken yet. People skills were not his strongest attribute. 'Hey,' Sam tried. Saying 'hey' was about as foreign to him, with its implied ease of communication, as Ukrainian. 'Hey,' he repeated, as stilted as the first time. 'Hey,' the man said back to him. Sam took note of the spatula in his hand and wondered what kind of domestic scene he had interrupted.

'Is Gracie home?' Sam asked, realizing he didn't know her last name.

'Why do you have hair all over your face?' The little girl looked up at him. 'Are you cold?'

'Gracie? Sure,' the man replied to Sam, after a pause and a look Sam caught (because he was as sensitive as a fly to such looks), that said 'Who is this guy and why is he asking for Gracie.' Then there was another moment — and at these times Sam really thought he might have superhero powers — the glimmer of an expression that could not be read as anything other than self-interest.

'I'm Kenny,' Kenny said, 'Kenny Pollock.' He said the last part with just a little more weight than the words warranted, as far as Sam was concerned. Then he reached out and shook Sam's hand. Judging by the crush of the handshake and the particular enthusiasm with which it was unleashed, Sam knew he hadn't misread anything. Spider-Man had nothing on Sam Knight.

But he wondered as he stepped inside, guided by Kenny with the earring and spatula, what on earth a frat boy like Kenny could find interesting about him. The little girl, still hovering under her father's arm, steadily eyed Sam and his beard. 'Can I touch it?' she finally asked after what Sam could feel was much deliberation.

'Are your hands clean?' Sam asked the girl, who nodded and then paused to examine her tiny hands.

'Gracie!' Kenny yelled. 'Got a young man here for ya.' Kenny turned and winked at Sam, a choice so shocking to Sam he almost jumped.

The three rounded the corner into the kitchen. Gracie was finishing off the last of the three pieces of bacon Kenny had placed on her plate. The eggs were already a memory. Jaden ran to her mother, who hugged and kissed her and then looked up guiltily. 'I guess I was really hungry,' she almost said. Instead she blurted out, 'Oh, my God.'

'Hey, Gracie,' Kenny bubbled, 'your friend — ' Kenny turned to him. 'Sorry, buddy, your name again?'

'Sam,' Sam said, his eyes only on Gracie. She was wearing a robe. She had probably changed her nightgown. Her toes were poking out of her slippers. Her hair was half in her face.

She was blushing furiously. She looked like a teenager. God, I want to kiss her, Sam thought. His further thoughts were more advanced, along the lines of disrobing her with his teeth, slowly licking her entire body, and politely screwing her brains out. The image of Gracie's lush, welcoming naked body stayed with Sam until Kenny had the nerve to break his trance by actually speaking. *Why do people need to talk so much?* Sam asked himself.

'So, Sam,' Kenny said to him, then turned to Gracie. 'This is the guy, right, Gracie? This is the one?'

Gracie was looking into Sam's eyes, sinking into his gaze. Did he ever blink? She'd read something about Scientologists not blinking; so when she and Kenny attended a Christmas party at the giant Church of Scientology in Hollywood (Kenny was wooing John Travolta to play the role of Madame Curie's husband, Mr. Curie) Gracie made a point of not blinking the whole night.

'Yeah,' she said. 'He's the one.' *Oh, screw it,* Gracie thought, *so I'm in love with a homeless man. There are worse tragedies.*

'Do you like to play?' Jaden asked Sam.

He looked down at her, sitting in her mother's lap, and smiled. 'My sister used to make me play with dolls,' he said, wincing at the memory, 'for hours and hours and hours. Days!'

Jaden burst out in giggles at her vision of his memory and burrowed deeper into her mother's robe.

'Great, listen.' Kenny turned to Sam. 'Gracie told me all about you, and, you know, your background, and I'd love to talk to you sometime. In fact I made a little breakfast here, as you can see. Why don't you join us?'

'I'm going to get dressed,' Jaden said. 'I'm not proper.' She didn't take her eyes off Sam as she slid from her mother's embrace and breezed sideways past him. And then, finally, she turned on her tippy toes and ran up the stairs.

'Kenny and I . . . ' Gracie wanted to explain to Sam. She pointed at Kenny, then to herself, then back and forth again.

'What she's trying to tell you is that we're married,' Kenny said. 'But not for much longer. I've got a serious, serious girlfriend, who's incidentally an international superstar, but that's not why I love her, not even a little bit, and well, look at you and Gracie, this is great. Really great.'

Gracie realized that Kenny still thought Sam was the 'rubber man' — the man who made hundreds of millions in rubber, the man who owned his own G-5.

Gracie burst out laughing.

'What?' Kenny asked, befuddled, looking at her with a slightly wounded expression.

Gracie just shook her head. She couldn't answer him and laugh and swallow the rest of her food at the same time.

The two men watched her laugh, her hands

403

flat on the counter, her head shaking from side to side.

And then Sam started to smile.

'Sam,' Gracie said, looking at him. Her eyes were red, rimmed with tears. 'Kenny wanted to talk to you, you know, about business. Your business.'

'My business,' Sam said rather than asked.

Gracie smiled. He was game.

'Yes, you know, rubber,' she said.

'Oh, the rubber business,' Sam said. 'Oh, I couldn't. It's far too dull.'

'Not at all,' Kenny said. 'I, personally, would be fascinated. I'm interested in all kinds of . . . rubber . . . things.'

'Kenny would be fascinated,' Gracie promised.

'Not many people are,' Sam shrugged. 'But I'd be happy to bring you up to speed. You know, we're having a little problem on the manufacturing side. The Indonesians, you know.'

Kenny put his arm around him. 'This is gonna be great,' he said. 'You ever think about the film business?'

'All the time,' Sam said.

'Are you kidding?' Gracie asked. 'He doesn't stop talking about the film business.'

Kenny rubbed his hands together. 'This is great,' he repeated.

Sam put his hand on Kenny's shoulder. 'Listen, Kenster,' he said, not knowing where the moniker had come from. 'You think I could talk to Gracie here for a minute?'

Kenny nodded eagerly. And stood there.

'Alone?' Sam asked. Kenny put his hands up

(including the one still holding the spatula).

'Right, right, no problem, take your time.' He scooted out of the kitchen and onto the deck, where Gracie could see him pretending to find the Pacific Ocean interesting.

'Listen — ' Gracie turned back to Sam. ' — I want to apologize again — '

'Lavender got hurt last night,' Sam said.

Gracie's face traversed a spectrum of emotions until it landed on panic.

'This morning. They said she's going to be all right,' he said. 'She's in the hospital. I thought you should know.'

Gracie's mouth squeezed into a grimace. 'How?'

'She got hit by a car. Early this morning.' Even as he said the words, he felt the muscles in his throwing arm twitch.

'The ambulance,' Gracie said. Her hand found her mouth and she began to cry. Sam put his arms around her as she buried her face into his chest.

'She's going to be fine,' he said. Why was he promising her what he didn't know to be true?

Gracie nodded. 'She's going to miss her graduation,' she said.

'You knew about that?' he asked. It wasn't like Lavender to trust the residents with personal information.

Gracie nodded, then let her head submerge into his chest once more.

Sam stroked her hair as her breathing eventually settled. Even now, surrounded by the taint of tragedy, he felt a burgeoning feeling —

Oh, fuck, Sam thought to himself. How can I be horny at a time like this?

He let Gracie go. 'I've gotta run,' he said. She was staring at him with her big, dark eyes. He wanted to stay there and stroke her hair and kiss her eyelids and run his hands all over her body. And that's why he was leaving.

Gracie nodded and listened to his footsteps as he walked away; she heard the clap of the door closing behind him.

She stared for what felt like a long time out the kitchen window when she noticed, there for all to see, the green blanket.

Sitting on top of the blanket was a lanky, well-dressed blond man, hooked up to an iPod. The Malibu Masturbator. His hands were seated nicely on his knees.

There was something on his face.

Gracie got out Joan's binoculars, always at the ready on the kitchen counter should someone really interesting (read: gorgeous and male) turn up on the beach.

She looked through the binoculars, finally finding her subject after drifting back from the pier.

He had a bandage across his nose. His eyes were bruised.

'Hey,' Kenny said, as he loped back into the kitchen, swinging the spatula like a baseball bat. 'Where'd your friend go?'

'He had to run,' Gracie said. 'Business to attend to.'

Kenny nodded solemnly. He looked about as disappointed as a child who's dropped ice cream out of his cone. 'Of course. But I want to set something up with him. Hook me up. Can you put together a dinner or something?'

Gracie shrugged.

'Do this for me,' Kenny said. 'Come on.' Apparently Gracie didn't respond fast enough. 'You know, this was the problem with our marriage. You just didn't support me enough.'

'I didn't . . . what?' Gracie turned toward him.

'It's the wives who decide everything.' Kenny was making a point with his spatula. 'It's the wives who determine the social status of the husband — the wives who can make or break a man. And you just didn't try hard enough.'

He punctuated his point, brandishing the spatula like a sword.

'I didn't try hard enough,' Gracie said.

'That's right, you didn't,' Kenny said, jumping in. 'We should have had dinner parties once a week. We should have had people over to play tennis every Sunday. And not just any people, like your friends — real people, like the Murdochs, the Spielbergs, the Katzenbergs, all the damned 'bergs — '

'Being head of a studio isn't good enough for you?' Gracie asked.

'Gracie. Don't be stupid,' Kenny snorted. 'All studio heads get fired. It's just a matter of time. But if I were friends with Rupert or Steven or Jeffrey, well, that goes a long way in this town. Why do you think I fell in love with Britney?'

'To help your career?' Gracie asked. She had passed anger and was now heading into bemusement.

'Damn right,' Kenny said. 'I mean, I do love her with all my heart, but, you know, this is going to blow me up big-time.'

Gracie nodded and wondered if she appeared at all interested.

'Did Spielberg date Madonna?' Gracie finally asked.

'He's been married to two actresses,' Kenny said.

'Geffen?'

'Married to Cher, I think.'

Gracie nodded, again. 'Maybe you're on to something, Kenny,' she finally said.

'It's got nothing to do with the movies, you know,' Kenny said. She realized he was being defensive. Kenny's last two pictures had been major flops. A third one? He'd be packed up and sent on his way.

'Sure,' Gracie said. 'It never does.'

Gracie thought about the demise of her marriage, she thought about Lavender's accident. She thought about her age.

She decided that she was going to sleep with Sam tonight, whether he wanted to or not. All of the signs could be read. There was no time to waste.

28

Lots of Stuff to Do Tonight

Gracie recalled the conversation she'd had with Joan as she left the house that evening.

'Where are you going?' Joan asked. She was on the couch, her reading glasses on. Gracie couldn't tell if she was reading *The Atlantic Monthly* or *The New Yorker*, but she looked vaguely annoyed as she often did when reading about social injustice or governmental abuse. Gracie was dressed casually but carefully — she had chosen clothes she could take on a hike, but made sure they were in colors flattering to her skin tone and body type.

She looked good enough, she knew, to raise the question of suspicion in Joan's mind.

'I'm going for a walk,' Gracie had said.

'A walk,' Joan repeated back to her, as if informing her friend that the mere thought of going for a walk on a balmy, slightly breezy evening in Malibu was suspect.

'I'm going to sleep with the homeless man,' Gracie admitted. Lying was not her strength.

'Oh, okay, fine,' Joan said, getting back to whatever magazine article was provoking her. 'Just make sure you're back at a decent hour.'

'If you need me, I'll be lying on the trail behind the Colony,' Gracie called out as she opened the front door, 'screwing my brains out.'

Joan raised her hand over her head, her fingers and thumb forming the universal 'okay' sign.

★   ★   ★

Sam had a few loose ends to tie up at the Kennicot house, so he stopped there before heading home.

He let himself in through the back door, as he had done for almost fifteen years. The silence in the home told him that Mrs. Kennicot was upstairs, presumably taking a nap. He looked for the little Filipino nurse, who never left her side, except to come downstairs to watch her Spanish-language soap operas if Mrs. Kennicot was sleeping during the day.

The Filipino nurse had left some food out for him on the kitchen table. Mostly, she made hot dogs. He was kind of hoping when they hired her that she'd be making some more, well, cultural fare.

Sam sat down and ate two of the hot dogs with no bun, nothing. She had made six for him — she was a bad cook, but she was a generous bad cook.

He was stuck. He wanted to go upstairs to say good-bye to Mrs. Kennicot. He had come to the conclusion that he had to take care of business tonight — if he waited any longer, the kid would probably be on a plane to another state, even another country. The sheriff, at the very least, had to keep him in town for two, three days to determine, to the best of his ability, what went down. After that, the kid would be free as a bird. The parents would buy their way into a college, maybe even buy a whole fucking building, and their little darling would get off scot-free.

While Lavender would miss her graduation.

Sam had checked in with J.D. earlier that day. J.D. had been on the phone to the nurses at the hospital every hour. Lavender's vital signs were steady, but she hadn't awakened yet. Not unusual when there's bleeding on the brain. They said she would, they said they thought she would. For sure.

Sam decided to leave a note for Mrs. Kennicot. She was going blind now, but the nurse could read it to her. He was pretty sure the nurse could read it to her. Her English was okay. Maybe she was smart enough to give J.D. the note if she couldn't read it.

Piss to hell, Sam thought, *this shit is so complicated. All I want to do is beat up the little fucker! Why should that be so hard?*

He wrote the note quickly, possibly illegibly. It said he had to leave suddenly, that he was sorry, that he would be grateful to her for the rest of his life. And he gave instructions to the nurse — where to find that thick lotion Mrs. Kennicot liked that they didn't stock at Sav-on, who to call to fix the old pipes under the kitchen sink (because he wouldn't be able to anymore). He left the name of the medication that worked best on her stomach problems. He thought the nurse might know, but just in case. He left the name of a lady in the Colony who could walk the dog.

Oh, fuck, Sam thought. *The fucking dog. I*

411

love that fucking dog. The dog's going to cry, I know it. Fucking Baxter.

Sam wiped his nose on the back of his hand as the screen door closed behind him.

The breeze hit him, raising the fine hairs on his forearms. He could hear the dog, his whine reaching him over the waves. The dog wanted to take a walk.

Do I have to say good-bye to Gracie? he asked himself. After all, he barely knew her. Wouldn't she think it was odd that he thought himself so important as to tell her he'd be leaving for a, well, extended period of time? But wouldn't she think it odd if she never saw him again?

Sam thought about it as he hopped the fence behind the tennis court and made his way down the trail behind the Colony.

He decided he wouldn't say good-bye. He'd let J.D. explain what had happened. It'd be better for her if he just disappeared.

★   ★   ★

Gracie made herself comfortable, pulling out the sleeping bag, draping a blanket she'd brought over it before settling down. Her first moments there could be broken down, incrementally — excitement brought on by lack of judgment, followed by self-doubt, followed by an increasing sense of dread, followed by fear, then terror, and finally, in a gesture of abandonment of what was left of her common sense, she decided that all was fine, she was perfectly safe, and it was normal for her to be sitting on top of this man's

412

sleeping bag, waiting for him to return from wherever he'd gone.

After a while, she lay back, watching the evening turn to night.

★   ★   ★

Sam walked up the trail. Besides packing, he wanted to dismantle his 'den,' take down the cardboard, the tent, roll up his sleeping bag nice and tight.

What he didn't expect to see were two white legs poking out from under his pup tent. He stopped. Then sighed and shook his head, but he could feel the smile creep onto his lips; he could feel it radiate into his chest.

Why was he smiling? He'd have to get rid of her. He had a job to do. Now he'd have to say good-bye. And now he was annoyed — he should be annoyed — she shouldn't just turn up any old time she pleased. It showed a lack of judgment, a lack of respect. A lack of common —

Geez, her legs look good, Sam thought as he came closer. He appreciated her small ankles. And those toes. He could see she was lying still, her face toward the sky. For a morbid moment, steel pierced his heart, and he thought she might be dead.

Then he heard the snoring.

He came upon her and watched her sleep. The small curve of her lips. The furrow between her brows softened. Her hands cupped over her belly, modest even in sleep.

He would have fallen in love with her right then, had he not already done so.

Sam sat down on the sleeping bag next to her. She moaned softly. He stretched out his legs and leaned back. She turned to her side, her back toward him. She snorted.

Ever so gently, in the smallest of motions, he maneuvered his body into a position he hadn't realized he'd missed so badly until he found himself in it.

He spooned her. He buried his nose in her hair; his lips were a breath away from her neck. He placed his arm around her waist and slid his hand beneath her breasts, curving under her belly.

Spooning, he thought, was dangerous business.

The comfort level was almost unbearable. Sam had to fight the surge of adrenaline that told him this situation was fight or flight, code red, highest alert.

He was in the middle of the wrestling match between emotion and physiology when she spoke.

'For crying out loud, just enjoy it,' she said.

His laugh came out like a bark. 'You are one scary woman,' he said.

Gracie turned her whole body toward his. 'Oh, you have no idea,' she said. 'There are women out there who make me look like a lost kitten.'

'Don't introduce me to them,' he said. They were face-to-face. Sam could feel her breasts pushing against his chest. He was lucky to be able to talk at this point.

He didn't know whether to be embarrassed or proud that he was sporting a hard-on that would've been able to chop wood.

He chose proud. He maneuvered himself into her hip.

'Not a chance,' she said, 'they'd eat you alive. And what would be left for me?'

'Only this,' he said, and he took her hand and placed it on his chest.

'Chest hair?' Gracie teased. 'No, they'd take that out, too. With their teeth.'

'My heart,' he said.

He left her hand on his chest and put his hand on her face and drew her in, and she wondered how long she had lived without a kiss like that and how she didn't want to live without that kiss again.

★ ★ ★

'Maybe you should start up a dating service for women who want to date homeless men?' Will said. 'Call it 'Homeless Hunks,' 'Babelicious Bums.''

'I think she should keep it her very own secret,' Joan said. 'Why should anyone else have all the fun?'

Gracie had wandered in at about ten o'clock that morning. Will had already dropped in with a tray of Coffee Bean and Tea Leaf (because that's where all the cute guys landed in the morning after their Malibu overnights) and Joan had made scraps out of the *New York Times*. First she divided the paper into sections. Then sections into piles. Then, she read each pile. Then, she took out her orange-handled shears and cut out the articles that would be most likely to push her into a suicidal funk, and she'd proceed to paste those to the refrigerator, which at this point seemed to groan under the weight of headlines such as REFUGEES KILLED AT CHECKPOINT, or JOBLESS RATE SOARS. Abu Ghraib had its own section, on the freezer.

Now, Gracie wasn't what you'd call an oversexed person. She hadn't been to a Sting concert since his famous quote claiming to have sex for three hours at a time, which seemed both painful and wasteful — why, you could learn rudimentary Spanish in three hours — you could knit a baby blanket — cook a four-course meal! She was at the high middle of the bell curve in terms of sexuality — she'd never tried sex with a woman (they don't have penises, unless they purchase them — and then, what's the point?), she wasn't familiar with vibrators and was, frankly, scared of electrocuting herself, or whatever happens to someone if a battery falls out within a three-inch radius of her vagina. She had never tried a threesome. She'd never been to a swingers party. She'd never even had a one-night stand.

But what she had under her belt now was that the night before, and into the wee hours of the morning, she'd had between four and five bouts of sex. Not just sex — but outdoor sex! She'd turned from a relative prude into a crazed exhibitionist.

'What's this 'between four and five'?' Joan asked.

'Let me answer,' Will said, raising his hand before Gracie had a chance to speak. 'He didn't come on the fifth time.'

'You are good,' Gracie said.

'I'm a man,' Will said. 'A man who regularly has between four and five bouts of sex. The only problem is, I never get taken out to dinner. Lefty's cheap.'

Joan looked at him.

'His hand won't pay,' Gracie explained. Joan nodded, her mouth forming a perfect O. 'Sad,' she said.

'Not really,' Will said. 'I don't have to kick myself out of bed early in the morning because I've made yet another horrible mistake.'

Gracie settled down on a stool. The pleasant but very real soreness between her legs caused her to stand suddenly.

Will looked at her knowingly. 'You might want to take it a little more slowly,' he said.

'Wow,' Joan said. 'It hurts to sit. Lucky for you.'

Gracie held on to the kitchen counter and lowered herself onto the stool. She felt as though the inside of her body was now on the outside. She remembered feeling this way once or twice before — in high school, and then again, in the early days with Kenny.

The very early days.

'I'll be needing coffee,' she said, reaching her hand out while Will slipped a cup of coffee into it.

'And Tylenol?' Joan asked.

'No,' Gracie said thoughtfully. 'You play, you pay.'

Will and Gracie touched their coffee mugs together in an uncivilized toast.

'Oh, by the way, girls,' Gracie said, 'Sam is definitely not a murderer. We chatted in between rounds.'

'Quite the opposite, I think,' Will said. 'He's the architect of your pleasure.'

And then he sighed.

★　★　★

There are always signs, Gracie thought, that marked the end of an era. And as Gracie perused the latest *Us Magazine*, she could feel that this was the beginning of the end. Will was standing next to her, holding her up. She stared through her sunglasses, taking in the disaster unfolding before her. Her hands were shaky, her knees weak. Her breathing had become shallow and labored.

'It says here he's a dancer,' Will said. 'She's getting plump — she should really stay away from those Whoppers.'

Gracie and Will were standing in front of the Malibu newsstand. *Us Magazine* had arrived moments before; the clerk had just cut the twine wrapped around the stack of new magazines.

On the cover was Britney Spears. And her new love, a boy dancer with the plucked appearance of someone who often finds vaginas none too interesting. A boy dancer named 'Billy.'

'Billy, don't be a hero,' Will said, having opened the magazine and begun devouring its contents. 'It says here he is five-nine and 146 pounds. And he likes chocolate. And doing The Vogue.'

He looked at Gracie. 'We're perfect for each other.'

Nowhere in the magazine was a mention of Britney's former beau, Gracie's soon-to-be ex, Kenny Pollock. What the magazine did say was that Britney had been lying low for the last month or so, nursing herself back to health after a bad bout of food poisoning combined with a sprained ankle.

'He's going to kill himself,' Gracie said.

'Maybe he doesn't know yet,' Will said.

'Maybe,' Gracie said. But she knew that Kenny knew — and she wondered why she cared.

29

The Bloody Denouement

Sam was no break-and-enter artist, and never had been. Burglary wasn't in his nature. He didn't have the gene and hadn't experienced the deprivation that would cause him to steal. He was fine with having few possessions of his own; he knew what too many possessions did to a person. The more possessions one had, the more headaches. The math was simple.

But here he was, wearing a pair of Mrs. Kennicot's nylons over his head, crawling through a half-open window on the side of a house. Here he was, creeping down a hallway, looking like Freddy Krueger's less stable cousin. Here he was, opening first one door, then another, searching for his stinking-rich, stinking-asshole quarry.

Sam had been watching the house since late afternoon. He had parked his bike outside of the Colony gate at the north end and had sat across from the house, hidden by trees and trash cans. He had even packed a sandwich, to stave off hunger as he hunkered down.

The father had left with his driver at about six o'clock in the evening. Word from the security gate, from a nervous Tariq, was that the father was headed on an unexpected business trip, leaving his only, felonious son to fend for himself. How would he survive, Sam wondered, with only two fully stocked refrigerators, a brand-new Range Rover, cash, credit cards, and a wine cellar filled with exclusive California cabernets and sublime Bordeaux? The kid didn't stand a chance.

Sam didn't see a clock, but he knew it was after midnight; he was intimately acquainted with the changing colors of the night sky. Sam crept past the living room, where he saw a body lying on the couch. He went closer, out of a sense of keen curiosity and sexual interest. She was a beautiful girl, young, soft skin, long legs akimbo. Her cell phone resting open on her stomach. A half-empty (or could it be seen as half-full? Sam wondered) bottle of vodka on the floor, leaning against the couch.

Sleeping Beauty was out for the night.

Sam continued on, up a flight of stairs. He figured the kid would be staying in a bedroom with a view. He didn't figure wrong.

The view was spectacular. It was the first thing he'd noticed. There was the Pacific Ocean in widescreen. The windows curved up so that even stars were visible beyond the moonlight.

Motherfucker, thought Sam. *I sleep outside, and his view is better than mine.*

Sam could see the black spikes of hair with bleached tips, slick with gel, sticking up over a large chair that was more expensive, Sam knew, than it looked. The kid was facing the ocean. The tableau felt strangely pensive to Sam, and looking back, he should have felt something.

There was no music on. No light except for the half moon.

It was at this moment that Sam should have put it all together. The mood was wrong. The atmosphere did not correspond to the subject matter.

The last thing he remembered was taking two steps forward before he felt the blow to the back of his head.

No, thought Sam, that's not really true. He remembered thinking as his legs gave out from underneath him, betraying him, he remembered thinking — *Shit. Somebody's going to see me with Mrs. Kennicot's nylons on my head.*

Sam did not want to be seen as a pervert.

* * *

'What'd you expect me to think?' J.D. said, as he brought him water. 'You're wearing Mrs. Kennicot's drawers on your head. A grown man.'

'Jesus Christ,' Sam said, rubbing the knot at the base of his skull. 'What the hell did you hit me with?'

J.D. lifted his industrial-strength black loafer before slipping it onto his foot.

'A shoe? I was knocked out by a shoe?'

J.D. shrugged. 'It's all I had. You work with what you got. You okay?'

J.D. was standing over Sam, who was sitting against a wall in the kid's room. Sam could see his reflection in J.D.'s thick glasses. The nylons were up on top of his head. He knew he looked about as ridiculous as he could without actually being in a parade.

Sam looked over toward the chair. The kid hadn't moved. It suddenly occurred to Sam that J.D. had killed him. J.D. had beaten Sam to the punch.

'He's not dead,' J.D. said, reading Sam's mind. Sam noticed he was wearing gloves — the kind that women wash their dishes with. Sam would bet a fifty that those gloves would be missed by J.D.'s wife come the morning.

Sam looked at him, questioning.

J.D. walked over to the chair and spun it around so that the boy was facing Sam.

Except his eyes were turned up toward the back of his skull. His mouth was hanging open in time-honored village-idiot fashion. Sam could detect a bit of drool where his lips met in the corner.

Sam was struck by how young he looked without the ubiquitous dark sunglasses.

'Not even seventeen yet,' J.D. said, reading his mind again. Sam saw the small box on the floor beside the chair. Took in the rubber band tied around the kid's arm. He knew there was a needle lying on the floor somewhere.

Then it occurred to Sam. 'What the hell are you doing here?' he asked J.D. 'And why the fuck did you hit me?'

J.D. smiled. 'This little bastion of society here called this veteran of a foreign war a nigger once,' he said, pointing at his chest. 'My plan was to wait 'til after retirement to do some collateral damage on his ass, but then there was the incident with Lavender. It just needed to be done.'

Sam put up his hand.

'And you?' J.D. asked.

'I don't like the way he drives,' Sam said. 'So I thought I'd break his hands for him.'

J.D. sniffed. 'Lord, this does have some impact on my plan.' He nodded his head toward the kid, who was on a sightseeing tour of Heroin Town.

They looked at each other.

'He's going to lose that arm eventually,' Sam said. 'See that?' He pointed to the kid's arm, which was noticeably smaller than the other. 'The muscles're atrophied. He's got about six more months.'

J.D. smiled.

'You ever going to come to my house for barbecue?' J.D. asked as they exited through the front door.

'I might just do that.'

They looked up at the sky.

'It's always beautiful here,' J.D. said.

Sam nodded.

★ ★ ★

Sam awakened to a boot on his chest. The boot was attached to the leg of one of the largest examples of masculinity he had ever seen. Even from his vantage point, staring up at this redwood of a man, he could see the chest as wide as the front end of a truck, the neck so large it made him think of Earl Campbell's thighs, the curved, reflective sunglasses, the shaved head, all pockmarks and sunburned skin.

'Morning,' Sam said as the boot slid up to the vicinity of his Adam's apple.

'You're trespassing,' the sheriff said. He had a surprisingly gentle voice. Sam wondered if the voice served as the raison d'être for the rest of his appearance.

'Not to be a bother, but . . . you're standing on my throat,' Sam coughed. He squinted, not so much for the reflection of the sunlight in the sheriff's glasses, but the pain in the back of his head that reminded him of a time not so long ago when he'd been accosted with a different type of footwear.

'We've been looking for you,' the sheriff said. He didn't move.

Sam stared at his reflection in the sunglasses and found himself wishing he'd gotten rid of that damned knife.

★   ★   ★

Gracie had called and left messages for Kenny at work, in his office, on his cell phone, at what once was the house they shared together. His assistant didn't know where he was. He hadn't shown up to the staff meeting this morning — which wasn't an entirely unusual occurrence. But then, in a fit of genius, Gracie had called his trainer and found out he hadn't shown up at their regularly scheduled appointment, either.

This was serious. Kenny never missed an appointment with his trainer, a bald egomaniac with the features of a Weimaraner. Gracie was almost afraid — and Will was almost buoyed — by the thought that Kenny might have offed himself.

At that moment Gracie had decided she would make the ultimate sacrifice for someone living in Malibu: She would get into her car and drive to where she figured she could find Kenny — under the sheets in their old bed at the house in Brentwood. Thirty minutes later, she drove up to the large wooden gates, which were closed, and tried to remember the numbers to the gate code. She pushed the intercom button. No one answered.

Finally she remembered. The gate code corresponded to Kenny's birthday. She wondered why she never thought this strange, why, in all the years they'd been together, her birth date had never been considered.

She pushed the buttons and waited for the gates to slowly open.

★　★　★

Gracie knocked on the front door, then let herself in. The house appeared empty, but as she listened she could detect the whir of the dishwasher in the kitchen. She thought that Ana must be there and felt a surge of nostalgia. She was surprised at the tears she felt welling in her eyes. She missed her housekeeper more than she missed her house — more than she missed her husband.

She walked into the kitchen, and there Ana was, absentmindedly wiping the kitchen counter as she stared out into the backyard, at the tennis court. She hadn't heard Gracie walk in.

'What does a girl have to do to get a cup of coffee around here?' Gracie asked.

Ana turned and looked at her, her face glowing from the exertion of wiping the same counter for what Gracie would guess (if her past job performance was any indication of her present one) was about twenty minutes. Gracie loved Ana for many reasons; her work ethic was not one of them.

Ana swooped Gracie up in her arms, then grabbed her hands and did a little dance.

'You're coming back to Mr. Kenny?' she asked, as she held Gracie's face in her hands.

Gracie tried to shake her head no, but Ana was holding firm.

'He need you, Miss Gracie,' she said.

'Kenny's divorcing me, Ana,' Gracie reminded her.

'Men,' Ana said, releasing her. 'You see that girl?'

Gracie nodded.

'She not bad girl, Miss Gracie,' Ana said, 'but she so young.' She shook her head. 'Men.'

'She was nice?' Gracie had to know.

'Oh yes, Miss Gracie,' Ana said. 'And very beautiful, no?'

'No,' said Gracie. She was beginning to sour on the whole Ana thing.

'Very young,' Ana said, as though this would make Gracie feel better.

'I have diaphragms older than her,' Gracie agreed. Which would have been true, had she still been using one. Ana smiled and nodded.

'Is the mister around?' Gracie asked.

Ana's face went dark. She shook her head again and said something in Spanish which included a lot of 'por Dios' allusions.

'Upstairs?' Gracie asked.

Ana said a few more 'por Dios's' and then pointed toward Heaven.

30

The House That Crime Built

He hated that house. The black car had driven up past the iron gates, past that lawn that the 49ers could've played their games on. Sam had avoided looking up at what he regarded as the Forbidding Fortress until the car stopped. And then. He peered at it through the tinted windows, like an anxious child. There it was. Almost two hundred years old. Made of stone brought over from Nevada. Built by itinerant workers. Survived earthquakes. Survived fires. Survived his family. Hell, generations of the San Francisco Knights.

He'd forgotten how big it was.

Sam had dressed in a suit and tie to accommodate the lawyers, who'd double-teamed him as he was taken to the Malibu Sheriff Station. Tweedle-Dee and Tweedle-Dum — speaking at a clip, their small, shiny shoes distracting him with their nervous tap-tap-tapping as he signed himself out. These midgets-in-pinstripes represented other midgets, in the Bay Area, who represented his family. The law firm had more than four names. He dearly wanted them to stop talking.

They'd put him on a plane, alone, after he reassured them that he was capable of reading his given name on a white card, which a driver would be holding up in the San Francisco airport. Sam didn't ask questions. He would have gone anywhere to have avoided further contact.

The suit was waiting for him in the hotel. As were the shoes, which pinched his ankles with every step. They were his size, the size that he once was, anyway. Years of walking on the beach had thickened his soles. His feet had spread.

The shoes were pretty, though. An Italian name was embossed on the bottom. And the leather was thick. If he wore them down, they could probably get him through the next winter. He wondered if he could keep them.

As he'd gotten dressed that morning, he thought again about what that sheriff had told him.

'Your family's looking for you.'

Sam had looked at him. Puzzled. Twenty years without a family makes one forget. *What family?* he thought. *Not my family.*

'They want you to come home,' he said.

Sam tried to listen to him talk. But he felt sorry about the pock-marks. This boy's life must have been miserable in high school, he thought. He looked at the nameplate on that chest. FERRIS. O. T. FERRIS.

What name starts with an O? Sam thought. Otis? Oral? (Oh, good Christ.)

'Plane leaves tonight,' the sheriff said. 'We've been charged with babysitting.' He spit out that last part. 'Like we got nothing better to do.'

'What's your name?' Sam asked. He wasn't

thinking straight yet — and also, he wanted to avoid the topic of his family. At least until the mental picture became clearer. Who was his family? Who was left?

'Omar,' the sheriff said.

'Thank God,' Sam replied as the sheriff pushed him into the back of his patrol car.

★   ★   ★

Sam looked at the driver, who had leaped from the car and was walking over to his door. The man wore a dark hat and had an unreadable face. Sam wondered if he was in on it.

The driver opened the door.

Sam stayed in the backseat.

'Sir?' The driver stuck his head in the open door. Sam wondered how much he knew.

'I don't want to go in there,' Sam said.

The driver stood, chewing his lower lip, as though weighing his options. Sam knew this was bothersome to the man — after all, he was just doing his job.

'C'mon, now,' the driver finally said. 'They're not going to hurt you.'

The thought occurred to Sam that the driver must work for his family — and that he might think that Sam, given the evidence of the last twenty-five years or so, was crazy.

'I'm not crazy,' Sam said as he remained seated, his arms folded against his chest. He longed to be back on that plane. He should have taken another of those little gin bottles. They were cute, those bottles. But were they practical?

431

Could he have used them for something else? What could they possibly store?

He wanted to go home.

'Oh, I've been working for your family for fifteen years,' the driver said, chuckling. 'I know you're not crazy.'

★ ★ ★

'Are you crazy?' Gracie had asked Kenny. She could see the tips of his hair pointing out from beneath the sheets. He groaned and turned over.

'Get up,' she said, pulling the sheet down. *Frette sheets*, she thought, as she tugged on them. *The finest money can buy*. She wondered if she could make off with a couple of them.

'The dailies look great.' His voice came out in shards. 'D'you see those numbers?'

Gracie shook her head, then pushed at Kenny's big, lumpy body. He was wearing boxer shorts and a tank top. He'd gained weight. He looked like Tony Soprano, without the body hair, and more important, without the animal sex appeal.

She wondered at the fact that she used to have sex with this man. It was like looking at your childhood home — what once seemed so overwhelming was now small and inconsequential.

'See you at the Oscars,' Kenny said, his words a slur.

She rolled him, using all of her strength, off the edge of the bed. He hit the floor. The ground shook. She heard a slight groan.

432

'Film's going all the way,' he continued.

By the time she'd hopped off the bed, Kenny had fallen back asleep. Gracie sat on the floor next to what used to be their marriage bed and stared at her sleeping almost-ex husband.

Finally she spoke. 'Kenny,' Gracie said, 'I want to talk to you. I — we never really talked. You wanted out. I was in shock. I just . . . felt I had to agree. And the truth was, I did have to agree. What kind of marriage did we have, anyway? Kenny, I have grown up. And it's been an eye-opener, a real kick in the face. But you know what? I like myself now. I didn't like myself when I was with you. It's not like you abused me. You weren't a bad guy, really. You never hit me or called me names. But every day, there was just a little more flesh cut from my body, every day, just a tiny piece of my soul would splinter. I was breathing, moving, talking, smiling. (Did you ever look at my smile, Kenny? I was all teeth. All teeth and my eyes were like coal, lifeless.) I was living. But I didn't live. It's almost as though I was dying, one cell at a time. There goes a brain cell, there goes my skin, my muscle, my bone. My heart. So I want to thank you. I really do. When you asked me for a divorce, I thought I would die. I thought it was the end. That no one would want me around. That I could never be without you. Without your name. But I lived, Kenny. I live now. I lost everything I didn't need. And I found everything I ever wanted.'

Gracie looked over at Kenny as a tear rolled down her cheek. Kenny snorted and rolled over. 'Also, I hate you,' she said to him. 'And I'm

433

having sex with the most extraordinary man,' Gracie continued. 'Five times — well, a little less than five times . . . '

She shuddered as the nerve endings along her spine awakened at the memory. She savored the feeling for a moment — how many women her age were having the kind of sex that made her feel like listening to Grace Jones albums and smoking Marlboros?

'Later,' she said at the jolt of electricity between her legs.

Gracie looked back at Kenny, on his side, fetal position. And wonder of wonders, she felt sorry for him. She crawled on her hands and knees over to him and reached out, her fingers lightly skimming the top of his hair.

'It's going to be okay,' she said to the man who had broken up their marriage via cell phone and left her for a chicklet. 'It's going to be okay,' she continued softly, her hand on his face. He turned and snuggled his cheek into her palm and stayed there.

★　★　★

Sam walked up the stairs to the immense front doors and hesitated. He turned back to look at the driver before knocking. The driver nodded his head, like a father to a son just starting first grade. 'Go 'head,' he seemed to say.

Sam stood there for a moment, and just as his hand reached up — to knock, to ring the doorbell — he wasn't sure how to make his next move — a man answered the door. He was wearing a suit with a high collar. His posture was so erect it had the effect of leaning back. He was old now, but he hadn't always been.

'Charles,' Sam said.

'Sir,' said the butler. 'May I say, it's good to see you.'

Sam reached forward with his hand and gripped the old man's hand, which was stronger than anyone had a right to expect. He had been middle-aged when Sam left; Charles had to be about eighty years old —

'Eighty on this very Sunday, sir,' Charles said.

'That's what I figured,' Sam said. 'Man, you're old, Charles. But what does that make me?' He was feeling better about his mysterious home-coming.

'Not a young man anymore, sir,' Charles said. 'Come inside, they're expecting you.'

'Any idea what this is about?' Sam asked. As long as he focused on Charles, he resisted that dizzy feeling. Charles was his anchor here.

'I'm afraid it's your mother, sir,' Charles said.

Sam drew a breath in slowly. 'She's not — '

'She'd like to see you,' Charles said. 'And I wish you would have shaved. That beard looks like roadkill. If I may say so, sir.'

* * *

He followed Charles past the living room, down a hall, past a powder room he dearly would have loved to use (but was too intimidated), past the old ballroom where he used to race Charles in go-carts, to the sitting room his mother preferred

435

even as a young woman avoiding her husband (Sam didn't blame her) and two children (Sam wasn't too keen on this part) and making her way to the top of the various Bay Area charity boards.

She looked small. Shockingly small, to Sam. His mother was a larger-than-life person, always — not only in his memory but to anyone who came in contact with her. The tatty overstuffed chair nearly swallowed her body. There were tubes running from her nose to an oxygen tank. There were others in the room as well — those who were suits, but she was the center of his, and their, attention.

Her face was pale, covered with makeup and powder. Even at this age, the most beautiful debutante in San Francisco's history had retained her vanity.

'You know I don't like facial hair,' she said. And she had retained her sharp tongue. 'Charles, you know I don't like a beard.'

'I know, mum,' Charles replied in a long-suffering voice. 'It would have been difficult to strap him down and straight-razor him, mum. He does look to have about forty pounds on me.'

Sam's mother said something that sounded an awful lot like 'harrumph' and waved her hand, and Charles left the room, but not before stealing a wink at his former charge. 'Knock her dead,' he whispered as he passed by. 'Please.'

Sam started laughing. His mother looked at him, her brilliant blue eyes having lost nothing of their sheen and well-bred intelligence — and overriding impatience.

'So. You're alive,' she said. She coughed, and Sam saw the team of suits jump out of their chairs at once in a flurry to get her a glass of water.

'Sit!' she said after her coughing fit. Sam had stood still as the lawyer butterflies flapped around him.

Sam looked around for an appropriate spot.

'Not you,' she said. 'You, come over here.' She tapped the floor next to her with her cane. 'We're going to have a little mother-son talk.'

She coughed again, and the lawyers jumped up again, and then she yelled 'Leave!' and they scurried out the door, wordless, their briefcases attached to their ribs, carried like footballs. Sam started to leave. 'Not you!' she said, pointing at him.

'You can't spank me,' he found himself saying to his mother.

'Like hell I can't,' she said. Her sudden flash of smile made Sam feel guilty as hell, and he wondered about what kind of son would leave his mother for as long as he had.

★   ★   ★

Gracie brewed coffee for Kenny in her former kitchen and watched him as he sat in the kitchen cubby, looking out the window into his beloved backyard, where, in his dreams and sometimes in reality, the famous and rich and fabulous would gather and drink and laugh and play a few sets.

She placed a cup of coffee (in his favorite massive white cup) in front of him, then sat

437

quietly next to him, and waited. What am I doing? Gracie wondered. She wondered at this strange sense of loyalty she had to Kenny. Because the room was silent, save for the buzzing sound coming from the deluxe, oversize (everything in the house was oversize, including the ex-husband) Sub-Zero refrigerator, Gracie could think out her actions; she could play amateur psychologist to herself. Finally, she smiled, a client she could relate to!

At the root of her sudden desire to take care of her husband was Lou's death. She looked at Kenny, who sighed, then nipped at his coffee like a bird picking at a blade of grass. She was sitting there because she was concerned that Kenny, too, would kill himself. How could she live with herself if she'd driven off and he was discovered the next day with a belt around his neck, swinging from the showerhead? What would she tell her daughter?

Not that the showerhead could take that kind of weight, Gracie thought. Let's be real.

She put her hand over his and squeezed. He looked at her and smiled a weak version of his lopsided grin.

'What kind of coffee did you use?' he asked.

'What?' Gracie asked.

'Was it in the white container or the black one?' he asked. 'Because I like the black container better. The Kona — we fly it over from that place in Hawaii. Sherry Lansing told me about it. She loves her coffee. You know, she called me. To see how I was doing.'

Gracie yanked her hand back from his as

though she'd been touching something disgusting. Like an ex-husband who can't get out of the way of his marriage-eating narcissism.

'I think I'm going to go independent,' Kenny said. 'Yeah, that sounds good.' He was nodding his head. He hadn't noticed that Gracie had snatched her hand away.

'The studio's folding?' Gracie asked. She wanted every last detail.

'No, no,' Kenny said. 'Nothing like that. I mean, there won't be a studio per se after all the . . . things are sold off. You know, the movies, the development, the phones, those bookshelves we put in, the, ah, staplers. Pencils. No, I'm going to form my own company. After all the, you know, legal stuff gets sorted out.'

'Legal stuff?'

'Coupla lawsuits. Nothing that'll stick. Let's hope,' he said, crossing his fingers.

'So that's good for you, then,' Gracie said.

'Great for me,' Kenny said. 'You know, I was never really able to fly with Lou around. I feel like I can do anything now.'

'Wow,' Gracie said, her mouth hanging open just enough to make her look mentally challenged. 'Wow, wow, wow,' she continued.

'You know,' Kenny said as he walked Gracie to the front door, 'that Britney thing was meaningless. To me.'

Gracie looked at him.

'I hated to break her little heart. I mean, she's just a kid,' he continued. 'But like I told her, 'Hey, I just can't be, like, 'The Wife Of,' you know?' '

'Right,' Gracie said, nodding. Was she starting to get a headache? She could hear her teeth grinding.

'I'm no Mr. Spears,' Kenny said.

'Certainly not,' Gracie said. She had a feeling of déjà vu and realized — this is how she felt when she fell into conversations with crazy people panhandling outside supermarkets.

★　★　★

'Hey!' Kenny called out to her as she started to drive away. He poked his head in the window. 'How's your guy, your man — what's his name?'

'Sam,' Gracie said, 'Sam Knight.'

'Yeah, that's it,' Kenny said. 'Listen, I'm crazy busy, but I'd sure like to talk to him about, you know, an investment opportunity. There's this film — Angelina Jolie is attached, she plays a World War II fighter pilot — '

'Kenny,' Gracie said. She wanted to finally come clean with him. And then she thought about the fact that there were likely *no* female fighter pilots in World War II. 'Sam . . . has no money. And when I say *no* money, he literally doesn't have a dollar in his pocket.'

Kenny looked at her. Gracie couldn't read his expression. Disappointment? Disgust? Gas?

'Kenny, he's homeless,' Gracie said finally. Kenny frowned, his lower lip curling out, like a rebellious five-year-old.

'Believe me, I know it sounds weird,' Gracie said. 'But take it from me. The only things Sam has in this world are a sleeping bag and a few books. And, like, I'm not talking Hemingway or Proust. And yet I think I love him.'

Gracie thought it was a bold move to profess her love of someone else to her former husband. Bold and maybe a little mean. She smiled.

'Gracie,' Kenny said, 'this is really low of you.'

Gracie nodded. She knew.

'And I don't find it funny in the least. I know we're broken up, but the least you can do is help out the father of your daughter.'

Gracie couldn't believe it. Kenny was playing the Father-of-Your-Daughter card.

'Kenny, I'm not screwing with you,' she said, exasperated. 'Sam Knight doesn't have a penny to his name.'

'Gracie,' Kenny replied in his blustery studio-head manner. 'Do you use lightbulbs?'

Gracie looked at him. It seemed an odd question, and she was again reminded of the crazy guy —

'How about razor blades?'

'Kenny . . . you're scaring me — '

'And you've heard of polyester?'

Gracie nodded. Her fight-or-flight reaction was teeming —

'Velcro?'

'I really have to get back. Jaden's waiting for me — ' She started to roll away —

'Gracie.' Kenny put his arm in the window and grabbed the steering wheel. 'Don't tell me you've never heard of Knight Industries.'

★ ★ ★

441

Sam was back in his hotel room, at the St. Francis on top of Nob Hill. Not two blocks from his childhood home (had he actually had a childhood). He looked down from his perch on the fourteenth floor and surveyed all that his family had once owned, generations ago. He could find all the answers to his life from up on his exalted perch. The vantage point brought him a degree of peace; looking down, he knew why he had escaped, first to Vietnam and then to a life without means.

He'd told his mother, in their quarter-century mother-son tête-à-tête, that growing up, listening to the adults argue about business, the onus of owning all they surveyed, left him with more than a bad taste in his mouth. As a child, he was ignored for such concerns. He learned to resent the fact that his parents cared more about what was going on outside their home than who was tucking their children in at night.

His mother had told him that she'd loved him, of course, but she had only raised him the way she'd been raised; she knew no better nor no worse. If he was neglected, she'd said, it's only because she must have been herself.

He'd nodded; he knew this was true. 'Age has a way of beating the truth into you,' she'd said. 'The Great Humbler, the Powerful Humiliator — Age!' She shook her fist at the high stone ceiling.

And then she'd coughed until Sam had reached out to punch the bell to notify the nurse. She'd slapped his hand away.

Which is when she'd told her son she wanted

to leave everything to him. Everything. All of it. The real estate, the majority shareholdership, the tangled mass of company titles. She spun the tale of the last twenty-five years, and it had become clear to Sam that she'd endured many heartaches — his leaving the family, her husband's death, the disappointment his sister had brought to her.

'She wants it, you know,' his mother told him.

'I don't believe that,' Sam said. He remembered his sister teaching him to read, though she was only a few years older than he; he remembered her tying his shoes, tucking his napkin under his chin; he remembered her letting him sleep next to her when he grew afraid in that big house — and there was much to be afraid of. He wasn't the only beneficiary of her kindness; she saved wounded pigeons, she wouldn't even take her shoe to a cockroach.

'She's married for the third time,' his mother said, 'and each time it gets worse. I don't even know this one's name.'

'What happened to her?' he asked. Suddenly his heart hurt. For himself, for his sister, for this woman, his mother.

His mother's hand fluttered up by her face and made a gesture like a bird flying away. He could see that his sister had hurt her just as much as he had.

'She wants it all,' his mother said. 'And I'm not going to give it to her.' She sniffed.

'She has children?' he asked.

'Three,' his mother said. 'And two grandkids.'

'You miss them,' he said.

His mother shrugged and looked away; the way her mouth turned down at the corners told him everything.

'Great-grandkids, isn't that something,' Sam said.

His mother grunted.

'Mother, I don't want your money. You know me, I wouldn't know what to do with all of it. I think about 'stuff' and I get nervous. I've never settled down, never had children, never made a woman happy — '

He cut himself off.

'She hasn't come to see me,' his mother said. 'She doesn't care. Look at me, all these tubes, strangers taking care of me, how can she not care?'

And then Sam heard a sound coming from his mother; it was a sound he was familiar with from war. All humans were capable of this sound; they just didn't know it until they'd lost a beloved friend, a parent. Worse — a child.

Tears spilled out over her cheeks, taking the powder on her face with them, rolling down like tiny snowballs. She wiped furiously at her eyes with her fragile hands, as though angry at the outburst of unfamiliar emotion.

'I'm dying, you know,' she told her son.

'I'm sorry,' he said, and he really was. He put his large, weathered hand over hers. The bones were tiny and her skin was thin and translucent; he felt as though he was holding a paper fan.

'Oh, I don't want your pity,' she said. 'Look at me, I'm so old. And I hate this place, frankly. You think I didn't want to run off? I could've left

. . . so many times. I could've left you and your sister. And you know what? I would have been happier.'

Maybe, thought Sam, *there's a time in the lives of all parents when they feel they can be honest with their children. It's a shame it usually comes too late.*

'I'm a prisoner. Worse — I'm a goddamned cliché — an old bird in a gilded cage,' she coughed. She looked him in the eye and he saw the strength of the life that was still there. Her tears had dried. There was a spark. 'So tell me. What's it like out there in the big world?'

For the next hour, he regaled her with tales of the life he'd chosen. He had been the closest of observers; what he hadn't known until that moment was that he could also tell the stories of the people whose lives crisscrossed his own — whether he had just watched them, conversed superficially with them, befriended them. Or slept with them. He knew the rich as well as the poor, the relentlessly happy (his mother said, 'Ooh, I hate that kind! What're they so goddamned happy about?') as well as the deeply depressed (to which she said, 'Ugh. Depression means too much time on your hands!'); he knew their dreams, their aspirations, their darkest desires, regrets, their fears. He was a walking encyclopedia of the knowledge that comes from living by one's wits, surviving on the edge of civilization, being a part of it, and yet apart from it. He knew many things about the human experience, but not so many on a personal level. He had not experienced heartbreak, had not experienced fatherhood, was not a veteran of domesticity.

He paused for a moment.

'Samuel? What is it?' his mother asked. She peered at him with the eyes he was so afraid of as a child, for he knew they saw everything.

'It's nothing,' he said, shaking off the feeling.

'Oh, no,' she said, 'you can't get away with that. I don't see you for twenty-five years and you shut down? You dare close yourself off to a dying woman?'

She leaned in. 'Who'm I gonna tell? Saint Peter?'

'You've got a point, Mother,' he said. And then. 'I've found someone. Or, really, she found me.'

'Who's her family?' The old lady couldn't stop herself. She raised one of those fan hands to her mouth and shook her head.

Sam laughed. 'She's got a four-year-old daughter,' he said. 'And an ex-husband. I guess that's family.'

'A divorcée?' The old woman acted shocked, put her hand to her chest. He could see her blood beating through the veins under her blouse.

'Afraid so.' He leaned in to his mother. 'You know, there's a lot of that going around.'

His mother clicked her tongue against the roof of her mouth and shook her head disapprovingly. And then laughed.

'Thank God your father died before I could divorce him,' she said. 'That's one less sin for me.'

Then her hand shot out and grabbed his, and Sam was surprised by the intensity of her grip. For that moment, she was not old and frail — for that moment, she was strong.

'Grab her,' she said to him, staring holes into his eyes. 'You grab that girl.'

And then she leaned back again.

'And for God's sakes, shave that beard. You were my beautiful, beautiful boy, you look like a damned grizzly.'

Before he left, Sam kissed his mother's upturned cheek, as tender an act as they'd ever experienced. She made him promise to return to her, with 'his girl.' She asked him a few more questions about her, and then her aqua eyes drooped. She didn't fight him when he hit the bell. The nurse came in, glared at Sam, and wheeled her away.

He watched her, trailed by tubes and the large tank, looking like an amateur underwater diver, and Sam knew in his soul that this was the last time he would see his mother.

Charles slipped his sister's phone number into Sam's hand before the driver whisked him back to the hotel.

31

Just Who is This Guy?

Gracie drove down Pacific Coast Highway from Brentwood. The sky had turned gray and cloudy, blending in with the water so that it was difficult to know where one started and the other began.

Okay, she thought, so maybe it's true. Maybe Sam Knight does come from a successful family. Not just a successful family, but one of those families who owned part of American History. She pictured an old San Francisco family — what would that mean? Nob Hill society? All the Ghirardelli chocolate you could ask for? She shook her head. It couldn't be.

Kenny had dragged her back inside the house to show her the research his assistant had compiled. The day she told him that she'd been 'dating' a 'billionaire,' he was determined to find out exactly who this guy was. Once he got a name, he started with the search engines . . . et voilà, pages upon pages about the Knight family, long of San Francisco and environs. They owned everything from a macaroni and cheese empire to several TV stations. The woman who ran the family with an iron fist (*Forbes*, March '82) was Sam's mother, according to Kenny. Her great-grandfather had staked his claim in the gold rush, then started buying up property in

San Francisco. He had lost his fortune and gained it back three times. Their family home was the oldest standing building in the area — it had survived the Great Fire, several earthquakes, the sixties.

Gracie had looked at the older woman's picture. She had Sam's forehead and possibly his chin — though his was hidden under a blanket of hair. There was something steely about her gaze that looked eerily familiar.

Was she reading into this?

The Forbes List stated that Sam Mère had two children — Sam Jr. and Penelope. Sam was thirty in 1982. There were no pictures of either.

The mere mention of the name 'Sam' was enough evidence for a dreamer like Kenny, someone who made his living making fake stories seem real — but not to Gracie. Until now she wondered why she hadn't asked Sam much about his past — and then the thought occurred to her: she'd been afraid to ask. What could he possibly tell her? About some horrible event that finally pushed him over the edge? About a long period of drug abuse? (Oh, my God, Gracie thought — needles!) His drinking problem? The family he left behind?

He was running away from something. That's all she had thought she needed to know.

She laughed at herself as the highway curved toward Big Rock and droplets of water hit her windshield. What kind of pathetic, desperate loser forgets to ask her homeless boyfriend about his past?

'Me,' she said out loud. 'Gracie Anne Peters.'

Gracie hesitated before she said the name 'Pollock.' She didn't need it anymore; she wasn't that person, she didn't wear the same size, like the same clothes, have the same hair, know the same acquaintances. So why would she keep the name?

Gracie Peters sped up, running a light at Carbon that was bent on turning red. Time to ask questions, she thought. Then, she said out loud, 'Time to get answers.'

⋆   ⋆   ⋆

Gracie parked her car in Joan's driveway, stepped outside, and was immediately set upon by the dogs whose names resembled expensive jewelry stores.

One was wagging its tail at Gracie even while depositing a steaming pile right in front of her passenger-side door.

'Cartier!' she heard Mrs. Boner exclaim. 'Come to Mommy!'

Gracie had had enough. She stomped over to where Mrs. Boner was bent over a chocolate Lab, smiling with her eyes closed as the dog tongue-kissed her cheek.

'You,' Gracie said to that face with the slash of frosted lipstick dividing her features in half. 'You, Monique Boner, will clean up your dog shit. Or I will — '

The woman looked at her. Her eyebrow cocked, her slash of a mouth twisted in a superior leer.

Gracie stuttered. 'I will — '

450

The woman looked off to the side and discharged a bored sigh.

'I will kill you,' Gracie said with a level of commitment she hadn't felt since her wedding vows.

The woman's eyes snapped back to face her.

'I will sneak into that mausoleum of yours when you and your husband are tucked away in your separate beds. I will poison your dogs. And I will slit your throat.'

The pink lower lip danced. She bit it to keep it from shaking. Her eyes stayed on Gracie.

'Tiffany,' she whispered. 'Cartier . . . '

Her voice trailed off.

'Lock your doors,' Gracie hissed. And then she walked back toward the house, veering around the side of the house toward the beach. The tide was high, even more so than normal, and she had to roll up her jeans and run to avoid getting drenched.

The beach was empty as far south as she could see. The lifeguard tower looked lonely in the gray afternoon, surrounded by empty trash cans. Even the ocean, moodier than usual because of the change of weather, was bereft of intrepid surfers bobbing in the tantrum of the storm waves.

Her feet made their way through the damp sand and onto the muddy path that Sam called home. She found herself walking past the old tennis court on the other side of the fence topped with barbed wire, which was so decrepit, the rusty spikes would have broken off in one's hand. She must have missed his spot, she thought. She back-tracked a few steps.

Nothing.

Gracie kneeled in the dirt and spread the underbrush with her hands. There was nothing there. She walked in circles, surveying the place she was sure to find Sam's sleeping bag, the cardboard box, his silly books.

There was nothing.

Gracie walked twenty feet in the other direction and then back again, then retraced her steps. She looked like an old hound dog with a busted sense of smell searching madly for the bird that dropped from the sky.

The gray clouds above her head had closed ranks, turning the sky almost black, dumping rain on Gracie as she slowly walked the path back to the beach. Her hair was slick against her cheeks as she found herself teetering toward the old telephone pole outside the lifeguard station.

At first she did not see him. The rain was coming down too hard and fast. Wiping it from her eyes served little purpose. Then there he was. Kneeling at his usual spot, but this time his head was tilted back, his arms wide open to the sky. The rain beating on his chest.

He looked like a human sacrifice.

She walked, dragging her body up beside his. She looked over briefly, but he did not look back. His eyes were closed, he swayed slightly to some inner melody.

Gracie dropped to her knees, sinking into the damp sand. She closed her eyes. And clasped her hands together.

Sam was never really one for prayer. Even in his darkest moments; even when he could hear the whir of bullets as they flew by his good-for-nothing helmet. Even when all around him boys were screaming for God's mercy.

But this flight had changed all that. The San Francisco to LAX route couldn't be more than forty-five minutes, but he could swear he lost about ten years of his life somewhere above Santa Cruz. A storm had hit suddenly and fiercely, forcing the plane into wind shear. They'd dropped from the sky — peanuts flew up in the air and rained down upon passengers, drinks went airborne, a stewardess hit the ceiling of the plane. 'What is happening?!' she screamed. 'What is happening?!'

Sam could have told her what was happening, if he'd been able to uncurl his tongue from the back of his throat. 'We're all going to die!' he would've screamed. The lady in the business suit next to him grabbed his arm and held tight, and the truth was, he was thankful she was there. He'd patted her hand, unsure if he was calming her down, or the other way around.

And then, within seconds, it was all over. The engines whined and the plane leveled off, and babies were hushed and the man in front of him got up to dry off his pants.

And this was when Sam swore to himself and God that if he lived through this flight, he was going to embark on something scarier than prison, more frightening than wind shear. He,

Samuel Jonas Knight Jr., was going to embark on a normal life.

After they had landed, Sam walked on unsteady legs back through the terminal, then turned and looked longingly back at the plane. He'd been spared, but he'd made a promise. Now, he would have a wife. A wife. A child. A dog. More children? Maybe.

He suspected that God had a sense of humor.

He smiled and tugged at his chin, then remembered that he had shaved his beard that morning.

Sam walked off with a slight catch in his stride from the blisters, cutting a dashing if slightly injured figure through the throng; a tall, clean-cut man who looked like a *GQ* cologne ad in his Armani suit and uncomfortable but practical Italian shoes.

32

The Sweetest Sound

Gracie pounded her shoes on the mat on the deck and shook the water from her hair before opening the sliding glass door and stepping into the small den. Joan was in the kitchen, sitting on a stool opposite the counter. Looking out at the late-August storm.

'I can't remember it raining here this early,' Joan said without severing her gaze. There were pots out on the stove, and two more on the kitchen floor. Leaks. The erratic dripping forming a tinny melody.

Gracie walked over to Joan and put her arm around her. 'Jaden's asleep,' Joan said. Gracie put her head next to her friend's and they both stared out the window onto the beach. The praying man had left, probably shortly after Gracie had walked away. Maybe the early rain was too much, overwhelming even for a man with clear God reception.

'I saw you,' Joan said. 'I just sat here, watched you for a few minutes. You looked so sad, Gracie, I couldn't take my eyes off of you — '

'He's gone,' Gracie said.

Joan took her hand, and they watched in silence as the rain continued to pour down; they watched as thunder rocked the house, and

counted the seconds until lightning hit, somewhere in the distance.

'Santa Monica Pier,' Gracie said, guessing
where the lightning had struck.

'Palos Verdes,' Joan replied. 'Did you hear
something?'

Gracie listened.

'Someone's at the door. I'll get it,' Joan said as
she slid from the stool. 'It'll be my exercise for
the day.'

The phone rang. 'Shoot,' said Joan as she
grabbed the phone and motioned for Gracie to
get the door.

Gracie moved around the pots on the floor,
just passing the stairs when she saw Jaden curled
up at the top of the landing.

'Jaden?' Gracie asked.

Jaden hopped up and leaped from the third
stair into Gracie's arms. 'Ooph,' Gracie said,
holding her child steady. 'What's this all about?'

'Mama, does it have to thunder?' she asked. 'I
can take the rain, but does it have to thunder?'

Gracie laughed, and with Jaden's legs secured
around her waist, walked to the front door.

She opened it and just spied the back of a man
walking away, in a suit too nice to be worn in a
thunderstorm. Wrong address, Gracie thought.

'Hey,' Gracie said, 'did you need something?'

The man turned and looked up at Gracie. His
hair was slicked back, the rain was coming down
hard, but his dark eyes lit up at the sound of her
voice.

'Gracie,' the man said, 'I'm back.'

It took Gracie a full second before she

recognized the voice.

'Mama, it's him,' Jaden said, 'it's your friend. But now he's bald on his face.'

'I know,' Gracie whispered without taking her eyes off Sam. 'I'm just getting used to the new look.'

Sam walked back, leaped up the front steps, then suddenly dropped on one knee, and Gracie called out to him, afraid that he had slipped —

Until she saw that he was holding up a ring.

Gracie put Jaden down.

'Mama, it's a ring,' she whispered.

'What are you doing?' Gracie asked him. Her hands were on her hips.

'I made a promise and I intend to keep it,' Sam said. 'I'm asking you to marry me.'

'This is crazy,' Gracie said. 'We haven't even been on a proper date.'

'Mama?' Jaden tugged at her shirt. 'Can I hold the ring?'

Sam was starting to look perplexed. 'You don't call what we did the other day a proper date?'

'More like an improper date,' Joan remarked. She was standing in the doorway.

'Jaden,' Gracie said, 'go inside.'

Jaden just looked at her. 'Not until I try on the ring.'

'Your wish is my command,' Sam said, slipping it on Jaden's finger. Her face glowed and she gasped.

'Give him back the ring, Jaden, and go inside. Now,' Gracie said. 'Don't make me count to three — '

457

'Don't make me count to three,' Jaden imitated, and Gracie made a move toward her. Jaden's eyes widened and she tossed the ring back to Sam and ran up the stairs and into the house.

Gracie couldn't see that Jaden had set up shop at the picture window facing the outside landing, watching their every move.

'It's my mother's engagement ring,' Sam said.

'My God, it's beautiful,' Joan said from the doorway. 'Did you steal it?'

'Joan,' Gracie said, 'inside.'

'I know, I know,' Joan said. 'Before you count to three.' She shut the door behind her.

'My mother gave it to me this morning,' Sam said. 'It had been my grandmother's before her. But she never did get along with her mother too much, so there's not too much sentimental value, to tell you the truth.'

The ring was an antique, of course. A large sapphire mounted in an elaborate platinum setting. The longer she looked at the ring, the harder it would be to refuse.

Gracie looked at Sam. With the beard, he was your typical ruggedly handsome movie-star type. Without it, he was breathtaking. For a brief moment, she thought he might be just too good for her. And then he stood and took her in his arms and kissed her. And she was reminded of all her stellar qualities.

After Sam released her, Gracie looked again at the ring, wondering what it would feel like on her finger. 'Keep it. Think about it, take your time,' he said. 'I'm not going away. Ever. Just

. . . don't take too long. I'm not getting any younger.'

And he kissed Gracie again and she realized that she wasn't thinking about her thighs or her scar or the way her hair frizzed up in the rain or any of those mean things she could say to herself — all she thought about was the moment, the kiss, their lips together. What was that feeling deep in her stomach?

Hope.

She turned and spied Joan and Jaden in the picture window.

'You see what you're in for?' Gracie asked. 'A house full of women.'

'I've lived on a dirt floor for twenty years,' Sam said. 'I think I can handle it.'

Gracie turned back and looked at him. His arms were around her waist. She ran a finger along the side of his face, slowly fingering his chin.

'You like it?' he asked.

'Yes,' she said. 'Yes. Yes. Yes.'

They kissed again, holding it long enough for him to slip the ring on her finger.

Epilogue

Mrs. Kennicot passed away a week after Sam's mother died. Sam was thankful that he'd had the opportunity not only to say good-bye to his mother but to talk about her, finally, to Mrs. Kennicot.

She'd gone in her sleep. The kind of death that we should all hold out for, Sam thought. One morning she just didn't wake up. No bells, no whistles, no fuss. And she'd already made the funeral arrangements. The Colony planned to plant a tree in her honor, after the memorial service. Lavender, who was back at work and feisty as ever, had informed him of the service shortly after her death.

He'd sure miss her.

Sam met with her two sons, who were young men the last time he'd seen them. But then, so had he been. They were going to sell the property. They wanted to know how much Sam thought it could sell for. Sam was up on all the Colony real estate deals — he seemed to be the filtering device for pertinent Colony intelligence.

Max, the baby of the family, now a college professor at Berkeley, had more of a sentimental heart. 'Do you think we should sell it, Sam?' he'd asked more than once. The older one, Jim, was a businessman in San Diego. There was no question in Jim's mind at all — the luxury of a man who thinks only in equations.

Sam gave them the numbers. He knew they could get a good price. He and Max shared a coffee at the local Starbucks before Max caught his plane back to Berkeley.

'You'll be sure to check out whoever buys the place, right, Sam?' Max said. 'Mom wouldn't want just anyone living there.'

Sam nodded. He knew this was true. As ramshackle as it was, she'd loved that old house.

'You know someone who'd be interested?' Max asked. 'Someone nice? With a family, maybe?'

Sam shook his head. 'Anyone who buys it would probably tear it down, Max.'

'I know,' Professor Max Kennicot said. 'But it doesn't seem right. It could be fixed up, you know. Hey, Sam. What's this about you getting married?'

Sam smiled. 'It happens to the best of us.'

'Sometimes the worst of us, too.' Max nodded, sipped his coffee. He had been married several times, Sam knew. 'My mom loved you, you know. I wish there was a way . . . '

'Yeah,' said Sam.

'She would've wanted it that way,' Max said. 'She'd want you to stay there forever.'

Sam had been sitting on something for a while. He looked at Max with his owlish face, the granny glasses. For a moment, in his wistful expression, he saw the boy he knew, smoking pot in his room, crying over a girl, waving good-bye as he went off to college.

'Max, my boy,' Sam said, 'I've got a little something to tell you.'

461

Sam, Gracie, Jaden, and Joan moved into Mrs. Kennicot's house three weeks later. J.D., Tariq, and Lavender, who sported a bandage around her head on which Jaden had colored a rainbow with Magic Markers, had assisted with the move. The escrow had been especially short, as it had been a cash offer. Sam thought about the look on Max's face when he informed him that his mother, richer than Croesus, had passed away, and against his wishes had left him just enough money to buy his dream house with a little padding for his dream future. Her daughter, her grandchildren and great-grandchildren, and various charities had received the bulk of the estate — just as Sam had hoped.

Sam and Max had made the deal that morning at Starbucks, based on a handshake. And then Sam had dropped him off at the airport.

'I still can't believe it,' Max said, shaking his head as his feet hit the curb at LAX and he popped his head back in the old station wagon window. 'Why would a guy like you spend all that time sleeping outside?'

'You ever try it?' Sam asked.

Max just laughed, shook Sam's hand, then turned and trudged toward the terminal, dragging his suitcase behind him.

★ ★ ★

The first night in their new, old home, Gracie and Sam curled up to sleep in what they laughingly referred to as the 'master' bedroom, Sam's arms and legs curved around Gracie's body.

'What's wrong?' Gracie asked finally. She knew Sam's eyes were still open, staring at the dark.

'Nothing,' he said. He stroked her hair, leaned up, and kissed her earlobe.

'Go ahead,' she said.

'Really?'

'Really.'

'God, I love you,' he said as he kissed her, relishing her warm breath, the slightest taste of her tongue. Her eyes were still closed as he got out of bed.

'I love you, too,' she said as she felt him leave the room. 'Side closet!' she called after him.

Sam went out to the front porch, loaded down with his old sleeping bag and a pillow, where a familiar face was waiting for him. Baxter.

'It's just you and me, Bax,' Sam said. The dog wagged his whole body, then sniffed around his ankles while Sam laid out his sleeping bag. After a good, long stretch, Sam slipped into his sleeping bag, secured his hands around his head, and stared up at the stars until the familiar, rhythmic sound of the waves lulled him to sleep.

The End . . .

Or is it?

Epilogue Two

A week after Gracie, Sam, Jaden, and Joan had moved in, Will and Cricket dropped by, separately, on a typically foggy Sunday morning. Cricket's three thousand kids stormed through the house like a swarm of African killer bees, with Cricket scurrying behind them bestowing psychobabble such as 'Rudy, what are you feeling when you hit your sister over the head with that vase? Are you feeling frustrated?'

Gracie was thankful that Sam was still out on his morning swim — going from sleeping alone on a bed of sand and rocks to a house full of screaming kids would likely have given him the bends.

'Now, it's not quite ready yet,' Gracie said to Will as he pushed past her five minutes later into the wood-paneled living room, which resembled the inside of the boat in that George Clooney movie where all the cute guys drowned. The life preserver on the far left wall didn't help matters.

'I can't breathe,' he said, flipping his sunglasses back down over his newly spray-tanned nose.

'Look, we've been through this before,' Gracie said. Her enthusiasm for the old house would not be deterred. When Sam had surprised her with the notion of buying the Kennicot place, she had demurred at first. She still had her heart set, somehow, on The Brown House. So she and

464

Sam had taken a drive to The Brown House. And guess what? The Brown House was now a private tennis court. And the oak trees in the back? The canopy of green hovering protectively over her baby? They now existed only in her cherished memories.

Luckily Gracie had grown fond of the Kennicot house — in fact, felt oddly protective toward the old place, as though she had to carefully preserve whatever moments it held, whatever secrets it sheltered.

'I need water,' Will said, his voice scratchy. He clutched at his scarf.

'I am not hiring you,' Gracie said.

Will went to sit down on one of Mrs. Kennicot's couches. It was Sam's favorite.

'What is this?' Will asked, jumping away from the dust that had sprayed out around him.

'A couch.'

'Well, there's something living in there — '

'I'm not hiring you,' Gracie repeated. 'You're too expensive and I want to try decorating this house on my own.'

Will looked at her as though she had just told him she was going to jump out of a speeding train. He put his hand to the side of his face. And stared at her. Finally he waved his hand dismissively.

'Fine, I'll do it for free!'

Gracie looked at him. Will's least favorite four-letter word was 'free.'

'Now, I want you to meet someone,' he said, his voice becoming softer. 'Come in, honey,' he called out. Gracie thought she detected a bit of a blush in Will's cheeks and then decided the spray tan had turned blotchy.

'Gracie, this is Aristo,' Will said as he turned toward the vision who had just walked into the living room. He was in his thirties, had short, thick dark hair, skin that reminded Gracie of olive oil and hot sun and a Mediterranean breeze, and light-green eyes that reached back generations.

'He's Greek,' Will said, rubbing the sheen on Aristo's arm lightly. Aristo smiled, his teeth as white as the shirt he wore, his sleeves rolled up to the elbow, revealing forearms that should have been bronzed and mounted. Gracie thought they'd make very nice bookends.

Aristo put his hand out. Gracie shook his hand. Dry and warm and capable.

Will had not taken his eyes off Aristo, but continued to speak to Gracie.

'Aristo means 'best,'' he murmured.

'Well, any idiot can see that,' Gracie said.

'He's a sailor by trade,' Will said. 'Can you believe it? I found him working as a waiter in that Greek restaurant on Third. I was tired, I was having a shitty day, none of my fabrics had come in, I started to order the souvlaki, and I looked up and . . . there he was. This . . . angel.'

Aristo put his arm around Will's waist and squeezed.

'Gay Kryptonite,' Gracie said.

Will was looking into Aristo's eyes. He looked back at Gracie. 'What?'

'I said, 'Here Comes the Bride.'' Gracie smiled.

466

Will blushed for the second time in his life and planted a kiss on Aristo's cheek. And then he clapped his hands and went right back to business. 'I'm returning on Monday with painters in tow. We need to lighten this place up. It's like the Poseidon Adventure in here, I swear to God.' He thought for a second, putting his index finger to his chin. 'I'm seeing a light . . . '

'Green?' Gracie asked.

Will and Aristo stayed awhile for espressos, but only because Gracie begged. It was clear the boys were quickly bored with company that included anyone but the two of them, and they departed arm in arm ten minutes later.

Cricket stayed a little while longer, running back and forth, chasing this blur and that until she had to depart to a birthday party, which would hopefully solidify her chances of getting her oldest into an exclusive Brentwood private school. She had bought a three-hundred-dollar cashmere sweater at Fred Segal for the little girl, though she was unsure of the spelling of the child's name. And really, unsure whether the child was in fact a girl or a boy.

Cricket fretted until Gracie unwrapped the gift and reassured her that the sweater was unisex. Finally she gathered up her brood and left. The house had never been more peaceful.

A moment later, Jaden insisted on visiting the dreaded pet store across the highway. The pet store, which sported several signs that read: OUR CAMERAS ARE THEIR [SIC] WATCHING YOU!, featured purebred puppies in glass containers. Gracie called them puppy-quariums.

Jaden loved to press her nose up against the glass and tap her fingers on the smudged surface and 'play' with the muted, high-priced fur balls on the other side. Gracie wasn't crazy about the place; the signs were not only misspelled but offensive to Gracie's sensibilities, and a chew toy there could easily cost twenty dollars. She rarely ventured near it.

Sam was not yet back from his morning swim, so there was no one to back Gracie in her argument against visiting the pet store.

'Don't you like puppies, Mommy?' Jaden asked. 'Who doesn't like puppies?' She seemed genuinely perplexed.

'Can you say 'puppy mill,' Jaden?' Gracie tried to joke as she tossed out bagel remnants.

But Jaden just stared at her and crossed her skinny arms over her chest and stared some more, and Gracie finally buckled after twenty minutes of silent, relentless staring.

The pet store was filled with browsers. Jaden tapped on the glass cage of a particularly adorable mini-dachshund until Gracie was finally able to drag her away with the promise of a gumball from a machine outside.

Jaden ran toward the gumball machine, then stopped. 'Mommy, books!' Jaden cried, pointing her arm toward the once-empty establishment next door.

Gracie caught up to her and looked inside. There was new life and a new sign: MALIBU BOOKS. She peered through the windows, expecting to see mostly spiritual titles or self-help books for one's colon but instead saw

. . . Philip Roth. Richard Russo. Coffee table art books. The new Anne Tyler title.

She grabbed Jaden's hand and pushed the door open. And exhaled. For here was a genuine bookstore. Intimate as a dear aunt's living room. A tall, angular fellow wearing a fedora at the register. Jaden ran toward the back, where Gracie could see a whimsically decorated children's section.

'Nirvana,' Gracie whispered to herself.

She followed Jaden, who had already opened a book and was being complimented on her choice by a woman with a gray bob and reading glasses sliding down her nose.

There was another mother there, holding her child on her lap, reading to her. Gracie was bending over Jaden's shoulder to examine her choice when she heard:

''Do belly buttons hold our bodies together? What if we unbuttoned our belly buttons? Would we explode? What if . . . ?''

Gracie's words to Jaden caught in her throat. She looked over at the woman sitting next to her.

The woman was reading her book. Gracie's book.

Gracie scooped Jaden up with the promise of buying the book that was still in her hand and made her way to the front of the store. The tall fellow at the cash register, the type that should be seen at any self-respecting bookstore, had flung off his hat and was running his fingers through his hair and muttering to himself.

'Excuse me,' Gracie said, 'I couldn't help noticing . . . ' He looked up at her.

'You have some titles by . . . Gracie Peters?'

'Children's books,' he said. He started tapping away at his computer. 'Yes, we have a few of her titles. Ah, *Question Boy*. Quite a few people like that one.'

Gracie grinned at him. And grinned.

'Is it out of stock?' he asked. 'Would you like to order it? We can have it for you within — '

'Mommy, *you're* Gracie Peters!' Jaden declared.

'I'm Gracie Peters,' Gracie said to the clerk. She could not stop herself from grinning. She looked like one of those dullards who stands behind the president at town hall meetings.

'A local author!' the clerk said, showing signs of life. 'Listen, we're new here. If you want to do a book signing sometime . . . '

'A book signing?' Gracie asked.

'You're not supposed to write in books,' Jaden said.

'Are you working on something new?' the clerk asked.

Gracie looked at him. And then she heard a tapping at the picture window facing the parking lot. She and the clerk looked up. Sam was standing outside the bookstore waving to her. His hair was combed back, still wet from the ocean. Grooves formed around his eyes at the sight of her.

'Sam!' Jaden said before she ran out the door and into his arms.

Gracie looked over at her daughter, laughing as she was being hoisted onto Sam's shoulders. She looked back at the clerk. She wondered if he sensed why she was crying now. There was no sadness. Her sadness had been replaced by something infinitely more powerful.

'I am writing a new book,' Gracie said finally. 'It's called *What Do I Love?*'

Really . . . The End.

We do hope that you have enjoyed reading this large print book.

Did you know that all of our titles are available for purchase?

We publish a wide range of high quality large print books including:
Romances, Mysteries, Classics
General Fiction
Non Fiction and Westerns

Special interest titles available in large print are:
The Little Oxford Dictionary
Music Book
Song Book
Hymn Book
Service Book

Also available from us courtesy of Oxford University Press:
Young Readers' Dictionary
(large print edition)
Young Readers' Thesaurus
(large print edition)

For further information or a free brochure, please contact us at:
Ulverscroft Large Print Books Ltd.,
The Green, Bradgate Road, Anstey,
Leicester, LE7 7FU, England.
Tel: (00 44) 0116 236 4325
Fax: (00 44) 0116 234 0205

Other titles published by
The House of Ulverscroft:

LEFT BANK

Kate Muir

Olivier and Madison Malin are glittering inhabitants of Paris's exclusive neighbourhood, the Left Bank. The Malins' life in their grand apartment with their daughter is the stuff of dreams. Madison is an American film star: she's beautiful and talented. Her husband, Olivier, darling of the sophisticated Left Bank, craves adoration (and is a little too willing to return it) . . . Everything seems perfect, until a new English nanny, Anna, appears at the doors of their Rue du Bac apartment. Gamine and artless, Anna unwittingly sets in motion a chain of events that will gravely endanger the Malins' daughter and their charmed lives — in ways no one could have foreseen.

OLD SCORES

Bernardine Kennedy

At sixteen, Maria Harman feels confused, resentful and bitter. She has always known she was adopted — a longed-for daughter amid three sons — but she has never understood her mother's disdain for her. Finola Harman's abuse, her older brothers' bullying and her father's lack of intervention have led to a life of misery. For, although hardened to her mother's contempt, Maria craves her love. Her solace comes from her warm-hearted, slow-witted brother Eddie, and her involvement with local bad boy Davey Allsop, until a tragic accident destroys even that . . . And slowly, as the truth of Maria's true parentage is revealed, the dysfunctional Harman family is thrown into chaos with potentially fatal consequences.

BRAND NEW FRIEND

Mike Gayle

When Rob's girlfriend asks him to leave London and live with her in Manchester, it means leaving behind his best mate in the entire world. Believing that love conquers all and confident that he'll meet new mates, Rob takes the plunge. Six months in, and yet to find even a drinking buddy, Rob realises that making friends in your thirties is not easy, so his girlfriend places an ad in the classifieds. Three excruciatingly embarrassing 'bloke dates' later, he's on the verge of despair . . . until his luck changes. There's just one problem. Apart from knowing less than nothing about football and the vital statistics of supermodels, Rob's new friend has a huge flaw. She's a girl . . .

WELCOME TO THE GREAT MYSTERIOUS

Lorna Landvik

Diva Geneva Jordan has performed for millions on stage, screen and television, but her current leading role is in Minnesota. She has agreed to look after her thirteen-year-old nephew, a boy with Down's syndrome, while his parents take a vacation. Geneva and her sister, Ann, are as different as night and day, and Geneva remembers she had a family before she had a star on her door. Accustomed as she is to playing the lead, finding herself a supporting actress in someone else's life is unexplored territory for Geneva. Then, the discovery of a scrapbook that she and Ann created long ago starts her thinking of things beyond fame, and looking for answers outside the spotlight's glow . . .